An Evangelical Apologetic of

The

Pilgrim's Progress

by John Bunyan

Themes & Issues

Barry E. Horner

A GREAT CHRISTIAN BOOKS publication
Great Christian Books is an imprint of Rotolo Media
160 37th Street Lindenhurst, New York 11757
(631) 956-0998
www.GreatChristianBooks.com
email: mail@greatchristianbooks.com
ISBN 978-1-61010-999-4 Paperback

Horner, Barry E., 1936-
Themes and Issues of the Pilgrim's Progress / by Barry E. Horner
p. cm.
A "Reformation Press" book by Great Christian Books
GREAT CHRISTIAN BOOKS an imprint of Rotolo Media
ISBN 978-1-61010-999-4
Recommended Dewey Decimal Classification: 234
Suggested Subject Headings:
1. Religion—Christian literature—Pilgrim's Progress
2. Christianity—The Bible—Soteriology
I. Title

The cover design for this title is by Michael Rotolo (www.michaelrotolo.com). This book is quality manufactured in the United States on premium, archival quality acid-free paper stock. To discuss the publication of your Christian manuscript or out-of-print book, please contact Great Christian Books. www.greatchristianbooks.com.

MANUFACTURED IN THE GREAT UNITED STATES OF AMERICA

TABLE OF CONTENTS

JOHN BUNYAN
PJ Shields

PREFACE

OVER the last few years, interest in seminars that I have conducted on *The Pilgrim's Progress* has greatly increased. Hence, it has been a privilege to speak at churches, family camps, colleges, and seminaries, in England, Australia, New Zealand, and many parts of America. During the course of these meetings, I have been stimulated in a large measure by the intense interest that has been shown in the substance of John Bunyan's allegory. On many occasions people have wanted to talk for hours on the numerous intricacies of Bunyan's weaving. So often I have been stimulated by various enquiries concerning details of the text, and related doctrinal matters, and as a result have been forced to do further study. However, there have been those times when people asked the same questions time and time again. Then there have been those who have admitted their prior misunderstanding of what Bunyan purposed to teach, and as a result have become so enthused and captivated by the depth of Bible teaching that he intended.

Through all of this, and it is very much an ongoing journey, many matters have arisen which I felt needed clarification before an evangelical world that sadly, to its shame, hardly knows Bunyan. Hence, this book is the product of such concern. While some chapters may include more scholarly substance than others, it is felt that all of the issues raised are of considerable importance. I do not apologize for being critical of the general aura of Bunyan studies during this twentieth century which, while contributing much with regard to textual and historical matters, has yet been politely distant, even sometimes disdainful, concerning evangelical warmth born of evangelical doctrine, which for Bunyan was unquestionably of supreme concern.

This writer reveres the ministry of John Bunyan principally because of the Bedford preacher's unswerving commitment to the gospel of God's sovereign grace as well as his winsome portrayal of that truth. If anyone loses sight of this priority, for whatever reason, he emasculates the allegory of its most vital feature. The reality is that at an academic level, many want to admire Bunyan selectively, while at the same time repudiating his doctrine as passé. In this situation, such assessments are usually filtered through the presuppositions of subjective liberalism or neo-orthodoxy.

However the biblical truth of *The Pilgrim's Progress* stands firm, whatever modern man may say. Therefore, the need of the hour is not detachment grounded upon the pretense of scholarly objectivity, but the recovery of that intelligent and heartfelt pursuit of the truth which does not stop short of personal embrace. Rather it acknowledges Bunyan as a whole, and gives the Bedford tinker that regard which esteems his evangelical truth priority above all else.

Barry E. Horner

THE
Pilgrim's Progreſs
FROM
THIS WORLD,
TO
That which is to come:
Delivered under the Similitude of a
DREAM
Wherein is Diſcovered,
The manner of his ſetting out,
His Dangerous Journey, And ſafe
Arrival at the Deſired Countrey.

I have uſed Similitudes, Hoſ. 12:10.

By *John Bunyan.*

Licenſed and Entred according to Order.

LONDON,
Printed for *Nath. Ponder* at the *Peacock*
in the *Poultrey* near *Cornhil*, 1678.

Original Title Page, First Edition

THE WRITINGS OF JOHN BUNYAN

FOR one hundred and fifty years, the standard publication of *The Works Of John Bunyan* has been the three volume set edited by George Offor. More recently *The Banner of Truth Trust* has reprinted this work, except that *A Map showing the Order and Causes of Salvation and Damnation* has been omitted. The original Offor edition contained fifty-nine separate compositions, though it appears that even this warmly appreciative editor had serious doubts about the inclusion of *An Exhortation To Peace And Unity.* In deference to the judgment of others he included it, yet expressed eight reasons why he questions its authenticity, and even offers the suggestion that it was written by Paul D'Anvers, a leader among London Baptists who opposed Bunyan's views on baptism.[1]

More recently, *Oxford Press (Clarendon)* has completed the publication of a totally new edition of Bunyan's writings, though sadly, it is very expensive. This scholarly production commenced with the publication of the definitive text of *The Pilgrim's Progress* in 1960, edited by J. B. Wharey and later revised by Roger Sharrock. Subsequently *Grace Abounding to the Chief of Sinners* was published in 1962, then *The Holy War* in 1980 and *The Life and Death of Mr. Badman* in 1988. Finally in 1994, the thirteen volume set of Bunyan's *Miscellaneous Works* was completed. In this overall Oxford Edition enterprise, the late Roger Sharrock was the General Editor.

In the Oxford Edition, it should be noted that the more recently discovered *Profitable Meditations*, first published in 1661, is included.[2] On the other hand, *An Exhortation To Peace And Unity*, *Reprobation Asserted,* and *Scriptural Poems* have been omitted. With regard to *Reprobation Asserted*, John Brown, Bunyan's foremost biographer to date, rejected the work as spurious.[3] Richard Greaves has written an article in which he cautiously agrees with this opinion. He also declares: "Henri Talon and G. B. Harrison rejected Brown's arguments and instead

---

1 John Bunyan, *The Works of John Bunyan*, ed. George Offor, II, pp. 742-3. John Brown likewise expressed considerable doubt concerning the authenticity of this work, *John Bunyan*, pp. 433-4.

2 John Brown, *John Bunyan*, pp. 161-2.

3 Ibid., p. 228.

affirmed Bunyan's authorship, whereas Roger Sharrock, while rejecting Brown's arguments as inconclusive, decided after a more intensive analysis that the work was, in fact, not Bunyan's."[4] In this regard, one thing remains certain, and it is that quite apart from this disputed work which represents high Calvinism, considered in more detail in Chapter 9, Bunyan's convictions concerning the sovereignty of grace remain both pervasive and substantial.

With regard to *Scriptural Poems*, Offor writes: "This very interesting little volume of poems, we believe, has not been reprinted since the year 1701, nor has it ever been inserted in any edition or catalog of Bunyan's works. . . . The style and substance of these scriptural poems are entirely Bunyan's."[5] On the other hand, Graham Midgley, editor of Volume VI of the recent Oxford Edition, and no doubt with Sharrock's agreement, omits this work.[6] It has to be admitted that based on Midgley's evidence, together with the supporting opinion of John Brown, this rejection seems warranted.

ACKNOWLEDGMENT

As the years pass, indebtedness has grown with regard to those who, out of love for the truth of God as Bunyan expressed it, have contributed in so many encouraging ways. In particular, I must mention my wife Ann, Jeff Kendal, John and Leona Heffelfinger, and Galen Johnson, as well as the late Henry and Naomi Ansell, and John Coleman.

---

4 Richard Greaves, *John Bunyan and English Nonconformity*, p. 185. In this essay Greaves also responds to an article by Paul Helm in *The Baptist Quarterly*, XXVIII, April, 1979, pp. 87-93, which, with considerable persuasion, attempts to defend Bunyan's authorship of *Reprobation Asserted*. Refer here to Chapter 9, pp. 153-8.

5 Bunyan, *Works,* II, p. 386.

6 John Bunyan, *The Miscellaneous Works of John Bunyan*, "The Poems," ed. Graham Midgley, VI, pp. xxii-xxv.

CHAPTER ONE

Why The Pilgrim's Progress Is A Book For Our Time!

THE first edition of *The Pilgrim's Progress* in 1678 was an immediate runaway bestseller, at least amongst the common populace within England and then beyond its shores. As a result, publisher Nathaniel Ponder became increasingly troubled with numerous attempts to pirate the work and infringe upon his license. Three editions were published within the first year, and by the time of Bunyan's death in 1688, thirteen editions overall had produced at least 100,000 copies. Even in 1686, eight years after the first edition, Bunyan could not refrain from expressing, in the introductory poem of Part II, his delight at such unparalleled and international success.

> My Pilgrim's book has travell'd sea and land,
> Yet I could never come to understand
> That it was slighted, or turn'd out of door
> By any kingdom, were they rich or poor.
> In France and Flanders, where men kill each other,
> My Pilgrim is esteem'd a friend, a brother.
> In Holland too, 'tis said, as I am told,
> My Pilgrim is with some worth more than gold.
> Highlanders and wild Irish can agree
> My Pilgrim should familiar with them be.
> 'Tis in New England under such advance,
> Receives there so much loving countenance,
> As to be trimm'd, new cloth'd, and deck'd with gems
> That it may show its features and its limbs,
> Yet more; so comely doth my Pilgrim walk,
> That of him thousands daily sing and talk.[1]

---

[1] John Bunyan, *The Works of John Bunyan*, ed. George Offor, III, p. 169.

During the 1690's several booksellers placed exceptionally large orders including two of approximately 10,000 copies.[2] Thus *The Pilgrim's Progress* became, "by far the most popular work of seventeenth-century prose fiction."[3]

Although the eighteenth century Great Awakening under Whitefield and Wesley spawned an even more widespread enthusiasm, again amongst multitudes of the lower classes, acceptance within "cultured" and "refined" circles was still reluctant. Even William Cowper could reflect this hesitancy when, in anonymously endorsing the *The Pilgrim's Progress*, he writes:

> I name thee not, lest so despised a name
> Should move a sneer at thy deserved fame.
> Yet, e'en in transitory life's late day
> That mingles all my brown with silver gray,
> Revere the man whose PILGRIM marks the road,
> And guides the PROGRESS of the soul to God.[4]

However, the early nineteenth century saw a sudden burst of learned enthusiasm such as is acknowledged by Lord Macaulay: "*The Pilgrim's Progress* is perhaps the only book about which, after the lapse of a hundred years, the educated minority has come over to the opinion of the common people."[5] Thus, through to the early part of the twentieth century, more often only the highest praise could be offered to Bunyan, such as in 1928 by the esteemed historian G. M. Trevelyan, commenting, to begin with, on the allegory's opening paragraph:

> Of all the works of high imagination which have enthralled mankind, none opens with a passage that more instantly places the

---

[2] W. R. Owens, "The reception of *The Pilgrim's Progress* in England," *Bunyan in England and Abroad*, eds. M. van Os and G. J. Schutte, pp. 91-2.

[3] N. H. Keeble, "'Of him thousands daily Sing and talk': Bunyan and his reputation," *John Bunyan, Conventicle and Parnassus*, ed. N. H. Keeble, p. 245.

[4] William Cowper, *The Poetical Works of William Cowper*, p. 308. It is noteworthy that in this poem titled "Tirocinium; or a Review of Schools," the author recommends the popular allegory as part of his preferred curriculum in providing Christian private tuition, which method of education he recommends in preference to attendance at relatively less edifying public schools.

[5] Lord Macaulay, *Macaulay's Lives of Bunyan and Goldsmith*, p. 22.

> reader in the heart of all the action that is to follow; not Homer's, not Milton's invocation of the Muse; not one of Dante's three great openings; not the murmured challenge of the sentinels on the midnight platform at Elsinor—not one of these better performs the author's initial task. The attention is at once captured, the imagination aroused. In these first sentences, by the magic of words, we are transported into a world of spiritual values, and impressed at the very outset with the sense of great issues at stake—nothing less than the fate of a man's soul. . . . He [Bunyan] shines, one of the brightest stars in the firmament of English literature. Yet he never had an ambition in anything he wrote save to turn poor sinners to repentance.[6]

But on into the remainder of this century there has gradually spread, like cloud shielding the light, a dullness concerning the heart of Bunyan that leaves us only with academic infatuation for his literary talent and embroilment in the historic facts of Puritan life, while the substance of his predominant evangelical concern seems more and more lost to view.

Is The Pilgrim's Progress Presently Valid?

So why then should *The Pilgrim's Progress* be enthusiastically recommended to modern man as this sophisticated twentieth century draws to an uncertain close? Why indeed, when a survey of readers by Columbia University Press in 1950, designed to identify the most boring of all literary classics, revealed that *The Pilgrim's Progress* by John Bunyan ranked at number one! (*Das Kapital* by Karl Marx ranked at number thirteen).[7] More recently a survey of 17-year olds in the USA indicated that less than one in seven could

---

6 G. M. Trevelyan, "Bunyan's England," *The Review Of The Churches*, July, 1928, pp. 319, 325. In 1912 a whole window of stained glass panels at Westminster Abbey was devoted to *The Pilgrim's Progress.* At the dedication it was declared: "This window is not only a valuable addition to the art which enriches and distinguishes this temple of fame, it also commemorates one of the most powerful books written by one of the greatest saints. But chiefly this work is a memorial of one of the saints who through 'Grace abounding to the chief of Sinners' still continues his ministry to man, and will from this spot witness to the vital truths of the Gospel to the fundamental facts of Christian experience, and to the growing catholicity of Christian men all over the world." John Brown, *John Bunyan*, p. 491.

7 David Wallechinsky, Irving Wallace, and Amy Wallace, *The Book of Lists*, pp. 218-219.

identify the book.[8] Further, why in this enlightened and secular age should we ever consider a biblical allegory that is over three hundred years old, that is so militantly Protestant and of the very essence of English seventeenth century Puritan thought? And again, why should we give so much as the time of day to a writing that was authored by an unlearned mender of pots and pans who lacked even a secondary education?

Why? Because all of these responses are but symptoms of biblical Christianity in present decline, of soul lethargy that shuns mind stimulation, of blinding modernity. They indicate a condition of pervasive spiritual dullness and indifference that requires not a capitulation to further drifting, but rather a heeding of Jeremiah's exhortation to backslidden Israel: "Ask for the ancient paths, where the good way is, and walk in it; and you shall find rest for your souls" (Jer. 6:16).

Of course we hasten to add that such a rallying call is not to past tradition and antiquarian loyalties. But we do strenuously maintain that there is a desperate need for Christian churches today to return to, "the faith which was once for all delivered to the saints" (Jude 3), and that Bunyan's classic allegory is ideally suited for stimulating such a recovery in its faithful undergirding of essential Bible truth. Yes, as shall be made more clear in detail, *The Pilgrim's Progress* must be suitably presented to this modern secular generation while keeping in view the media and image consciousness of today that Bunyan never remotely dreamed about. Nevertheless we would vigorously contend that *The Pilgrim's Progress* is an ideal and proven medium for reaching our present generation. Seminar experience has demonstrated this point over and over again. What is needed is passionate recommendation, communication, and proclamation of the peerless allegory. And in so doing the Word of God, and the gospel in particular, will be set forth with a purity and power that will prove to be both uncommonly refreshing and effectual. Recently, during a seminar conducted by this writer, between sessions a man confessed that his wife had recently left him. Then he added: "However, in spite of participation in counseling, this teaching of John Bunyan's has been far more helpful."

---

[8] Diane Ravitch and Chester E. Finn, jun., *What do our 17-years olds know?* cited by Christopher Hill, *A Tinker And A Poor Man*, pp. 372-373.

Some Necessary Qualifications.

Because literary awareness is at an all time low within Christendom, it has become necessary to deal first with certain misunderstandings which a previous generation would not have entertained. For instance, this writer has heard on several occasions the opinion expressed that *The Pilgrim's Progress* was an account of the Pilgrim Fathers' journey from Europe to America! At other times some have confused John Bunyan with Paul Bunyan, the American folklore hero! And multitudes have, on eventually studying this great classic, freely confessed their former ignorance concerning what *The Pilgrim's Progress* really taught. Hence, four qualifications are given here for the purpose of clearing the air and allowing Bunyan's real intentions and content to stand out with biblical clarity.

1. The Pilgrim's Progress was not primarily written for children.

The Christian book market is becoming increasingly flooded with simplified versions of *The Pilgrim's Progress* that are apparently designed to make the allegory appealing to children and toddlers. Not surprisingly, some have been led to believe that *The Pilgrim's Progress* was principally written for children, and nothing could be further from the truth since it is definitely an adult book that deals with a multitude of very adult situations. Luther scholar Gordon Rupp confirms this estimate when he describes how, "Coleridge called it [*The Pilgrim's Progress*] a compendium of evangelical doctrine, and we shall be wise not to treat it as a long outmoded pious book for children."[9] For a more detailed consideration of this misunderstanding refer to Chapter 19.

2. The Pilgrim's Progress was not written for academic study.

John Bunyan and his writings have proved to be a happy hunting ground for twentieth century academics who, while repudiating his Calvinistic doctrine and literalist understanding of the Bible, have bowed to his natural abilities and analyzed his person and works from a multitude of perspectives. These include:

a. Literary criticism, concerning style, sources, influences, and allegorical structure.
b. Historical investigation, concerning a turbulent, revolutionary seventeenth century.

---

[9] Gordon Rupp, *Six Makers of English Religion, 1500-1700*, p. 98.

c. Psychological analysis, concerning Bunyan's puritan mores and supposed sensitive psyche.
d. Political theory, concerning secular partisan conflicts, class struggles, and influences.
e. Theological appreciation, concerning a biblicist Puritan era that is usually assessed from a modern skeptical perspective.

For a more detailed consideration of these areas of specialist study refer to Chapter 18. However, Bunyan's fundamental purposes in writing *The Pilgrim's Progress* were spiritual and pastoral as his introductory and concluding poems so clearly indicate. He desired to gain the attention of the listless and indifferent, and even bait them with his engaging style. His concern was for the souls of men, both the lost in commending Christ to them at the Wicket-gate, and authentic Christians in encouraging them to persevere toward the Celestial City.

3. The Pilgrim's Progress is not merely a simple gospel tract.

While the gospel pervades the allegory as a whole, in Part One 10.5% of the text is concerned with the beginning of the allegory up to Christian's reception at the Wicket-gate and conversion, while 89.5% of the text takes us from the Wicket-gate up to the conclusion at the Celestial City. As the title plainly suggests, *The Pilgrim's Progress* is chiefly about the progress of a Christian pilgrim.

4. The Pilgrim's Progress is not a non-doctrinal moral novel.

Truncated versions of *The Pilgrim's Progress* are inevitably pruned of the more doctrinal discourse sections. However, it comes as a surprise to the serious student of the allegory to discover that Bunyan deals with theological issues with considerable precision and detail. Dr. J. Gresham Machen perceptively writes of, "that tenderest and most theological of books, the *Pilgrim's Progress* of John Bunyan, . . . that is pulsating with life in every word."[10]

The Essential Purposes of The Pilgrim's Progress

From the outset, and in view of the preceding disclaimers, it would seem important to declare positively, in a summary fashion, what in essence John Bunyan intends to communicate in *The Pilgrim's Progress* that is below the surface of his allegorical style.

---

[10] J. Gresham Machen, *Christianity and Liberalism*, p. 46.

In the concluding poem of Part One he challenges his readers as follows:

> Take heed also, that thou be not extreme,
> In playing with the outside of my dream:
> Nor let my figure or similitude
> Put thee into a laughter or a feud.
> Leave this for boys and fools; but as for thee,
> Do thou the substance of my matter see.[11]

Hence, the obvious question that has to be considered here is, what does Bunyan mean when he directs the reader to the "substance" of his allegory? Clearly it involves the essence of his biblical emphases, and it is suggested that these concern four recurring themes.

a. The gospel of the Lord Jesus Christ's saving, substitutionary righteousness, as the ground of the advancing pilgrim's justification and sanctification.
b. Progressive sanctification, from entrance at the Wicket-gate by means of transforming conversion to entrance into the Celestial City with resultant glorification.
c. Church fellowship under faithful pastoral leadership, as the only sure place of earthly refuge and support for pilgrims in transit.
d. Anticipation of ultimate deliverance from the evil and trials of this world, along with future glory in the presence of Christ, when entrance is gained at the Celestial City.

THE PILGRIM'S PROGRESS IS THOROUGHLY BIBLICAL

Even a casual acquaintance with *The Pilgrim's Progress* will reveal its biblical solidity. C. H. Spurgeon has vividly described this intrinsic quality as follows:

> Read anything of his [Bunyan's], and you will see that it is almost like reading the Bible itself. He had studied our Authorized Version, . . . he had read it till his whole being was saturated with Scripture; and, though his writings are charmingly full of poetry, yet he cannot give us his *Pilgrim's Progress*—that sweetest of all prose poems,—without continually making us feel and say, 'Why, this man is a living Bible!' Prick him anywhere; and you will find that his blood is

---

[11] Bunyan, *Works,* III, p. 167.

Bibline, the very essence of the Bible flows from him. He cannot speak without quoting a text, for his soul is full of the Word of God.[12]

As a Montage of Bible truth

Aside from the basic marginal Scripture references which Bunyan supplies, there are countless other biblical passages that are almost seamlessly woven together. Often this montage is so smooth that the reader may be unaware that the Bible is in fact being quoted. Consider just one instance, when Evangelist reappears to discover Christian paralyzed with fear as he cowers under the threatening sheer slopes of the mountain, in reality Mt. Sinai, that separates him from the village called Morality. Evangelist's first words of stern enquiry are, "What doest thou here?"[13] Christian's only response is shameful silence since he has departed from the narrow way. But does this not recall a similar Old Testament scene, that of the prophet Elijah having fled from wicked Jezebel to a desert cave, where the word of the Lord addresses him in a similarly shameful situation, "What doest thou here, Elijah?" (I Kings 19:9 KJV). In this case, Bunyan gives no Scripture reference even though the specific biblical situation is clearly implicit. Hence, it is possible to study *The Pilgrim's Progress* without being fully aware of the biblical content that is being assimilated.

As a Multi-level Composition

It would also be true to say that Bunyan has incorporated levels of biblical understanding in *The Pilgrim's Progress* which account for its appeal within a wide range of age levels. There is the *basic* level of graphic spiritual adventure which is so captivating for young children and simply identified by character and situation names. There is the *biblical* level which transcends the allegorical framework so that the broad panorama of redemption is identified. There is the *doctrinal* or substantial level which deals with such categories as justification, imputation, Christ's person and work, the church, the world, sanctification, glorification, etc.

As a Systematic Presentation of Bible Truth

Hence, it is perhaps most significant of all that Bunyan's use of Scripture is ultimately systematic rather than indiscriminate. He

---

[12] C. H. Spurgeon, *C. H. Spurgeon's Autobiography*, IV, p. 268.

[13] Bunyan, *Works*, III, p. 94.

uncompromisingly presents a unified body of doctrine that clearly portrays the great truths of God, man, sin, Jesus Christ, grace, redemption, sanctification, the final judgment, glorification, etc. Nowhere is this emphasis clearer than in Bunyan's many-faceted presentation of the gospel. In Christian is mirrored Bunyan's own distinctive saving embrace of Christ with its disjunction between the Wicket-gate and the Place of Deliverance (refer to Chapter 6), whereas in Hopeful's testimony we have the process of conversion described in its more normative expression. Immediately following this comes the contrast of Ignorance's faith in a false gospel, that is his trust in an infused (inner) righteousness that produces justifying personal works of righteousness.

In all of this Bunyan is adamant that only the imputed substitutionary righteousness of Jesus Christ, received through faith alone, is able to reconcile any sinner to God. In full agreement with Luther, he insists that this gift of justifying righteousness is of the very essence of the gospel. And it is for this reason, this pervasive gospel centrality, that *The Pilgrim's Progress* is of such great importance for these days of clouded doctrine, for it is not only thoroughly biblical, but also truly evangelistic.

THE PILGRIM'S PROGRESS HAS PROVEN UNIVERSAL APPEAL

In the 1986 edition of *The Norton Anthology of English Literature*, a somewhat paradoxical comment is made. It is that while "*The Pilgrim's Progress* is no longer a household book [as it formerly was]," yet it remains "the most popular allegory in our literature."[14] Now as to this more recent fall in popularity, further consideration will later be given to this concern. However, though this definitive manual describes *The Pilgrim's Progress* as the most popular *allegory* even at the present, it is proposed that this acknowledged recognition and circulation involves wider dominance.

It is Second Only to the Bible

While both William Shakespeare and Bunyan's contemporary rival John Milton may have cause to challenge in the field of general literary stature, even they cannot offer a single title that equals Bunyan's sustained universal popularity with regard to the circulation of his magnum opus. In other words, it is no

[14] M. H. Abrams. ed., *The Norton Anthology of English Verse*, I, pp. 1857-1858.

exaggeration to claim that *The Pilgrim's Progress* remains the most popular and widest circulating single piece of English literature, allegory or otherwise, outside of the Bible.[15] And this being so, such a book continues to merit careful study.

Leading Bunyan scholar Roger Sharrock has written in this vein as follows:

> *The Pilgrim's Progress* is a book which in three hundred years of its existence has crossed most of those barriers of race and culture that usually serve to limit the communicative power of a classic. It has penetrated into the non-Christian world; it has been read by cultivated Moslems during the rise of religious individualism within Islam, and at the same time in cheap missionary editions by American Indians and South Sea Islanders. Its uncompromising evangelical Protestantism has not prevented it from exercising an appeal in Catholic countries. But to English readers it is bound to appear as the supreme classic of the English Puritan tradition.[16]

It has Suckled Close to the Bible

However, is this world-wide popularity simply due to an appealing simplicity of style contained within an arresting allegorical form? Surely the answer to this question must be in the negative if these two elements are all that we perceive Bunyan's method to be. For as well as style and form, he has forged a biblical epic that has suckled close to the most popular book in all of human history, that is the Bible. Here is the primary cause of the Bedford tinker's unrivaled success. In *The Cambridge History of English Literature* this conclusion is well supported. "There are now versions of *The Pilgrim's Progress* in no fewer than one hundred and eight [now 200] different languages and dialects, so

---

[15] N. H. Keeble writes: "No other seventeenth-century text save the King James Bible, nothing from the pen of a writer of Bunyan's social class in any period, and no other puritan, or, indeed, committed Christian work of any persuasion, has enjoyed such an extensive readership." John Bunyan, *The Pilgrim's Progress*, Oxford World's Classics, ed. N. H. Keeble, p. ix. In the eighteenth century Benjamin Franklin writes that "it [*The Pilgrim's Progress*] has been more generally read than any other book, except perhaps the Bible." *The Autobiography Of Benjamin Franklin*, p. 53. Also refer to Keeble's excellent review of Bunyan's rise in popularity in, "'Of him thousands daily Sing and talk': Bunyan and his Reputation." *John Bunyan: Conventicle and Parnassus, Tercentenary Essays*, ed. N. H. Keeble, pp. 241-263.

[16] John Bunyan, *The Pilgrim's Progress*, ed. Roger Sharrock, p. 7.

that it is no mere poetical figure to say, as has been said, that it follows the Bible from land to land as the singing of birds follows the dawn."[17]

It Merits Optimistic Recognition

What then is the point for us today concerning this sustained though fading universal recognition? It is simply that the present neglect of *The Pilgrim's Progress* ought to be cause for acknowledgment of contemporary impoverishment rather than fleeting patronage of a past literary curiosity that is believed to contain only outmoded theology. But further, it is our belief that such repentance ought to be evidenced by an awakening to the need of freshly impassioned proclamation of Bunyan's classic. The favorable judgment of the last three centuries is not something that should be lightly tossed aside. Perhaps the fault really lies with a modern generation that is neglectful of history, sensually intoxicated, mentally lazy, biblically illiterate, and rebellious toward God. However, more particularly, even evangelical Christianity has turned from its Godly heritage to imbibe a mess of man-centered religious pottage.

Nathaniel Hawthorne recognized this deterioration within Christendom even during the middle of the nineteenth century so that he was stimulated to write his short parody of Bunyan's allegory titled *The Celestial Railroad*. In it he caricatures the prevailing interest of nominal Christians in desiring to travel, not now by means of a narrow trial strewn way, but rather a more comfortable rail journey that promises the same destination by means of a less laborious form of transportation.[18] But more than such insightful satire is required at this hour.

However true such an analysis may be concerning the subtle seduction of the church by the world, the assessment of *The Pilgrim's Progress* for the future by Cambridge scholar, George Sampson ought to be seriously pondered and optimistically embraced.

> There is no need to say anything about the book by way of criticism; for its characters, its scenes and its phrases have become a common possession. Of course in every age there has been, and there always will be, the kind of superior person who disdains it.

---

[17] A. R. Ward and A. R. Waller, *The Cambridge History of English Literature*, VII, p. 177.

[18] Nathaniel Hawthorne, *The Celestial Railroad*, 20 pp.

> Such people are naught. *The Pilgrim's Progress* goes on forever. Creeds may change and faith may be wrecked; but the life of man is still a pilgrimage, and in its painful course he must encounter the friends and the foes, the dangers and the despairs that Bunyan's inspired simplicity has drawn so faithfully that even children know them at once for truth.[19]

THE PILGRIM'S PROGRESS HAS WINSOME CHARACTER

In alluding to Jesus Christ's command to the disciples Peter and Andrew, "Follow Me, and I will make you fishers of men" (Matt. 4:19), John Bunyan includes the following lines in his introductory poetic apology to *The Pilgrim's Progress*:

> You see the ways the fisherman doth take
> To catch the fish; what engines doth he make!
> Behold! How he engageth all his wits;
> Also his snares, lines, angles, hooks and nets.
> Yet fish there be, that neither hook nor line,
> Nor snare, nor net, nor engine can make thine:
> They must be grop'd for, and be tickled too,
> Or they will not be catch'd, whate'er you do.[20]

The evangelistic rationale here is clear, unambiguous, and somewhat bold. Even though persuasion as a broad category may be open to abuse through extreme and gimmicky application, nevertheless gospel truth ought to be presented in a manner suitable to the sensitivities and peculiarities of the audience. In particular, let the indifferent masses be more than baited; rather let them even be massaged a little; let the truth be so packaged that it arouses attention, awakens curiosity, stimulates interest, goads reaction, and promotes response.[21] In this same poem Bunyan continues:

> Art thou for something rare and profitable?
> Wouldest thou see a truth within a fable?

---

[19] George Sampson, *The Concise Cambridge History of English Literature*, p. 375.

[20] Bunyan, *Works*, III, p. 85.

[21] Beyond any doubt, Bunyan was a strict Calvinist, yet on the other hand here we note his innovative approach to the communication of the truth of God. For a more detailed consideration of this matter refer to Chapters 16-17.

Art thou forgetful? Wouldst thou remember
From New-Years-Day to the last of December?
Then read my fancies, they will stick like burs,
And may be to the helpless, comforters.

This book is writ in such a dialect,
As may the minds of listless men affect;
It seems a novelty, and yet contains
Nothing but sound and honest gospel strains.[22]

Again the judgment of history is that this imprisoned pastor's goal was achieved beyond his most extravagant hopes. From the outset of its publication, *The Pilgrim's Progress* has captivated successive levels of society, except for the latter part of this twentieth century. The following engraving by J. D. Watson of the last century well illustrates this universal popularity. It represents a scholar coming

The early popularity of The Pilgrim's Progress

---

[22] Bunyan, *Works*, III, p. 8

out from under the Sign of the Peacock, the address of Bunyan's publisher, Nathaniel Ponder. There is also a more rustic character with a whip in one hand and money in the other who is going into the shop, while standing beside the door are a gay gallant and a fair lady, schoolboys, serious men and women, all busily reading their copy of the best selling allegory.

It is Doctrinally Winsome

From a slightly different perspective, that is concerning Bunyan's doctrinal emphasis, poet Samuel Coleridge describes his appeal in this regard as follows:

> This wonderful work [*The Pilgrim's Progress*] is one of the very few books which may be read over repeatedly at different times, and each time with a new and a different pleasure. I read it once as a theologian—and let me assure you that there is great theological acumen in the work—once with devotional feelings—and once as a poet. I could not have believed beforehand that Calvinism could be painted in such exquisitely delightful colors.[23]

It is Biblically Arresting

The question then that faces us today is whether this acknowledged appeal of the past is adequate for the present. While admitting the original attractiveness of Bunyan's style and content, is it nevertheless suitable for an age that has moved from typography to television, from discourse to sound-bites, from objectivity to subjectivity, from facts to feelings, from reality to sensuality, from tradition to modernity? In other words, can an old-fashioned literary garment, though popular in its time, yet wear well and admirably in the present and therefore be communicated today in a manner that is up-to-date, faithful to Bible truth, and equally enchanting? The undoubted conviction of this writer is, with the weight of history on his side, that *The Pilgrim's Progress* can be effectively communicated by teaching and proclamation that is both passionate and persuasive; indeed when a person, gifted of God, brings forth the Word of God that Bunyan has so marvelously enshrined in his allegorical style, he will find it quite easy for him to move into the mode of preaching and proclamation. One of the prime reasons for reduced interest has simply been misunderstanding about the essential message of

---

[23] Roger Sharrock, ed., *Bunyan, The Pilgrim's Progress, A Casebook*, p. 53.

the tinker preacher; when the truth has been pointed out in teaching and seminar settings, time and time again the enthusiastic response has been astonishment at what Bunyan is really saying, especially in terms of the gospel, sanctification, local church life and pastoral leadership.

THE PILGRIM'S PROGRESS SPEAKS TO THE SPIRITUAL NEEDS OF THE HOUR

Unfortunately, as mentioned earlier, *The Pilgrim's Progress* has more recently been perceived in the last half of this century as a book more suitable for children since it has been thought to be designed to present simple Bible truth in an imaginative, adventuresome, even fairy tale manner. However, such an assessment is far from the truth. One has only to consider the variety of cast characters to realize that no child of few years in this life could fully comprehend the developed traits, both perverse and godly, that are embodied in these mostly adult persons. When we understand that Faithful is propositioned by a seductress, that Christian is inclined to commit suicide, and that Hopeful has a fleeting appetite for mammon, only then do we begin to grasp that *The Pilgrim's Progress* is about perennial adult problems that can only be dealt with by means of God's timeless gospel remedy.

If someone suggests that *The Pilgrim's Progress* is quite outdated and incapable of addressing the complex struggles of our technological and sophisticated generation, this writer simply responds with a series of questions that goes something like this: "Do you know of anyone today who could be designated as a Mr. Worldly-wiseman or a Mr. Save-self? Amongst your neighbors or friends at work, do you recognize a Mr. Money-love or a Mr. Love-lust? In your experience in church life, have you ever encountered a Pastor Two-tongues who says one thing and believes another? Do you know religious people who could be just as boldly hypocritical as Talkative? Have you occasionally met a real Christian who, like Hopeful, is so buoyant and encouraging in the midst of trying circumstances?" On so many occasions, people who hear this challenge grin as they acknowledge that times have not really changed, at least with regard to the basic character of man.

Hence, there are the best of reasons for maintaining that *The Pilgrim's Progress* is well able to address the spiritual torpor and ignorance of these modern times. In particular it confronts the growing corrosion of evangelical Christianity from a number of perspectives.

There is the Need of Clear Proclamation of the Gospel

While the Apostle Paul was zealous in upholding the truth of the gospel with great exactness (Gal. 1:6-9; 2:4-5, 14-16), present evangelism has degenerated into mere abstract, sentimental and relational encounter with an ill-defined Christ. In particular, the modern gospel has blurred the centrality of the atonement and the fundamental moral conflict between God and man addressed by the doctrine of justification by faith alone.

However, *The Pilgrim's Progress* calls us back to this Pauline gospel precision. Bunyan was a great admirer of Martin Luther, and especially the reformer's commentary on Galatians.[24] It is no surprise then to discover the Bedford pastor was rooted and grounded in that same gospel of free justification. The conversion testimony of Hopeful and the detailed dispute between Christian and Ignorance are model expositions of the nature of both true and false conversion, and the gospel as God's gift of imputed perfect righteousness received through faith alone.

There is the Need of Clear Proclamation of Sovereign Grace

Avoid the emotive terms of "Calvinism" and "Arminianism" if we will, yet in this century the Christian ground swell has been predominantly toward the powers of human autonomy at the expense of the sovereignty of God. Free-will doctrine has dominated the frontiers of evangelism, and thus it ought to be no surprise that the resulting harvest has produced a large number of doubtful conversions and spiritual stillbirths.

However in this arena Calvinist Bunyan has much to teach us. Again we quote from Samuel Coleridge. "Calvinism never put on a less rigid form, never smoothed its brow and softened its voice more winningly than in *The Pilgrim's Progress.*"[25] Yes, the portrayal of the Man in the Iron Cage, with its emphasis on reprobation, is extremely sobering. Even so, the doctrines of human inability and sovereign grace, and the clear distinction between the particular elect of God and the reprobate simply flow forth as part of a larger canvas; these truths are taught integrally rather than topically.

---

[24] Bunyan, *Works*, I, §§ 129-130, pp. 40-41.

[25] Sharrock, ed., *Pilgrim's Progress, Casebook*, p. 54.

Nevertheless, in Bunyan's overall ministry, there is no logical constriction regarding the free offer of the gospel, but rather the most passionate, repeated, reasoned and entreating gospel invitations. It ought not to surprise us that C. H. Spurgeon, such a lover of the doctrines of sovereign grace, in having so large an admiration for Bunyan should likewise manifest that same unfettered evangelistic zeal.

There is the Need of Clear Proclamation of Sanctification

In this century, two conservative evangelical movements have promoted deviant views of practical Christian sanctification that have resulted in varying degrees of widespread confusion, conflict, and carnality. The influence of the classic English Keswick/Higher Life Movement has been pervasive in numerous convention centers. It has erroneously taught that justification through faith is paralleled by sanctification through faith or passive surrender to the Holy Spirit.[26] The influence of the Pentecostal/Charismatic Movement has been even more influential toward the end of this century, and it has been particularly intrusive in many denominational associations and individual church fellowships. It has erroneously taught that advanced sanctification should come by means of a sudden, cataclysmic, post-conversion baptism in the Holy Spirit evidenced by certain phenomena such as speaking in tongues.

To both of these emphases, *The Pilgrim's Progress* speaks with clarifying freshness and honesty. The allegory's basic format, that is of a journey requiring advancement toward a heavenly destination, is a most graphic representation of the biblical pattern of encountering "conflicts without and fears within" (II Cor. 7:5), of "pressing on toward the goal for the prize of the upward call" (Phil. 3:14), of "growing in the grace and knowledge of the Lord Jesus Christ" (II Pet. 3:18). Bunyan's title is most apt. It is not *Pilgrimage on the High Road* or *The Phenomenal Pilgrim*, but *The Pilgrim's Progress* concerning participation in an endurance race that involves both "entangling encumbrances" and the goal of embrace of Jesus Christ at the "breasting of the line" (Phil. 3:12-14; Heb. 12:1-2). The denial of such ongoing struggle and conflict in the Christian life is both self-delusive and spiritually counter-productive.

---

[26] Refer to J. C. Ryle, *Holiness*, and B. B. Warfield, *Perfectionism*.

There is the Need of Clear Proclamation that Honors God

In his poetic introduction to *The Pilgrim's Progress,* Bunyan indicates just how sensitive he was to criticism of his allegorical method. He sought advice from pastoral colleagues. He did not rush into publication. He considered biblical standards of communication. And he eventually decided to go to print and let history be the final arbiter. Of course the verdict of universal approval has been in for some time, and without question there has never been any ongoing criticism with regard to Bunyan's literary style in terms of it being irreverent or lacking in spiritual taste.

Yes, there are moments of very droll humor, though these are far outweighed by the more numerous scenes of transfixing seriousness. But there are never found vain or flippant expressions, never coarseness or vulgarity,[27] especially when the person and work of God are concerned. Of course numerous objectionable and worldly characters are described, and with such clarity that one becomes convinced that their names are simply pseudonyms for specific acquaintances of the author. However, these are also representative of contemporary personality traits that equally pervade this twentieth century.

There are just as many Obstinates and Pliables and Mr. Worldly-wisemans and Talkatives abounding today. Our fashions and accents may have modified over the past three hundred, yet as Bunyan so convincingly demonstrates, the essential characteristics of man prove to be unchanging. And this is why *The Pilgrim's Progress* continues to be ongoing in its popularity, for it communicates with reverence and contemporaneity—that is provided it is suitably proclaimed.

There is the Need of Clear Proclamation that is Competitive

Many of life's choicest experiences have come to us, not so much by means of self-discovery as through the recommendation and enthusiastic persuasion of a friend. For instance, consider the case of a particular foreign cuisine in which formerly we expressed no

---

[27] There is one occasion when Christian and Hopeful are fleeing from Doubting Castle where, in using the key named promise to open the final gate, we are told, "but that lock went damnable hard, yet the key did open it," Bunyan, *Works*, III, p. 143. However this was not a slip born of a blaspheming past. Bunyan's point is that the damning confinement of Doubting Castle was very resistant to the fleeing escapees.

interest whatsoever—perhaps, say, Indian curry dishes. But then a friend presses us to join him at an Indian restaurant for a sample dinner, and so we indifferently accept his gratuitous invitation. His description of the menu is rapturous. But still we are unmoved, that is until we sample the distinctive fare and suddenly awaken to the delights of a whole new world of taste.

Now as a convert to this new type of food, and thus desirous that others be likewise persuaded, ought we simply be content with thinking that all our friends need do is read an Indian recipe book, obtain the curry powder and spices at an import food store, and then proceed to cook an Indian dinner themselves? No, of course not! We need to enthuse our friends, even as we were, through persuasive communication that awakens the listless to a whole new world of delicious enjoyable food. Of course the ingredients must be intrinsically good and appetizing, that is competitive in a world of food. And of prime importance is the necessity for various recipes to be well prepared, and promoted with fervent recommendation.

And so it is with *The Pilgrim's Progress* at this time. It is a neglect of responsibility today to believe simply that it is sufficient for Bunyan's allegory to be available on bookstore shelves. It would certainly be a neglect of responsibility to suggest that the Bible only needs to be made available in bookstores; otherwise preaching and personal evangelism would be regarded as quite superfluous. However, as the Bible does need proclamation, so does *The Pilgrim's Progress* to this present, spiritually dull generation. As a spiritual classic it is essentially good and appealing. History proves just how supremely competitive it really is. Yes, contemporary taste has degenerated. But this is only all the more reason why better food ought to be offered. *The Pilgrim's Progress* needs skillful and applicatory exposition that awakens the lethargic in their souls to a new spiritual taste sensation!

The truth remains that twentieth century man is on a pilgrimage, whether he recognizes it or not, though it is a sad journey to behold. Gordon Rupp describes it this way.

> Modern man, in the ruins of Hiroshima and Nagasaki, in the prisons of Europe, in the cities of Hungary [writing in 1957], knows as poignantly as Christian the dilemma of human existence. But modern man, unlike Christian, has no book in his hand, he has no faith in Evangelist, and a heavenly city seems to him much more likely to be a mirage. The God-dimension is missing, and he does his thinking in a curious parody of Christian verities. He too moves along a road of human experience: meets mishap and disaster:

> knows what comforts comradeship and love, joy and laughter, may bring: knows the besetting impact of evil and temptation: moves inexorably towards the lonely experience of dying. But he cannot answer the question 'Whence?' or 'Whither?'[28]

However, it is the Bible truth of *The Pilgrim's Progress* that can direct him to the answers.

THE INITIATIVE OF GOD IN SAVING SINFUL MEN

It is expected among men that he which giveth the offence should be the first in seeking peace; but, sinner, betwixt God and man it is not so; not that we loved God, not that we chose God; but "God was in Christ, reconciling the world unto himself, not imputing their trespasses unto them." God is the first that seeketh peace.

What sayest thou now, sinner? Is not this God rich in mercy? Hath not this God great love for sinners? Nay, further, that thou mayest not have any ground to doubt that all this is but complementing, thou hast also here declared that God hath made his Christ "to be sin for us, who knew no sin, that we might be made the righteousness of God in him." If God would have struck at anything, he would have struck at the death of his Son; but he "delivered him up for us freely; how shall he not with him also freely give us all things?" (Rom. 8:32).

But this is not all. God doth not only beseech thee to be reconciled to him, but further, for thy encouragement, he hath pronounced it, in thy hearing, exceeding great and precious promises; "and hath confirmed it by an oath, that by two immutable things, in which it was impossible for God to lie, we might have a strong consolation, who have fled for refuge to lay hold upon the hope set before us." (Heb. 6:18-19; Isa. 1:18; 55: 6-7; Jer. 51:5).

John Bunyan
Saved by Grace
Works, I, p. 350

---

[28] Rupp, *Six Makers of English Religion*, p. 101.

CHAPTER TWO

Biblical Reality Through Allegory

WHILE *The Concise Oxford Dictionary* defines an "allegory" as "a story in which the meaning or message is represented symbolically,"[1] John Bunyan in *The Pilgrim's Progress* has a much broader understanding in view. Within the introductory and concluding poems of Part One are to be found eight terms in all which describe his style. They are "allegory," "similitude," "metaphor," "parable," "figure," "type," "fable," and "shadow." In other words, to force his method into a too technical literary definition is inevitably to bring about an invalid suggestion of inconsistency or contradiction.

Let it simply be stated that *The Pilgrim's Progress* is a literary life and truth representation that, though painted on a broad canvas, yet incorporates a blend of various stylistic elements; these include dialogue, muse, poetry, characterization, emblem, droll humor, fantasy, drama, saga, intrigue, polemic, spiritual romance, and mystery. The weaving together of these items also incorporates continuity, contrast, and progression that anticipate a glorious yet sober climax, and so fulfillment of the author's spiritual purposes.

BUNYAN'S JUSTIFICATION OF HIS ALLEGORICAL STYLE

Again, both the introductory and concluding poems of Part One give a comprehensive explanation of his rationale for what was, in Puritan circles, a true literary novelty. The following list of nineteen arguments that Bunyan proposes in support of his allegorical method is especially the product of his interaction with early critical assessments, particularly at a pastoral level.

Concerning the Introductory Poem

1. Apparent darkness of style, as some suggest, may yet yield fruit.

---

[1] R. E. Allen, ed., *The Concise Oxford Dictionary*, p. 30.

2. Hard souls need a stimulating and softening literary style.
3. Difficult souls can only be snared by appropriate equipment.
4. Treasure is often contained in a tawdry casket.
5. "Feigned" or invented and contrived words have made truth to sparkle.
6. Metaphors, types, and shadows have been used by God to communicate solid truth.
7. Impartial men will admit that truth in a covering is better than untruth cased in silver.
8. Paul does not forbid the use of parables.
9. This use of allegory is not extreme, but rather appropriate to the truth.
10. This style is equal to accepted dialogue and principally committed to the truth.
11. This style is found in Scripture and does not smother truth.
12. This style commends the reality of Christian pilgrimage.
13. This style stimulates the forgetful and listless.
14. This style arouses inquisitiveness.
15. Beneath the veil of literary form is substance.
16. Nuggets and veins of truth justify disposable dross.

Concerning the concluding poem

17. The style, though open to abuse, displays good when rightly interpreted.
18. The unveiled outward figure reveals helpful substance.
19. The unwrapped ore-like form discloses the gold of biblical truth.

BUNYAN'S PURPOSES WITH HIS ALLEGORICAL STYLE

While we might desire to discover some grand, ambitious design which compelled Bunyan to commence writing *The Pilgrim's Progress*, yet he tells us in his introductory poem to Part One that such was not the case. He appears to have been well into the composition of *The Heavenly Footman*,[2] in prison of course, when

---

2 Posthumously published in 1698 based on I Corinthians 9:24, this small work similarly uses the pilgrimage motif to represent the

suddenly the sparks of an idea flashed into his fertile mind, more as a literary challenge to his sanctified spirit than anything else, so that it gradually flamed to a point of dominance. He tells us he also shunned the bad produce of idleness. Did he then form some noble missionary vision in his thinking whereby he might confront an ungodly world that needed the truth via literary titillation? No, for Bunyan tells us quite honestly that he wrote simply, "mine own self to gratify."[3] Nevertheless, like a woman spinning flax, he describes how, "as I pull'd it came; and so I penn'd it down,"[4] till it rapidly grew in size.

However, knowing something of the spiritual earnestness of Bunyan, which he in genuine humility would be most reluctant to boast about or put to writing in some congratulatory sense, we must surely read between the lines here and attribute to him a more specific and edifying purpose, even if almost unconscious, than he is prepared to admit. Clearly the introductory poem was written when Part One had been completed and publication was imminent. Nevertheless, its concluding lines are a strong statement of several purposes that need to be appreciated by both the reader in general and the teacher of *The Pilgrim's Progress* in particular. They are as follows:

He Intended to Gain the Attention of the Indifferent

As a pastor, Bunyan was an astute observer of his fellow man and the world of nature as well. And by means of this capacity for keen perception he both learned many lessons and was sufficiently flexible in making application that always kept within the bounds of holy propriety. Convinced Calvinist though he was, yet Bunyan did not hesitate to write as follows concerning winsomeness in evangelistic outreach which he learned, not only from skillful fishing (Matt. 4:19) as already mentioned, but also "fowling" or bird hunting. Such means he considered to be perfectly legitimate.

> How does the fowler seek to catch his game
> By divers means! All which one cannot name:
> His gun, his nets, his lime-twigs, light and bell:
> He creeps, he goes, he stands; yea, who can tell

Christian as being encouraged to avoid dallying and rather run with preparation toward heaven.

3 John Bunyan, *Works*, III, p. 85.

4 John Bunyan, *The Pilgrim's Progress*, eds. Wharey and Sharrock, p. 312.

Of all his postures? Yet, there's none of these
Will make him master of what fowls he please.
Yea, he must pipe and whistle, to catch this,
Yet if he does so, that bird he will miss.[5]

Nevertheless, with regard to this present century great discernment is certainly needed here concerning the critical question that immediately comes to mind about what is appropriate enticement. And when is "piping" and "whistling" legitimate and illegitimate? Bunyan, while incorporating modest literary amusement in some of his writings, would doubtless abominate modern gimmickry in ministry such as that of "Christian comedy" and the entertainment syndrome so prevalent in contemporary local churches. The Bunyan Meeting was quite strict and sober by today's standards.[6] Even so, the dry and witty humor of *The Pilgrim's Progress* does seem to indicate how moderately far he would go with his "hunting," and no further. Most likely this indicates the limit of his spiritual "stalking."

However, it ought to be readily understood that sobriety in the allegory does far outweigh the lighter occasions. This proportion is evident in the totality of Bunyan's ministry including his other writings. The moments of very droll expression are far eclipsed by the periods of intense seriousness. Certainly both the commencement and conclusion of the allegory are exceedingly sober. As already mentioned, there is not the slightest hint of coarseness or worldly banter.

He Intended to Communicate Biblical Reality Through Allegory

In a world that frantically attempts to avoid reality by immersing itself in fantasy or diversionary escapades, whether through television, science fiction, music, drugs, or a hundred other indulgences, Bunyan presents us with a reverse scenario. He is passionately concerned that men and women should be confronted with the biblical reality concerning themselves that they so desperately seek to evade. This he does by engaging their attention with enticing allegory that suddenly turns our amusement and

---

[5] John Bunyan, *Works*, III, p. 86.

[6] Richard Greaves explains: "Those admitted to church membership, according to Bunyan, were those who were 'for separating from the unconverted and open prophane, and for building up one another an holy Temple in the Lord, through the Spirit'", *John Bunyan*, p. 127.

enjoyment into a sober reminder about truth and real life and sin and God and guilt and our ultimate destiny.

Of course the reader of *The Pilgrim's Progress* can still purposely avoid Bunyan's warning and determine only to "play with the outside of his dream," as he puts it, though he does so at his own peril along with Bunyan's condemnation of such foolishness. Lord Macaulay has significantly written that, "Bunyan is almost the only writer who ever gave to the abstract the interest of the concrete."[7] Surely this is the wonder and intrigue and captivating quality that continues to appeal to even the twentieth century reader, provided he will spend sufficient time to give the gifted pastor of Bedford a fair hearing.

Modern man increasingly engrosses himself in flights of fancy, many of which he has yet to awaken from; his only prospect is the depressing jolt of a return to hard-core reality, and often before a yawning grave. On the other hand, Bunyan invites his audience to take a flight of fancy into reality and thus not awaken with the same necessary wrenching adjustment. Yes, he reveals the reality about sin and guilt and ultimate judgment, not fantasy, and that can be profoundly disturbing. Yet the honest person senses that this revelation has integrity in spite of its allegorical form. But furthermore, Bunyan reveals the reality, not of necessary resignation to the status quo, but rather the glory of the gospel alternative that transfers the awakened sinner to the kingdom of God's grace. When Bunyan concludes, "So I awoke, and behold it was a dream,"[8] he does not deflate us. He is simply stripping away the allegorical form and leaving us with the unchanging gospel truth of biblical revelation.

He Intended to Communicate Truth Through Novel Form

On several occasions the Son of God indicates that at times his servants lacked that proper initiative and shrewdness which the children of the Devil only too frequently manifested (Matt. 10:16; Luke 16:1-9; cf. Josh. 9:3-27). However, it is doubtful if the Bedford tinker could be charged with being negligent in this regard. In the introductory poem of *The Pilgrim's Progress* are the lines:

---

[7] Roger Sharrock, ed., *Bunyan, The Pilgrim's Progress, a Casebook*, p. 68.

[8] Bunyan, *Works*, III, p. 166.

Art thou for something rare and profitable?
Wouldest thou see a truth within a fable?
Then read my fancies, they will stick like burs,
And may be to the helpless comforters.[9]

So the wily literary artist declares here both his spiritual priority and alluring strategy.

1. The priority of truth.

Amidst the solicitous carnival atmosphere at Vanity Fair, and even the proverbial gaiety that this scene has established, yet the intractable commitment of Christian and Faithful to the pilgrim way without the slightest deviation is certainly representative of Bunyan's own consecration to biblical Christianity. What is it that keeps the two transients from sampling the wares, either to the left or to the right? The answer is in the response of both pilgrims to the hucksters' solicitations, "We buy the truth."[10] Of course no such merchandise was on sale, though the visitors were not slow to recommend this rare commodity in the face of much opposition.

So for Bunyan truth, that is Bible truth about God, man, sin, and grace that could not possibly communicate error, objective and concrete truth, is his chief concern, even though in this instance it is packaged with such an engaging exterior.

2. The strategy of attractive literary form.

To read only *The Pilgrim's Progress* might lead one to conclude that this style is representative of the author in general, and nothing could be further from the truth. The works of Bunyan as a whole convey a far more sober spirit, though no less lacking in imaginative expression. Even *The Holy War*, and certainly *The Life And Death Of Mr. Badman,* are not so impregnated with subtle and serious wit. Most often Bunyan is direct, intimate and solid, combining evangelistic fervor, pressing application with close doctrinal reasoning while at every hand he is unflinching in his defense of the truth of Scripture. Like his mentor Martin Luther, he throbs with life and is never dull.

However *The Pilgrim's Progress* is distinctive because it is aimed at a difficult and resistant market. Who specifically comprises this audience? According to the introductory poem of Part One, it is

---

[9] Ibid., p. 87.

[10] Ibid., p. 128.

the slothful, blind, forgetful, listless, melancholy, etc. This being so, then what enticement is offered? It is fancies, novelty, riddles, amusement, but not in an overwhelming measure so that the truth is all but lost sight of. No, there is enough bait to cause the fish to bite, but the hook of truth remains substantial just below the surface.

He Intended to Persuade the Reader to Become a Traveler

It is true as George Offor writes that, "all mankind are pilgrims; all are pressing through this world."[11] Nevertheless, the problem remains that all of mankind are not headed in the same direction, and it is this matter of destiny that causes Bunyan, so anxious for the souls of men, to set them earnestly upon a very specific and unique course. So again in the introductory poem of Part One is to be found an invitation for the spiritually adventurous to become travelers.

> This book will make a traveler of thee,
> If by its counsel thou wilt ruled be;
> It will direct thee to the Holy Land,
> If thou wilt its directions understand.[12]

However, this spiritual travel agent is not one to recommend the journey without having first tasted of the route heavenward himself. *Grace Abounding to the Chief of Sinners* is a faithful publicity testimonial and brochure, though unlike recruiting posters it does not describe the cost in small print, but rather with bold honesty. On the other hand, the resting places and forward scenery portrayed in full graphic color are enough to allure any serious pilgrim.

From another perspective, one of the recurring elements in this whole matter of allegorical journeying, of progress to a destination, is that of recapitulation. On numerous occasions the major pilgrims are to be found recollecting their former experiences, either to prove their authentic status, or to reassure themselves and fellow travelers; "Thus far the Lord has helped us" (I Sam. 7:12). All in all, Bunyan is intently involved in stimulating his readers to move and not be static. He is very sympathetic to the backsliding of a Christian or the slowness of a Little-faith insofar as they

---

11 Ibid., p. 1.

12 Ibid., p. 87.

resume progress. But the inertia of a Simple, Sloth, or Presumption is greatly distressing to him.

He Intended to Animate the Reader to Become an Arriver

For the Apostle Paul it was not enough for sinners to be converted unto Christ through his ministry. Rather he never ceased to be concerned about the safe arrival home of these saints into the very presence of the Lord Jesus Christ. So to the Thessalonians he writes: "For what is our hope or joy or crown of exultation? Is it not even you, in the presence of our Lord Jesus at his coming?" (I Thess. 2:19). With a similar interest Bunyan writes in *Grace Abounding to the Chief of Sinners* to his readers: "I now once again, . . . do look yet after you all, greatly longing to see your safe arrival into the desired haven. . . . The milk and honey is beyond this wilderness. God be merciful to you, and grant that you be not slothful to go in to possess the land."[13]

So in *The Pilgrim's Progress*, this same long-term goal is even more graphically portrayed. It is not an allegory about "successful" evangelistic crusades, but rather the faithful shepherding of souls who enter the Wicket-gate unto their safe reception in the Celestial City. The dominant perspective of the major pilgrims is not merely that of present sanctification, but God's consummate "eternal glory in Christ" of which we have had but a small taste (I Cor. 2:9; 13:12; I Pet. 5:10). Typical of this priority is Bunyan's rapturous final description of the Celestial City and his envious editorial remark at the entrance of Christian and Hopeful into that holy metropolis of heaven: "I wished myself among them."[14]

BUNYAN'S CRITICS AND HIS ALLEGORICAL STYLE

The introductory poem of Part One of *The Pilgrim's Progress* makes it abundantly clear that the initial criticism of such a novelty was more a matter of moral propriety and Christian suitability rather than literary correctness of style or doctrinal orthodoxy. However, a change of emphasis has now taken place and reached a point where the classic is regarded more as a literary specimen of an outdated species that is chiefly suitable for the endless mining of historic minutia, exotic stylistic speculation, and antiquarian conjecture. The one common factor that unites this delving is a

---

[13] Ibid., I, pp. 4, 5.

[14] Ibid., III, p. 166.

studied avoidance of any commitment to the truth of Bunyan's message.

Roger Sharrock describes this development in a very honest and revealing fashion as follows:

> The greater part of the writing about *The Pilgrim's Progress* in the eighteenth, nineteenth, and into the twentieth century, was in the nature of pious commentary and moral exhortation, much of it by writers in the Free Church tradition. For a book that lay in the window-seat with the Bible there was no possibility of pure literary criticism; that was only to come, like the concept of 'the Bible designed to be read as Literature', in the decadence of the English religious tradition.[15]

What a confession this is! One could hope that this writer does indeed mean that the "pure literary criticism" of today is in fact a symptom of deep-seated "decadence." But most disturbing of all is the inference that a "pious" regard for *The Pilgrim's Progress* inhibited "pure literary criticism." Herein lies, from the pen of the quintessential twentieth century Bunyan scholar, a frank, albeit misguided confession that objective study is only possible when there is personal detachment from Bunyan's evangelical substance. Mind you, it matters not if a scholar has a strong socialist/secularist/theologically liberal commitment, by which he is openly revisionist in his approach to Bunyan's writings; in that case, such "scholarship" is acceptable and even roundly applauded!

Seventeenth Century Criticism of Bunyan's Allegorical Style

History appears to have delivered its verdict that Bunyan's own apology for his novel allegorical style has been vindicated. The poetic defense of Part One is thorough and persuasive, especially insofar as convincing Christians are concerned, that is those who are sensitive about capitulation to worldliness. Furthermore, it ought to be remembered that prior to 1678 when *The Pilgrim's Progress* was first published, the author had incurred strong opposition from some Baptist leaders concerning his *Differences In Judgment About Water Baptism No Bar To Communion* published in 1673. However, let it be repeated, this difference of opinion was about appropriateness rather than literary style.

At the time of Bunyan's increasing popularity, he also manifested a restrained creative boldness that certainly challenged the more staid of his Puritan acquaintances. In 1664 he had published his

---

[15] Sharrock, *Pilgrim's Progress, a Casebook*, p. 20.

Map Spewing The Order And Causes Of Salvation, an uncommon chart for his time.[16] In the third edition of *The Pilgrim's Progress* published in 1679, there was included "The Sleeping Portrait" as it became known, surely with Bunyan's approval, being a drawing of himself dreaming his dream. It also depicted Christian progressing from the City of Destruction toward the Wicket-gate.[17] This was bold iconography. Yet with the likely endorsement of John Owen,[18] as well as multitudes of common people, the debate subsided giving way to astonishing distribution, acceptance and blessing. As John Brown writes: "The fact that three editions were thus called for within a year, shows that *The Pilgrim's Progress* leaped at a bound to that popularity which it has retained.[19]

Eighteenth Century Criticism of Bunyan's Allegorical Style

However, such initial renown fell more within the ranks of the less cultured strata of society. Christopher Hill explains that, "*The Pilgrim's Progress* was a best-seller from the start among the middling and poorer sort, though despised by the literary establishment."[20] While Dr. Samuel Johnson attributed great merit to the work in 1773, yet the prevailing consensus amongst the sophisticated classes was, as David Hume expressed in 1757, that such writing was in poor taste.[21] Even as late as 1784 William Cowper thought it best to refer to Bunyan's classic, though appreciatively, yet with anonymity. In considering the elements of a good education he includes the allegory, yet makes the following explanation:

> I name thee not lest so despised a name
> Should move a sneer at thy deserved fame.[22]

---

[16] However William Perkins had published a similar diagram in the previous century.

[17] John Bunyan, *The Pilgrim's Progress*, eds. Wharey and Sharrock, pp. xxxviii-xxxix, 353-354.

[18] Christopher Hill, *A Tinker And A Poor Man*, p. 198.

[19] John Brown, *John Bunyan*, p. **251.**

[20] Christopher Hill in, *John Bunyan And His England*, eds., Lawrence, Owens, and Sim, p. 15.

[21] Keeble, *Conventicle and Parnassus*, pp. 247, 248.

[22] William Cowper, *Cowper's Poetical Works*, p. 308.

Nevertheless, the amalgam of *The Pilgrim's Progress* with the dawning evangelical awakening was a fruitful marriage indeed. As a result, the "reading of Bunyan contributed to the conversion or rededication of many who were, or would become, dissenting ministers. Leaders of the Evangelical Revival and of Methodism were inspired by him, returned to him often, and recommended him constantly."[23]

George Whitefield, JohnWesley, Howel Harris, and John Newton, but to name a few, were all enthusiasts for Bunyan's pen. For instance, in 1768, Newton writes to some Christian ladies as follows:

> Soon after I returned [to Olney] from Yorkshire, I began to expound the *Pilgrim's Progress* in our meetings on Tuesday evenings; and, though we had been almost seven months traveling with the pilgrim, we have not yet left the House Beautiful; but I believe [we] shall set off for the Valley of Humiliation in about three weeks. I find this book so full of matter, that I can seldom go through more than a page, or half a page at a time. I hope the attempt has been greatly blessed among us; and for myself, it has perhaps given me a deeper insight into John Bunyan's knowledge, judgment, and experience in the Christian life, than I should ever have had without it.[24]

However, it needs to be pointed out that up to this point, estimates of *The Pilgrim's Progress* were based primarily upon biblical substance, even though there was fascination with the captivating novel style and background.

Nineteenth Century Criticism of Bunyan's Allegorical Style

While, to apply the words concerning Bunyan's Lord and Master, "the common people heard him gladly" (Mark 12:37), during the 1830's there came forth a remarkable number of opinions from notable literary critics and essayists expressing a previously unknown appreciation of *The Pilgrim's Progress.* For instance classical scholar and educationist Thomas Arnold writes: "I hold John Bunyan to have been a man of incomparably greater genius than any of them [i.e. of the Anglican divines and theologians], and to have given a far truer and more edifying picture of Christianity. His *Pilgrim's Progress* seems to be a complete reflection of Scripture, with none of the rubbish of the

---

[23] Keeble, *Conventicle and Parnassus*, p. 249.

[24] John Newton, *Works*, VI, p. 37-38.

theologians mixed up with it." In the same manner, Samuel Coleridge, Walter Scott, and Thomas Macaulay also heaped praise on the author then dead for over 140 years. Similarly Robert Southey joined this parade of recognition, writes Keeble: "That the poet laureate [Southey] should not feel it beneath his dignity to write a hundred page introduction to *The Pilgrim's Progress* implicitly testified to Bunyan's new-found status."[25]

Yet at this apex of esteem, there also seems to have been injected a move of emphasis, as earlier noted, from evangelical substance to style and background for its own sake. And it ought not to escape notice as well that as a rationalistic approach to the Bible began to infect Christendom in general, so this change of emphasis with regard to *The Pilgrim's Progress* seemed to run in parallel with a birth of supposed "higher" critical enlightenment. Thus in 1880 J. A. Froude, while declaring Bunyan to be distinguished as an "English Man Of Letters," yet suggests a more accommodating approach to the universal concept of pilgrimage than the more specific Puritan model:

> His [Christian's] experience is so truly human experience, that Christians of every persuasion can identify themselves with him; and even those who regard Christianity itself as but a natural outgrowth of the conscience and intellect, and yet desire to live nobly and make the best of themselves, can recognize familiar footprints in every step of Christian's journey.[26]

So by 1905 Robert Bridges can patronizingly comment:

> It is pleasanter to write about Bunyan without reference to his theology. . . . Bunyan himself would have been horrified to find that the secret of his fame was literary excellence, yet without that he would have perished long ago. In this regard his book [*The Pilgrim's Progress*] is like Milton's epic [*Paradise Lost*], which was at first esteemed for its plot and theological aspect, and now is read in spite of them. . . . Overpraise will do his [Bunyan's] reputation no service; and his theology needs so much allowance that anything which dislocates him from his time does him vast injury.[27]

Sad to say, for the decades that have followed, with few exceptions, this new emphasis upon various aspects of style and background

---

[25] Keeble, *Conventicle and Parnassus*, p. 254.

[26] J. A. Froude, *Bunyan, English Men Of Letters*, pp. 154-155.

[27] Sharrock, *Pilgrim's Progress, a Casebook*, pp. 114-115.

rather than evangelical content has remained of the essence of Bunyan scholarship.

Twentieth Century Criticism of Bunyan's Allegorical Style

To assess the overall merits of a new automobile today requires a complex of appreciative skills. Manufacturing excellence, aesthetics, performance, and purpose are all inseparable elements necessary for a true judgment to be made. This is not to say that all of these factors necessarily may be of equal importance. However, if the vehicle's appearance is said to be poor while the intended purpose is strictly utilitarian, then the opinion of the aesthetic analyst becomes of minor importance. And if the standard of manufacture is only mediocre while the purpose of the vehicle is totally fulfilled, then of what use is it to pronounce that the vehicle is poor on the grounds of one criteria? So it is especially the case today with regard to the assessment of *The Pilgrim's Progress*. Many a secular scholar applies a distinctive area of analysis to the famous allegory while in fact this particular enquiry is of minor importance when considered in the light of Bunyan's essential purposes.

1. *The neglect of Bunyan's purposes.*

There are six closely related elements that confront the modern reader of the famous allegory in the realm of Bunyan studies. They are literary style, history, psychology, sociology, theology, and experience, the last two mentioned being preeminent according to Bunyan's stated purposes. However, the great danger is that a contemporary analytical approach may, for instance, very easily focus on the first two of these elements and give them unwarranted prominence. And sad to say, so much of modern criticism of Bunyan reveals its fatal weakness at this point. Often a literature savant will be found to be woefully ignorant of theology as a dynamic of the soul, or a specialist in history will, while having some appreciation of theology, usually from a liberal perspective, be quite ignorant with regard to Bunyan's biblical reasons for his Calvinism. Yet the literary and historical essays of this eclectic genre pour forth unabated and are nevertheless elevated to considerable heights in the forum of scholastic investigation.

2. *The neglect of Bunyan's evangelicalism.*

Thus, most conspicuous by its absence in Bunyan studies today has become that evangelical sympathy with the Bedford pastor's experience that most likely, as Sharrock has intimated, would be regarded as a disqualification for objective study. Mind you, antipathy toward Bunyan's literalist understanding of the Bible would be thought of as no hindrance whatsoever. Furthermore, in this same vein another failure today is the avoidance of the expressed purposes of Bunyan in writing *The Pilgrim's Progress,* especially in any practical sense. Indeed it might not at all be ridiculous to suggest that any modern scholar who experientially identified with Bunyan's gospel might be in danger of academic ostracism!

Of course the problem here is that to consider seriously such a realm is to enter immediately into the area of biblical authority, biblical theology, and resultant personal application. If one agrees with Bunyan, according to his understanding of Scripture, that the predicament of sinful human souls is of supreme importance, and that the evangelical gospel is man's only remedy, then such matters rise far above mere literary style so that academic burrowing of fanciful proportions becomes of far less importance. In this scenario, allegory is a bridge and not an end in itself; literary style is a vehicle that is far transcended in importance by the substance of the gospel freight and ultimate heavenly destination.

3. *The developing critical spirit.*

But the literary quibbling continues. Even during the nineteenth century Macaulay wrote:

> *The Pilgrim's Progress* undoubtedly is not a perfect allegory. The types are often inconsistent with each other; and sometimes the allegorical disguise is altogether thrown off. The river, for example, is emblematic of death; and we are told that every human being must pass through the river. But Faithful does not pass through it. He is martyred in reality, not in shadow, but in reality, at Vanity Fair.[28]

However the simple answer here is that the river represents the normal encounter with death. There are abnormal encounters such as with Enoch and Elijah to which an angel on the river shore refers, as well as martyrdom.

More recently in this century, concerning Christian's sudden discovery of the key called promise, Keeble seems to join with Sharrock in suggesting that such a turn of events is "fictionally

---

[28] Sharrock, *Pilgrim's Progress, a Casebook*, pp. 69-70.

implausible."[29] However Bunyan has experience in mind here so that this thought is most believable. When a Christian is depressed, his Bible at hand may yet be remote to him. This was Bunyan's own experience as he relates in *Grace Abounding*: "I have sometimes seen more in a line of the Bible than I could well tell how to stand under, and yet at another time the whole Bible hath been to me as dry as a stick; or rather, my heart hath been so dead and dry unto it, that I could not conceive the least drachm of refreshment, though I have looked it all over."[30]

More harsh in tone is Brian Nellist in his analysis of the first scene at the house of the Interpreter:

> Interpreter . . . presents his emblems as though they were simple pictures but uses them to disconcert the beholder as though they were hieroglyphs. For example, Christian sees first a man with lifted eyes, book in hand, the world behind him, pleading with men, while a golden crown hangs over his head. 'Christian witness,' we may think. The hero only confirms his naivety in our eyes by asking, 'What means this?'. Yet the interpretation provided is more perplexing than the emblem itself: 'This is one of a thousand; he can beget children, travail in birth with children, and nurse them himself when they are born.' This static figure, moreover, grotesquely distorted, eyes upwards, mouth on the level, back to the world ('Where is the audience, then?'), this is the authorized guide 'in all the difficult places thou meetest with in the way.' If the pictures were in themselves puzzling, their sequence increases our bemusement.[31]

And on and on read the irritated comments. That such remarks could be considered scholarly is difficult to conceive since they hardly merit notice. Doubtless Bunyan intends to make his readers think and dig. The fifth scene in the house of the Interpreter concerning the persevering valiant pilgrim concludes with such a prod.[32] Is Christian "naive"? Yes, since, having recently entered the Wicket-gate, he represents a new rather than a mature believer.

---

[29] John Bunyan, *The Pilgrim's Progress*, ed. N. H. Keeble, p. 275.

[30] Bunyan, *Works*, I, p. 50.

[31] Brian Nellist, "*The Pilgrim's Progress* and Allegory," *The Pilgrim's Progress: Critical And Historical Views*, ed. Vincent Newey, pp. 140-141.

[32] Christian simply declares: "I think verily I know the meaning of this," without any unfolding of this meaning being given. Bunyan, *Works*, III, p. 100.

Here is portrayed the ideal pastor, likened to a spiritual midwife, after the model of John Gifford, who, now represented as Bunyan by the Boehm statue at the corner of St. Peter's Green in Bedford, hardly represents a "grotesque" stance. Surely it is obvious that "the world behind him" refers to his own spiritual priority since he is next described as if "pleading with men," that is the world.

In conclusion, Gordon Wakefield describes Ignorance to have "been judged one of Bunyan's artistic failures. His fate is perplexingly severe. It almost dims the glories of the pilgrims' entry into the Celestial City."[33] But what are the grounds of such judgment? With Wakefield it is not difficult to discover since he confesses not only to being at odds with Bunyan's doctrine, specifically the gospel and his Calvinism which are set against the preferable Arminianism of John Wesley, but also to having an apparent sympathy with universalism.[34] On the other hand, no doubt Bunyan's sober conclusion has in mind the teaching of Jesus Christ as reflected in Matthew 7:21-23, where many will, with shockingly misplaced confidence, be spurned by this same Judge Jesus at the Great Assize!

4. The preferable Bunyan perspective.

What then would be Bunyan's response to all of this? It is this writer's opinion that he would be scathing in his denunciation of such learned "playing with the outside of my dream" while studiously avoiding, even sneering at "the substance of my matter."[35] It is one thing to love *The Pilgrim's Progress* for a multitude of reasons, whether sentimental or academic; it is quite another to love the truth of the allegory. Herein lies the distinguishing factor whereby the evangelical Christian alone has true fellowship with the blessed tinker.

[33] Gordon Wakefield, *Bunyan the Christian*, p. 89.

[34] Ibid., pp. 48-49, 76.

[35] Bunyan, *Works*, III, p. 167.

CHAPTER THREE

The Bible and The Pilgrim's Progress

IN spite of frequent depreciatory remarks at a contemporary scholarly level concerning John Bunyan's "literalist" and "Calvinist" regard for the Bible, and that in a century when the authority of Scripture has waned in influence, the truth is that his understanding of the Book of God was quite representative not only for his time, but also of that stream of evangelical Christianity that continues to the present time. Concerning the seventeenth century, J. A. Froude writes:

> No doubts or questions had yet risen about the Bible's nature or origin. It was received as the authentic word of God Himself. . . . No one questioned it, save a few speculative philosophers in their closets. The statesman in the House of Commons, the judge on the Bench, the peasant in a midland village, interpreted literally by this rule the phenomena which they experienced or saw.[1]

But now, in this era of modern Bunyan studies, Roger Sharrock snidely writes not only of Bunyan's "reliance on the literal text of the Bible," but also his "intense, peculiar reading of Scripture [that] has guided the structure of his narrative [in *The Pilgrim's Progress*]."[2] He further comments: "In Bunyan's spiritual sickness {his conversion struggles related in *Grace Abounding*] the extreme Protestant idea of the Bible as the Word of God was always present to him. Like the majority of Puritan Englishmen of his day, he believed that each verse of the Bible, taken out of its context, still held a message of truth." Bunyan, in fearing that he had committed the unpardonable sin and perhaps identified himself with Judas, draws the comment: "Here we see the remarkable way in which

---

1 J. A. Froude, *Bunyan*, p. 4.

2 John Bunyan, *The Pilgrim's Progress*, ed. Roger Sharrock, pp. 11, 25.

the tradition of bibliolatry harmonized with the psychological temperament of Bunyan."[3]

Also consider Richard Greaves' opinion which, in a pejorative style, implies a reluctance to admit what is patently clear, namely verbal inspiration of the original manuscripts as the prevailing belief of the Puritans along with a normative literalist hermeneutic:

> In practice [but not in principle?], most Nonconformists treated Scripture *as if* [emphasis added] it were infallible, though without addressing this issue. For the most part they were content to think of the Bible as the perfect rule of faith and obedience, the authority of which was divine, at least to the extent that the Spirit suggested the words and aided the authors in expressing their thoughts. . . . In contrast several Dissenters enunciated a view closer to that expressed in our own century by such neo-orthodox theologians as Karl Barth and Emil Brunner.[4]

But John Owen did address the issue of the divine nature of Scripture in great detail.[5] Further, the evidence supplied hardly proves a seventeenth century neo-orthodox existentialist approach to fallible manuscripts, as the Bible being a scratchy record and witness that directs man to Christ as revelation.[6] Such a view

---

[3] Roger Sharrock, *John Bunyan*, p. 64. It is worth noting that Sharrock converted to Roman Catholicism in 1951.

[4] Richard Greaves, *John Bunyan And English Nonconformity*, pp. 30-31. Monica Furlong takes a similar approach when, somewhat patronizingly, she comments: "The more relaxed way he [Bunyan] talks of God and of scripture later in his life, together with what little we know of the religious development of individuals, suggests a move away from literalism into a deeper understanding of the deeper truth of metaphor," *Puritan's Progress*, p. 147.

[5] Greaves does make reference to Owen's profession of verbal inspiration, though not to his substantial work titled, "Three Treatises Concerning The Scriptures," Owen, *Works*, XVI, pp. 281-476.

[6] This is precisely how Emil Brunner regards the Bible. "Everyone has seen the trade slogan 'His Master's Voice.' If you buy a gramophone record you are told that you will hear the Master Carusso. Is that true? Of course! But really his voice? Certainly! And yet—there are some noises made by the machine which are not the master's voice, but the scratching of the steel needle upon the hard disc. But do not become impatient with the hard disc! For only by means of the record can you hear 'the master's voice." So, too, is it with the Bible. It makes the real Master's voice audible—really His voice, His words, what He wants to

would have been anathema to Bunyan, Owen, *et al,* who strenuously opposed Quaker subjectivism and upheld the Bible as a concrete and propositional revelation.[7]

The Bible is Inerrant and Truthful

In *A Relation Of My Imprisonment*, Bunyan describes his encounter with Paul Cobb, Clerk of the Peace in Bedford, at the commencement of his imprisonment, in which he was exhorted to submit to the Church of England. The exchange concerning Bunyan's claim to have the gift of preaching continues as follows:

> *Cobb.* But, said he, how shall we know that you have received a gift?
>
> *Bun.* Said I, Let any man hear and search, and prove the doctrine by the Bible.
>
> *Cobb.* But will you be willing, said he, that two indifferent persons shall determine the case, and will you stand by their judgment?
>
> *Bun.* I said, Are they infallible?
>
> *Cobb.* He said, No.
>
> *Bun.* Then, said I, it is possible my judgment may be as good as theirs. But yet I will pass by either, and in this matter be judged by the Scriptures; I am sure that is infallible, and cannot err.[8]

In approaching the doctrine of the Trinity, Bunyan recommended the impeccable nature of Scripture to be of first priority: "Suffer thyself, by the authority of the word, to be persuaded that the scripture indeed is the word of God; the scriptures of truth, the words of the holy one; and that they therefore must be every one

---

say. But there are incidental noises accompanying, just because God speaks His word through the voice of man. . . . Therefore the Bible is all His voice, notwithstanding all the disturbing things, which, being human, are unavoidable." Emil Brunner, *Our Faith*, pp. 19-20.

7 Refer to J. I. Packer, "John Owen on Communication from God" in relation to Barth's view of Scripture, *A Quest for Godliness*, pp. 81-96.

8 John Bunyan, *The Works of John Bunyan*, ed. George Offor, I, p. 59.

true, pure, and for ever settled in heaven."[9] Thus for Bunyan, the Bible is verbally and plenarily inspired, the result being that it is thoroughly truthful and inerrant; his numerous references to John 10:35 give added support to this contention.[10]

The Bible is Inerrant and Truthful as a Copy of the Original

On one occasion, Bunyan was castigated by a Cambridge scholar since, unlike himself, he did not have access to "the original," presumably the Greek and Hebrew texts. Bunyan enquired if the scholar had the "the very self-same original copies." In responding "No, . . . but we have the true copies of those originals," Bunyan then asked, "How do you know that?" The scholar answered, "Why, we believe what we have is a true copy of the original." To this Bunyan concluded, "Then, so do I believe our English Bible is a true copy of the original."[11]

This understanding of biblical authority, insofar as it applies to present translations, is virtually identical with that annunciated in Article X of *The Chicago Statement On Biblical Inerrancy* produced in 1978: "We affirm that inspiration, strictly speaking, applies only to the autographic text of Scripture, which in the providence of God can be ascertained from available manuscripts with great accuracy. We further affirm that copies and translations of Scripture are the Word of God to the extent that they faithfully represent the original."[12] Of course for Bunyan, we know that he was familiar with both the Geneva Bible and the King James Bible; on one occasion he refers to Tyndale's version.[13]

The Bible is the Only Sure Guide for Salvation and Life

Concerning Bunyan's personal life, *Grace Abounding To The Chief Of Sinners* is saturated with instances of the Bible being his one and only guide. In the midst of doubts, fears, and struggles, even concerning the mysteries of the Bible itself as a young

---

9 Ibid., p. 386.

10 References to John 10:35 include, *Works*, I, §§ 195, 209, 245, pp. 31, 33, 37-38. Other references to his belief in the authority of Scripture include, I, §§ 96-7, 186, pp. 17, 29-30; also II, p. 601.

11 Ibid., III, p. 767.

12 Normal L. Geisler, ed., *Inerrancy*, p. 496.

13 Bunyan, *Works*, I, p. 695.

believer, Scripture is the undoubted final authority. Hill describes the Bible as "Bunyan's sheet-anchor, his defense against despair and atheism."[14] When making his defense on trial at the commencement of his imprisonment, this foundational resort to the Bible becomes vividly apparent, especially in his upholding of nonconformity. However, *The Pilgrim's Progress* gives the most graphic representation of this principle. It is the book in Christian's hand, clearly the Bible, by virtue of its divine character, that alone is able to guide the pilgrim through many trials and testings to the Celestial City.

As Roger Sharrock comments, "*The Pilgrim's Progress* is soaked in the imagery of the Bible and deeply pervaded by the Puritan belief that the Bible provided the key to every problem of life and thought."[15] So Bunyan himself confesses:

> Wouldst thou know what thou art, and what is in thine heart? Then search the Scriptures and see what is written in them (Rom. 1:29-31; 3:9-18; Jer. 17:9; Gen. 6:5; 8:21; Eph. 4:18), with many others. The Scriptures, I say, they are able to give a man perfect instruction into any of the things of God necessary to faith and godliness, if he hath but an honest heart seriously to weigh and ponder the several things contained in them.[16]

Further, in his pocket volume titled *Christian Behavior* published in 1674, Bunyan supplies copious biblical references to justify his instruction concerning the godly duties of family life, especially with regard to relationships among husband, wife, children, and servants. Then follows a consideration of neighbors and the sins that inhibit a godly testimony before them such as covetousness, pride, and uncleanness. In conclusion, Bunyan addresses the believer whose zeal has cooled: "I know thou wilt be afflicted with a thousand temptations to drive thee to despair, that thy faith may be faint, &c. But against all them set thou the word of God, the promise of grace, the blood of Christ, and the

---

[14] Christopher Hill, *A Tinker And A Poor Man*, p. 169.

[15] Bunyan, *Pilgrim's Progress*, ed. Sharrock, p. 23.

[16] Bunyan, *Works*, III, p. 708.

examples of great backsliders that are for thy encouragement recorded in the scriptures of truth."[17]

The Bible in Tension with Bunyan Studies Today

The forgoing obviously reveals an inevitable conflict that arises between Bunyan's regard for the Bible and modern liberal scholarship. Even in 1928, G. B. Harrison could pompously write:

> Puritanism is an unattractive creed, and its holiness is not beautiful. . . . With the [modern] change of attitude towards the Old Testament the Puritan dogma has crumbled. If there was no first Adam, there was no actual compact between him and God; the sacrifice on Calvary ceases to be the bloody retribution for Adam's sin, and a new interpretation must be sought if the Bible is to be regarded as a record of God's dealings with man. It is difficult for an educated man in the twentieth century, accustomed to see the natural laws of God revealed through the microscope, to realize the full horror of literal belief in the Old Testament; but it is illustrated very clearly in the development of the mind of John Bunyan. . . . Many of his books survive as little more than curious examples of an extinct theology. But four stand out—*Grace Abounding*, *The Pilgrim's Progress*, *Mr. Badman*, and *The Holy War*—perennial monuments of a man who was greater than his creed.[18]

But over seventy years hence, the evangelical cause with an authoritative Bible and a redeeming Christ is very much alive while modernity is more jaded, especially in the moral sphere, and not nearly so attractive in its fading bloom. Bunyan's analysis of human nature and his biblicist gospel remain true when the heart of contemporary man is honestly plumbed.

BUNYAN'S INTERPRETATION OF THE BIBLE

The hermeneutic of John Bunyan is classically Protestant even if not perceived as such in terms of the more loose principles of contemporary interpretation. According to Bernard Ramm, Luther replaced "the four-fold system [historical, allegorical, anagogical, tropological] of the scholastics" with "the literal principle."

---

[17] Ibid., II, p. 574.

[18] G. B. Harrison, *John Bunyan: A Study in Personality*, pp. 11, 13, 185.

Likewise Calvin "rejected allegorical interpretation . . . [calling it] Satanic because it led men away from the truth of Scripture. . . . 'Scripture interprets Scripture' was a basic conviction. . . . This meant many things. It meant *literalism* (as defined in this book) in exegesis with a rejection of the medieval system of the four-fold meaning of Scripture."[19]

So in the seventeenth century, the Reformation hermeneutic is thoroughly embraced by the Puritans. J. I. Packer confirms this point when, in naming their governing principles, he lists the first as follows. "Interpret Scripture literally and grammatically. The Reformers had insisted, against the medieval depreciation of the 'literal' sense of Scripture . . . that the literal—i.e., the grammatical, natural, intended—sense was the only sense that Scripture has. . . . The Puritans fully agreed."[20] Thus Bunyan seems to have well understood this matter as the following exchange, again taken from *A Relation Of My Imprison*ment with Mr. Justice Foster, indicates.

Fost. He told me that I was the nearest the Papists of any, and that he would convince me of immediately.

Bun. I asked him wherein?

Fost. He said, in that we understood the Scripture literally.

Bun. I told him that those that were to be understood literally, we understood them so; but for those that were to be understood otherwise, we endeavored so to understand them.

Fost. He said, which of the Scriptures do you understand literally?

Bun. I said this, 'He that believeth shall be saved.' This was to be understood just as it is spoken; that whosoever believeth in Christ shall, according to the plain and simple words of the text, be saved.[21]

---

19 Bernard Ramm, *Protestant Biblical Interpretation*, pp. 54, 58.

20 J. I. Packer, *A Quest For Godliness*, p. 101.

21 Bunyan, *Works*, I, p. 53. The subjective and selective use of the literal principle here is not totally consistent with the essential Protestant principle that *all* of Scripture be interpreted literally. Refer to Ramm,

Of course Bunyan can write *Solomon's Temple Spiritualized*, but at the same time he explains, "I have, as thou by this little book mayest see, adventured, as this time, to do my endeavor to show thee something of the gospel-glory of Solomon's temple: that is, of what it, with its utensils, was a type of; . . . I may say that God did in a manner tie up the church of the Jews to types, figures, and similitudes."[22] So John R. Knott, jun., rightly concludes:

> Bunyan would have seen no inconsistency between his strong commitment to the literal truth of biblical narrative and his increasing interest in the 'spiritual' or 'mystical sense of Scripture. He operated within the Protestant tradition that acknowledged only one, literal sense and saw 'spiritual' interpretations [applications?] as, in the words of Elizabethan Puritan William Whitaker, 'not various senses, but various collections from one sense, or various applications and accommodation of that one meaning.'"[23]

BUNYAN'S EXPERIENCE WITH THE BIBLE

The Period up to His Conversion

Grace Abounding To The Chief Of Sinners is a remarkably clear window on the soul of John Bunyan, and that unclouded by abnormal neuroses as some declare who are not experientially acquainted with the Christian gospel. The role of the Bible in this account is extremely pervasive, and the author's initial interest in the Word of God, however casual it might be, would take us back to his earliest unrecorded days as a child while growing up in a turbulent religious society. In this regard, Bunyan's mention of some early schooling would presuppose Bible instruction of some sort.[24] Up to his marriage after military service, he recounts, "the thoughts of religion were very grievous to me; I could neither

---

Protestant Biblical Interpretation, pp. 89-96; Packer, *'Fundamentalism' and the Word of God*, pp. 102-106.

22 Ibid., III, p. 462.

23 John R. Knott, jun., "'Thou must live upon my Word': Bunyan and the Bible," *John Bunyan, Conventicle and Parnassus*, ed. N. H. Keeble, p. 162. U. Milo Kaufmann makes the same point about Bunyan's hermeneutic, *The Pilgrim's Progress and Traditions in Puritan Meditation*, pp. 25-41.

24 Bunyan, *Works*, I, § 3, p. 6.

endure it myself, nor that any should; . . . I was now void of all good consideration, heaven and hell were both out of sight and mind."[25] Then his new wife recommended some Christian books which gained a reading, and he followed this by regular church attendance. Subsequently he began to read the Bible and with some pleasure, so that curiosity was aroused and guilt stimulated. At first only historical passages appealed rather than doctrinal epistles,[26] but then, "I began to look into the Bible with new eyes, and read as I never did before; and especially the epistles of the apostle Paul were sweet and pleasant to me; and, indeed, I was then never out of the Bible, either by reading or meditation; still crying out to God [like Christian], that I might know the truth, and the way to heaven and glory."[27]

In his quest for peace with God, he tells us that in searching from Genesis to Revelation, he came upon many perplexing questions. "Then darkness seized upon me, . . . blasphemous thoughts were such as also stirred up questions in me, against the very being of God, and of his only beloved Son; as, whether there were, in truth, a God, or Christ, or no? And whether the holy Scriptures were not rather a fable, and cunning story, than the holy and pure Word of God?"[28] Yet, on numerous occasions we read, "These words [of Scripture] broke in upon my mind . . .," or "that Word came in upon me," or, "That scripture did also tear and rend my soul." Then comes conversion:

> I remember that one day, as I was traveling in the country and musing on the wickedness and blasphemy of my heart, and considering of the enmity that was in me to God, that scripture came in my mind, He hath 'made peace through the blood of his cross' (Col. 1:20). By which I was made to see, both again, and again, and again, that day, that God and my soul were friends by this blood; yea, I saw that the justice of God and my sinful soul

[25] Ibid., § 10, p. 7.

[26] Ibid., § 29, p. 9.

[27] Ibid., § 46, p. 11.

[28] Ibid., § 96, p. 17.

could embrace and kiss each other through this blood. This was a good day to me; I hope I shall not forget it.[29]

The Period Following His Conversion

The subsequent period of struggle, lasting from two to three years, yet must be understood as being watered by the influential, stimulating, and solid biblical ministry of John Gifford, Bunyan's pastor and mentor, as well as Martin Luther via his *Commentary on Galatians*. In the midst of spiritual wrestling that oscillated between fervent hope and near despair, yet many great biblical issues arose in the Bedford tinker's soul about which he sought biblical resolutions. For instance, concerning his yielding to temptation, was he to be likened to apostates Esau and Judas rather than Peter? Had he committed the unpardonable sin? Throughout all of this, the Word of God continues to erupt in Bunyan's soul. He is constantly studying the Bible and recollecting its truth, yet there are those more notable times when, as he puts it, "suddenly this sentence bolted in upon me," or "this word took hold of me," or "scripture would come running after me," or "then did that scripture seize upon my soul," or "this scripture would strike me down as dead," or "now was the word of the gospel forced upon my soul," or "that scripture fastened on my heart." In these instances, Bunyan happily understands their coming at him as divine intervention. He also writes: "That piece of a sentence darted in upon me, 'My grace is sufficient.' At this methought I felt some stay, as if there might be hopes. But, oh how good a thing it is for God to send his Word! . . . Therefore I still did pray to God, that he would come in with this Scripture more fully on my heart."[30] Then follows assurance and stability when, "that was brought to my remembrance, he [Christ] 'of God is made unto us wisdom, and righteousness, and sanctification, and redemption' (I Cor. 1:30)."[31]

This resultant peace and rest in Bunyan's soul, at his "Place of Deliverance," led to formal membership in the Bedford non-conformist church, his "Palace Beautiful," then the commencement

---

29 Ibid., § 115, p. 20. Refer to Chapter 6 where Bunyan's conversion is considered in greater detail.

30 Ibid., §§ 204, 206, p. 32.

31 Ibid., § 230, p. 36.

of itinerant preaching. Thus in all of this, the Word of God remained pre-eminent in Bunyan's personal life and ministry. However, this is not to suggest that he never experienced further instability since he later confesses: "I have sometimes seen more in a line of the Bible than I could tell how to stand under, and yet at another time the whole Bible hath been to me as dry as a stick; or rather, my heart hath been so dead and dry unto it, that I could not conceive the least drachm of refreshment, though I have looked it 'all' over."[32]

THE BIBLE IN THE PILGRIM'S PROGRESS

One of the most remarkable features of *The Pilgrim's Progress* is the author's ability to blend Scripture into his narrative in such a way that the reader is often unconscious of his absorption of Bible truth. John R. Knott, jun. puts it this way: "The influence of the Bible upon *The Pilgrim's Progress* is so pervasive that one must be alert to it continuously even when Bunyan does not point to specific biblical passages with citations in the margin."[33] Nevertheless, in addition to more direct references to the Bible, there is a variety of emblems that adds color and also speaks of distinctive biblical functions. They include:

The Book in the Hand of Christian

In the opening scene of *The Pilgrim's Progress*, Christian simply appears with "a book in his hand" that is clearly the cause of the ensuing "great burden upon his back."[34] Remembering that Christian is a distinct portrayal of Bunyan, the parallel in *Grace Abounding To The Chief Of Sinners* is most likely that occasion already noted when, having begun to study the more historical parts of the Bible, he then advances to admiration of Paul's epistles. In refuting a licentious friend named Harry as well as the antinomian Ranters at that time, he declares: "The Bible was precious to me in those days."[35]

---

32 Ibid., p. 50.

33 Knott, jun. "Bunyan and the Bible," *John Bunyan, Conventicle and Parnassus*, ed. Keeble, p. 165.

34 Bunyan, *Works*, III, p. 12.

35 Ibid., I, § 45, p. 11.

This inscripturated revelation is then described, by means of Evangelist's direction, as "a shining light" which is, according to II Peter 1:19, "the prophetic word made more sure, . . . a lamp shining in a dark place." Christian's book is then mocked by Obstinate, toyed with by Pliable, and repudiated by Mr. Worldly-Wiseman.

The Parchment-Roll Provided by Evangelist

The inscribed exhortation is, "Fly from the wrath to come", which originates from the ministry of John the Baptist (Matt. 3:7). The Christocentric context of this passage (Matt. 3:3, 11-12) suggests that this flight be toward Christ at the Wicket-gate. The exhortation here is but a faithful evangelist's expansion of the truth that is in Christian's hand.

The Inscription Over the Wicket-gate

The invitation, "Knock and it shall be opened unto you" is in fact the inscripturated invitation of the Lord Jesus Christ (Matt. 7:7-8), represented by Good-will.

The Instruction at the House of Interpreter

The Interpreter is the Holy Spirit who is inseparably associated with the Word of God. It is He who makes the Word "living and powerful" (Heb. 4:12), who communicates and illuminates the truth (II Tim. 3:16), and especially as it concerns the person and work of the Lord Jesus Christ (John 15:26). Thus Interpreter is, as Good-will declared, "he [who] would shew him excellent things."[36]

The Instruction at the Palace Beautiful

This faithful local church ministers the Word of God by means of exhortation, instruction, edification, and the Lord's Table.

1. *The exhortation of Palace leadership.*

Prudence, Piety, and Charity give wholesome instruction as a result of considering Christian's cases of conscience.[37]

---

[36] Ibid., pp. 97-98.

[37] Most likely these ladies represent those saints who gave Bunyan early guidance, not feminine leadership, *Works*, I, §§ 37-41, p. 10-11.

2. The fellowship supper.

This memorial banquet involves reminiscing about the person and work of the pilgrim's Lord.

3. The records in the study.

Here focus is placed upon the great saving works of God by His warrior Son and through His faithful servants, as well as prophetic instruction.

4. The sword of the Spirit.

This accouterment is the Word of God according to Ephesians 6:17 which is but a more militant version of Christian's book that is to be used both defensively and offensively.

The Key Called Promise in Christian's Bosom

This key, revealed at Doubting Castle, is a representation of the light of truth or promises of the Word of God which the Spirit of God brings to mind; as a result the darkness of despair is cast out (Ps. 119:130).

The Exhortation of the Shepherds at the Delectable Mountains

This pastoral scene represents another provision of spiritual nourishment via local church ministry; it involves the truth of Scripture imparted by knowledgeable, experienced, watchful, and sincere men of God.

The Nourishment from the Gardener at Beulah Land

Here appetizing food is provided, again the Word of God, which is mediated by the Gardener, another pastoral representation. This nourishment is particularly satisfying for senior pilgrims who are longing to gain entrance into the Celestial City.

The Inscription over the Gate of the Celestial City

This quotation from Revelation 22:14, "Blessed are they that do his commandments, that they may enter in through the gates into the City," is a warning that pretenders will not be admitted. Only those who have believed the Word and obeyed it will gain entrance.

THE BIBLE IN BUNYAN'S PROGRESS

Hence this magisterial dominion of Scripture in *The Pilgrim's Progress*, void of focus through Aristotle or Plato via Oxford or Cambridge, yet subject to tutelage by Luther and Gifford, and probably Owen and Dell, is representative of Bunyan's intention to embody the principle of *sola scriptura* in all of his ministry:

> Wherefore 'I will not take' of them [the learned] 'from a thread even to a shoe-latchet, – lest they should say, We have made Abram rich' (Gen. 14:23). . . . What you find suiting with the Scriptures take, though it should not suit with [the learned] authors; but that which you find against the Scriptures, slight, though it should be confirmed by multitudes of them [the learned]. Yea, further, where you find the Scriptures and your [learned] authors jump [agree], yet believe it for the sake of Scripture's authority. I honor the godly [learned] as Christians, but I prefer the Bible before them; and having this still with me, I count myself far better furnished than if I had without it all the libraries of the two universities. Besides, I am for drinking water out of my own cistern; what God makes mine by the evidence of his Word and Spirit, that I dare make bold with.[38]

THE GLORY OF RIGHT CHURCH FELLOWSHIP

Church fellowship, or the communion of saints, is the place where the Son of God loveth to walk; his first walking was in Eden. Church fellowship rightly managed, is the glory of the world. No place, no community, no fellowship, is adorned and bespangled with those beauties as is a church rightly knit together to their head, and lovingly serving one another.

John Bunyan
The Desire of the Righteous Granted
Works, I, pp. 757-8

[38] Bunyan, *Works*, III, pp. 398-9.

CHAPTER FOUR

The Concept of Progress in Pilgrimage

THE title of John Bunyan's classic allegory, *The Pilgrim's Progress*, is pregnant with meaning insofar as a comprehensive understanding of his essential purpose is concerned. It immediately identifies the composition as a connected whole that, fittingly without chapter divisions as is the case with many of the author's writings, is designed to be understood in continuity and not a piecemeal fashion.

Furthermore, the reader is straightaway impressed with the guiding principle of movement that offers the prospect of journeying, of scenic change, of variation in pace, of challenging encounter, of blessed arrival. At the same time this immediacy confronts us with life-relatedness that is grounded upon a vital cause of such importance that nothing less than the undivided attention of a man's immortal soul must be employed.

Thus pilgrimage is to advance from the secular to the sacred, from this ugly world to that of holy beauty to come, with commencement finding timeless expression in the opening line, "As I walked through the wilderness of this world, I came upon a certain place."[1] To begin with we are captivatingly introduced to Bunyan's own journeying and then its representation by Christian. Hence the title guides us to the beginning of the journey which aptly portrays the world as one in which we all presently groan. Such a beginning is not chronological but rather theological; it is the pit in which we all find ourselves (Isa, 51:1).

The Pilgrim who Progresses

According to *The Concise Oxford Dictionary*, a "pilgrim" is "a person who journeys to a sacred place for religious reasons, a

---

[1] John Bunyan, *The Works of John Bunyan*, ed. George Offor, III, p. 89.

person regarded as journeying through life, a traveler,"[2] as represented by the Pilgrim Fathers who immigrated to New England. That the Puritans, and Bunyan in particular, happily identified with this title of "pilgrim" is readily understandable if one recalls the biblical truth that Christians are, among other titles, called to be "strangers and pilgrims" (I Pet. 2:11; Heb. 11:13 KJV), and "sojourners" (I Chron. 29:15; Ps.39:12) while on earth. So William Haller comments that "the vocation of the elect [Puritans] was to go through this life as pilgrims."[3]

The Progress of the Pilgrim

While the modern understanding of "progress" as improvement and advancement may come quickly to mind at this point, nevertheless Philip Edwards challenges this idea with regard to Bunyan's original intent. He musters considerable authority when he explains: "In fact, Bunyan's 'progress', correctly quoted by the *Oxford English Dictionary* under sense 1, means, quite neutrally, traveling, a movement from one place to another, how Christian got from this world to the world which is to come."[4]

However, if this perspective is correct at this juncture, then two problems arise that must be addressed. First, if "progress" simply means traveling and movement, then it would seem that Bunyan is guilty of a tautology, as if in fact the title of his work should read, "The Pilgrim's Pilgrimage." Second, and this seems to carry more conclusive weight, the whole allegory is full of indications of advancement that include the quality of improvement, which meaning is certainly a possible seventeenth century alternative in *The Oxford English Dictionary*. Consider some examples of this internal evidence.

1. To journey from the City of Destruction to the Celestial City is more than travel; rather it is advancement of the highest kind, from sin to salvation, from earth to heaven.
2. There is advancement in many doctrinal issues and especially with regard to an expanding revelation concerning the gospel and sanctification. Consider the more extensive, detailed and doctrinally profound later discourse that takes place on the Enchanted Ground.

---

[2] R. E. Allen, ed., *The Concise Oxford Dictionary*, p. 902.

[3] William Haller, *The Rise of Puritanism*, p. 190.

[4] Philip Edwards, 'The Journey in *The Pilgrim's Progress*,' *The Pilgrim's Progress, Critical and Historical Views*, ed. Vincent Newey, p. 111.

3. There is a geographic sense of moving on to higher and safer ground that offers blessing as opposed to many valley trials. A point is reached by Christian and Hopeful at the land of Beulah where certain earlier evil influences, such as the Valley of the Shadow of Death, Giant Despair and Doubting Castle, become out of reach to the pilgrims in their maturity.[5]
4. There is evident spiritual improvement in the three leading pilgrims, and especially with regard to Faithful and Hopeful. Christian, although like Peter in temperament, yet becomes wiser, such as with regard to his mature analysis of Little-faith while conflicts multiply.
5. The number of pilgrims who commence the journey is reduced as the later stages are reached, though this order is reversed in Part Two. So at the Delectable Mountains the Shepherds declare: "For but few of them that begin to come hither, do show their face on these mountains."[6]

The Specificity of Progress on Pilgrimage

For today, the name of *The Pilgrim's Progress* has become more than the title of a definitive, timeless Christian classic. Rather it now has, in its historic popularity, taken on the aura of a life motif in general that need not be taken too seriously in terms of its strict biblical stance. The dominant theme of life as a religious journey is cordially appreciated while the author's literalist approach to the Bible and Calvinism is, out of respect for his fame, patronizingly regarded as *passé* theology. Such an approach is by no means meant to suggest that his allegory is of little worth for today. Quite to the contrary, his teaching as literature is appreciated as a wonderful mine for modern extrapolation.[7] Yet at the same time this approach must be filtered through a grid of modern biblical presuppositions that are in reality diametrically opposed to Bunyan's essentially evangelical convictions.

---

[5] Bunyan, *Works*, III, p. 161.

[6] Ibid., p. 144.

[7] This patronage has mined a wide variety of themes that are remote from Bunyan's expressed purposes. A few examples include the class struggles and sectarian conflicts of the seventeenth century, historical investigation into a turbulent era, Puritan studies, feminism, the psychology of conversion and despair, literary structure, and linguistic analysis, etc.

One recent biography of Bunyan is by Gordon Wakefield, a modern English Methodist scholar who, in his decidedly interpretive account, quite plainly reveals his fundamental doctrinal differences with the Bedford tinker. Concerning Bunyan's "too narrow view" of the gospel he writes:

> It was one of the errors of Puritanism that everyone must undergo conversion through conviction of sin and the agonized cry of the Philippian gaoler [Acts 16:30]. . . . [Bunyan believed that] apart from Christ and the divine grace through him there is only 'a just God, a sin revenging God, a God that will by no means spare the guilty'. In Christ there is infinite mercy and a love which passes knowledge and grace to cover all sin. This seems appallingly exclusive and discouraging to 'virtuous and godly living'. Bunyan rules out so many whom the consensus of God-fearing humanity would regard as lights in their generation. . . . Most will be left outside though they approach in hope and confidence. This would not worry Bunyan since Calvinism does not expect universal salvation.[8]

Yet from a more general perspective, Wakefield is correct when he describes the innateness in life of Bunyan's journey theme as follows: "Behind us all is the journeying instinct of humanity. . . . We are on a journey whether we like it or not from birth to death. . . . The journey is the truest metaphor of life."[9] Nevertheless, for Bunyan these definitions would be lacking in biblical specificity. His title, *The Pilgrim's Progress*, incorporates three connected key elements, namely departure, transition, and arrival according to the historic, sans liberal and universalist, interpretation of Scripture. Certainly the life of Abraham is illustrative of this principle, for having departed from Ur of the Chaldeans, the patriarch's life becomes a "looking for the city which has foundations, whose architect and builder is God" (Heb. 11:9-10). In the same vein, the nation of Israel, having departed from Egypt, wanders in transition until the time appointed for its arrival in Canaan under the leadership of Joshua (Judg. 2:1).

However, Bunyan has something in mind that is even more significant than these narrative events. Certainly he uses a narrative motif himself to convey his message. But his essential point is that it is the human soul in all of its militant alienation from God that must depart, through the sovereignty of grace, from its enmity and

---

8 Gordon Wakefield, *Bunyan the Christian*, pp. 48-49, 76.

9 Ibid., pp. 72-73.

bondage, make transition through an opposing wilderness world, and finally arrive acceptable in the presence of a holy and gracious heavenly Father. Here is the reality of Bunyan's allegory, the substance of his shadows, the concreteness of his imagination, the vital nerve of his title.

THE ORIGIN OF THE PILGRIMAGE MOTIF

Because Bunyan makes no pretense at being a scholar and openly confesses his lack of formal learning, many have attempted to discover, assuming some derivation of his concept, exactly what sources he used to obtain his style. The literary excellence of his composition, that is its attractive simplicity of style, have led these same people to suspect that such a popular work could not possibly have originated from a poor, uneducated tinker. Bunyan himself experienced charges that his allegory was not original. As a result, in 1682 at the publication of *The Holy War*, he penned the following apologetic poem:

> Some say the Pilgrim's Progress is not mine,
> Insinuating as if I would shine
> In name and fame by the worth of another,
> Like some made rich by robbing of their brother.
> Or that so fond I am of being sire,
> I'll father bastards; or, if need require,
> I'll tell a lie in print to get applause.
> I scorn it: John such dirt-heap never was,
> Since God converted him. Let this suffice
> To show why I my Pilgrim patronize.
>
> It came from mine own heart, so to my head,
> And thence into my fingers trickled;
> Then to my pen, from whence immediately
> On paper I did dribble it daintily.
>
> Manner and matter too was all mine own,
> Nor was it unto any mortal known,
> 'Till I had done it. Nor did any then
> By books, by wits, by tongues, or hand, or pen,
> Add five words to it, or write half a line
> Thereof: the whole, and every whit, is mine.[10]

[10] Bunyan, *Works*, III, p. 374.

Now while we support the integrity of Bunyan at this point, nevertheless it will help to consider the relative validity of certain factors which may have impinged upon him without detracting from the originality of his allegory.

The Seventeenth Century Literary Antecedents

Just as investigation into Bunyan's doctrine, both in general and with regard to *The Pilgrim's Progress*, has been minimal, so the study of his possible literary antecedents has been prolific. George Offer, admittedly very sympathetic to the renowned author, made an extensive study of this matter during the first half of the previous century. Amidst numerous suggested parallels, one is worth mentioning since it was, according to Bunyan himself, most influential in his early spiritual development. It concerns the dialogue structure of *The Plain Man's Path-way to Heaven* by Arthur Dent which, in *Grace Abounding*, he declares to have been a legacy that his first wife shared with him, and he found pleasing.[11]

Yet concerning this Offer writes:

> It is singular that no one has charged him with taking any hints from this book, which is one of the very few which he is known to have read prior to his public profession of faith and holiness in baptism. . . . This volume must have been exactly suited to the warm imagination of Bunyan. It had proved invaluable to him as a means of conversion; but, after a careful and delightful perusal, no trace can be found of any phrase or sentence having been introduced into Pilgrim's Progress.[12]

Thus Offer concludes as a result of the whole of his investigation:

> Every attempt has been made to tarnish his [Bunyan's] fair fame; the great and learned, the elegant poet and the pious divine, have asserted, but without foundation in fact, or even in probability, that some of his ideas were derived from the works of previous writers. . . . 'It came from his own heart.' The plot, the characters, the faithful dealing, are all his own. And what is more, there has not been

---

[11] Ibid., I, p. 7. This popular presentation of gospel truth underwent twenty editions during the period of 1600-1640. It is comprised of discussion between Theologus (a divine), Philagathus (an honest man), Asunetus (an ignorant man), and Antilegon (a caviler, petty objector).

[12] Ibid., III, pp. 44, 45.

> found a single phrase, a sentence borrowed from any other book, except the quotations from the Bible, and the use of common proverbs. To arrive at this conclusion has occupied much time and labor, at intervals, during the last forty years.[13]

Of course this assessment has not stopped the literati of today from endeavoring to discover pillaged sources. However, concerning present scholarly conclusions re the genesis of Bunyan's essential idea, Christopher Hill sums up the matter as follows:

> Much printer's ink has been spilt in the search for antecedents for *The Pilgrim's Progress*. I shall merely try to summarize what I take to be the present position. The concept of life as a pilgrimage goes back far into the Middle Ages, if not further. All attempts to tie Bunyan down to a single model have failed. The idea was common property in the fifteenth to seventeenth centuries.[14]

The Thorough Absorption of Biblical Truth

In Richard Greaves' study of Bunyan's theology according to the major heads of Christian doctrine, there is one important area which he fails to consider that, strangely enough, has been little written about in this century. This omission concerns the Bedford pastor's regard for the Bible.[15] Of course the reason for this omission may be that Bunyan's attitude toward Scripture is so patently obvious and dominant that it goes without saying.

His works convey an astonishing understanding of the content of the English Bible. And of course *The Pilgrim's Progress* presents a near seamless weaving of the sacred text as has no other comparable work. But to move to the more doctrinal aspect of this matter, to use modern parlance, his understanding of the Bible was "literalist" and "fundamentalist," which terms his modern literary critics use pejoratively. On the other hand, the biblical liberalism and cultural relativism of today would receive from Bunyan just as severe a broadside of condemnation as did the Latitudinarians and Quakers of his time.

---

[13] Ibid., p. 30.

[14] Christopher Hill, *A Tinker and a Poor Man*, p. 201.

[15] Richard Greaves, *John Bunyan*, 176 pp, being a published doctoral thesis. A more recent doctoral thesis by Pieter de Vries has been published under the title of *John Bunyan on the Order of Salvation*. This work, in briefly and correctly assessing Bunyan's high view of Scripture, is highly recommended; its heartfelt sympathy for Bunyan's overall doctrine is refreshing while uncommon.

Hill is accurate in his description of the importance of the Bible for the well instructed tinker, though he does also reflect the diminished sympathy that the modern spirit of literary scholarship has for his fervent evangelical doctrine. To quote him again more fully: "The Bible is Bunyan's sheet-anchor, his defense against despair and atheism. He would have been lost if he had abandoned it. This accounts for what seem today some of the less attractive features of Bunyan's thinking – his emphasis on hell-fire, or the inherent sinfulness of children, his racism and sexism."[16]

Not that Bunyan was unaware of spurious ministry in his day. Learned clergy led multitudes astray then just as they do today. So he responded with fiery warning:

> You who muzzle up your people in ignorance with Aristotle, Plato, and the rest of the heathenish philosophers, and preach little, if anything, of Christ rightly; I say unto you, that you will find you have sinned against God, and beguiled your hearers, when God shall, in the judgment-day, lay the cause of the damnation of many thousands of souls to your charge, and say, He will require their blood at your hands (Ezek. 33:6)[17]

The Subjective Experience of a Questing Soul

The chief interior source of the substance of *The Pilgrim's Progress* is the author's self-exposure of his hyper-sensitive soul. This Puritan inclination for heart searching was based on Paul's exhortation to pilgrims to, "test yourselves to see if you are in the faith; examine yourselves!" (II Cor. 13:5). In Bunyan's case he chronicled his intense analysis of himself in *Grace Abounding To The Chief Of Sinners*, and it is this spiritual autobiography which becomes an indispensable tool for a right understanding of *The Pilgrim's Progress*. Roger Sharrock explains that:

> *Grace Abounding* deals almost wholly with the development of his inner religious feelings; there are hardly any references to persons or places. Bunyan discards any attempt at literary adornment in order to achieve an absolutely naked rendering of his spiritual history. . . . The movement into allegory serves to naturalize and familiarize Bunyan's religious perceptions to us. . . . But *The Pilgrim's Progress* still retains the sense of personal urgency: it is his tremendous need to find a righteousness not his own [like Luther] by which to be saved that we encounter in the very first paragraph, and which is

16 Hill, *Tinker and a Poor Man*, p. 169.

17 Bunyan, *Works*, III, p. 716.

the force irresistibly driving Christian along the road to his final entry into the Celestial City.[18]

Christopher Hill, while expressing his reliance upon Sharrock, adds:

> Perhaps the most significant prototype of *The Pilgrim's Progress* is *Grace Abounding*. The state of desperation in which the Pilgrim finds himself at the beginning of the story (GA, § 9) mirrors that of Bunyan throughout *Grace Abounding*. The wicket-gate had been anticipated in Bunyan's dream of his exclusion from the company of the godly in Bedford (GA, §§ 53-5). The Slough of Despond recalls Bunyan finding himself 'as on a miry bog that shook if I did but stir' (GA, § 82). Christian's fear that Mt. Sinai would fall on his head recalls Bunyan's fear that the church bells or steeple might fall on him whilst watching bell-ringing (GA, § 33-4). The blasphemies whispered to Christian by a devil in the Valley of the Shadow of Death echo those which Bunyan himself had been tempted to utter. Hopeful is as influenced as Bunyan had been by the text 'My grace is sufficient for thee' (GA, §§ 204-6, 213). The 'very brisk lad' called Ignorance, and Mr. Brisk in Part II, remind us that Bunyan himself had been a brisk talker in matters of religion (GA, §§ 16, 29-32, 37).[19]

The Personal Cultivation of Natural Ability

Had Bunyan been formally trained at either Oxford or Cambridge, his natural intellectual ability leaves little doubt that he would have fulfilled a brilliant academic course. Providentially this was not to be, and the distinctive result was a life of freshness and originality that was not subject to the structuring of classical studies or Aristotelianism or any other school of philosophy, except that of the school of Christ with its only textbook, the English Bible.

Notwithstanding his lack of secular schooling, there is evidence of a very determined spirit that sought improvement through self-tutelage, though John Gifford, William Dell and John Owen seem to have been welcome guides. The poems in Part Two of *The Pilgrim's Progress* show a marked improvement in style over those contained in Part One. Add to this an inventive frame of mind and the result is variegated personal expression that results in a *Map Showing the Order of Salvation and Damnation*, emblematic

[18] John Bunyan, *The Pilgrim's Progress*, ed. Roger Sharrock, pp. 10-11.

[19] Hill, *Tinker and a Poor Man*, pp. 206-7.

poems for children, a flute hewn in prison from a chair leg, a metal fiddle fashioned according to his own metal-working skills, mental acuity in doctrinal reasoning and debate, close friendship with Sir John Shorter, the Lord Mayor of London, and an invitation to sit as a member of the Corporation of Bedford which he declined. These and other admirable, colorful, and innovative characteristics portray a man who possessed exceptional abilities. John Bunyan had no need to borrow his creativity from other sources.

THE BIBLICAL ORIGIN OF THE PILGRIMAGE MOTIF

Within the Bible there are many possibilities with regard to the concept of progress in pilgrimage that is so integral to *The Pilgrim's Progress.* To select a primary source here is not easy, and it is this writer's opinion that a combination of biblical texts and scenes best explains Bunyan's essential concept of a spiritual journey. For a man so saturated with Scripture, it is to be expected that a montage of Scriptural expeditions would form the basis of his allegorical idea. Yet six strands of influence seem to emerge from the multitude of biblical examples that describe spiritual traveling in a wilderness world.

The Patriarchal Journeying of Abraham

In Hebrews 11:8-10, 13-16; 13:14 we certainly have a major declaration of the journeying characteristic of Abraham who, "when he was called, obeyed by going out to a place which he was to receive for an inheritance; and he went out, not knowing where he was going. . . . for he was looking for the city which has foundations, whose architect and builder is God" (Heb. 11:8, 10; cf. Gen. 11:28-12:5). This same spiritual adventure is described in Joshua 24:2-3, as well as by Stephen in Acts 7:2-4. It is quite possible that Bunyan associated Ur of the Chaldeans with the City of Destruction, especially since, when Christian and Faithful are being escorted to the gates of their glorious destination, the accompanying angels declare, "You are going now to Abraham, Isaac, and Jacob, and to the Prophets."[20]

The Flight of Lot from Sodom

The City of Destruction is paralleled by Sodom when Christian warns his wife and children that, "our city will be burned with fire from heaven . . . fire and brimstone"(Gen. 19:23-28), even as

---

[20] Bunyan, *Works*, III, p. 164.

Christian's escape is akin to Lot's flight when he flees for his life. Significantly, the Great Fire of London occurred in 1666, just prior to that period when Bunyan probably commenced his writing of *The Pilgrim's Progress*. Thus, "he [Christian] looked not behind him, but fled towards the middle of the plain" (Gen. 19:17). At the Palace Beautiful, Christian testifies to Charity that he warned his loved ones, "'but I seemed to them as one that mocked,' and they believed me not" (Gen. 19:14). Then, just beyond the silver mine at the Hill Lucre, Christian and Hopeful encounter the monument to Lot's wife with its inscription, "Remember Lot's wife" (Luke 17:32), on account of her "looking behind her" (Gen. 19:26).[21]

The Exodus Journeying of the Nation of Israel

The pilgrimage of Israel from Egypt to Canaan, with the intervening wilderness sojourn, is frequently described in terms of "the way" (Ex. 32:8; Josh. 24:1-17) or "the straight [right KJV] way" (Ps. 107:4-7). So Evangelist enquires of Christian, having been detoured by the counsel of Mr. Worldly-Wiseman, "How is it, then, that thou art so quickly turned aside? For thou art now out of the way."[22] At the Wicket-gate Good-will warns Christian of many ways ahead, but "thou may'st distinguish the right from the wrong, the right only being straight and narrow."[23] Faithful advises Christian that Pliable "hath forsaken the way."[24] Christian exhorts Faithful, on account of Demas' seductive overtures, "Let us not stir a step, but still keep on our way."[25] At By-Path-Meadow, "the souls of the pilgrims were much discouraged because of the way" (Num. 21:4).[26] Then, having been led astray by Vain-confidence, the pilgrims are exhorted, "Let thine heart be towards the highway, even the way that thou wentest, turn again" (Jer. 31:21).[27] Before the hospitable Shepherds Christian enquires, "Is there in this place any relief for pilgrims that are weary and faint in the way?" (Deut. 25:17-18).[28] Following release from the

---

[21] Ibid., pp. 89, 90, 108, 137.

[22] Ibid., p. 94.

[23] Ibid., p. 97.

[24] Ibid., p. 117.

[25] Ibid., p. 136.

[26] Ibid., p. 138.

[27] Ibid., p. 139.

[28] Ibid., p. 144.

Flatterer's net by an angel, the pilgrims are asked, "if they had not of those Shepherds a note of direction for the way?"[29] After discipline, they "went softly along the right way."[30]

The Spiritual Journeying of the Psalmist

The definitive passage here is Psalm 23:3-4. In v. 3 David is a pilgrim who declares, "He guides me in the paths of righteousness for His name's sake." Then in the Valley of the Shadow of Death, lamenting Christian hears a voice ahead of him, "Though I walk through the valley of the shadow of death, I will fear no evil; for thou art with me."[31] The Psalms are full of references to life as a spiritual journey, whether a "way" (Ps. 1:1, 6; 2:12; 5:8; 119:32, 102; 142:3) or "path" (Ps. 16:11; 27:11;119:35, 105; 142:3) or "walk" (Ps. 56:13; 101:2; 116:8-9;138:7; 143:8).

The Redemptive Journeying of Jesus Christ

Undoubtedly Jesus Christ is the entrance to the way at the Wicket-gate (John 10:7), while at the same time he is the person of Good-will.[32] However, at Vanity Fair Bunyan weaves in the incarnate journey of the Son of God with the explanation, "The Prince of princes himself, when here, went through this town to his own country, and that upon a fair day too; yea, and as I think, it was Beelzebub, the chief lord of this fair, that invited him to buy of his vanities; yea, would have made him lord of the fair, would he but have done him reverence as he went through the town."[33] This appears to portray Jesus Christ as traveling from the Celestial City, through Vanity Fair, toward the Place of Deliverance and the Wicket-gate. Overall, John 14:6 describes this redemptive journeying: "I am the way, and the truth, and the life; no one comes to the Father, but through Me." (cf. Isa. 40:3; John 16:28; Eph. 4:10).

---

[29] Ibid., p. 151.

[30] Ibid.

[31] Ibid., p. 115.

[32] Ibid., p. 190. In Part II, at the Place of Deliverance, Great-heart explains to Christiana and company the atoning deed that is displayed before them: "The pardon that you and Mercy, and these boys have obtained, was obtained by another, to wit, by him that let you in at the gate; and he hath obtained it in this double way. He has performed righteousness to cover you, and spilt blood to wash you in."

[33] Ibid., p. 127.

The Allegorical Journeying of the Apostle Paul

To the church at Corinth, Paul gives the following exhortation, "Know ye not that they which run in a race run all, but one receiveth the prize? So run, that ye may obtain" (I Cor. 9:24 KJV). Based upon this verse, Bunyan produced a further allegorical work entitled *The Heavenly Footman*, with the exhortation to his readers, "Arise man, be slothful no longer; set foot, and heart, and all into the way of God, and run, the crown is at the end of the race."[34] Concerning this work Sharrock comments: "Gradually, as if Bunyan cannot help himself, the metaphor turns from a cross-country race into a long journey."[35] Further consider Paul's understanding of his earthly ministry as a "course" to be obediently completed, according to his commissioning (Acts 20:24; II Tim. 4:7).

THE MARKET DAY OF THE SOUL

The first day of the week is the Christian's market day, that which they so solemnly trade in for soul provision for all the week following. This is the day that they gather manner in. To be sure the seventh day sabbath is not that. For of old the people of God could never find manna on that day (Ex. 16:26).

John Bunyan
The Seventh-Day Sabbath
Works, II, p. 382

---

[34] Ibid., p. 380.

[35] John Bunyan, *The Pilgrim's Progress*, eds. James Blanton Wharey and Roger Sharrock p. xxxii.

CHAPTER FIVE

The Gospel in The Pilgrim's Progress

OF all the emphases concerning the truth of God incorporated in *The Pilgrim's Progress*, none is equal in importance to Bunyan's multifaceted representation of the authentic Christian gospel. In these days of spiritual declension as the twentieth century concludes, this foundational evangelistic thrust in allegorical form is of crucial importance since the contemporary presentation of the gospel has become so diluted of truth, and as a consequence so anemic, as to be in many cases utterly disqualified. On the other hand, in Chapter 7 it will be maintained that the predominant concern of *The Pilgrim's Progress* is with regard to sanctification rather than salvation, thus an apparent though unreal contradiction seems to arise. The gospel is of supreme importance, yet sanctification is the major thrust of *The Pilgrim's Progress*.

The explanation is this, that while the gospel is foundational to *The Pilgrim's Progress* as a whole, it is also of the essence of initial salvation and the ground of resultant sanctification. This formal distinction between salvation and sanctification on the one hand, and the inseparable relationship between salvation and sanctification on the other, is one which not only the sixteenth century Reformers upheld, but also their seventeenth century descendants. In this regard Bunyan was no exception. He explains this vital matter most clearly when, through the animated response of Christian to Ignorance, he yet expresses his own conviction concerning the gospel, both its root and fruit, very dogmatically:

> Ignorance is thy name, and as thy name is, so art thou. . . . Ignorant thou art of what justifying righteousness is, and as ignorant how to secure thy soul, through the faith of it, from the heavy wrath of God. Yea, thou art also ignorant of the true effects of saving faith in this righteousness of Christ, which is, to bow and win over the heart

to God in Christ, to love his name, his Word, ways, and people, and not as thou ignorantly imaginest.[1]

Hence, throughout *The Pilgrim's Progress* the gospel is a pervasive saving and sanctifying reality that manifests itself according to three related and important perspectives.

The Pilgrim's Progress is Christocentric

Comprehensive proof of this assertion is provided in Chapter 11. Furthermore, even a cursory review of the contents of Bunyan's *Works* will only reinforce the pervasive aspect of this claim. One might say, to coin an expression derived from Spurgeon, that if the tinker's "blood was bibline," then it circulated by means of a Christ animated heart. Of course the Christ that Bunyan worshiped was truthfully revealed in the totality of the New Testament including both the Gospels and the Epistles of Paul. In *The Pilgrim's Progress* he is most frequently designated as the "Lord of the Hill," that is the sovereign Savior of that hill called Calvary where full atonement for sinners was made.[2]

To begin with, like Bunyan's own experience recorded in his autobiography *Grace Abounding to the Chief of Sinners*, Christian's early vision of Christ is ever so dim, and even at the Wicket-gate, which he was formerly unable to see. Thus his initial perception of the gospel was, although effectual, yet very basic. But following the revelation of the grace of Christ at the house of Interpreter and the Place of Deliverance, the pilgrim's accelerated passion is to "see him alive that did hang dead on the cross,"[3] that is to "see him as he is" (I John 3:2), and this glorious goal he confesses to the enquiring inhabitants of the Palace Beautiful.

The Pilgrim's Progress is atonement centered

The pre-eminence of Christ for Bunyan is not measured simply in terms of perfectly wedded deity and humanity, not his divine incarnate person only but also his saving work and atoning sacrifice. Further, granted that Christ has come to deliver man from his overwhelming predicament, his hopeless bondage to sin

---

1 John Bunyan, *The Works of John Bunyan*, ed., George Offor , III, p. 158.

2 The expression "Lord of the Hill" is used on eight occasions and in context refers to that Hill where Christian looked at the cross and was released of his burden, Bunyan, *Works*, III, pp. 105-7, 109-10, 143.

3 Ibid., p. 108.

and consequent judgment, more specifically the allegorist considered it of crucial importance as to how it is possible for a holy God to maintain His integrity and at the same time save the sinner. In simple terms, how could a just God pardon the ungodly? This was not so much a concern of the Latitudinarians and Quakers of Bunyan's day who stressed an inward and gradual work of renovation in cooperation with grace that Christ's atonement provided, resulting in justifying works. The Roman Catholic view of justification was virtually identical at this point.

However, for Bunyan the moral issue concerning God's holy character (Is. 6:1-3) was vital since, to deal rightly with sin, satisfaction of His offended righteousness was absolutely necessary. Thus Richard Greaves comments:

> The necessity of an atonement was based by Bunyan upon the assumption that grace could only be extended to the sinner in a way which was not contradictory to divine justice, hence the rhetorical question was asked: 'If the Promise, and God's grace without Christ's Blood would have saved us, wherefore then did Christ die?' For Bunyan there could be no thought of even the theoretical possibility that God could be gracious and merciful to sinners without an atonement for their sins.[4]

Hence in *The Pilgrim's Progress* this penal, satisfactory, substitutionary understanding of the atonement is of pervasive importance, just as it is in *Grace Abounding*.

Of course, as with Luther and the other Reformers, the doctrine of Paul in particular was of crucial significance here. Concerning his own experience, the Bedford pastor relates in his autobiography:

> One day, as I was passing in the field, and that too with some dashes on my conscience, fearing lest yet all was not right, suddenly this sentence fell upon my soul, Thy righteousness is in heaven; and methought withal, I saw, with the eyes of my soul, Jesus Christ at God's right hand there, I say, as my righteousness; so that wherever I was, or whatever I was adoing, God could not say of me, He wants [lacks] my righteousness, for that was just before him. I also saw, moreover, that it was not my good frame of heart that made my righteousness better, nor yet my bad frame that made my righteousness worse; for my righteousness was Jesus Christ himself, the same yesterday, and today, and forever (Heb. 13:8). Now did

---

[4] Richard Greaves, *John Bunyan*, p. 36.

> my chains fall off my legs indeed, I was loosed from my affliction and irons, my temptations also fled away.[5]

Hopeful also tells of the advice he received from Faithful: "He told me, that unless I could obtain the righteousness of a man that never had sinned, neither mine own, nor all the righteousness of the world, could save me. . . . He bid me say to this effect, God be merciful to me a sinner, and make me to know and believe in Jesus Christ; for I see, that if his righteousness had not been, or I have not faith in that righteousness, I am utterly cast away." Finally revelation from Christ breaks through as he confesses: "From all which I gathered, that I must look for righteousness in his [Christ's] person, and for satisfaction for my sins by his blood. . . . And now was my heart full of joy, mine eyes full of tears, and mine affections running over with love to the name, people, and ways of Jesus Christ."[6]

The Pilgrim's Progress is Justification Centered

When Christian's clothing of filthy rags, being representative of his shabby righteousnesses (Isa. 64:6), is taken away at the Place of Deliverance and replaced with a free coat, all of this being as a result of his look of faith at the crucified Christ, Bunyan graphically portrays the essential truth of the Reformation doctrine of justification by faith alone. Christian further explains to Formalist and Hypocrisy: "As for this coat that is on my back, it was given me by the Lord of the place whither I go; and that . . . to cover my nakedness with. And I take it as a token of his kindness to me; for I had nothing but rags before."[7]

The Latitudinarian, Edward Fowler,[8] a future Bishop, with whom Bunyan strenuously disputed over this matter in his *Defense Of The Doctrine Of Justification*, maintained that justification before God was a cooperative work whereby the sinner and

---

[5] Bunyan, *Works*, I, §§ 229-230, pp. 35-36.

[6] Ibid., III, pp. 154-156.

[7] Ibid., p. 104.

[8] Christopher Hill describes "Latitudinarians" as "liberal, rational, middle-of-the-road men." He explains that in Edward Fowler's *The Design of Christianity*, this Anglican moderate not only rejected the doctrine of imputed righteousness, but also propounded that, "a holy and a moral life was possible for everyone, because the principles of such a life were written in the hearts of all men." *A Tinker and a Poor Man*, p. 130.

internal grace produced justifying works. This synergistic gospel, being much like that of Roman Catholicism, meant that man was saved through gradual moral improvement. To this, and in stark contrast, Bunyan upheld an objective rather than a subjective atonement whereby the believing sinner, by looking to Christ's complete and satisfactory sacrifice, was justified and accredited with Christ's perfect righteousness. Pieter de Vries is right when he comments: "Bunyan was a staunch advocate of the forensic nature of justification. God clothes us with the righteousness that lies altogether outside ourselves and resides solely in the person of Christ. . . . The grounds of salvation lie in the work of Christ *for* us and not in that of the Holy Spirit *in* us."[9] In contrast, Fowler maintained that cooperation with infused and subjective grace was the ground of human works that obtained progressive justification. On the other hand, for Bunyan, faith in objective grace, that is the Calvary atonement outside of the sinner, was also works based, but these works were exclusively those of Christ's doing and dying.

In the detailed dispute between Christian and Ignorance on the Enchanted Ground, this objective/subjective conflict concerning the atonement is at the heart of their disagreement. Ignorance declares: "I believe that Christ died for sinners; and that I shall be justified before God from the curse, through his gracious acceptance of my obedience to his law. Or thus, Christ makes my duties, that are religious, acceptable to his Father, by virtue of his merits; and so shall I be justified."[10] To this Christian responds:

> Thou believest with a false faith; because it taketh justification from the personal righteousness of Christ, and applies it to thy own. . . . This faith maketh not Christ a justifier of thy person, but of thy actions; and of thy person for thy action's sake, which is false. . . . [T]rue justifying faith puts the soul, as sensible of its lost condition by the law, upon flying for refuge unto Christ's righteousness, which righteousness of his is not an act of grace, by which he maketh, for justification, thy obedience accepted with God; but his personal obedience to the law, in doing and suffering for us what that required at our hands; this righteousness, I say, true faith accepteth, under the skirt of which, the soul being shrouded, and by it presented as spotless before God, it is accepted, and acquit from condemnation.[11]

---

9 Pieter de Vries, *John Bunyan on the Order of Salvation*, pp. 147, 148.

10 Bunyan, *Works*, III, p. 158.

11 Ibid.

In response to this, Ignorance recoils with the objection, "What! Would you have us trust to what Christ, in his own person, has done without [outside of[12]] us? This conceit would loosen the reigns of our lust, and tolerate us to live as we list; for what matter how we live, if we may be justified by Christ's personal righteousness from all, when we believe it?"[13] Such a response is not unlike that of Paul's hypothetical opponent in Romans 6:15.

THE SCENES OF THE GOSPEL

During the course of *The Pilgrim's Progress* there are numerous areas of focus where the content of the gospel is portrayed with distinctive emphasis. When this truth is considered as a whole, it can be concluded with the greatest certainty that the biblical gospel has abiding significance for the Christian; it is not merely initiatory, but perennially glorious.

Evangelist directs Christian to the Wicket-gate

While reading the Bible in the City of Destruction causes Christian to experience an increasing load of guilt, it is Evangelist who first directs him to the gospel by way of his exhortation to flee toward the Wicket-gate, even though at that stage the distressed pilgrim is too dim of sight to identify this entrance into the narrow way. However, it is "yon shining light," or "a lamp shining in a dark place" that shows the way ahead to Jesus Christ, "the morning star" (II Pet. 1:19). Upon his arrival at the Wicket-gate, the burdened pilgrim is confronted with a gospel montage, that is Jesus Christ as the door (John 10:9), the way (John 14:6), and Good-will (Luke 2:14). Thus his course is set and a short way ahead, at the Place of Deliverance, the clarity of the gospel of free grace through an imputed righteousness results in assurance that his sin has been borne away (Ps. 103:12). As Christian travels

---

12 Bunyan's meaning of "without" means the more archaic "external to" rather than the modern "exclusive of." Refer to *The Oxford English Dictionary*. Further support for this meaning is found in Bunyan's *Gospel Truth's Opened* where he distinguishes between a subjective and an objective atonement, even though in this instance he is opposing Quaker doctrine. "The new, false Christ, is a Christ crucified within, dead within, risen again within, and ascended within, in opposition to the Son of Mary, who was crucified without, dead without, risen again without, and ascended in a cloud away from his disciples into heaven without them (Acts 1:9-11)." *Works*, II, pp. 134-5.

13 Bunyan, *Works*, III, p. 158.

onward, numerous incidents cause him to recall his hope in a crucified Christ. These include boasting about his coat to Formalist and Hypocrisy, the supper at the Palace Beautiful, and his subsequent victory over Apollyon when he is strengthened by eating bread and drinking from the bottle of wine given to him by his former companions, Discretion, Prudence, Piety, and Charity.

Evangelist Rescues Christian From a False Gospel

The seduction of Christian by Mr. Worldly-Wiseman is countered by the greater pastoral interest of Evangelist who exposes this charlatan's fraudulent gospel. Such a deceitful evangel, supposedly offering burden relief by means of Legality at the Village Morality just beyond a "high hill," is in fact encouragement to attempt the impossible, that is the scaling of Mt. Sinai so as to attain its demands of a perfect righteousness (Gal. 5:3). Thus Mr. Worldly-Wiseman, while denouncing Christian's book as well as free grace through the cross, is a proclaimer of "justification by the works of the law" (Rom. 3:20; Gal. 2:16). Further, this false gospel or "administration of death" (II Cor. 3:7-11) only results in condemnation. Nevertheless Evangelist redirects Christian toward Christ at the Wicket-Gate with words of encouragement: "[Y]et will the man at the gate receive thee, for he has good-will for men."[14]

Christian's Encounter With the Wicket-gate

Although the apparent disjunction between the Wicket-gate and the Place of Deliverance is a reflection of Bunyan's particular experience, explained in detail in Chapter 6, it ought to be understood that biblically speaking, and the author of *The Pilgrim's Progress* would heartily agree here, this entrance is the great gospel transition point from darkness to light, from condemnation to justification, from the broad road leading to destruction to the narrow road leading to eternal life (Matt. 7:13-14). Entrance requires a felt load of guilt before God and an earnest response to the gospel invitation (Matt. 7:7); this is simple though earnest faith in the Lord Jesus Christ as the only way of salvation and reconciliation with God (Matt. 11:28; John 14:6). The gospel, when seriously approached, is not complex, but it does demand the prerequisite of a "broken and a contrite heart" (Ps. 51:17). Furthermore, in progressing beyond this gate, this same

---

[14] Ibid., p. 96.

gospel retains ongoing importance since entrance through the Wicket-gate has become the fundamental insignia of a bona fide pilgrim, and by this means the illegitimacy of Formalist and Hypocrisy, and Ignorance, is identified.

If the specifics of the atonement seem to be missing at this juncture, Christian is certainly pulled through the Wicket-gate by the nail-pierced hands of Goodwill, who is later identified in Part Two as Jesus Christ.[15]

The House of Interpreter

Of the seven scenes that instruct Christian, two in particular have a gospel emphasis that, being communicated by the Holy Spirit, enlarge the understanding of the new pilgrim concerning the narrow way along which he now travels.

1. The distinction between the law and the gospel.

This second scene, concerning the dusty room, illustrates the distinction between the law and the gospel which Bunyan, according to the particular influence of Luther, believed to be of great importance. In simple terms, the new Christian is to understand that having been initially saved by the gospel, he will also be maintained and sanctified by the gospel, and not the law. As he puts it, unlike the gospel, "it [the law] doth not give power to subdue."[16] Elsewhere Bunyan writes:

> That thou mayest know the nature of the love of Christ, . . . be much in acquainting of thy soul with the nature of the law, and the nature of the gospel (Gal. 3:21). . . . The law is a servant, both first and last, to the gospel (Rom. 10:3-4): when therefore it is made a Lord, it destroyeth: and then to be sure it is made a Lord and Savior of, when its dictates and commands are depended upon for life.[17]

2. The grace of Christ conquers the assailed heart.

This fourth scene, concerning the inextinguishable blaze, illustrates the surpassing greatness of the sustaining grace of Christ in the face of Satan's furious attempts to douse the flaming soul that has been ignited in the first place by Christ (Rom. 5:20). As Bunyan explains, "This is Christ, who continually, with the oil of

---

[15] Ibid., p. 180.

[16] Ibid., III, p. 99.

[17] Ibid., II, p. 28.

his grace, maintains the work already begun in the heart."[18] In other words, gospel grace began the work in the soul, and only gospel grace can uphold that work in the soul to the end.

The Palace Beautiful

This representation of a faithful non-conformist church indicates the pastoral centrality of the gospel in a number of ways. To begin with, there is careful investigation by the Palace Beautiful inhabitants as to whether Christian has had an authentic encounter with the gospel via the Wicket-gate, and that his new affections reflect genuine conversion. In testifying that he has occasional spiritual victories, Christian points out that these are obtained through meditation on the cross and his coat.

However, it is at supper time, when the Lord's Table is so graphically portrayed, that the gospel is seen to be of such sustaining influence for the residents. Here the details of Christ's atonement are explained in graphic and applicatory detail as the household partakes of "fat things, and with wine that was well refined."[19] In conversation around the table, they discussed that he [the Lord of the hill], had been a "great warrior" involving "the loss of much blood."[20] Further, "he had stripped himself of his glory, that he might do this for the poor. . . . They said moreover, that he had made many pilgrims princes, though by nature they were beggars born, and their original had been the dunghill."[21] Even at his departure, the strengthened pilgrim is given gospel tokens for the frequent and nourishing remembrance of Christ's saving work.

Faithful's Conversion and Witness

Convinced by Christian's witness at the City of Destruction that he should go on pilgrimage, Faithful is propositioned by Wanton just outside the Wicket-gate. In resisting her, presumably he is also snatched in through the gate by Good-will as was Christian and thus savingly joined to Christ. In being at first inclined toward the seductive proposal of Old Man Adam the first, he incurs the severe condemnation of Moses yet is delivered by the man with holes in his hands and side.

---

[18] Ibid., III, p. 100.

[19] Ibid., p. 109.

[20] Ibid.

[21] Ibid.

Up to this point Faithful's apprehension of Christ seems weaker than that of Christian, though strengthening seems to rapidly increase as he disputes with Talkative and witnesses at Vanity Fair. Here he explains to Hopeful in the plainest possible terms that only the saving perfect righteousness of the Lord Jesus Christ, received for justification through faith alone, could save him. This gospel witness and Faithful's subsequent martyrdom made a considerable impression upon the town of Vanity, as is evident in Part Two when Christiana finds fellowship there, and the populace is reported to have become less aggressive towards pilgrims.

Hopeful's Conversion and Witness

This testimony of conversion given to Christian on the Enchanted Ground is the model presentation of the gospel in *The Pilgrim's Progress*. In contrast with Christian's experience, there is no disjunction here between conversion and assurance. A summary of this testimony is as follows:

1. Worldly intoxication without guilt.
2. Conviction commences in various circumstances.
3. Self-reformation attempted with religious duties.
4. Conviction strengthens through Scripture truth.
5. Consultation with Faithful.
    a. He needs a perfect righteousness.
    b. The Lord Jesus is the only righteous man.
    c. Believe on the Lord Jesus for justification.
6. Objections to Faithful's invitation.
    a. It is presumptuous to come to Christ.
    b. What is it to come to Christ?
7. Christ is revealed from heaven and invites.
8. Objections to Christ's invitation.
    a. I am a great sinner.
    b. What is it to believe?
9. Embrace of Christ as saving righteousness.
10. Confession of Christ to Christian.

The Testimony of Ignorance

The stark contrast between the gospel attested to by Hopeful and that of Ignorance subsequently discussed at the Enchanted Ground is of the highest importance to Bunyan. Described as "a very brisk lad" at his first meeting with Christian and Hopeful, Ignorance is immediately identified as an apostate since he strenuously defends his entrance into the narrow way by means of "a little crooked lane,"[22] and not via the Wicket-gate. He is firmly religious and intent on entering the Celestial City. When the three pilgrims are reacquainted at the Enchanted Ground some distance ahead, the ensuing detailed dispute between Christian and Ignorance may be likened to Paul's animated concern for the purity of the gospel in Galatians 1:6-9; likewise for Bunyan, at this point essential truth is at stake (Gal. 2:5).

As considered earlier in this chapter, the controversy may be reduced to a question as to whether justification is by an objective, imputed and complete work of Christ crucified outside of man, or a subjective, infused, and cooperative work with Christ within the heart of man. Ignorance is constantly stressing his trust in what is going on within his heart, good thoughts, etc., so that he objects to the suggestion that he is a thorough sinner. Thus, he believes in a collaborative work with grace in his life whereby good works are produced that result in gradual justification before God. Christian is emphatic that faith alone must lay hold of what Christ has completed as an atonement on Mt. Calvary outside of the sinful heart. However, Ignorance is unwavering in his belief in a mystical gospel to the end, and it is significant that when he finally arrives at the entrance to the Celestial City, he declares his qualification for entrance to be, not Christ's righteousness but, "I have eat and drank in the presence of the King, and he has taught in our streets [Luke 13:26]."[23]

THE DOCTRINE OF THE GOSPEL

At this point, those today who merely have a sentimental, and broad evangelical regard for *The Pilgrim's Progress* will, when they correctly understand what Bunyan's gospel doctrine is all about, find themselves on the horns of a dilemma. Either they will have to walk away from their literary hero since their contemporary grasp

---

22 Ibid., p. 146.

23 Ibid., p. 166.

of the gospel is admitted to be radically different from that portrayed in the famous allegory, or else they will have to change their understanding of the gospel in such a way that it will be likened to a theological Copernican revolution. For instance, the contemporary terminology that expresses Christian conversion as, "inviting Jesus Christ into your heart" will not mesh with Bunyan's representation of the Gospel. It is more akin to the Roman Catholic gospel where justification is by infused grace.

First and foremost, Bunyan was a thorough biblicist who very conscientiously sought the truth in Holy Scripture for himself without relying upon many secondary sources. Of course, he had no knowledge of the original languages, and made no pretense that he did; however in no way did he disparage those more scholarly Puritans who were of like precious faith. Nevertheless his devotion to the English Bible was primary since he openly confessed his preference for not drawing from the wells of other men. Even so, other influences did impinge upon him, all of course claiming biblical roots. These shaped his theology in a secondary sense, particularly with regard to the gospel, while at the same time it must be acknowledged that Bunyan was very much his own man and not one to fall in line with a system of doctrine for the sake of loyalty and acceptance in some church association. The primary influences upon Bunyan's doctrine of the gospel are now considered as follows:

Presupposition Concerning Sin

Bunyan's understanding of sin, its historic commencement in the Garden of Eden and universal consequences, is classically biblical and orthodox. He believed in an original, historic Adam who fathered the sinful human race:

> He [Adam] . . . made them [his children] sinners—'By one man's disobedience many were made sinners.' (Rom. 5:19). . . . [H]e [Adam] was the conduit pipe through which the devil did convey off his poisoned spawn and venom nature into the hearts of Adam's sons and daughters, by which they are at this day so strongly and so violently carried away, that they fly as fast to hell, and the devil, by reason of sin, as chaff before a mighty wind."[24] Elsewhere he writes of a person presently being, "under the wrath of God because of original sin (Rom. 5:12).[25]

---

[24] Ibid., I, p. 505.

[25] Ibid., II, p. 166.

Thus he believed in the doctrine of original or congenital sin whereby even from birth and the cradle sin is inherently present.

Furthermore, "[sin] is that which hath stupified and besotted the powers of men's souls, and made them even next to a beast or brute in all matters supernatural and heavenly (II Pet. 2:12). For as the beast minds nothing but his lusts and his belly, by nature, so man minds nothing but things earthly, sensual, and devilish, by reason of iniquity."[26] This pollution is not only universal but thorough and has resulted in man being infected in all of his faculties, intellect, will, and affections, so that every individual can only move with the freedom of this corrupt nature. "[Sin] has alienated the will, the mind, and affections, from the choice of the things that should save it, and wrought them over to a hearty delight in those things that naturally tend to drown it in perdition and destruction (Col. 1:21)."[27] Consequently, man retains no inherent ability to take pleasure in and obey the righteousness of God, such as via "free-will."[28] Any holy response on man's part, even saving faith, can only be generated by particular grace sovereignly imparted (Eph. 2:8).[29]

Martin Luther

It is not difficult to understand Bunyan's feelings of spiritual kinship here with the great Reformer Martin Luther. As a tinker, newly married, he became increasingly aware of his own inner ungodliness; the misery was excruciating. Moreover he then read a book that described this struggle and at the same time prescribed the remedy with great animation and jealous regard for the supremacy of free and sovereign grace. Hence, it is not surprising that Bunyan wrote in *Grace Abounding* concerning Luther's *Commentary On Galatians* that, "I found my condition, in his experience, so largely and profoundly handled, as if his book had been written out of my heart. . . . I do prefer this book of Martin Luther upon the Galatians, excepting the Holy Bible, before all the

---

[26] Ibid., p. 512.

[27] Ibid.

[28] "[I]t is no error to say, that a man naturally has Will, and a Power to pursue his will, and that as to his salvation [his own way]. But it is a damnable error to say that he hath will and power to pursue it, *and that in God's way* [emphasis added].' Ibid., p. 241; cf. also pp. 312, 756.

[29] Ibid., p. 134.

books that ever I have seen, as most fit for a wounded conscience."[30]

Of course, as an Augustinian monk, Luther had faced the same struggle concerning his inward corruption and the great question as to how reconciliation might be made with a righteous God. So it seems that Bunyan felt forever indebted to Luther for his ministration of gospel truth, especially its description in Pauline terms of the free, objective, substitutionary "righteousness of God" (Rom. 1:17), that is "the gift of righteousness" (Rom. 5:15), or "the righteousness which is by faith" (Rom. 9:30). To illustrate this dependance on Bunyan's part, consider the conclusion of that turbulent period of over two years following his conversion when he came to a point of immediate enlightenment and stability. In *Grace Abounding* he writes:

> [S]uddenly this sentence fell upon my soul, *Thy righteousness is in heaven*; and methought withall, I saw, with the eyes of my soul, Jesus Christ at God's right hand; there, I say, as my righteousness. . . . Now did my chains fall off my legs indeed, I was loosed from my affliction and irons, my temptations also fled away; . . . So when I came home, I looked to see if I could find that sentence, *Thy righteousness is in heaven*; but could not find such a saying, wherefore my heart began to sink again, onely that was brought to my remembrance, he *of God is made unto us wisdom, righteousness, sanctification, and redemption*; by this word I saw the other Sentence true (I Cor. 1:30).[31]

Now compare Luther's *Lectures on Galatians* where he comments on, "For we through the Spirit, by faith, are waiting for the hope of righteousness" (5:5):

> I conclude that perfect righteousness has been prepared for me in heaven. . . . in this hope I am strengthened against sin and look for the consummation of perfect righteousness in heaven. . . . [Devout Christians] know that they have eternal righteousness, for which they look in hope as an utterly certain possession, laid up in heaven, when they are most aware of the terrors of sin and death; and that they are the lords of everything when they seem to be the poorest of all.[32]

---

[30] Ibid., I, §§ 129-130, p. 22.

[31] Ibid., I, §§ 229-30, p. 72,

[32] Martin Luther, *Luther's Works*, 27, pp. 22, 27. Cf. a similar comment on 2:15-16, p. 225.

Thus it is the Reformer from Wittenberg rather than Calvin from Geneva that made such an indelible impression, and there is general agreement that this influence persisted throughout the length of the tinker's ministry. Although Bunyan was a strong predestinarian, there was a doctrinal motif that guided him which was far more influential than divine determinism, namely the reign of grace. Richard Greaves describes this dominion of gospel grace as follows:

> The influence of Luther on Bunyan's concept of the nature of God can be seen especially in Bunyan's view of God fundamentally in terms of the wrath–grace dichotomy rather than in terms of the Calvinist emphasis on the sovereign will of God. The controlling motif in Bunyan's theology was not the more philosophical principle of the divine will exercising supreme control in the universe, but the more personal and experiential conflict which raged in both the convicted sinner and the converted pilgrim who sensed on the one hand the dread of God whose wrath could not be mitigated because of the wrong done to his holiness and justice, and on the other hand the all-sufficient grace of a God whose love and mercy had triumphed in the salvation of his elect.[33]

How then does this perspective find its outworking in *The Pilgrim's Progress*? It is evidenced in a consideration of the far greater degree to which sin and grace find emphasis in contrast with the sovereignty of divine will. Of course this is not an either/or situation but rather a mater of primacy, and in this respect, beyond doubt, *The Pilgrim's Progress* does manifestly give greater place to that sovereignty of grace which is greater than all our sin (Rom. 5:20). It is the grace of *sola scriptura*, *sola christos*, *sola fide*, of free justification, of imputed righteousness.

Law and Gospel

This emphasis clearly confirms the dominant influence of the German Reformer over the Bedford pastor, and as Hill points out, along with the impact of John Foxe, John Owen, and William Dell.[34] For Luther, law and gospel were antithetical, reactive, though both in necessary tension. Law, as the declaration of God's perfect righteousness, thunders against incapacitated sinful man. More than that, it magnifies and arouses sin in whatever crevice it

---

[33] Greaves, *John Bunyan*, p. 155.

[34] Hill, *A Tinker And A Poor Man*, pp. 157-160.

hides. It offers no extenuating circumstances, no middle ground, no relativity, no truce, only relentless and accusatory demand.

On the other hand grace rightly quenches and satisfies and has dominion overall that the law requires. It justly pardons sinners and thereby silences the condemnatory voice of the law. Whatever the law is able to arouse and terrify through guilt, grace is able to cleanse, quench and bring peace through pardon. The law, as represented by Moses, is a ministry of condemnation and death while grace, as embodied in Jesus Christ, is a ministry of free righteousness and life and peace (John 1:17; Rom. 5:1, 17-21; II Cor. 3:7-18).

So in *The Pilgrim's Progress* there are several indications of the major importance of this truth for Bunyan. Mr. Worldly-Wiseman counsels Christian to lose his burden at the Village of Morality just beyond "yonder high hill."[35] However, this representation of Mt. Sinai only thunders at the pilgrim's attempt to scale the impossible heights of the law. Then at the house of Interpreter, the second scene there is a precise portrayal of the opposite roles of law and grace. The dusty room is man's thoroughly polluted heart which the sweeper only magnified. But then the damsel sprinkles the settling and cleansing influences of the gospel.

Further on Faithful is inclined to heed Old Man Adam the first. For this reason Moses mercilessly and repeatedly beats him down until Christ comes to the rescue and drives away the accuser. Surprisingly, although Bunyan deals with this whole doctrinal matter in great detail in his *The Doctrine Of The Law And Grace Unfolded* published in 1659,[36] and that in modified covenantal terms when he refers to the covenant of works and the covenant of grace, yet he declines to use these covenantal designations in any way in *The Pilgrim's Progress* later published in 1678, as well as Part Two in 1684. This may well have been for the purpose of not involving his readers with more intricate terminology.

Calvinism

In consideration of more exact doctrinal definitions, while it is unquestionably true that Bunyan was a strict Calvinist, yet to be far more precise he was really a predestinarian as was Luther, probably being more familiar with the German's *Bondage Of The Will* than the Frenchman's *Institutes Of The Christian Religion*.

---

35 Bunyan, *Works*, III, p. 94.

36 Ibid., I, pp. 492-575.

Bunyan's Works express no regard for Calvin that is comparable to his confessed reliance upon Luther. In this vein Greaves explains:

> On this Lutheran foundation Bunyan built an essentially Calvinistic superstructure with the ideas which he assimilated from the writings of Bayly and Dent,[37] the teaching of Gifford and Burton, his ministerial association with men such as Owen [and Dell], and his contact in general with the recurrent and often controversial discussion of basic Christian principles which absorbed the minds of so many in the seventeenth century. . . . In the Westminster Confession and the writings of Owen, to use two obvious examples, predestination was a doctrine derived from the prior principles of the absolute sovereignty of the divine will and the concomitant decrees pronounced by that will, whereas in the writings of Bunyan the doctrine of predestination originated primarily in a soteriological concern, with men being predestined more on the basis of foreknowledge [forelove, not prescience?] and gracious love than as the result of abstract philosophical principles. In order that predestination be accomplished there had to be the effectual and irresistible calling of those predestined to glory, and in stating this doctrine Bunyan continued to draw upon his Calvinist mentors and associates. The remainder of his soteriology manifested consistent if not especially noteworthy Calvinist influence.[38]

From a twentieth century perspective, Bunyan would undoubtedly be regarded as a thoroughgoing, five point baptistic Calvinist rather than a Lutheran, and especially with regard to church structure and the ordinances. His belief in unconditional particular election, and rejection of free will as popularly understood, would mark him out as very different from the broad stream of evangelical Christendom.[39] Greaves also indicates that Bunyan seems to have professed belief in a limited or definite atonement while not writing at length on this issue as did his friend John Owen.[40] Refer to Chapter 9 for a more detailed consideration of this matter of sovereignty, election, and free will.

However, when we come to *The Pilgrim's Progress*, the author, while dealing with issues related to the sovereignty of God in many instances, yet causes his tone in most cases to be mellow and winsome rather than direct and dogmatic as in his other writings.

---

[37] Ibid., p. 7.

[38] Greaves, *John Bunyan*, pp. 156-157.

[39] Ibid., pp. 51-61.

[40] Ibid., pp. 41-45.

This bares out the comment of Samuel Coleridge that, "Calvinism never put on a less rigid form, never smoothed its brow and softened its voice more winningly than in *The Pilgrim's Progress*."[41] However, what are these more gentle representations of a gospel that exalts in the truth that salvation is wholly of the grace of God? There is the simple expression, "But as God would have it," which explains the ability of Christian to regain his lost sword, though almost vanquished, and give Apollyon a deadly thrust.[42]

Likewise following the martyrdom of Faithful, Bunyan relates, "But he that overrules all things, having the power of their rage in his own hand, so wrought it about, that Christian for that time escaped them, and went his way."[43] Then there is the despairing Reprobate in the Iron Cage, refer to Chapter 10, who explains that, "God has denied me repentance. His Word gives me no encouragement to believe; yea, himself hath shut me up in this iron cage; nor can all the men in the world let me out. O eternity! eternity! how shall I grapple with the misery that I must meet with in eternity!"[44] The Shepherds declare to Christian and Hopeful, concerning the status of the way ahead, that it "is safe for those for whom it is to be safe; but transgressors shall fall therein (Hos. 14:9)."[45]

However, with more specific regard to the gospel, Bunyan makes it quite clear that a saving understanding of this message is only possible by means of sovereign revelation from heaven. When Hopeful seeks counsel from Faithful in Vanity, he is told to go to Christ, at which Christian asks of his companion on the Enchanted Ground, "And did the Father reveal his Son to you?" Hopeful responds, "Not at the first, nor second, nor third, nor fourth, nor fifth; no not at the sixth time neither." Then, having related how he eventually believed, Christian responds, "This was a revelation of Christ to your soul indeed."[46]

In the succeeding incident, when Christian disputes with Ignorance, at the conclusion of this encounter Hopeful interrupts

---

[41] Roger Sharrock, ed., *Bunyan, The Pilgrim's Progress, A Casebook*, p. 54.

[42] Bunyan, *Works*, III, p. 113.

[43] Ibid., p. 132.

[44] Ibid., p. 101.

[45] Ibid., p. 143.

[46] Ibid., pp. 155, 156.

with the question as to whether "he [Ignorance] ever had Christ revealed to him from heaven." Ignorance is offended at such a doctrinal emphasis to which Hopeful responds: "Why, man! Christ is so hid in God from natural apprehensions of the flesh, that he cannot by any man be savingly known, unless God the Father reveals him to them."[47] To Bunyan then the grace of God and His uncompromised sovereignty are inseparable elements (Rom. 11:5-6). He portrays the gospel in *The Pilgrim's Progress* as being strongly urged upon all men, yet the authentic embrace of this saving message will ultimately and only be the response of those, "as God would have it."

Conclusion

There is no doubt that John Bunyan's preaching, teaching, and writing had a vibrant quality about them, not unlike the animation and intensity one senses when reading the writings of Luther. Such a style was both infectious and captivating insofar as his hearers were concerned. And it is important to ask why? For instance, consider Bunyan's concluding exhortation in his *A Few Sighs From Hell*, based upon an exposition of Luke 16:19-31 concerning the destiny of Dives and Lazarus:

> Reader, here might I spend many sheets of paper, yea, I might upon this subject write a very great book, but I shall now forbear, desiring thee to be very conversant in the Scriptures, 'for they are they which testify of Jesus Christ' (John 5:39). The Bereans were counted noble upon this account: 'These were more noble than those in Thessalonica, in that they received the Word with all readiness of mind, and searched the scriptures daily' (Acts 17:11). But here let me give thee one caution, that is, have a care that thou do not satisfy thyself with a bare search of them, without a real application of him whom they testify of to thy soul, lest instead of faring the better for they doing this work, thou dost fare a great deal the worse, and thy condemnation be very much heightened, in that though thou did read so often the sad state of those that die in sin, and the glorious estate of them that close in with Christ, yet thou thyself shouldst be such a fool as to lose Jesus Christ, notwithstanding thy hearing, and reading so plentifully of him.[48]

Such Pauline earnestness demonstrates a vital, heartfelt compassion that is to be found in all of Bunyan's writings, and yet

---

[47] Ibid., pp. 155, 158.

[48] Ibid., pp. 709-710.

sadly is so rare today. Greaves provides some help in our search for the reason for this fervency. It provokes careful thought concerning what ought to be at the heart of our gospel proclamation at this needy hour:

> Because grace was [Bunyan's] dominating motif, his thought retained a personal element which was often lacking in the writings of many Calvinists, notably those of Owen and the *Westminster Confession.* This sense of personal contact and vibrancy was, however, perhaps due more to the style of his writing than to his concern with grace; yet the concept of grace must be considered an important contributing factor to this personal element which pervaded his writings, since grace per se lent itself to a more personal treatment than did, for example, the more abstract concepts of sovereignty and will which were the basic principles of contemporary Calvinist theology. It was precisely this personal and living quality which made his sermons and writings so popular, for through the spoken and the printed word he made the workings of divine grace come alive.[49]

HOW TO RUN TO THE KINGDOM OF CHRIST

Well then, sinner, what sayest thou? Where is thy heart? Wilt thou run? Art thou resolved to strip? Or art thou not? Think quickly, man, it is no dallying in this matter. Confer not with flesh and blood; look up to heaven, and see how thou likest it; also to hell! If thou dost not know the way, inquire at the Word of God. If thou wantest company, cry for God's Spirit. If thou wantest encouragement, entertain the promises. But be sure thou begin by times; get into the way; run apace and hold out to the end; and the Lord give thee a prosperous journey. Farewell.

John Bunyan
The Heavenly Footman
Works, III, p. 394

---

[49] Greaves, *John Bunyan*, pp. 159-160.

CHAPTER SIX

The Conversion of Christian

IN today's conservative evangelical environment, readers of *The Pilgrim's Progress* could easily be forgiven for assuming that the conversion of Christian occurred at the Place of Deliverance where, having gazed at the uplifted cross, his burden was loosed from off his back. Yet it may come as a surprise to these same readers, even as it did to this writer several years ago, to discover that, beyond doubt, John Bunyan understood the conversion of Christian to have taken place earlier at the Wicket-gate. Hence, first let us consider the proof of this assertion, and then attempt to understand Bunyan's conception of conversion with regard both to his own life and to the order of these particular narrative events.

The Evidence of Christian Given Assurance by Good-will

Upon Christian having passed through the Wicket-gate, he is assured by Good-will, "An open door is set before thee, and no man can shut it."[1] Surely this reference to Revelation 3:7-8 is indicative of the new pilgrim's security, obtained at conversion, that will reassure him on his journey.

The Evidence of Christian at the House of Interpreter

In accord with John 15:26, Good-will at the Wicket-gate, being representative of Jesus Christ, directs Christian to proceed toward the house of Interpreter, which is representative of the ministry of the Holy Spirit. The substantial instruction which Christian then receives is very much reflective of the teaching and illuminating ministry of this same Holy Spirit (John 7:37-39; 14:26; 15:26; 16:13-15), in conjunction with the Bible that Christian has in hand. However, such teaching in Scripture clearly has reference to the Holy Spirit's instructive ministry in the life of the believer.

---

[1] John Bunyan, *The Works of John Bunyan*, ed. George Offor, III, p. 97.

Hence the sequence of these events, particularly the fact that this revelation immediately precedes Christian's arrival at the Place of Deliverance, is Bunyan's portrayal of that teaching as being most suitable for a new believer.

At the fourth scene in the house of Interpreter, Christian observes not only Satan attempting to quench the fire of grace *already burning* in a true pilgrim's heart, but also the greater and more effectual outpouring of Christ's oil of grace which triumphantly maintains the blaze. In this regard Christian is told, "This is Christ, who continually, with the oil of his grace, maintains the work *already begun in the heart* [emphasis added]."[2] This explanation would only make sense if Christian had already been converted.

The Evidence of the Illegitimacy of Certain Pilgrims

When Formalist and Hypocrisy tumble over the wall called Salvation, Christian questions their legitimacy since they have not made entrance through the Wicket-gate. They are rebuked with a quotation from John 10:1, not because they ignored the Place of Deliverance, but rather because they avoided the legitimate gospel door or Wicket-gate at the head of the way, which is obviously Jesus Christ.[3] In the same manner Ignorance is recognized as being an illegitimate pilgrim by Christian, not because he ignored the Place of Deliverance, but because he also did not commence his journey through the Wicket-gate.[4]

Of course it could be objected that the authentic pilgrim Hopeful, originating from the town of Vanity, apparently did not make an entrance through the Wicket-gate. In reply, this is no more a problem than the fact of Faithful appearing not to be accoutered with necessary armor available at the Palace Beautiful. In the case of Hopeful, Bunyan takes liberty with his allegorical form so that this pilgrim is converted through the gospel preaching and witness of Faithful prior to his martyrdom.

The Evidence of Good-will's Testimony to Christiana

In Part Two of The Pilgrim's Progress, Christiana, with her four sons and Mercy, eventually arrives at the Wicket-gate as they follow in the steps of Christian. There, having sought pardon for

---

[2] John Bunyan, *Works*, III, p. 100.

[3] Ibid., p. 103.

[4] Ibid., p. 146.

their sins, they are told by the Keeper of the Gate, or Good-will: "I [Christ, see next paragraph] grant pardon, . . . by word and deed; by word in the promise of forgiveness, by deed in the way I [Christ] obtained it." Then we are told that this Keeper, "had them up to the top of the gate and showed them [at a distance] by what deed they were saved, and told them withal that that sight they would have again as they went along in the way, to their comfort."[5]

The Evidence of Great-heart's Testimony About Good-will

In Part Two, when Christiana and her company arrive at the Place of Deliverance, their escort Great-heart gives explanation of the atoning deed that was described immediately following their entrance through the Wicket-gate. "The pardon that you and Mercy, and these boys *have attained*, was obtained by another, to wit, by him that let you in at the gate; and he hath obtained it in this double way. He has performed righteousness to cover you, and spilt blood to wash you in."[6]

The Evidence of *Grace Abounding To The Chief Of Sinners*

In Bunyan's spiritual autobiography, *Grace Abounding to the Chief of Sinners*, he describes dreaming of his miserable and cold isolation, obviously as an unbeliever, on the dark side of a mountain that faces an opposite sunny mountain. The only means of access to warm relief is through the narrow gap of a dividing wall that extends along the dividing valley. After much struggle and repeated effort, Bunyan passes through. He then gives the following interpretation: "The [sunny] mountain signified the church of the living God [cf. I Tim. 3:15]."[7] Sharrock incorrectly identifies this as the tinker's entrance into the local nonconformist Bedford congregation, which reception is far more certainly portrayed at the Palace Beautiful.[8] On this occasion, Bunyan's prime quest was for the light of the saving grace of God, not local church membership. Bunyan continues:

---

5 Ibid., p. 180.

6 Ibid., p. 190.

7 Ibid., I, §§ 53-6, pp. 12-13.

8 John Bunyan, *The Pilgrim's Progress*, eds. James Blanton Wharey and Roger Sharrock, p. 315.

> The sun that shone thereon, [was] the comfortable shining of his merciful face on them that were therein; the wall, I thought, was the Word, that did make separation between the Christians and the world; and the gap which was in this wall, I thought, was Jesus Christ, who is the way to God the Father (John 14:6; Matt. 7:14). But forasmuch as the passage was wonderful narrow, even so narrow, that I could not, but with great difficulty, enter in thereat, it showed me that none could enter into life, but those that were in downright earnest.[9]

The context in *Grace Abounding*, and especially the quote of Matthew 7:14, obviously regards this incident as a preview of Bunyan's conversion, which is also graphically replicated at the Wicket-gate.

The Evidence of *The Strait Gate*

In *The Strait Gate*, a treatise based upon Luke 13:24 published two years before *The Pilgrim's Progress*, Bunyan comments:

> There is the door of faith, the door which the grace of God hath opened to the Gentiles. This door is Jesus Christ, as also himself doth testify, saying, 'I am the door,' &c. (John 10:9; Acts 14:27). By this door men enter into God's favor and mercy, and find forgiveness through faith in his blood, and live in hope of eternal life.[10]

At this point George Offor adds the editorial comment: "How delightfully but solemnly is this illustrated in *The Pilgrim's Progress*, [that is in] the Wicket-gate at the head of the way, at which the poor burdened sinner must knock and obtain an entrance by Christ the door."[11]

The Evidence of Spurgeon's *Around the Wicket Gate*

In C. H. Spurgeon's tract *Around the Wicket Gate*, wholly based upon *The Pilgrim's Progress*, he identifies with halting pilgrims who draw near to the way of salvation and yet, for various reasons, do not pass through the entrance gate, that is the Wicket-gate:

---

9 Bunyan, *Works*, I, § 55, pp. 12-13.

10 Ibid., p. 365.

11 Ibid.

> Millions of men are in the outlying regions, far off from God and peace; for these we pray, and to these we give warning. But just now we have to do with a similar company, who are not far from the kingdom, but have come right up to the Wicket-gate which stands at the head of the way of life. . . . He who does not take the step of faith, and so enter upon the road to heaven, will perish. It will be an awful thing to die just outside the gate of life. Almost saved, but altogether lost![12]

Clearly Spurgeon understood the Wicket-gate scene to be the place of conversion for Christian.

CAN CHRISTIAN'S CONVERSION BE CLEARLY LOCATED?

In asserting that Christian's conversion took place at the Wicket-gate, we would add that this has certainly been the prevailing opinion amongst the more notable commentators on *The Pilgrims' Progress*, including George Offor, W. Mason, George Cheever, John Kelman, etc. However, a recent scholar has, to a certain degree, challenged this point of view with the following comment: "From the fact that Bunyan, in *The Pilgrim's Progress*, Part Two, had the sealing of the Spirit occur, allegorically, before Christiana's entry through the Wicket-gate, we may learn that we had better be on our guard against attaching too much significance to the order in which Bunyan arranged his scenes."[13]

In response, it appears quite clear from the text that Christiana's entrance through the Wicket-gate is the occasion of her conversion, as was the case with her husband. However, prior to this, Christiana receives a visitor in the City of Destruction who passes on to her a letter from the King of the Celestial City that invites her to go on pilgrimage. Who then is this messenger who identifies himself as Secret? Probably he represents "the angel of the LORD" who responds to Manoah's question in Judges 13:18 KJV, "What askest thou thus after my name, seeing it is secret?", as well as the reference to, "The secret of the LORD is with them that fear him; and he will shew them his covenant" (Ps. 25:14), as de Vries suggests.[14] Thus Christiana is to hold this letter close to her bosom, frequently read it, sing it as a song, and present it as validation at the gate of the Celestial City.[15]

---

[12] C. H. Spurgeon, *Around the Wicket Gate*, p. 3.

[13] Pieter de Vries, *John Bunyan and the Order of Salvation*, p. 207.

[14] Ibid., p. 206.

[15] Bunyan, *Works*, III, p. 174.

Now there is an obvious similarity between this item and that of the roll which Christian received at the Place of Deliverance, "the assurance of his life and acceptance at the desired haven."[16] Further, according to a marginal reference to Ephesians 1:13, Bunyan, to some degree, associates this roll given to Christian with the sealing of the Holy Spirit. However, it should be understood that Christian's *perception*, newfound stability, and heightened assurance at the Place of Deliverance reflects that which had already been established, concerning the work of the Holy Spirit, at the Wicket-gate. In fact Bunyan gives no clear, definitive exposition regarding the sealing of the Holy Spirit in terms of a more momentary understanding which many Calvinists understand by this expression. Hence de Vries is correct when he concludes: "Surveying the whole we can say that Bunyan related being sealed with the Spirit to the whole field of personal, spiritual experience. Spiritual life, whatever measure of it there was, was to be seen as a fruit of the sealing work of the Spirit."[17] Therefore, when we consider the letter of invitation given by Secret to Christiana before her conversion at the Wicket-gate, we do not associate it with a sealing of the Spirit usually related with conversion. Rather it represents that prevenient work of the Spirit which offers hope, encouragement, and promise that will be formally inaugurated at the Wicket-gate (I Pet. 1:1-2). Support for this understanding of Bunyan here is found in a segment of his poetic discourse entitled *A Discourse of the Building, &c., of the House of God*. Here are addressed those who qualify for the judgment of God and thus are distressed:

> But bring with thee a certificate,
> To show thou seest thyself most desolate;
> Writ by the master, with repentance seal'd,
> To show also that here thou would'st be heal'd,
> By those fair leaves of that most blessed tree,
> By which alone poor sinners healed be;
> And that thou dost abhor thee for thy ways.
> And wouldst in holiness spend all thy days;
> *And here be entertained; or thou wilt find*
> *To entertain thee here are none inclin'd.*[18]

---

16 Bunyan, *Works*, III, p. 106.

17 **de Vries**, *Order of Salvation*, p. 208.

18 Ibid., II, p. 580.

Thus the desolate are invited to come to the church for salvation, and bring with them a certificate of invitation that Jesus Christ has offered. This is clearly a preceding work of the Spirit being productive of repentance that *leads* to spiritual healing, conversion.

THE CONVERSION OF CHRISTIAN ACCORDING TO JOHN BUNYAN

In *The Holy War* published in 1682, military metaphor, familiar to the author, is used to describe the recapture by King Shaddai of the City of Mansoul that has been subject to the tyrannical reign of giant Diabolus. The actual campaign represents Christian conversion, and George Offor more specifically relates several incidents here to Bunyan's own conversion portrayed in *Grace Abounding.*[19] This being so, it ought not to surprise us if Bunyan similarly incorporates his own experiences into the conversion experience of Christian.

Why Does Christian Retain His burden?

While the author of *The Pilgrim's Progress* definitely portrays Christian as being converted at the Wicket-gate, yet release from this pilgrim's burden does not occur until he, having been instructed at the house of Interpreter, then gazes at the uplifted cross at the Place of Deliverance. To twentieth century Christians, this may seem a conflicting order of events. What then is Bunyan's intention here? What does this purposed hiatus represent? What is this post-conversion experience at the Place of deliverance?

The Opinion of C. H. Spurgeon

Consider once again the opinion of C. H. Spurgeon at this point who, as a devoted student and admirer of *The Pilgrim's Progress*, was second to none in his esteem for Bunyan. Yet this did not mean that he was in agreement with every detail concerning the tinker's allegory.[20] In fact he disagreed with two features that relate

---

[19] Ibid., III, p. 278-83, 289, 292, 295-7, 299, 302-3.

[20] This writer also, while having the most affectionate regard for Bunyan's ministry and specifically his literary magnum opus, has a disagreement with one feature of *The Pilgrim's Progress* It is that at the River of Death Christian and Hopeful cross over together; indeed Hopeful is very much a helping companion as they encounter this fearful trial. However for the Christian, death is always a solo experience. Perhaps Hopeful is intended to represent that loving assistance and encouragement which an earthly friend in Christ can offer to a departing saint.

to the gospel, namely the initial directing of Christian to the shining light, and the placing of the cross beyond the Wicket-gate.

1. The sermon illustration.

In a sermon based upon I Corinthians 2:2, Spurgeon comments:

> By the way, let me tell you a little story about Bunyan's *Pilgrim's Progress*. I am a great lover of John Bunyan, but I do not believe him infallible; and the other day I met with a story about him which I think is a very good one. There was a wise young man; so he thought, 'If I am to be a missionary, there is no need for me to transport myself far away from home; I may as well be a missionary in Edinburgh.' . . . Well, this young man started, and determined to speak to the first person he met. He met one of those old fishwives; those of us who have seen them can never forget them, they are extraordinary women indeed. So, stepping up to her, he said, 'Here you are, coming along with your burden on your back; let me ask you if you have got another burden, a spiritual burden.' 'What!' she asked; 'do you mean that burden in John Bunyan's *Pilgrim's Progress*? Because, if you do, young man, I got rid of that many years ago, probably before you were born. But I went a better way to work than the pilgrim did.
>
> The evangelist that John Bunyan talks about was one of your parsons that do not preach the gospel; for he said, 'Keep that light in thine eye, and run to the wicket gate.' Why, man alive! That was not the place for him to run to. He should have said, 'Do you see that cross? Run there at once!' But instead of that, he sent the poor pilgrim to the Wicket-gate first; and such good he got by going there! He got tumbling into the slough, and was like to have been killed by it,' 'But did not you,' the young man asked, 'go through any Slough of Despond?' 'Yes, I did; but I found it a great deal easier going through with my burden off from the commencement of the pilgrimage. If he meant to show what usually happens, he was right; but if he meant to show what ought to have happened, he was wrong. We must not say to the sinner, 'Now, sinner, if thou wilt be saved, go to the baptismal pool; go to the Wicket-gate; go to the church; do this or that.' No, the cross should be right in front of the Wicket-gate; and we should say to the sinner, 'Throw thyself down there, and thou art safe; but thou art not safe till thou canst

cast off thy burden, and lie at the foot of the cross, and find peace in Jesus.[21]

2. The sermon illustration and the Wicket-gate.

Now while we would agree with Spurgeon's criticism to some extent, it ought to be pointed out that, assuming that Bunyan understood the Wicket-gate to be a representation of Christ as the "door" (John 10:7, 9), or "way" (John 14:6), then the exhortation of Evangelist was not altogether wrong. However, for a man so opposed to Quakerism as was Bunyan, the initial directive to follow the shining light was perhaps surprising. Though concerning this point, it is certain that he had in mind, "Thy word is a lamp unto my feet, and a light unto my path" (Ps. 119:105), and "the prophetic word made more sure, to which you do well to pay attention as to a lamp shining in a dark place, until the day dawns and the morning star arises in your hearts" (II Pet. 1:19), as his marginal references indicate. In other words, the shining light was the illuminated Word of God which would lead to the dawning of Christ in the heart of the prospective Christian. Even so, the lack of clarification concerning the Wicket-gate and the subsequent Place of Deliverance is certainly misleading, though could this be the reason why greater explanation is given in the account of Part Two concerning the conversion of Christiana, her four sons, and Mercy?

John Bunyan's Conversion as a Model for Christian

However, it is important to understand that the conversion of Christian in *The Pilgrim's Progress* is undoubtedly a reflection of Bunyan's own experience, and herein lies the essential reason for the distinctive order of events that we are studying. Bunyan's tortuous and complicated conversion, unlike that of Spurgeon, involved an approximate period of up to four years, commencing with his first marriage in 1649 and continuing to 1653 when he was received into membership by the nonconformist church at Bedford. The definitive description of this period is Bunyan's own intense unveiling of his tender soul in *Grace Abounding to the Chief of Sinners*, and especially Paragraphs 15-235.[22] To some more recent critics, this testimony is extreme and indicative of a warped psyche born of strict Calvinism and a too literal

[21] C. H. Spurgeon, *Metropolitan Tabernacle Pulpit*, XLVI, pp. 211-2. Refer also to similar criticism by Spurgeon in a sermon on I Corinthians 12:28, *Metropolitan Tabernacle Pulpit*, XIII, p. 593.

[22] Bunyan, *Works*, I, pp. 7-36.

understanding of the Bible.[23] However, in rejecting any mere secular psychological explanation of this classic confession, or the patronizing claim that Bunyan was too hard on himself, we would counter that modern day reticence in the realm of honest soul-searching, before the presence of a holy God, is a better explanation of the skepticism of these times toward this account. Consider then three significant aspects of Bunyan's self-revelation in *Grace Abounding* that provide a basis for understanding the conversion of Christian in *The Pilgrim's Progress*.

1. There is a degree of progression in Bunyan's conversion.[24]

Having read his wife's Christian books with interest (§ 15), he then reads the Bible, first the narrative sections (§ 29), then with growing appreciation the Epistles of Paul (§§ 45-6). His early reformation of manners (§§ 28-31) is followed by a desire for light as opposed to his present darkness (§§ 53-6), yet assaults of the devil cause him to despair (§§ 101-2). He is also troubled in prayer with goading from the devil and wandering thoughts (§§ 107-8). Yet encouraged by the gospel, he is also discouraged by Satan (§§ 109-10). Then comes a definite and assured trust in Christ (§§ 113, 115-6). Subsequent sitting under John Gifford's ministry strengthens his soul (§§ 117-8). Still wounded in conscience, understanding and comfort come from Luther's commentary on Galatians (§§ 19-30). Nevertheless, he is tempted to sell Christ, yet in weakness, given grace brings victory (§§ 132-4). He struggles with the possibility of falling from grace and the sins of professors (§§ 194-208). He is still troubled by the state of Esau yet comes to some understanding of his not being of the same reprobate spirit (§§ 212-28). Then light floods his soul with resulting stability based upon a more sure trust in Christ's perfect imputed righteousness (§§ 229-35).

2. There is a striving with many questions in Bunyan's conversion.

Will he leave his sins and go to heaven, or have his sins and go to hell? (§ 22). Were the Ranters' claims to licentious freedom and perfection true? (§§ 44-5). Would it be possible to accomplish a

---

[23] John Stachniewski, *The Persecutory Imagination*, pp. 1-216. But how does one account for the remarkable ongoing popularity of Bunyan's testimony? This writer recalls a new Christian commenting, having just read *Grace Abounding*, "Why pastor, that book is about me!"

[24] Bunyan, *Works*, I, pp. 7-36. Paragraph numbers only follow in this section.

miracle by faith? (§ 51). Was he one of God's elect, or a reprobate? (§§ 58-61). Are the Mohammedan and pagan lost? (§ 97). Was Paul a deceiver? (§ 98). Might he have committed the unpardonable sin against the Holy Spirit? (§§ 103, 153, 174, 180-1, 189). Was Jesus Christ both God and man? (§ 122). Was his sin like that of Judas? (§§ 158-60). Did he have the mark of Cain? (§ 165). Could the blood of Christ be sufficient to save his soul? (§ 203). What is the meaning of certain warning passages in Hebrews? (§§ 196, 208, 223-8).

3. There is a struggle with ambivalence in Bunyan's conversion.

The latter part of this unsettled period in Bunyan's early Christian life involved extremes of oscillation. He describes how, "I should be sometimes up and down twenty times in an hour, yet God did bear me up." (§ 191, cf. §§ 194-8, 203-5, 208). But then comes release and stability to his still burdened and wavering soul as he suddenly grasps a clear understanding of the perfect substitutionary righteousness of Jesus Christ: "Now did my chains fall off my legs indeed, I was loosed from my affliction and irons, temptations also fled away; . . . Oh, I saw my gold was in my trunk at home [heaven]! In Christ, my Lord and Savior! Now Christ was all; all my wisdom, all my righteousness, all my sanctification, and all my redemption [I Cor. 1:30]." (§§ 228-32).

Christian's conversion represents that of John Bunyan

When we consider then the sequence of events in *The Pilgrim's Progress* whereby Christian encounters the Wicket-gate, the house of Interpreter, and the Place of Deliverance, we discover a close parallel with the conversion of Bunyan himself.

1. Concerning the Wicket-gate.

Here Christian, like wavering Bunyan, is yet pulled through and thus enters into the narrow way with the gift of eternal life, that is through Jesus Christ (Good-will) who is, according to the allegory, a composite representation of the "door," the "doorkeeper," and the "good-shepherd" (John 10:3, 7, 11, 14). At this point the pilgrim has no deep understanding of the atonement, and uncertainty remains, yet his face is set heavenward. Early in *Grace Abounding*, Bunyan describes his conversion as follows:

> I remember that one day, as I was traveling into the country and musing on the wickedness and blasphemy of my heart, and considering of the enmity that was in me to God, that scripture

> came in my mind, He hath 'made peace through the blood of his cross' (Col. 1:20). By which I was made to see, both again, and again, and again, that day, that God and my sinful soul could embrace and kiss each other through this blood. This was a good day to me; I hope I shall not forget it.[25]

In George Offor's edition of Bunyan's *Works*, this early experience of c. 1650, is related in *Grace Abounding* under the editorial subheading, "His [Bunyan's] conversion and painful exercises of mind, previous to his joining the church at Bedford."[26] Certainly, according to Bunyan's perception of himself, a burden remained at this point, causing instability, spasmodic assurance, even as with Christian, though the comment of Kelman here is helpful: "It will be observed that Christian does not take with him the love of sin, but only the weight of sin. . . . The practical lesson of it is, in Dr. Whyte's words, 'get into the right way and leave your burden to God.' It is thus that the laboring and heavy-laden find rest unto their souls."[27]

2. *Concerning the House of Interpreter.*

Here Christian, like unenlightened Bunyan as a new believer being edified through Pastor John Gifford, receives profitable instruction for his journey. So in *Grace Abounding* we are told, "At this time, also, I sat under the ministry of holy Mr. Gifford, whose doctrine, by God's grace, was much for my stability."[28] It is significant that the first room in Interpreter's house displays a portrait of the godly pastor as epitomized by Gifford, thus following very closely, as we have just considered, the sequence of events described in *Grace Abounding*. For Christian, the burden remains while the balm of instruction is applied; and so he continues to struggle with temptation, various questions, and fluctuating stability related to hope and fear; and so it was the case with Bunyan until the cross came into clear view.[29]

Cheever comments concerning this condition:

---

[25] Ibid., § 115, pp. 19-20.

[26] Ibid., p. 10. This heading incorporates §§ 37-116.

[27] John Kelman, *The Road*, I, p. 47. Many a new Christian, whose sins have been dealt with at the Wicket-gate, unnecessarily carries a burden representative of uncertainty concerning their forgiveness.

[28] Bunyan, *Works*, I, p. 20.

[29] Ibid., I, pp. §§ 117-228, pp. 20-35.

> "Young Christians are very apt to expect entire relief from all their burdens and a complete deliverance from sin the moment they are got within the Wicket-gate, the moment they have come to Christ. But very often this expectation is not realized, and then they faint and become disheartened or filled with gloomy doubts.[30]

However, it ought to be noticed that Bunyan does critically address this period of spiritual turbulence that plagued him for up to four years, and he offers two principal reasons for its presence in the initial years of his Christian life. First, his prayer in the face of present trouble only focused upon the present. Rather, he adds, "I also should have prayed that the great God would keep me from the evil that was to come. . . . I do beseech thee, reader, that thou learn to beware of my negligence, by the affliction that for this thing I did for days, and months, and years, with sorrow undergo."[31] Second, he tempted God, as if making a bargain, or looking for a sign as did Gideon (Judg. 6-7). Once, when he was troubled as his wife was experiencing birth pangs, he prayed that her suffering would subside and thus become proof of his prayer being heard. But later he realized, "I should have believed his word, and not have put an *if* upon the all-seeingness of God."[32]

3. *Concerning the Place of Deliverance.*

Here Christian, like enlightened Bunyan as a stabilized and assured believer, gains a much clearer understanding of the atonement with all of its attending benefits, and especially that of the saving substitutionary righteousness of Jesus Christ. Thus the burden of doubt falls away: "Then was Christian glad and lightsome, and said with a merry heart, 'He hath given me rest by his sorrow, and life by his death.'"[33] So after approximately four years of restlessness, Bunyan tells us how he himself was similarly delivered, c. 1653, "from the guilt that, by these things, was laid upon my conscience, . . . from the very filth thereof; for the temptation was removed, and I was put into my right mind again, as other Christians [not unbelievers] were."[34] Does Bunyan then endorse his own experience as a normal post-conversion

---

[30] George Cheever, *Lectures on The Pilgrim's Progress*, p. 162.

[31] Bunyan, *Works*, I, §§ 237, 239, p. 37.

[32] Ibid., § 243, p. 37.

[33] Ibid., III, p. 102.

[34] Ibid., I, § 114, p. 19.

experience? Not at all, for rather he seems to perceive it as none too common and an unnecessary sequence. It represents a failing rather than a biblical norm. We saw earlier how Spurgeon would agree with this assessment.

Hence Bunyan incorporates his own testimony into the narrative of *The Pilgrim's Progress* as a help to those who, like himself, have needlessly floundered. Certainly he would know nothing here of what is presently referred to by Pentecostals and Charismatics as a post-conversion "baptism of the Holy Spirit," even though Bunyan was undoubtedly delivered through the sanctifying agency of the Comforter. Such a thought is foreign to the totality of his writings. Further, his experience and that of Christian are atonement centered rather than pneumatic in emphasis. However, Bunyan does gladly acknowledge several benefits that accrued to him as a result of his rescue from his prolonged trial. They are:[35]

(a) His appreciation of the being, glory, compassion, and holiness of God and Christ was greatly enlarged, especially in the light of his former fits of atheism and perplexity, with resulting humiliation.

(b) The Scriptures were perceived as more wonderful and awesome, particularly their finality in offering either bliss or woe, being the very keys of the kingdom of heaven.

(c) The details of the promises of God were found to be more delightful in the light of his wrestling with the threatening justice of God.

(d) Former hesitancy in faith with the promises of God was replaced with a bold readiness to believe and claim the invitation and generosity of Christ as described in John 6:37.

(e) Because great sins draw out great grace, so, from the depths, he was led to see the loftier heights of God's grace, love, and mercy, being greater than the capacity of his heart could comprehend.

4. *Concerning assurance.*

The experience of Christian in the sequence of the three events just described is clearly seen to be Bunyan's imposition of his own early struggles as a believer upon *The Pilgrim's Progress*. It is not claimed to be the biblical norm as his confession above readily

---

[35] Ibid., §§ 244-52, pp. 37-38.

proves. However, it seems clear that upon his entrance into authentic Christian life, Bunyan lacked sufficient assurance to produce steadiness in his soul. Only after prolonged struggle and exposure to faithful instruction did he reach a point of stability and confidence in Christ's substitutionary atonement. In contrast with this distinctive experience, refer to Hopeful's more normative testimony at the Enchanted Ground.

Pieter de Vries is of a similar opinion when he concludes: "In *The Pilgrim's Progress* [in this sequence of events] . . . Bunyan symbolically intimated that in his opinion a longer or shorter period of time will elapse between coming to Christ and possessing the comfort and assurance that one's sins are forgiven. We find the same in *The Holy War*. After Mansoul had been invaded by Emmanuel's troops, there was not immediately joy in the hearts of Mansoul's citizens."[36]

Richard Greaves provides the following comment that, while making too much of an apparent conflict because he does not give enough weight to the gospel embraced at the Wicket-gate, yet he does arrive at the right conclusion. "Theologically the delay between entering the gate and the activities at the cross is intolerable, but it is experientially verifiable for Bunyan and various fellow Calvinists. The early stages of the pilgrimage do not bring unrelieved assurance," at least, we might add, in every case such as this.[37] In addition, Greaves helpfully draws attention to a portion of *Law and Grace* in which Bunyan describes this particular early period of struggle following conversion.[38]

Christian's Conversion and Contemporary Evangelism

In terms of the climate of evangelism today, and the penchant that Christians have for commonly calling upon unbelievers to "make a decision for Jesus Christ" in a very momentary sense, such a modern scenario does not help us understand the concept of conversion in *The Pilgrim's Progress*. As stated earlier, Spurgeon's criticism of Bunyan is essentially correct, though it could have been expressed with a little more caution, even as the fishwife's disagreement was not fully warranted. The Bible does urgently call upon sinners to repent and believe in Jesus Christ at a point of

---

[36] Pieter de Vries, *John Bunyan on the Order of Salvation*, p. 193, 197-9.

[37] Richard L. Greaves, ed., 'I Will Pray with the Spirit; The Doctrine of Law and Grace Unfolded.' *Miscellaneous Works*., II, p. xxxv.

[38] Bunyan, *Works*, I, pp. 548-50.

time, without delay (Mark 1:14-15; Acts 3:19; 17:30-31; 26:20). This crucified Savior is to be the exclusive focus of the seeking sinner.

Yet are we not sometimes carnal in our eagerness to declare precisely when that true faith in Christ was expressed? Certainly Spurgeon recounts a very specific moment regarding his own conversion,[39] and it appears that even Bunyan came to a saving knowledge of Jesus Christ at a particular period, which he recounts in *Grace Abounding*.[40] However, in this latter instance, the ensuing struggle of four years has tended to blur the more biblical description and sequence of conversion that Spurgeon upheld, and indeed is reflected in the testimony of Hopeful.[41]

Of course the problem here is closely related to those which we often face in the natural world, and they are a variety of pre-natal irregularities and birthing problems that contrast with the normal delivery process. Some babies, indeed a considerable proportion, come forth from the womb with textbook precision. However, others are born with degrees of struggle and limitations of health that are later corrected. So we ought to view Bunyan and Spurgeon in this light. Such an idea is in no way intended to detract from radical and manifest conversion, and obscure the evident spiritual life and fruit that distinguish between the saved and the unsaved. In this respect, Bunyan himself is the clearest possible example of conversion leading to radical change in his interests and lifestyle.

However, perhaps we are presently in need of discerning spiritual midwives in the life of local churches. Even so, whether we side more with Spurgeon or Bunyan in this matter, and most likely this will be according to our own experience, is it not manifest godliness and true affections that are the essential birthmarks of authentic conversion, and not merely a precisely defined regimen in spiritual delivery?

---

[39] C. H. Spurgeon, *C. H. Spurgeon's Autobiography*, I, pp. 97-115.

[40] Bunyan, *Works*, I, pp. 19-20.

[41] Ibid., III, pp. 153-6.

CHAPTER SEVEN

Sanctification in The Pilgrim's Progress

DURING the later end of the nineteenth century and on into this modern era, two widespread conservative evangelical movements have promoted deviant views of practical Christian sanctification that have resulted in varying degrees of confusion, conflict, and carnality. The influence of the English Keswick Movement, though now considerably modified and less distinctive, has been pervasive in numerous convention centers throughout the world. It had erroneously taught that justification by faith is paralleled by sanctification by faith or passive surrender to the dominion of the Holy Spirit.[1] The impact of the recent Pentecostal/Charismatic Movement has probably been even more influential, and certainly more intrusive in many denominational associations and fellowship groups. It has erroneously taught that sanctification comes by means of a sudden and cataclysmic post-conversion experience, a baptism in the Spirit that is often identified by phenomena such as expressed ecstasy and the evidence of speaking in tongues.

To both of these emphases, *The Pilgrim's Progress* speaks with clarifying freshness and honesty. The allegory's basic format, that of a journey requiring advancement toward a heavenly city, is a

---

1 A more recent representation of this teaching is to be found in Ruth Paxon's *Life on the Highest Plane* where the believer is to obey Romans 6:13 and thus, "'Yield' '*yield*,' 'YIELD'–by a definite, intelligent, voluntary act of the will the believer must choose Christ as his new Master and yield himself to Him as Lord." p. 237. This writer can well remember attending a number of Keswick conventions in Australia and England many years ago where, after the customary exposition of Romans 5-8, Christians were prompted to come forward to signify their decisive yielding and surrender to the Holy Spirit so that He might live the Christian life for them. The call was, "to let go and let God" by an act of faith in divine enabling, at the neglect of emphasizing the biblical responsibility of believers to use appointed means of grace.

most graphic representation of the biblical pattern of encountering "conflicts without and fears within" (II Cor. 7:5), of "pressing on toward the goal for the prize of the upward call" (Phil. 3:14), of "growing in the grace and knowledge of the Lord Jesus Christ" (II Pet. 3:18). Bunyan's title is most apt. It is not *Pilgrimage on the High Road* or *The Phenomenal Pilgrim*, but *The Pilgrim's Progress* concerning participation in an endurance race that involves both disturbing "sinful encumbrances" and the goal of embrace of Jesus Christ at the "crossing of the line" (Heb. 12:1-2). The denial of the normalcy of such ongoing struggle and conflict in this present Christian life, while interspersed with periods of joyful confidence, is both self-delusive and spiritually counter-productive.

SANCTIFICATION IN THE PILGRIM'S PROGRESS

In the Wharey and Sharrock edition of *The Pilgrim's Progress* published by Oxford Press (Clarendon), the text of Part One is comprised of 5,607 lines. Of these, 10.5% cover that first period from the commencement at the City of Destruction until Christian progresses to knock at the Wicket-gate. The 89.5% remainder of the lines covers that second period from Christian's passage through the Wicket-gate until the disposal of Ignorance to hell from outside the gates of the Celestial City. The obvious significance of these facts is that while over 10% of the text deals with the time that leads up to Christian's conversion, nearly 90% of the text expounds upon the progressive sanctification of Christian through periods of wilderness buffetings and blessings.

In other words, *The Pilgrim's Progress* is not primarily an evangelistic presentation, even though it most definitely has an evangelistic thrust; rather it is an allegorical tract that focuses upon the authentic journey of a bona fide Christian, and especially his distancing of himself from the City of Destruction and its agents, and his advancement toward the Celestial City by means of its agents. Both the negative and positive elements here are of the very essence of biblical sanctification.

The response to the Higher Life Movement

The term "Higher Life Movement" is used simply as a broader title that not only includes the English Keswick Movement and its emphasis on impacting Romans 5-8 upon Christian lives, but also the European and American antecedents of this ministry. The Boardmans, the Pearsall-Smiths, Bishop H. G. Moule are but a few representatives of an emphasis on practical sanctification which had a sweeping influence upon evangelical Christendom during the turn of the century and onwards.[2] At that same time, another Anglican Bishop, J. C. Ryle of Manchester, who Spurgeon rated as the most stalwart evangelical minister of the Church of England of his time, wrote a classic book entitled *Holiness* which vigorously though graciously challenged the biblical basis of Keswick type ministry. In his introduction to that volume he succinctly asks seven questions which suggest, from a right understanding of Scripture, negative responses.[3] They are:

1. Is faith the one thing needful for sanctification?
2. Is practical exhortation to holiness to be neglected?
3. Is language about present perfection in holiness with warrant?
4. Is it true that Romans 7 does not describe the mature saint?
5. Is the teaching of "Christ in us" given proper emphasis?
6. Is a distinction between conversion and consecration proper?
7. Is sanctification a yielding rather than an active conflict?

In reply to the last mentioned question Ryle comments:

> A holy violence, a conflict, a warfare, a fight, a soldier's life, a wrestling, are spoken of [in Scripture] as characteristic of the true Christian. It would be easy to show that the doctrine [of passive yielding] is utterly subversive of the whole teaching of such tried and approved books as *Pilgrim's Progress*, and that if we receive it we cannot do better than put Bunyan's old book in the fire! If Christian in *Pilgrim's Progress* simply yielded himself to God, and never fought, or struggled, or wrestled, I have read the famous allegory in vain.[4]

---

[2] For a good survey of this "Higher Life Movement," refer to D. M. Lloyd-Jones, *The Puritans: Their Origins And Successors*, pp. 316-325. For greater detail refer to B. B. Warfield, Perfectionism, pp. 216-311.

[3] J. C. Ryle, *Holiness*, pp. xvii-xviii.

[4] Ibid., pp. xvi-xvii. Ryle further adds: "[T]he expression 'yield yourselves' is only to be found in one place in the New Testament, as a duty urged upon believers. That place is in the sixth chapter of Romans, and there within six verses the expression occurs five times. (See Romans 6:13-19.) But even there the word will not bear the sense

Indeed it would be more true to say that *The Pilgrim's Progress* most naturally speaks to all of Ryle's questions in a manner that fully supports his teaching on both justification and progressive sanctification. In this regard the Bishop continues concerning the real doctrinal heart of the problem: "The plain truth is, that men will persist in confounding two things that differ—that is justification and sanctification. In justification the word to be addressed to man is believe—only believe; in sanctification the word must be 'watch, pray, and fight.' What God has divided let us not mingle and confuse."[5] This vital matter will be subsequently dealt with in greater detail.

The Response to the Pentecostal/Charismatic Movement

This more contemporary development has emphasized a post-conversion "baptism with the Holy Spirit" that is often said to be evidenced by "signs following" such as speaking in tongues and healing, etc. Other additional related aberrations have been similarly phenomenological and usually sensual such as "slaying with the Holy Spirit," "healing of the memories," "exorcism," "word of faith prosperity," "word of knowledge prognostication," "extra-biblical revelation," "holy laughter," etc. While this movement has required belief in the gospel as being mandatory for Christian conversion, yet it has only been so in a very rudimentary and even mechanical sense. The transcending experience, insofar as being empowered for Christian living is concerned, has commonly been the supernatural "baptism with the Holy Spirit." Unfortunately the pneumatic pursuit here has been more for the animation and felt power of the Holy Spirit than the pursuit of the righteousness of God through Christ.

To this whole scenario *The Pilgrim's Progress* speaks in necessary theocentric, moral, and remedial terms. It magnifies the gospel of grace through free justification as God's supreme saving work rather than as some perfunctory transaction. It relates power for sanctification to regeneration and justification rather than some phenomenal experience that is subsequent to conversion. It exalts in the wonder of moral transformation at the very depths of a sinner's being rather than bodily stimulation. It emphasizes man

---

of 'placing ourselves passively in the hands of another.' Any Greek student can tell us that the sense is rather that of actively 'presenting' ourselves for use, employment, and service. (See Rom. 12:1.)" Ibid.

[5] Ibid., p. xvii.

becoming conformed to God's holy image particularly as embodied in the Lord Jesus Christ.

It is certainly true that for the first four years of Bunyan's Christian life he struggled with doubts, fears, and frequent spiritual ambivalence. Yet his deliverance from this instability was not due to some Spirit baptism but, as he records in *Grace Abounding*, on account of an awakening to the certain knowledge that Christ's imputed righteousness had been credited to his heavenly account.[6] Further, Bunyan relates that this period of early instability was abnormal and due to spiritual negligence on his part.[7] For greater detail on this matter refer to Chapter 6.

The Response of Biblical Sanctification

By sanctification is meant that resultant work of regeneration and justification whereby the "new creation [or species] in Christ" (II Cor. 5:17) manifests increasing holy likeness to his divine Progenitor. This sanctification, being progressive, is to be distinguished from that definitive or declarative sanctification which is complete at the time of the sinner's conversion (I Pet. 2:9).[8] Ryle gives his definition as follows:

> Sanctification is that inward spiritual work which the Lord Jesus Christ works in a man by the Holy Ghost, when he calls him to be a true believer. He not only washes him from his sins in His own blood [justification and redemption], but he also separates him from his natural love of sin and the world, puts a new principle in his heart, and makes him practically godly in life.[9]

He also includes the following twelve qualifying points to which are added parallels from *The Pilgrim's Progress*.[10]

1. *Sanctification is the invariable result of union with Christ.*

---

[6] John Bunyan, *The Works of John Bunyan*, ed. George Offor, I, §§ 229-32, pp. 35-36.

[7] Ibid., I, paras. 114, 244-52, pp. 19, 37-38.

[8] For a detailed consideration of "Definitive Sanctification" and its distinctive relationship with regard to "Progressive Sanctification," refer to John Murray, *Collected Writings of John Murray*, II, pp. 277-317.

[9] Ryle, *Holiness*, p. 16.

[10] Ibid., pp. 16-24.

Having passed through the Wicket-gate and concluded his period of instruction at the house of Interpreter which included much substance concerning Christ, Christian declares:

> Here I have seen things rare and profitable;
> Things pleasant, dreadful, things to make me stable.[11]

On leaving the Place of Deliverance, "Christian gave three leaps for joy, and went on singing."[12] Subsequent spiritual maturity in Christ is stimulated by frequent reflection upon his new coat and scroll.

2. *Sanctification is the inseparable result of regeneration.*

The authentic pilgrim, having been saved by Good-will [Christ], is in immediate need of the ministry of Interpreter [the Holy Spirit] and so is commended to his house. Later, in rejecting Apollyon's former dominion over him, Christian states: "I like his [Christ's] service, his wages, his servants, his government, his company, and country, better than thine."[13]

3. *Sanctification is the sure evidence of the indwelling Holy Spirit.*

When Christian recovers his roll [assurance] and thrusts it into his bosom "with joy and tears, . . .[then] how nimbly now did he go up the rest of the hill [Difficulty]!"[14] In other words, authentic assurance through the indwelling Spirit has victorious consequences (John 15:1-5, 8, 12-14; 26-27).

4. *Sanctification is the only sure mark of God's election.*

When Christian arrives at the gate of the Palace Beautiful, the initial investigation (for church membership) by the porter Watchful, along with Discretion, Prudence, Piety, and Charity, is intended to discover if Christian has the marks of a true pilgrim, specifically from "whence he was, and whither he was going, . . . how he got in the way, . . . what he had seen and met with in the way, . . . his name."[15]

---

[11] Bunyan, *Works*, III, p. 102.

[12] Ibid., p. 103.

[13] Ibid., p. 112.

[14] Ibid., p. 106.

[15] Ibid., 106-107.

5. Sanctification is a thing that will always be seen.

Of Talkative it is said, concerning his lack of sanctification, "His house is as empty of religion, as the white of an egg is of savor. There is there, neither prayer, neither sign of repentance for sin. . . . he cheweth the cud, he seeketh knowledge, he cheweth upon the word; but he divideth not the hoof, he parteth not with the way of sinners."[16] Contrast the saintly demeanor of Christian and Faithful at Vanity Fair in the face of persecution.

6. Sanctification is a thing for which every believer is responsible.

Because Talkative lacks evidence of personal holiness, Faithful declares: "The proverb is true of you which is said of a whore, to wit, that she is a shame to all women; so are you a shame to all professors."[17] Even Christian and Hopeful are accountable for their negligence and thus disciplined because they yielded to the deceit of the Flatterer.

7. Sanctification admits of growth by degrees.

Faithful's early journeying is weak, yet at Vanity Fair he seems stronger in his testimony than Christian. When Christian and Hopeful arrive at Beulah Land, "wherefore this was beyond the Valley of the Shadow of Death, and also out of the reach of Giant Despair, neither could they from this place so much as see Doubting Castle."[18]

8. Sanctification depends on a use of Scriptural means.

Christian is variously strengthened in this regard, first with the Bible in his hand, then with fellowship by means of Faithful and Hopeful, as well as at the Palace Beautiful just before his encounter with Apollyon. In particular, at the armory, "they harnessed him from head to foot with what was proof [resistant to penetration], lest, perhaps, he should meet with assaults in the way."[19]

9. Sanctification does not exclude inward spiritual conflict.

Consider Faithful's inclination toward the overtures of Old Man Adam the first, which he eventually repents of and bemoans, "O

---

[16] Ibid., pp. 122-23.

[17] Ibid., p. 125.

[18] Ibid., p. 161.

[19] Ibid., p. 111.

wretched man [that I am]."[20] Also recall Hopeful's initial interest in the silver mine at the Hill Lucre, which he then repents of with the declaration, "I am sorry that I was so foolish, and am made to wonder that I am not now as Lot's wife."[21]

10. Sanctification cannot justify, yet it pleases God.

Having crossed the River of Death, Christian and Hopeful are royally welcomed as pilgrims who persevered yet their entrance into the Celestial City is by certificate only. Over the gate is the inscription, "Blessed are they that do his commandments, that they may have right to the tree of life, and may enter in through the gates into the city" (Rev. 22:14).[22]

11. Sanctification witnesses to character on the day of judgment.

However, the man who dreamed of this scene at the house of the Interpreter shamefully declared, "[M]y sins also came into my mind; and my conscience did accuse me on every side. . . . I was not ready for it."[23] On the other hand, as Christian and Hopeful draw near to the Celestial City, they are described as, "the men that have loved our Lord when they were in the world, and have left all for his holy name."[24]

12. Sanctification is necessary preparation for heaven.

Pastoral edification at the Palace Beautiful and Delectable Mountains has contributed holy preparation. By the time that Christian and Hopeful have progressed and reached Beulah Land, there further pastoral encouragement causes them to become lovesick out of desire for heaven, crying out because of their pangs, "If ye find my Beloved, tell him that I am sick of love" (S. of S. 5:8).[25]

SANCTIFICATION AND JUSTIFICATION

Unlike much contemporary evangelical practice, for Bunyan sanctification is not a soft option but rather a resultant necessity,

[20] Ibid., p. 118.

[21] Ibid., p. 137.

[22] Ibid., p. 165.l

[23] Ibid., p. 102.

[24] Ibid., p. 165.

[25] Ibid., p. 162.

the possibility of back-sliding notwithstanding. That is, while he was second to none in upholding the doctrine of justification by faith alone, yet he was adamant that justification did not stand alone, but rather was productive of a spiritually fruitful life. So he writes:

> Now, he that shall not only see, but receive, not only know, but embrace the Son of God, to be justified by him, cannot but bring forth good works, because Christ who is now received and embraced by faith, leavens and seasons the spirit of this sinner, . . . so then the soul being seasoned, it seasoneth the body; and the body and soul, the life and conversation. . . . For the true beholding of Jesus to justification and life, changes from glory to glory (II Cor. 3:18).[26]

In other words, justification and its exaltation of free grace is the ground and substance and root from which sanctification springs forth as the admirable flowering and fruitfulness of the gospel. Now the root is not the fruit and the fruit does not establish the root, though the root must give rise to fruit; therefore the root without the fruit is dead (Jas. 2:26), while the fruit without the root is counterfeit. This truth permeates the whole of *The Pilgrim's Progress*. Consider four examples:

a. In explaining to Talkative concerning the indications of a true work of grace in the heart, Faithful comments: "Now according to the strength or weakness of his [the true believer's] faith in his Savior, so is his joy and peace, so is his love to holiness, so are his desires to know him more, and also to serve him in this world."[27]

b. When Christian disputes with Formalist and Hypocrisy, they deride his strange coat, and thus he makes his defense: "[It is] as you say, to cover my nakedness with. And I take it as a token of his kindness to me; for I had nothing but rags before. And, besides, thus I comfort myself as I go."[28]

c. In Hopeful's testimony of his conversion, shared with Christian, he tells of how he finally understood that, "I must look for righteousness in his [Christ's] person, and for satisfaction for my sins in his blood." The result was, "it made me love a holy life, and long to do something for the

---

[26] Ibid., II, p. 507.

[27] Ibid., III, p. 124.

[28] Ibid., p. 104.

honor and glory of the name of the Lord Jesus; yea, I thought that had I now a thousand gallons of blood in my body, I could spill it all for the sake of the Lord Jesus."[29]

d. When Ignorance disputes concerning the essential nature of the gospel, Christian soberly responds: "Ignorant thou art of what justifying righteousness is, and as ignorant how to secure thy soul, through the faith of it, from the heavy wrath of God. Yea, thou also art ignorant of the true effects of saving faith in this righteousness of Christ, which is, to bow and win over the heart to God in Christ, to love his name, his Word, ways, and people, and not as thou ignorantly imaginest."[30]

SANCTIFICATION AND THE MEANS OF GRACE

For those of God's elect who have been regenerated and judicially reconciled to God through faith in Christ's imputed righteousness, there are made available means of grace whereby the new pilgrim is enabled to safely traverse this earthly wilderness (I Cor. 5:9-10). Indeed it is the journeying saint's responsibility to use these means, though some do more so than others. Little-faith neglects his provisions and progresses very slowly as a spiritual hypochondriac. On the other hand, Great-grace uses well and valiantly the equipment at his disposal, scars notwithstanding. So Ryle exhorts: "Our God is a God who works by means, and he will never bless the soul of that man who pretends to be so high and spiritual that he can get on without them."[31]

Perspective

By its very nature, pilgrimage is governed by departure, transition, and arrival. At any point on this continuum the degree of progress may be assessed by both a retrospective and prospective review of the journey; to do so is to gain a sense of encouragement, direction, and hope. So when Christian is challenged by Timorous and Mistrust to return to the City of Destruction on account of imminent danger, he reviews what is both behind him and ahead, and comes to the following

---

[29] Ibid., p. 156.

[30] Ibid., p. 158.

[31] Ryle, *Holiness*, p. 21.

conclusion: "To go back is nothing but death; to go forward is fear of death, and life everlasting beyond it. I will yet go forward."[32]

1. Retrospective journeying.

On several occasions the major pilgrims review their progress thus far, even as did Israel (Ps. 106:6-46), for the purposes of mutual edification (I Sam. 7:12) and being strengthened by the remembrance of God's keeping grace.

a. At the Palace Beautiful Christian is required to review his travels thus far as a means of indicating his legitimacy as a pilgrim.

b. When Christian catches up with Faithful they both reminisce concerning their individual experiences that are somewhat related to their individual strengths and weaknesses.

c. At the Enchanted Ground, drowsiness is combated when Hopeful shares in detail his testimony with Christian. This is in fact a comprehensive review of the gospel, which survey of the life of another pilgrim becomes instructive, by way of contrast, and encouraging.

2. Prospective Journeying.

Conversation and vistas concerning future glory are major incentives for perseverance. Arrival will undoubtedly be better than anticipation, for "we shall then know just as we have been fully known" (I Cor. 13:12), and "we shall see Him just as he is" (I John 3:2).

a. When Christian is unconverted, yet he is able to enthuse Pliable concerning "an endless kingdom to be inhabited and eternal life to be given us; there are crowns of glory to be given us, and garments that will make us shine like the sun in the firmament of heaven."[33]

b. At the Palace Beautiful, Christian is taken to the rooftop from where he gains a view of Immanuel's Land and is told that there the resident Shepherds will reveal to him a vista of the Celestial City. Then we read that on account of future

---

32 Bunyan, *Works*, III, p. 105.

33 Ibid., p. 91.

focus and renewed enthusiasm, "[n]ow, he bethought himself of setting forward."[34]

c. Upon concluding their visit with the Shepherds, Christian and Hopeful are taken to the top of the hill called Clear, and there through a telescope, with trembling hands, yet they discern the gate and some of the glory of the Celestial City. Thus, with singing and hope, they immediately set forth once again.

d. At the land of Beulah pilgrims obtain a more perfect view of the Celestial City and its radiant glory which only makes them all the more lovesick for arrival. The increasing brilliance becomes "so extremely glorious," that they have to wear dark glasses, or a veil (II Cor. 3:18).[35] They seem oblivious of the imminent River of Death.

The Truth of God

This comes by way of a variety of means although such media always communicate the truth of Scripture. Again, the pilgrim is responsible for attending to such an array of helps.

a. Christian is first described as a man with "a book in his hand,"[36] that is the Bible or Word of God. Its initial communication, being preparatory for gospel grace, is that of conviction of sin and the warning of imminent judgment.

b. When Christian asks Evangelist for knowledge of the way of escape, he is given a parchment roll on which is written, "Fly from the wrath to come (Matt. 3:7)."[37]

c. On meeting Formalist and Hypocrisy, Christian distinguishes between his walking according to "the rule of my Master" and their following after "laws and ordinances [Eph. 2:15; Col. 2:14]."[38] Under the New Covenant, Christian is "under the law of Christ" (I Cor. 9:21) and not subject to the law of Moses (Rom. 7:1-4).

d. At the house of Interpreter, Christian receives much illumination concerning vital doctrine. The instrument here is

---

[34] Ibid., p. 111.

[35] Ibid., p. 162.

[36] Ibid., p. 89.

[37] Ibid., p. 90.

[38] Ibid., p. 104.

the Holy Spirit since His particular ministry is that of guiding pilgrims "into all the truth" (John 16:13).

e. In the armory at the Palace Beautiful, Christian is equipped with the "whole armor of God," and "the sword of the Spirit, which is the word of God."[39] In other words, the Palace Beautiful or faithful local church is to teach Christian how to skillfully use that book in his hand (Eph. 6:17) lest he meet with assailing Apollyon!

f. By the time Christian is incarcerated in Doubting Castle he has hid much of the Word of God in his heart (Ps. 119:11). However, personal interest causes him to be forgetful, that is until fellowship on the Lord's Day morning brings about a fresh eruption of the promises of God into his consciousness that dispels despair.

Church Fellowship

For Bunyan personally, the fellowship of the local separatist church in Bedford had been of immense spiritual help and stimulation. Pastor John Gifford had given him much individual attention. Many of his portrayals of this encouragement in *The Pilgrim's Progress* overlap so that they collectively represent the church as a heavenly embassy upon earth.

a. Evangelist is but representative of one facet of the pastoral office. He points people to Christ, delivers them from religious charlatans such as Mr. Worldly-Wiseman, and nurses along new converts by means of encouragement and warning.

b. Help, who rescues Christian at the Slough of Despond, is a further portrayal of that pastoral nurture which Bunyan received from Pastor Gifford when, in studying the Scriptures, he increasingly wrestled with personal corruption.

c. The Palace Beautiful is, or ought to be, a major vehicle of grace for weary and assailed pilgrims. It provides strengthening fellowship in the truth about Christ, communion around the table of Christ, rest in the grace of Christ, weaponry to fight for Christ, and a vision of the consummated kingdom of Christ.

d. At the Delectable Mountains we have but another representation of the faithful separatist church, except that

[39] Ibid., p. 111.

even greater emphasis is placed on the importance of faithful shepherding through the ministry of Knowledge, Experience, Watchful, and Sincere.

e. Fellowship is of special importance when believers meet together on the Lord's Day. This is emphasized by Christian and Hopeful's release from Doubting Castle on Sunday morning, the day of resurrection and church life, the day of feasting on the promises of God, the day when the light of truth casts out the darkness of doubt and despair accumulated during the week.

Miscellaneous Means

These all go to prove just how much provision of grace there is for pilgrims. They are more than sufficient in subduing the snares and hellish devices of Satan. Furthermore, they are scattered throughout the journey to meet varying needs according to individual strength.

a. Help at the Slough of Despond is also an agent of prevenient grace, that is grace meted out to sinners who struggle toward Christ before conversion. However, Faithful was not similarly troubled at this juncture, for he perceived the alternative provision of stepping stones, or "wholesome instructions," that crossed this mire.

b. Angels or messengers make frequent appearances such as at the Place of Deliverance assisting Christian, then administering discipline when Christian and Hopeful are foolishly snared by the Flatterer. Further they encourage true pilgrims at the River of Death and escort them to the very gates of heaven.

c. The spring at the foot of the Hill Difficulty is most strategically placed, though not all ascending pilgrims such as Faithful are wise enough to drink there. As a result he becomes inclined toward the carnal proposal of Old Man Adam the first halfway up the Hill and reaps much pain for his neglect.

d. The Arbor halfway up the Hill Difficulty is a legitimate place for the modest refreshment of weary climbers, though it does at the same time test the flesh for indulgence. Hence, due to carnality, at this very place Faithful is mercilessly beaten by the accusatory Moses until rescued by Christ.

e. The tokens of "a loaf of bread, a bottle of wine, and a cluster of raisins"[40] supplied by the Palace Beautiful are obviously reflective of Lord's Supper imagery; they are to be carried by pilgrims since they represent that grace which is supplied as they recall Christ's atoning merits during their ongoing travels.

f. When Christian gingerly wends his way through the Valley of the Shadow of Death, he finds that his regular weapons of warfare are of little use. Hence he resorts to the instrument of "All-prayer" (Eph. 6:18) since he is devilishly tormented.

g. Memorials are warnings designed to deliver pilgrims from deceitful circumstances, such as the monument to Lot's wife which served as a deterrent re coveting after the Silver Mine at the Hill Lucre. Christian and Hopeful set up a similar pillar of warning at the stile leading to By-path Meadow.

SANCTIFICATION AND THE EXPERIENCE OF GRACE

As with the Puritans in general, Bunyan believed that authentic Christian experience was generated by the knowledge of Christian truth. J. I. Packer comments: "The starting point was their certainty that the mind must be instructed and enlightened before faith and obedience become possible. All the Puritans regarded religious feeling and pious emotion without knowledge as worse than useless. Only when the truth was being felt was emotion in any way desirable."[41] Therefore, concerning *The Pilgrim's Progress* it is obvious that "truth within a fable," as Bunyan describes it, is very prominent as the ground of Christian's hope at all stages along the way, and as a consequence productive of profound experiences that are especially rooted in the grace of God.

Consider just one example of many instances in *Grace Abounding* where the truth of the grace of God in Christ causes such an eruption of praise on the part of the author.

> Now I saw Christ Jesus was looked on of God, and should also be looked on by us as that common or publick person, in whom all the whole body of his elect are always to be considered and reckoned; that we fulfilled the law by him, died by him, rose from the dead by him, got the victory over sin, death, the devil, and hell, by him. Ah, these blessed considerations and scriptures, with many other of like

---

[40] Ibid., p. 111.

[41] J. I. Packer, *A Quest For Godliness*, pp. 69-70.

> nature, were in those days made to spangle in mine eyes, so that I have cause to say, 'Praise ye the Lord. Praise God in his sanctuary: praise him in the firmament of his power. Praise him for his mighty acts: praise him according to his excellent greatness' (Ps. 150:1-2).[42]

Here Bunyan vibrantly personifies sanctification through the contemplation and experience of grace.

Experience in Emotion

Of all the emotion expressed in *The Pilgrim's Progress* it is that which is stimulated by the grace of God in the gospel that seems to be the most passionate and pervasive. This truth is not to be comprehended in mere cerebral and matter-of-fact terms, but rather that which melts hardened souls and persuades them to be forever debtors to grace. While sin is proclaimed as exceedingly sinful, yet grace and mercy are heralded as being more abundant and powerful (Rom. 5:20-21). The effect of this truth upon Bunyan is exciting in the best sense of that term, causing him to be enraptured. So he communicates his ardent feeling in several scenes of his allegory. At the Place of Deliverance, with tears streaming down his face on account of a sudden surge of assurance, Christian ponders with astonishment, "Must here be the beginning of my bliss?"[43] Hopeful is likewise moved when confronted with the gospel: "Now was my heart full of joy, mine eyes full of tears, and mine affections running over with love to the name, people, and ways of Jesus Christ."[44] Here is emotion in its rightful place. Here is evident sanctification.

Experience in Singing

The first occasion of Christian singing is at the Place of Deliverance. Up to his entry at the Wicket-gate he had little to sing about. But now we read: "Then Christian gave three leaps for joy, and went on singing."

> Blest cross! blest sepulchre! blest rather be
> The man that there was put to shame for me![45]

---

[42] Bunyan, *Works*, I, §§ 234-35, p. 36.

[43] Ibid., III, p. 103.

[44] Ibid., p. 156.

[45] Ibid., p. 103.

Following the martyrdom of Faithful, Christian yet rejoices and chimes forth:

> Sing, Faithful, sing, and let thy name survive;
> For, though they kill'd thee, thou art yet alive.[46]

Then while being refreshed at the River of the Water of Life, both Christian and Hopeful sing in chorus:

> The meadows green, besides their fragrant smell,
> Yield dainties for them: and he that can tell
> What pleasant fruit, yea, leaves, these trees do yield,
> Will soon sell all, that he may buy this field.[47]

A further instance of this inclination for singing by the genuine pilgrim concerns the materially impoverished shepherd boy in Part Two who, while nourished with the herb Hearts-ease, yet happily sings:

> He that is down, needs fear no fall,
> He that is low, no pride:
> He that is humble, ever shall
> Have God to be his guide.[48]

So for Bunyan, the child of God has a new song to sing (Ps. 40:1-3), and such spontaneous worship is but further evidence of sanctification.

Experience in Instruction

For Bunyan, the idea of a pilgrim shunning teaching in a local church was not characteristic of a weak believer, but rather of one being related to Ignorance. A normal Pilgrim would delight in the food of God's sanctifying truth (Matt. 4:4; I Pet. 2:1-2). So at the house of Interpreter we observe Christian becoming earnestly involved in the truth which the Holy Spirit imparts. He is deeply interested in asking questions and responding with eager and thoughtful comment. Concerning the valiant man who thrusts his way into the stately palace, he seems to readily identify himself here as he smiles and asserts: "I think verily I know the meaning of

---

[46] Ibid., p. 132.

[47] Ibid., p. 138.

[48] Ibid., p. 206.

this."[49] The despairing man in the iron cage causes Christian to respond: "This is fearful! God help me to watch and be sober, and to pray that I may shun the cause of this man's misery!"[50] Thus he concludes that all seven scenes have put him in "hope and fear."

> Here I have seen things rare and profitable;
> Things pleasant, dreadful, things to make me stable
> In what I have begun to take in hand;
> Then let me think on them, and understand.[51]

At the Palace Beautiful further substantial instruction is found to be delightful; thus Christian is encouraged to press forward. When Evangelist reappears, yet more teaching is sought from him. Likewise the Shepherds impart further truth which Christian and Hopeful recommend:

> Come to the Shepherds, then, if you would see
> Things deep, things hid, and that mysterious be.[52]

Experience in Discipline

When the narrow way becomes rough to the feet of Christian and Hopeful, obviously by the design of the Lord of the way, this testing brings forth murmuring and grumbling, as was the case with Israel (Num. 21:4-5). Thus it is not surprising that the stile leading to By-Path-Meadow and Doubting Castle should appear at this point. The pilgrims' resultant imprisonment here is discipline built into their act of rebellion. As they shall learn from the Shepherds at the Delectable Mountains, it is only grace that delivers them from their folly. However, this whole incident is full of painful experiences reflective of Bunyan's own travail of soul. Yet the pilgrims become wiser for their trouble and thoughtfully take the initiative in warning others of lurking danger.

In a similar vein, Christian and Hopeful are subject to more direct discipline when they fall as easy prey to the Flatterer, and that in the face of warning from the Shepherds. As a result, they "lay bewailing themselves"[53] until rescued by an angel with a disciplinary whip in his hand. So the pilgrims submit to sore

[49] Ibid., p. 100.

[50] Ibid., p. 101.

[51] Ibid., p. 102.

[52] Ibid., p. 145.

[53] Ibid., p. 151.

chastisement, after which they "thanked him [the angel] for all his kindness, and went softly along the right way, singing."[54] This too was a profitable incident for their progressive sanctification.

Experience in Conflict

Immediately following the Place of Deliverance, naive Christian is confronted with the indifference of Simple, Sloth, and Presumption, and then the illegitimacy of Formalist and Hypocrisy. Thus he proceeds "sighingly and sometimes comfortable; also he would be often reading in the roll that one of the Shining Ones gave him, by which he was refreshed."[55] Christian is now naive no longer; he has advanced in his understanding of the counterfeit religious world about him and consequently has increased in sanctification. However when Apollyon is encountered, he learns concerning a different type of conflict. Residence at the Palace Beautiful has set him apart in a preparatory sense, but actual experience in spiritual warfare will substantially increase his sanctification or growth in holiness. Following the initial verbal encounter, the battle becomes more bloody and withering; Christian's own strength gradually fails until he seems all but defeated; but sovereign grace enables him to regather his lost sword. When Apollyon retreats, he leaves Christian standing his ground and more sanctified through this harrowing experience.

Upon entering the subsequent Valley of the Shadow of Death, we read that "Christian went on his way, but still with his sword drawn in his hand [and not in its scabbard as before]; for fear lest he should be assaulted."[56] Here the conflict changes in its character yet again. In this gloomy place the assaults are now more subtle and difficult to distinguish from personal thought processes. The redeemed spirit is devilishly tormented. So Christian resorts to the more appropriate weapon of "All-prayer" (Eph. 6:18). Eventually relief is anticipated when the resolute voice of Faithful is heard to be just ahead. So Christian's exit from this valley finds him to be a far more mature, though very imperfect, sanctified pilgrim, and that through the instrumentality of conflict.

---

[54] Ibid.

[55] Ibid., p. 104.

[56] Ibid., p. 114.

CHAPTER EIGHT

Law and Grace in The Pilgrim's Progress

IT is common today, as has always been the case, for great saints to be claimed as supporters of a particular doctrinal cause. This is especially so amongst conservative evangelical Christians with regard to mustering the agreement, say of Martin Luther, John Calvin, or more recently C. H. Spurgeon. It is sometimes claimed that while they have not expressly stated their commitment to such-and-such a position, yet it is obviously implied in related matters. The latter mentioned Baptist preacher of London is a case in point since he has been claimed as a premillennialist, post-millennialist, and amillennialist, and that in spite of the fact that he specifically aligned himself with historic premillennialism in general.[1]

A similar case is the question of John Bunyan and his commitment to the relationship between law and grace, and especially as it concerns certain Calvinistic emphases. Everyone wants John Bunyan on their side, and it may not be so pleasant to discover that he in fact does not hold to our darling position. And in any case, as Richard Greaves confirms, he is not the sort of person who neatly fits into certain defined categories.[2] For instance, some claim in

---

1 Dennis Michael Swanson, *Charles H. Spurgeon and Eschatology: Did He Have a Discernable Millennial Position?* Unpublished dissertation, The Master's Seminary, California. Internet sourced.

2 Richard Greaves, *John Bunyan*, p. 159. "No single theological label without careful qualification will fit Bunyan. He was bitterly opposed both to Arminianism and to Quakerism, and he was neither a moderate Calvinist nor a true Antinomian, although at certain points his doctrine was harmonious with Antinomian tenets. His foundation principles were basically Lutheran, but much of his theology was in full accord with the orthodox Calvinism of his period. His doctrine of the church and sacraments was neither Calvinist nor Lutheran but a heritage from the Independent-Baptist tradition, particularly the segment of that tradition of which he was a part."

agreement with Greaves, and they are by far in the majority, that Bunyan steered very close to antinomianism, while others do not.[3] Certainly, like Paul, no one has ever charged him with being a legalist! Of course in this realm, as we shall see, it often becomes a matter of definitions.

Influences Concerning Bunyan's Thought

At the outset, it needs to be reiterated that Bunyan was dominated more by Martin Luther than the emphases of John Calvin and the Westminster divines, so influential in England during Bunyan's lifetime. He was a friend of both John Owen[4] of the Westminster fraternal, and William Dell[5] who was decidedly

---

3 Richard Greaves states, "In *Law and Grace* Bunyan . . . on occasion . . . evinces Antinomian influence." He also documents the claims that Richard Baxter and Anthony Burgess more strongly judged Bunyan's treatise here as Antinomian. John Bunyan, 'I Will Pray with the Spirit; The Doctrine of Law and Grace Unfolded.' *Miscellaneous Works*, ed., Richard Greaves, II, p. xxxv. On the other hand Pieter de Vries writes, "R. L. Greaves' conclusion that Bunyan displayed Antinomian tendencies is in my opinion incorrect. . . . He rejected both Anti- and Neonomianism." *John Bunyan and the Order of Salvation*, p. 160.

4 John Owen moved from Anglicanism and the repudiation of Presbyterianism to Congregationalism. A posthumous treatise on *The Dominion Of Sin And Grace* based on Romans 6:14, published in 1688, seems to indicate his arriving at a view regarding law and grace much closer to that of Bunyan than might have been the case in his former years. He gives four reasons why the Christian is not under law. "1. The law *giveth no strength against sin* unto them that are under it, but grace doth. . . . 2. The law *gives no liberty of any kind*; it gendereth unto bondage, and so cannot free us from any dominion. . . . 3. The law *doth not supply us with effectual motives and encouragements* to endeavor the ruin of the dominion of sin in a way of duty. . . . It works only by fear and dread, with threatenings and terrors of destruction. . . . 4. *Christ is not in the law*; he is not proposed in it, not communicated by it,—we are not made partakers of him thereby. This is the work of grace, of the gospel. . . He [Christ] alone ruins the kingdom of Satan, whose power is acted in the rule of sin." ***Works***, VII, pp. 542-51.

5 William Dell, Master of Gonville and Caius College, Cambridge, rector of Yelden until ejected in 1662, was a pastoral friend of Bunyan's who eventually embraced independency and probably exerted considerable influence on the Bedford preacher. He was an antinomian, according to Christopher Hill, *A Tinker And A Poor Man*, p. 167. John Brown records a typical strong opinion. "If two or three Christians in the

not aligned with Westminster. Michael Mullett is correct when he writes: "Though the church he [Bunyan] joined was suffused with Calvinist thinking, Bunyan had also been strongly influenced by Luther, for whom justifying faith was more important than election and for whom predestination was not as explicitly salient as it became for the Calvinist school, especially in England."[6]

Development Concerning Bunyan's Thought

In the lives of many notable men of God, over a considerable period of ministry, it is noticed that a progress and maturity of thought develops, even a change of opinion; otherwise it must be concluded that views have been expressed that remain contrary to one another. Now such a perception of change must be based upon solid evidence, otherwise it could be charged that an author's opinions are being twisted to suit a preconceived notion. Yet in the case of Bunyan, particularly with regard to the subject at hand, it is this writer's opinion that there is conclusive evidence of a change of opinion over that thirty-two year period from the time of his first published writing in 1656, *Some Gospel Truths Opened, According To The Scriptures*, until his death in 1688. A clear case in point is as follows:

1. *Teaching in The Doctrine Of The Law And Grace Unfolded, published in 1659.*

Here Bunyan gives the most explicit exposition of his covenantal teaching, the emphasis being placed upon what he claims are the two essential covenants, the covenant of works and the covenant of grace, these terms being often used, though nowhere else in such a relentless way. Concerning the covenant of works, he writes: "The covenant of works or the law, here spoken of, is the law delivered upon Mount Sinai to Moses, in two tables of stone."[7]

---

country, being met in the name of Christ, have Christ Himself with His Word and Spirit among them, they need not ride many miles to London to know what to do. . . . What wild and woful work do men make when they will have the Church of God thus and thus, and get the power of the magistrate to back theirs, as if the new heavens wherein the Lord will dwell must be the work of their own fingers, or as if the New Jerusalem must of necessity come out of the Assembly of Divines at Westminster." *John Bunyan*, p. 75.

[6] Michael A. Mullett, *John Bunyan in Context*, p. 48.

[7] John Bunyan, *The Works of John Bunyan*, ed. George Offor, I, p. 498. The antithetical "covenant of grace" is the new covenant or bargain

However this point of origination is then qualified:

> But though this law was delivered to Moses from the hands of angels in two tables of stone, on Mount Sinai, yet this was not the first appearing of this law to man; but even this in substance, though possibly not so openly, was given to the first man, Adam, in the garden of Eden, in these words, 'And the Lord God commanded the man saying, 'Of every tree in the garden thou mayest freely eat: but of the tree of the knowledge of good and evil, thou shalt not eat of it; for in the day that thou eatest thereof thou shalt surely die' (Gen. 2:16-17). Which commandment then given to Adam did contain in it a forbidding to do any of those things that was and is accounted evil, although at that time it did not appear so plainly, in so many particular heads, as it did when it was again delivered on Mount Sinai; but yet the very same.[8]

Then follows proof of this assertion, that is the listing of instances where all of the ten commandments were upheld or broken from creation up to Mt. Sinai, that involves Pharaoh, Jacob, Abimelech, Ham, Cain, the Sodomites, etc. Concerning the sabbath or the fourth commandment given prior to the giving of the law at Mt. Sinai, Bunyan writes: "And we find the Lord rebuking his people for the breach of the fourth commandment (Ex. 16:27-29),"[9] that is just prior to their arrival at Mt. Sinai.

2. Teaching in *Questions About The Nature And Perpetuity Of The Seventh-day Sabbath, published in 1685.*

To begin with, it is interesting that while the terms "law" and "grace" are frequently used in this polemic directed against Seventh-day Baptists, especially the former, there is no mention of the covenant of works, and the covenant of grace is only referred to once. The frequently used terms are "the ministration of death/Sinai/condemnation" and "the ministration of the Spirit/gospel/righteousness," obviously drawing upon II Corinthians 3:7-11. However, there appears to be a definite change with regard to the question of the Mosaic law having any antecedents back to Adam. It must be said that in the most absolute and repeated terms, the fourth commandment is described as being strictly ordained for Israel, the time of that endowment being the

---

established by the blood of Christ, I, pp. 522-3, which is more reflective of Luther's law/gospel antitheses than those of the Westminster divines.

[8] Ibid., I, p. 498.

[9] Ibid., p. 499.

commencement of the wilderness wanderings. There is not one sentence that allows any latitude here.

Consider the following:

> Now as to the imposing of a seventh day sabbath upon men from Adam to Moses, of that we find nothing in holy writ either from precept or example. . . . But of this [sabbath] you see we read nothing, either by positive law, or countenanced example, or any other way, but rather the flat contrary; to whit, that Moses had the knowledge of it first from heaven, not by tradition. . . . The seventh day sabbath therefore was not from paradise, nor from nature, nor from the fathers, but from the wilderness, and from Sinai. . . . What can be more plain, . . . that the seventh day sabbath, as such, was given to Israel, to Israel ONLY [Bunyan's emphasis]; and that the Gentiles, as such, were not concerned therein![10]

It is readily acknowledged that Bunyan's vigorous defense of Sunday as the Christian's Lord's day, or the Christian holy day as he calls it, which has no continuity with the abolished Jewish Sabbath, takes on a rigid form which others, of a similar mind, would not endorse. For instance, he writes that, "Were I in Turkey with a church of Jesus Christ, I would keep the first day of the week to God, and for the edification of his people: and would also preach the word to the infidels on their sabbath day, which is our Friday."[11]

However, what then is the explanation of this evident change of opinion? Most likely it is that period of twenty six years separating the composition of these writings, that is between 1659 and 1685. Bunyan's understanding of the period from Adam to Moses has obviously modified. Certainly he seems to have come to the conclusion that the fourth commandment was not a creation ordinance. And this being the case, the publication date of 1678 for The Pilgrim's Progress should be kept in mind as we now consider the role of law and grace in its teaching.

THE ROLE OF THE LAW IN THE PILGRIM'S PROGRESS

In recalling the significance of Luther's influence upon Bunyan, it is not difficult to appreciate the Bedford preacher's indebtedness to the German reformer concerning the distinction between law and gospel. It is here that Bunyan obtains his essential

---

[10] Ibid., II, pp. 363, 365, 366.

[11] Ibid., p. 379.

understanding of two covenants that are virtually identical with the Mosaic and new covenants.

It is well to remember that, as Greaves points out,

> Luther was in no sense even remotely a covenant theologian. Furthermore, Luther's pronouncements on law and grace in his commentary on *Galatians* were made predominantly in the context of the doctrine of justification rather than on the place of the law in the life of a justified believer. Yet it seems more than coincidence that Bunyan's first treatise of theological importance, published as early as 1659, should be entitled *The Doctrine of the Law and Grace Unfolded*, echoing as it did the theme of Luther's commentary.[12]

In other words, the substance of Bunyan's teaching on law and grace was derived more from Luther, even though it was clothed with a certain limited covenantal dress that was fashionable in Puritan conversation in the seventeenth century.

As Illustrated in *The Pilgrim's Progress*

The role of the law or ten commandments here is very reflective of Bunyan's overall views which seem to have developed in a direction away from a certain Puritan emphasis in England that caused him at times to be charged with antinomianism, such as by Richard Baxter. This is not to say that Bunyan totally discarded the Law as being unnecessary for the child of God, but it is to indicate that in his opinion such a use, governed by Christian liberty, paled before the revelation of the incarnate righteousness of God through His blessed Son.

1. The stimulus of Christian's growing burden.

At the commencement of *The Pilgrim's Progress,* we discover that Christian already has a book in his hand and a growing burden on his back—in other words, the Bible in his hand is stimulating his guilt to a crushing extent. But what part of the Bible is he reading? Surely it is not only the ten commandments, but rather that more comprehensive revelation of the demands of God's perfect righteousness, as well as His promised judgment of sinners, discovered in the totality of both the Old and New Testaments (cf. Rom. 3:19-20 where, in context, "law" refers to the whole of the Old Testament).

---

[12] John Bunyan, *Richard L. Greaves*, p. 118.

In Christian's lament, "What shall I do to be saved?" there is the inference that the circumstances of Acts 2:36-7; 16:30-2 are indicated. That is, the means by which the Jews at Pentecost and the Philippian jailor were convicted are in mind—for instance, Peter's use of the Old Testament to bring about such conviction. In *The Doctrine of the Law and Grace Unfolded*, Bunyan refers to these two situations to explain the need of sinners to be convicted or made dead to their own righteousness by means of the old covenant, the covenant of condemning law.[13] We know that later, when Faithful will eventually heed Christian's warning to escape from the City of Destruction, so also Moses, consistent with his ministry of condemnation, threatens to burn down his house unless he flee.[14] So Christian experiences the awakening and accusatory ministry of the law of God in its broadest sense.

2. The threatenings of Mt. Sinai.

When Mr. Worldly-Wiseman counsels Christian to lose his burden at the Village Morality, just beyond the "high hill," he is in fact, as a latitudinarian minister of a false gospel of works, exhorting the seeking pilgrim to obtain the release of his burden by means of the fulfillment of the law of Mt Sinai. The recommendation of Mr. Worldly-Wiseman seems so plausible, so attainable, while in fact being utterly impossible. For Christian to scale successfully the "high hill" would require that perfect, total, and everlasting obedience to the law which the infinitely holy God requires. So the hill thunders, "As many as are of the works of the Law, are under the curse; for it is written, Cursed is every one that continueth not in all things which are written in the Book of the Law to do them (Gal. 3:10)."[15]

This scene also conveys Bunyan's belief that the proclamation of the gospel presupposes a necessary revelation of the judgment of God's righteousness before the saving character of His righteousness is made known. So he writes:

> [I]f thou wouldst know the authority and power of the gospel, labor first to know the power and authority of the law. . . . That man that doth not know the law doth not know in deed and truth that he is a sinner; and that man that doth not know he is a sinner, doth not

[13] Bunyan, *Works*, I, p. 543.

[14] Ibid., III, p. 119.

[15] Ibid., III, pp. 94, 96.

know savingly that there is a Savior. . . . If thou wouldst, then, wash thy face clean, first take a glass [mirror] and see where it is dirty.[16]

3. Law and grace at the house of Interpreter.

In the connected sequence of events in *The Pilgrim's Progress*, the scene of the dusty room that is swept clean occurs shortly after Christian has entered through the Wicket-gate and thus become an authentic child of God. Hence, in receiving instruction via the ministry of Interpreter, that is the Holy Spirit, the second room that Christian is shown is that which describes the contrasting roles of the law and the gospel. For Bunyan, like Luther, this is a vital distinction that needs to be firmly grasped for the purpose of pilgrims making satisfactory progress. Why is this so? Not because the law is a means of grace for the new believer, but rather because its recommendation by misguided zealots, such as Mr. Worldly-Wiseman, may delude the child of God into believing that the law will assist him in his journeying and growth in grace.

So following the man who sweeps the dusty room and only all the more arouses the pervasive filth, there comes the gospel messenger, the damsel who sprinkles water and thus subdues carnal corruption and facilitates cleansing. The point for Bunyan here is *not* that the pilgrim needs the sin-arousing influence of the law. Rather, as the allegorist well knows, sin in the life of a new believer is a reality that can be both a shocking and despairing discovery. Hence, the question arises as to *how* sin in the pilgrim is to be dealt with. For Bunyan, it is gospel grace alone that subdues carnal eruptions.

George Offor appreciates this point when he quotes George Cheever as follows:

> Christian well knew this in his own deep experience; for the burden of sin was on him still, and sorely did he feel it while the Interpreter was making this explanation; and had it not been for his remembrance of the warning of the Man at the gate he would certainly have besought the Interpreter to take off his burden. The Law could not take it off; he had tried that; and grace had not yet removed it, so he was forced to be quiet and to wait patiently. But when the damsel came and sprinkled the floor and laid the dust, and then the parlor was swept so easily, there were the sweet influences of the Gospel imaged, there was divine grace distilling as the dew, there was the gentle voice of Christ hushing the storm; there were the corruptions of the heart, which the Law had but

[16] Ibid., I, p. 494.

roused into action, yielding unto the power of Christ; and there was the soul made clean and fit for the King of glory to inhabit. Indeed this was a most instructive emblem. Oh that my heart might be thus cleansed, thought Christian, and then I verily believe I could bear my burden with great ease to the end of my pilgrimage, but I have had enough of that fierce sweeper, the Law. The Lord deliver me from his besom [broom]![17]

4. The Assault of Moses.

When Christian joins in fellowship with Faithful, this new companion recalls his own distinctive experiences. Following the carnal propositioning of Madam Wanton, another challenge to his flesh comes in his encounter, at the foot of the Hill Difficulty, with old Adam the First. His offer of fleshly comfort and security, including marriage to his three daughters, Lust of the Flesh, Lust of the Eyes, and the Pride of Life, causes Faithful to confess, "Why, at first, I found myself somewhat inclinable to go with the man, for I thought he spake very fair." Now while he eventually repudiates such an overture (II Tim. 2:22), yet as a result old Adam the First is aroused to enmity that leads him not only to pinch Faithful painfully, but also promise, "that he would send such a one after me, that should make my way bitter to my soul." So Faithful is soon assaulted by Moses, the embodiment of the law, who can only repeatedly assail the guilty pilgrim. To Faithful's cries for mercy, he pitilessly responds, "I know not how to show mercy." It is only when the man with the nail-prints in his hands comes along, the pilgrim's Lord, that Moses is beaten off.[18]

Not unlike the previous scene at the house of Interpreter, again Moses is the hound and ferret of unrighteousness, who responds at the merest whiff of sin. And once he catches the guilty sinner, like a dog having caught its prey, he endeavors to shake the captive to death! Is Faithful guilty? Yes, since for a time he had a hankering for old Adam the First's proposal. Hence that was enough for Moses to pursue his quarry. But Christ, in confronting Moses' "ministry of death, . . . [his] ministry of condemnation," beats him off by means of his "ministry of the Spirit, . . . [his] ministry of [saving] righteousness" (II Cor. 3:7-9). Thus Bunyan warns in *The Heavenly Footman*, "I will assure you, the devil is nimble, he can run apace, he is light of foot, he hath overtaken many, he hath turned up their heels, and hath given them an everlasting fall. Also

---

[17] Ibid., III, p. 99.

[18] Ibid., pp. 118-9.

the law, that can shoot a great way, have a care thou keep out of the reach of those great guns, the ten commandments."[19]

As Indicated in Other Works

1. The Doctrine of the Law and Grace Unfolded.

Reference has already been made to this early work. But one quote of Bunyan here is instructive concerning the role of the law in relation to the unbeliever.

> The new [grace] covenant promiseth thee a new heart, . . . but the old [law] covenant promiseth none; . . . [the new covenant promiseth] a new spirit, but the old covenant promiseth none (Ezek. 36:26). The new covenant conveyeth faith, but the old one conveyeth none (Gal. 3). Through the new covenant the love of God is conveyed into the heart; but through the old covenant there is conveyed none of it savingly through Jesus Christ (Rom. 5). The new covenant doth not only give a promise of life, but also with that the assurance of life, but the old one giveth none; the old covenant wrought wrath in us and to us, but the new one worketh love (Rom. 4:15; Gal. 5:6).[20]

2. Of the Law and a Christian.

This late work, posthumously published in 1692, was discovered in a broadsheet format which Offor suggests was probably designed, as was then the popular mode, to be "posted against a wall, or framed and hung up in a room,"[21] for ready consumption. Though brief, filling just over one page in Offor's edition, yet it presents us with the most mature expression of Bunyan's understanding of the role of the law in the life of a Christian.

Bunyan sees a contrast between the first giving of the law, in Exodus 19:16-20 where God revealed Himself with terror and severity, and the second giving of the law, in Exodus 34:1-8 where God revealed Himself as "merciful, gracious, longsuffering, and abundant in goodness and truth, keeping mercy for thousands, forgiving iniquity, transgressions and sins." Thus he expounds:

> My meaning is, when this law with its thundering threatenings doth attempt to lay hold on my conscience, shut it out with a promise of grace; cry, the inn is took up already, the Lord Jesus is here

[19] Ibid., p. 382.

[20] Ibid., I, p. 560.

[21] Ibid., II, p. 386.

> entertained, and here is no room for the law. Indeed if it will be content with being my informer, and so lovingly leave off to judge me [like the second giving of the law]; I will be content, it shall be in my sight, I will also delight therein; but otherwise, I being now made upright without it, and that too with that righteousness, which this law speaks well of and approveth; I may not, will not, cannot, dare not make it my savior and judge, nor suffer it to set up its government in my conscience; for by so doing I fall from grace, and Christ Jesus doth profit me nothing (Gal. 5:1-5). . . . [T]he Christian hath now nothing to do with the law, as it thundereth and burneth on Sinai, or as it bindeth the conscience to wrath and the displeasure of God for sin; for from its thus appearing, it is freed by faith in Christ. Yet it is to have regard thereto, and is to count it holy, just and good (Rom. 7:12); which that it may do, it is always whenever it seeth or regards it, to remember that he who giveth it to us is 'merciful, and gracious, longsuffering, and abundant in goodness and truth,' etc. (Ex. 34:6).[22]

To sum up, Bunyan does not discard the law in a total sense. But he rejects the law as a necessary judge of the conscience, as an adjunct system that the Christian requires (Rom. 7:1-4). However, if the law ministers of the essential good character of God, like the second revelation of the law to Moses, then that is profitable.

THE REIGN OF GRACE IN THE PILGRIM'S PROGRESS

As in Bunyan's works in general, so in *The Pilgrim's Progress*, the subject of "saving grace" and its resultant effects upon the life of a progressing pilgrim is the subject of exquisite and supreme delight to his soul. And the Bedford preacher's due should be given here in acknowledging his faithfulness, with regard to this subject, as it has similar dominance in Luther and the Apostle Paul. Thus he exalts in *Saved By Grace*: "O, when a God of grace is upon a

---

[22] Ibid., pp. 387-8. Also consider a similar explanation in *The Saint's Knowledge Of Christ's Love*, likewise published in 1692. Here Bunyan warns of, "not suffering the law to rule but over my outward man, not suffering the gospel to be removed one hair's breadth from my conscience. When Christ dwells in my heart by faith (Eph. 3:17), and the moral law dwells in my members (Col. 3:5), the one to keep up peace with God, and the other to keep my conversation in a good decorum: then am I right, and not till then. But this will not be done without much experience, diligence, and delight in Christ. For there is nothing that Satan more desireth, than that the law may abide in the conscience of an awakened Christian, and there take up the place of Christ, and faith." Ibid., p. 29.

throne of grace, and a poor sinner stands by and begs for grace, and that in the name of a gracious Christ, in and by the help of the Spirit of grace, can it be otherwise but such a sinner must obtain mercy and grace to help in time of need?"[23]

As Illustrated in The Pilgrim's Progress

Whereas so many of Bunyan's works explicitly eulogize the saving and reigning grace of God, yet *The Pilgrim's Progress*, while in no way diminishing this emphasis, yet cloaks it with the allegorical style. Thus it has somewhat to be unveiled, and that by a more analytical and encompassing investigation.

1. The grace of God in the gospel.

Christian's original name as a citizen in the City of Destruction was "Graceless." In such a condition he is directed by Evangelist toward Good-will at the Wicket-gate; this person by very name is the incarnate fount of "divine grace, Christ's mercy to sinners, revealed in the words used by the angels at the nativity (Luke 2:14; cf. Eph. 2:4, 7; II Thess. 2:16; I John 4:9)."[24] So with Pliable at his side, he tells his temporary companion of the relief and riches of grace (Eph. 1:18; 2:7) that are ahead for those who persevere. To the question of Pliable, "How shall we get to be sharers thereof?" Christian replies: "The Lord, the governor of the country, hath recorded, that in this book, the substance of which is, if we be truly willing to have it, he will bestow it upon us freely [gratis, by grace alone]."[25] Of course Mr. Worldly-Wiseman cannot offer any pilgrim the slightest particle of grace, notwithstanding his congenial attitude—only relief from his burden that is conditional on successfully scaling Mt. Sinai.

At the Wicket-gate, Good-will, who is Christ,[26] responds to Christian's request for entrance as follows: "I am willing with all my heart," so that as a consequence, "with that he opened the gate."[27] Here grace embraces the new pilgrim, literally by snatching him through the gate, from which point he will, "grow in the grace

---

[23] Ibid., I, p. 360.

[24] John Bunyan, *The Pilgrim's Progress*, ed. N. H. Keeble, p. 267. Refer to Bunyan's definition of grace that incorporates "good-will" in *Works*, I, p. 644.

[25] Bunyan, *Works*, III, p. 91.

[26] Ibid., III, pp. 180, 190.

[27] Ibid., p. 96.

and knowledge of our Lord and Savior Jesus Christ" (II Pet. 3:18). At the Place of Deliverance comes a larger revelation of grace that was, up till this point, dimly perceived. Here is embraced a collection of benefits that all originate from the look of faith at the atoning Christ. Of course Talkative desires stimulating conversation with Christian and Faithful concerning, "the need of Christ's righteousness, . . . the necessity of a work of grace in their soul, in order to eternal life. . . . a man can receive nothing except it has been given to him from heaven; all is of grace, not of works."[28] However this charlatan's understanding of "grace" is only based upon the problem of sin in others rather than himself.

Some time later, when Hopeful provides a testimony of his conversion while traversing the Enchanted Ground, he explains to Christian that in being tempted to quit praying and seeking for saving grace, yet he concluded he could, "but die at the throne of grace." But in further wrestling with the greatness of his sin, the Lord Jesus responded, "My grace is sufficient for thee."[29] Finally, the Lord Jesus is revealed from heaven (not discovered) according to gracious revelation. In contrast, the next encounter with Ignorance reveals a man who trusts, not in Christ sovereignly revealed and objectively believed, which belief is to him the doctrine of "distracted brains,"[30] but justifying works produced through his cooperation with grace. Christian roundly rejects this false gospel; it "is not an act of [cooperation with] grace, by which he [Christ] maketh, for justification, thy obedience accepted with God; but his [Christ's] personal obedience to the law, in doing and suffering for us that required at our hands."[31]

2. The grace of God as the pilgrim's dynamic.

The perseverence of Christian, in the midst of many trials, is based upon the stimulus of various means, tokens and supplies of grace. The authenticating roll, the mark on his forehead, and the embroidered coat are all indications of God's gracious and sovereign oversight that He will not forsake. Then at the house of the Interpreter, there is not only the damsel who sprinkles "the sweet grace of the gospel" in the polluted heart, but also the man behind the blaze in the fireplace that the Devil attempts to

---

[28] Ibid., p. 121.

[29] Ibid., p. 155.

[30] Ibid., p. 158.

[31] Ibid.

extinguish, that is "Christ, who continually, with the oil of his grace, maintains the work already begun in the heart."[32] Further along the journey, at the Palace Beautiful as well as the Delectable Mountains, the pastoral fellowship and edification are vital stimuli that continuously remind the pilgrim of redeeming grace. Recall the supper with Discretion, Prudence, Piety, and Charity, as well as the emblems of bread, wine, and raisins for sustained travel. These all project the ongoing significance and stimulation of the grace of Christ. Further consider Great-grace, the King's champion, a valiant warrior for the Lord. But note that it is the greatness of grace that makes him the defender of the faith that he is! In contrast, Little-faith, although an authentic pilgrim, yet neglects means of grace, such as in his traveling solo. Further consider the companionship between Christian, Faithful, and Hopeful where there is mutual encouragement in the grace of God.

From this it will be seen that for Bunyan, Moses and the law are not to tag along behind the converted pilgrim, like some necessary perennial goad and daily code. The language of Luther in his commentary on Galatians, in which the law can yet apply to the carnal believer,[33] is far more Bunyan's style, not the emphasis of *The Westminster Confession of Faith* where the law is, along with Christ, a rule for Christian living.[34] This is foreign to the spirit of

---

[32] Ibid., pp. 98-100.

[33] Luther comments on Galatians 3:25: "If therefore ye look unto Christ and that which he hath done, there is now no law. For he, coming in the time appointed, verily took away the law. Now, since the law is gone, we are not kept under the tyranny thereof any more; but we live in joy and safety under Christ, who now so sweetly reigneth in us by his Spirit. . . . As long then as we live in the flesh, which is not without sin, the law oftentimes returneth and doth his office, in one more and in another less, as their faith is strong or weak, and yet not to their destruction, but to their salvation. . . . [I]f I behold Christ, I am altogether pure and holy, knowing nothing at all of the law; for Christ is my leaven." *A Commentary on St. Paul's Epistle To The Galatians*, pp. 336-8. This comment certainly has the flavor of Bunyan about it, especially as he writes in *Of The Law And A Christian*.

[34] In *The Westminster Confession of Faith*, the law is not merely for times of carnality, but rather it is a revelation and code for the stimulation of righteousness, of "moral duties." That is, "as a rule of life, informing them [true believers] of the will of God and their duty, it [the ten commandments] directs and binds them to walk accordingly;" it "encourageth . . . a man's doing good," Philip Schaff, *The Creeds of Christendom*, III, pp. 640-3. In response to this, both Luther and Bunyan would claim that now, by means of a faith union, the Lord

The Pilgrim's Progress. Rather, it is grace in Christ that speeds the pilgrim along, it is grace in Christ that constrains him to keep looking heavenward, it is grace in Christ that is productive of spiritual fruit in his life (Rom. 7:4).

As Indicated in Other Works

The following excerpts span Bunyan's early to his later ministry. It is so obvious that the doctrine of grace dominated his thinking in such a way that it overwhelmed any legal emphasis that other Puritans manifested.

1. *The Doctrine of Law and Grace Unfolded.*

While some attention has already been given to Bunyan's law emphasis in this early writing published in 1659, the grace aspect should not be neglected, especially since it occupies well over twice the amount of text. The distinctive covenantal terminology in this work frequently speaks of a "covenant of grace" which is identified with such terms as, principally "the new covenant," but also "the second covenant," "the better testament," "the Son's covenant," "the blessed covenant," and "the gospel covenant." In this regard, it is important to note that this "second covenant" is to be distinguished from "the first covenant" in a consecutive and superior sense, but not as systematic covenantalism proposes, that is with one comprehensive covenant of grace under which a law or works covenant subsumes. Thus a man is either under a "covenant of works" or a "covenant of grace" in the same way that a man is under either the law or the gospel.

Thus in language reminiscent of Luther, Bunyan writes:

> [I]f these two be not held forth—to wit, the covenant of works and the covenant of grace, together with the nature of the one and the nature of the other—souls will never be able either to know what they are by nature or what they lie under. Also, neither can they understand what grace is, nor how to come from under the law to meet God in and through the other most glorious covenant, through which and only through which, God can communicate of himself grace, glory, yea, even all the good things of another world. . . . [T]he apostle [Paul] speaketh but of two covenants—to wit, grace

Jesus Christ is supremely and transcendently to be my code of moral duty, my rule of life, and my encouragement for good.

> and works—under which two covenants all are; some under one, and some under the other.[35]

By way of definition Bunyan declares: "The word 'grace,' therefore, in this scripture (Rom. 6:14), is to be understood of the free love of God in Christ to sinners, by virtue of the new covenant, in delivering them from the power of sin, from the curse and condemning power of the old covenant."[36] This grace covenant is between the Father and "the seed of Abraham; not the seeds, but the seed, which is the Lord Jesus Christ [Gal. 3:16]."[37] Thus Christ is the surety and mediator of the grace of this unchangeable covenant. "Whatsoever any man hath of the grace of God, he hath it as a free gift of God through Christ Jesus the mediator of this covenant, even when they are in a state of enmity to him, whether it be Christ as the foundation-stone, or faith to lay hold of him, mark that (Rom. 5:8-9; Col. 1:21-22)."[38]

How then is a man brought into this covenant of grace? He is, according to Bunyan's terminology, " killed" of any attachment to the covenant of works. "O, when the sinner is killed, and indeed struck dead to everything below a naked Jesus, how suitably then doth the soul and Christ suit one with another. Then here is a naked sinner for a righteous Jesus, a poor sinner to a rich Jesus, a weak sinner to a strong Jesus, a blind sinner to a seeing Jesus, an ignorant, careless sinner to a wise and careful Jesus."[39] Thus grace comprehends salvation as all of God through Christ while man is thoroughly guilty under the covenant of works, and at the same time totally impotent insofar as self-deliverance is concerned.

2. *Grace Abounding to the Chief of Sinners.*

The triumph of grace in Bunyan's spiritual autobiography published in 1666 is so evident even to a casual reader that it hardly needs further comment. The Preface reads:

> It is profitable for Christians to be often calling to mind the very beginnings of grace with their souls. . . . In this discourse of mine you may see much; much, I say, of the grace of God towards me. I thank God I can count it much, for it was above my sins and

---

[35] Ibid., I, pp. 493, 499-500.

[36] Ibid., p. 520.

[37] Ibid., p. 522.

[38] Ibid., p. 538.

[39] Ibid., p. 544.

> Satan's temptations too. . . . Oh, the remembrance of my great sins, of my great temptations, and of my great fears of perishing for ever! They bring afresh into my mind the remembrance of my great help, my great support from heaven, and the great grace that God extended to such a wretch as I.[40]

Following his conversion and introduction to the helpful biblical instruction of Pastor John Gifford, especially the exhortation to seek divine confirmation of its truthfulness, he confesses: "Wherefore I found my soul, through grace, very apt to drink in this doctrine, and to incline to pray to God that, in nothing that pertained to God's glory and my own eternal happiness, he would suffer me to be without the confirmation thereof from heaven."[41] However, the initial turbulent years brought an ambivalence of experience that could lead him to confess: "Wherefore, still my life hung in doubt before me, not knowing which way I should tip; only this I found my soul desire, even to cast itself at the foot of grace, by prayer and supplication."[42] At another time he recounts:

> Wherefore, one day as I was in a meeting of God's people, full of sadness and terror, for my fears again were strong upon me; and as I was now thinking my soul was never the better, but my case most sad and fearful, these words did, with great power, suddenly break in upon me, 'My grace is sufficient for thee, my grace is sufficient for thee, my grace is sufficient for thee,' three times together; and, oh! methought that every word was a mighty word unto me.[43]

Eventually the instability subsided, yet in retrospect Bunyan's perception of this trial is appreciative:

> I never saw these heights and depths in grace and love, and mercy, as I saw after this temptation. Great sins do draw out great grace; and where guilt is most terrible and fierce there the mercy of God in Christ, when showed to the soul, appears most high and mighty. . . . I had two or three times, at or about my deliverance from this temptation, such strange apprehensions of the grace of God, that I could hardly bear up under it, it was so out of measure amazing, when I thought it could reach me, that I do think, if that sense of it

---

[40] Ibid., pp. 4-5.

[41] Ibid., § 118, p. 20.

[42] Ibid., § 175, p. 28.

[43] Ibid., § 206, pp. 32-33.

> had abode long upon me, it would have made me incapable for business.[44]

3. Saved By Grace.

First published in 1675, this exposition of Ephesians 2:5, while continuing the emphasis of Luther upon the vital distinction between law and gospel (grace),[45] yet is very sparse in its covenantal mention of these doctrinal antitheses. However, when this terminology is used, it exactly parallels that used in *The Doctrine Of Law And Grace Unfolded*. Thus concerning the terms of salvation:

> [God] hath made all these things over to us in a covenant of grace. We call it a covenant of grace, because it is set in opposition to the covenant of works, and because it is established to us in the doings of Christ, founded in his blood, established upon the best promises made to him, and to us by him."[46]

Overall, there is typical extolling of the grace of God that includes its elective and prevenient aspects.[47]

A representative expression of Bunyan's passionate concern for this gospel truth is as follows:

> Thou Son of the Blessed, what grace was manifest in thy condescension! Grace brought thee down from heaven, grace stripped thee of thy glory, grace made thee poor and despicable, grace made thee bear such burdens of sin, such burdens of sorrow, such burden's of God's curse as are unspeakable. O Son of God! Grace was in all thy tears, grace came bubbling out of thy side with thy blood, grace came forth with every word of thy sweet mouth. Grace came out where the whip smote thee, where the thorns pricked thee, where the nails and spear pierced thee. O blessed Son of God! Here is grace indeed! Unsearchable riches of grace! Unthought-of riches of grace! Grace to make angels wonder, grace to make sinners happy, grace to astonish devils. And what will become of them that trample under foot this Son of God?[48]

---

44 Ibid., § 252, p. 38.

45 So, "works and grace, as I have showed, are in this matter opposite each to other; if he be saved by works, then not by grace; if by grace, then not by works (Rom. 11)." Ibid., p. 356.

46 Ibid., p. 349.

47 Ibid., pp. 351, 355.

48 Ibid., p. 346.

Concerning this passage, John Brown rightly comments: "We seem to see the tears welling up to his eyes and to hear his voice, tremulous with emotion, as we read this characteristic passage about the grace of Christ to men."[49]

Of particular significance at this point is Brown's recognition in this work of two instances where there seem to be preludes to the forthcoming *The Pilgrim's Progress.*[50] First is an expression of the future riches of grace that the believer can anticipate in a manner that is very reminiscent of Christian's description of these ravishing delights to Pliable.[51] Second, there is a variation of the scene at the house of Interpreter where Christ pours on the "oil of grace" so that the heart of the child of God might blaze in spite of Satan's extinguishing efforts. "O what an enemy is man to his own salvation! I am persuaded that God hath visited some of you often with his Word, even twice and thrice, and you have thrown water as fast as he hath by the Word cast fire upon your conscience."[52]

4. *The Saint's Privilege and Profit.*

In this posthumous work published in 1692, Bunyan explains:

> [T]he word grace shows that God, by all that he doth towards us in saving and forgiving, acts freely as the highest Lord, and of his own good-will and pleasure, but also for that he now saith, that his grace has become a king, a throne of grace. A throne is not only a seat for rest, but a place of dignity and authority. This is known to all. Wherefore by this word, a throne, or the throne of grace, is intimated, that God ruleth and governeth by his grace. And this he can justly do: 'Grace reigns through righteousness, unto eternal life, through Jesus Christ our Lord' (Rom. 5:21). So then, in that here is mention made of a throne of grace, it showeth that sin, and Satan, and death, and hell, must needs be subdued. For these last mentioned are but weakness and destruction; but grace is life, and the absolute sovereign over all these to the ruling of them utterly down. A throne of grace![53]

---

[49] John Brown, *John Bunyan*, p. 297.

[50] Ibid., pp. 296-7.

[51] Bunyan, *Works*, I, pp. 341-342.

[52] Ibid., p. 351.

[53] Ibid., p. 644.

COVENANT LAW AND GRACE IN THE PILGRIM'S PROGRESS

It is interesting to note that there are no explicit covenental references in *The Pilgrim's Progress*, and it is questionable if there are even any that are implicit. Richard Greaves attempts to describe Christian as under the covenant of works until he arrives at the Wicket-gate, but then confesses a difficulty:

> Christian is saved from damnation only because he is brought by Good-will (divine grace) into the new covenant, the covenant of grace. But the manner of entrance in *The Pilgrim's Progress* is more in keeping with Bunyan's experience as recorded in *Grace Abounding* than it is with Bunyan's [covenant] theology as it is set forth in *Law and Grace*.[54]

This is precisely so because Bunyan's experience in *Grace Abounding* is unquestionably paralleled with Luther's experience rather than Westminster covenant theology. Consider the Bedford tinker's soul excitement on reading the Wittenberg Reformer's *Commentary on Galatians*: "I found my condition, in his experience, so largely and profoundly handled, as if his book had been written out of my heart."[55] So the Luther scholar Gordon Rupp explains: "As Bunyan found his own heart written out in Luther's Galatians, so there is much of Luther in 'Grace Abounding' and in the 'Pilgrim's Progress.' Here is Luther, thinking of the Christian man as a St. George against the dragon - and coming very close indeed to the immortal conference between Christian and Apollyon."[56]

This is not to avoid the fact that in *The Doctrine Of The Law And Grace Unfolded* there is a major emphasis on the terms "covenant of works" and "covenant of grace," though Bunyan's exact meaning here has to be carefully distinguished. Concerning Bunyan's covenental beliefs, this early work, first published in 1659, is his most important writing, and that for an obvious reason. In this work, as in none of his other compositions, the terms "covenant of works" and "covenant of grace" are prolifically used, at least 115 times. Further, such synonymous

---

[54] John Bunyan, 'I will pray in the Spirit; The Doctrine of the Law and Grace unfolded,' *Works*, ed. Richard L. Greaves, II, pp. xxxiv-xxxv.

[55] Bunyan, *Works*, I, § 129, p. 22.

[56] **Gordon Rupp**, *The Righteousness Of God*, p. 347.

terms as "old/new covenant" and "first/second covenant" etc. are used over 140 times.

However, it needs to be carefully understood that Bunyan's repeated use of these expressions is not identical with that of the classic systematic definition whereby there is only one comprehensive covenant of grace under which subsume a variety of covenantal dispensations.[57] Consider that not once in *Law and Grace* is this meaning stated. And how is this to be accounted for? Simply by the fact that the distinction of Luther between law and gospel, not the covenantalism of the *Westminster Confession*, is the undergirding principle that is given a varied and covenantal dress.

The Covenant of Law

In *Law and Grace* Bunyan proposes: "The covenant of works or the law, here spoken, is the law delivered upon Mt. Sinai to Moses, in two tables of stone, in ten particular branches or heads. . . . [Y]et this was not the first appearing of this law to man; but even this in substance, though possibly not so openly, was given to the first man, Adam, in the garden of Eden."[58] However, as mentioned earlier, Bunyan's opinion at this point appears to change so that later, in *Questions About The Nature And Perpetuity Of The Seventh-day Sabbath*, the decalogue originated strictly by means of revelation to Moses. Often this "covenant of works" is described as the "covenant of law," the "old covenant," and the "first covenant." As such this covenant was established by God with man.

The Covenant of Grace

In *Law and Grace* the "covenant of grace" is variously described as the "covenant of the gospel," the "new covenant," and the "second covenant." It is a free, unchangeable, bargain covenant established exclusively between the Father and the Son in eternity past.

> [T]his covenant was not made with God and the creature; not with another poor Adam, that only stood upon the strength of natural abilities; but this covenant was made with the second Person, with

---

[57] Refer to "The Westminster Confession of Faith," Chapter VII, Philip Schaff, *The Creeds of Christendom*, III, pp. 616-618, also Herman Witsius, *The Economy of the Covenants Between God and Man*, I, pp. 291-324, published in 1677.

[58] Bunyan, *Works*, I, p. 498.

> the eternal Word of God; with him that was everyways as holy, as pure, as infinite, as powerful, and as everlasting as God. . . . This covenant or bargain was made in deed and in truth before man was in being.[59]

Man was excluded, contrary to systematic covenentalism where God and His elect are parties, and this again indicates, as Greaves rightly surmises,[60] Bunyan's identification with Luther in regard to preserving the gospel through the requirement of faith alone.

BUNYAN, LAW AND GRACE IN SUMMARY

John Bunyan, notwithstanding his variety of friends, was an individualist. His convictions concerning water baptism in relation to church membership are ample proof of this. In 1672 he writes in *A Confession Of My Faith, And A Reason Of My Practice*, "Touching my practice as to communion [church membership] with visible saints, although not baptized with water; I say it is my present judgment to do so, and am willing to render a farther reason thereof, shall I see the leading hand of God thereto."[61] (The next year in 1673 he then published, *Differences in Judgment about Water Baptism No Bar to Communion*.) Yet in this *Confession* just quoted, while he gives a very representative summary of his gospel convictions, even as they also relate to the believer, yet there is not so much as one mention of the tension that relates to the matter of law and grace. Rather he focuses on the main heads of the gospel. The reason, it would seem, is that while he was extremely sensitive to the plague and deceitfulness of sin, even as the decalogue of Moses could expose it, yet the glories of grace so abundantly available in Christ, that ministry of righteousness so in excess of the ministry of condemnation (II Cor. 3:9), caused him chiefly to focus on the incomparable superiority of the new covenant.

It is for this reason that Chrisopher Hill rightly declares, "Bunyan often skirted near antinomianism."[62] Indeed, it would seem that in terms of some of his opinions, he certainly was a mild antinomian. As indicated earlier, his views expressed in *Questions About the Nature and Perpetuity of the Seventh-day Sabbath*,

---

59 Ibid., pp. 522-3.

60 Richard L. Greaves, *John Bunyan*, pp. 106-7.

61 Bunyan, *Works*, II, p. 594.

62 Christopher Hill, *A Tinker And A Poor Man*, p. 86.

where the idea of the sabbath as a creation ordinance is expressly denied, indicate a rejection of the abiding significance of the fourth article of the Decalogue,[63] and especially its association with Moses and Israel. However it is this writer's conviction that, in this instance, such a charge of "mild antinomianism" is in fact a complement that any faithful gospel preacher ought to covet. If the Apostle Paul suffered a repeated charge from his Jewish opponents, it was that he was exhorting the Jews "to forsake Moses . . . [and] the Law" (Acts 21:21, 28), and thus embrace antinomianism. There is no instance of Paul being labeled even a mild legalist. And the same could likewise be said of John Bunyan.

Martyn Lloyd-Jones, commenting on Romans 6:1, makes a very searching application concerning the charge of antinomianism that the Apostle Paul, Martin Luther, and for us John Bunyan, appear to have endured:

> The true preaching of the gospel of salvation by grace alone always leads to the possibility of this charge being brought against it. There is no better test as to whether a man is really preaching the New Testament gospel of salvation than this, that some people might misunderstand it and misinterpret it to mean that it really amounts to this, that because you are saved by grace alone it does not matter at all what you do; you can go on sinning as much as you like because it will redound all the more to the glory of grace. That is a very good test of gospel preaching. If my preaching and presentation of the gospel of salvation does not expose it to that misunderstanding, then it is not the gospel. Let me show you what I mean. If a man preaches justification by works no one would ever raise this question. . . . Nobody has ever brought this charge [of antinomianism] against the Church of Rome, but it was brought frequently against Martin Luther. . . . It was also brought against George Whitefield two hundred years ago. It is the charge that formal dead Christianity—if there is such a thing—has always brought against this startling, staggering message, that God 'justifies the ungodly', and that we are saved, not by anything that we do, but in spite of it, entirely and only by the grace of God through our Lord and Savior Jesus Christ."[64]

---

[63] Walter J. Chantry seems to suggest this antinomian tendency when he writes, obviously in defense of the Westminster Confession of Faith understanding of the Christian sabbath: "It would be difficult to endorse all of his [Bunyan's] specific arguments in this article, *God's Righteous Kingdom*, p. 138.

[64] D. Martyn Lloyd-Jones, *Romans, Exposition of Chapter 6, p. 8-10.*

Yet many gospel preachers today have never known such a charge of even mild antinomianism, and this being so, they ought to ask themselves, “Why is this so?” John Bunyan has certainly suffered this accusation, and he is to be admired for it.

PERSEVERANCE IN JESUS CHRIST

What is the safe state of the saints as touching their perseverance? They shall stand though hell rages, though the devil roareth, and all the world endeavoreth the ruin of the saints of God, though some through ignorance of the virtue of the offering of the body of Jesus Christ, do say a man may be a child of God today, and a child of the devil tomorrow, which is gross ignorance; for what? Is the blood of Christ, the death of Christ, the resurrection of Christ, of no more virtue than to bring in for us an uncertain salvation? Or must the effectualness of Christ's merits, as touching our perseverance, be helped on by the doings of man?

Surely they that are predestinated are also justified; and they that are justified, they shall be glorified (Rom. 8:30). Saints, do not doubt of the salvation of your souls, unless you do intend to undervalue Christ's blood; and do not think but that he that hath begun the good work of his grace in you will perfect it to the second coming of our Lord Jesus (Phil. 1:6). Should not we, as well as Paul, say, I am persuaded that nothing shall separate us from the love of God, which is in Christ Jesus (Rom. 8:38-39). O let the saints know, that unless the devil can pluck Christ out of heaven, he cannot pull a true believer out of Christ. When I say a true believer, I do mean such a one as hath the faith of the operation of God in his soul.

John Bunyan
The Law and Grace Unfolded
Works, I, p. 565

CHAPTER NINE

Sovereignty, Election, and Free Will

EVEN a cursory study of *The Pilgrim's Progress* would lead one to conclude that John Bunyan gives little emphasis to explicit references concerning the doctrine of the sovereignty of God and related matters. On the other hand, many of Bunyan's other writings do plainly and forcefully refer to what are designated as Calvinism or the doctrines of sovereign grace. So what is the reason for this variation? To what extent is there implicit teaching on the sovereignty of God in *The Pilgrim's Progress*, and how does it find more direct expression in the Bedford pastor's other writings?

When one considers the stated purposes of Bunyan in the opening and concluding poems of the famous allegory, it becomes obvious that in consideration of his alluring method, he purposely avoided a direct and full-blooded presentation of explicit Calvinism in much the same way as a fisherman must use appropriate bait to gain a catch, and even, as Bunyan puts it, resort to some "groping" and "tickling."[1] To some this approach may appear as capitulation, a yielding to non-offensive evangelism that obscures and dishonors God's sovereignty in salvation; but Bunyan would probably respond along the lines of J. C. Ryle at this point, who wrote: "A man must first go to the little Grammar-school of Repentance and Faith, before he enters the great University of Election and Predestination."[2]

However we must also consider the comment of Samuel Coleridge in this regard who, having read *The Pilgrim's Progress*, happily confessed that, "I could not have believed beforehand that

---

1 John Bunyan, *The Works of John Bunyan*, ed. George Offor, III, p. 86.

2 J. C. Ryle, *Old Paths*, p. 473.

Calvinism could be painted in such exquisitely delightful colors."[3] Here then is a clue that leads us to the conclusion that Bunyan's Calvinism is not really suppressed as was initially suggested. Rather, according to stylistic intention, he portrays the doctrines of sovereign grace in *The Pilgrim's Progress* more integrally than in a systematic manner, more intrinsically than formal definitions.

THE SOVEREIGNTY OF GOD IN THE PILGRIM'S PROGRESS

The Sovereignty of Good-will at the Wicket-gate

"So when Christian was stepping in, the other [Good-will, having opened the gate] gave him a pull."[4] This exertion of Good-will, who is in reality Jesus Christ,[5] is suggestive of the sovereignty of the Son of God over not only Captain Beelzebub and his assailing hosts but also Christian. The true entrant into the kingdom of the Lord Jesus is indeed "a brand plucked from the fire" (Zech. 3:2) by that same Christ. So James Inglis comments:

> The pull given by Good-will . . . shows that while we are saved by grace through faith, the faith is not of ourselves, but it also is the gift of God (Eph. 2:18).
>
> Why was I made to hear thy voice?
> And enter while there's room;
> When thousands make a wretched choice,
> And rather starve than come.
> 'Twas the same love that spread the feast,
> That sweetly forced us in,
> Else we had still refused to taste,
> And perished in our sin.[6]

God's Sovereignty Over the Man in the Iron Cage

This sixth scene at the house of Interpreter is one of the most sobering in *The Pilgrim's Progress*, and the reason for this is not difficult to discover. While the topic as a whole is dealt with in

---

3 *Bunyan, The Pilgrim's Progress, A Casebook*, ed. Roger Sharrock, p. 53.

4 Bunyan, *Works*, III, p. 96. Greaves sees electing grace here since, "[n]o would-be pilgrim had the ability to open the gate." *John Bunyan and English Nonconformity*, p. 197.

5 Refer to Ch. 6, pp. 85-6.

6 John Bunyan, *The Pilgrim's Progress*, notes and memoir by James Inglis, p. 22.

detail in Chapter 10, it is sufficient to note here that this despairing reprobate declares, "God hath denied me repentance. His Word gives me no encouragement to believe; yea, himself hath shut me up in this iron cage; nor can all the men in the world let me out. O eternity! eternity! How shall I grapple with the misery that I must meet with in eternity!"[7] The essential problem is that God has sovereignly abandoned this wretch; human autonomy and free will cannot save him; his case is hopeless. Thus Christian's fearful response is acceptance of the warning that such a situation presents.

"But as God would have it"

This expression and similar utterances are mentioned on three occasions, all of which reflect a trust that God in His sovereignty is able to preserve his children in the most oppressive of circumstances, and in site of pilgrim frailty.

1. Christian is delivered from Apollyon.

The fierce encounter between Christian and Apollyon reaches a dramatic climax when the doughty pilgrim nevertheless becomes weary in combat and finds himself knocked to the ground. As a result his sword, representative of his only offensive weapon, the Word of God (Eph. 6:17), flies from his hand. Drawing close for the *coup de grâce*, Apollyon boasts, "I am sure of thee now," with the result that Christian "despaired of Life." Then we read, "but as God would have it," the pilgrim was enabled to regain his sword and give Apollyon a "deadly thrust, which made him give back, as one that had received his mortal wound."[8] Clearly Christian's ultimate hope is the sovereignty of God, "for the Lord is able to make him stand" (Rom. 14:6).

2. Christian is delivered from Vanity Fair.

Following the martyrdom of Faithful, Christian is remanded back to prison. Then we are told that, "there [he] remained for a space; but he that overrules all things, having the power of their rage in his own hand, so wrought it about, that Christian for that time escaped them [the counselors of the town of Vanity], and went his way."[9] So again Christian experiences the power of God's

---

7 Bunyan, *Works*, III, p. 101.

8 Ibid., p. 113,

9 Ibid., p. 132.

deliverance, for: "The LORD has established His throne in the heavens, and His sovereignty rules over all" (Ps. 103:19). However, it ought to be understood that this evidence of sovereign grace in the preservation of Christian was no less manifest in the agony and departure of martyred Faithful.

3. Christian is delivered from Faint-heart, Mistrust, and Guilt.

Following a brief encounter with Turn-away, Christian is stimulated to introduce discussion with Hopeful about Little-faith, who was so brutally beaten by the three rogues, Faint-heart, Mistrust, and Guilt. After detailed interaction concerning this weak though authentic pilgrim, Christian relates that he also had previously known the fury of these three assailants. He confesses: "I found it a terrible thing. These three villains set upon me, and I beginning, like a Christian, to resist, they gave but a call, and in came their master. I would, as the saying is, have given my life for a penny; but that, as God would have it, I was clothed with [tested] armor of proof."[10] Yet once more Christian is delivered solely by God's sovereign intervention, even as the psalmist who declares: "They [the wicked] band themselves together against the life of the righteous and condemn the innocent to death. But the LORD has been my stronghold, and my God the rock of my refuge" (Ps. 94:21-22).

Sovereign Grace Along the Narrow Way

When the pilgrims meet the four Shepherds at the Delectable Mountains, namely Knowledge, Experience, Watchful, and Sincere, Christian enquires: "How far is it thither [to the Celestial City]?" A Shepherd responds: "Too far for any but those that shall get thither indeed." Christian further asks: "Is the way safe or dangerous?" Another Shepherd replies: "[It is] safe for those for whom it is to be safe; 'but transgressors shall fall therein' (Hos. 14:9)."[11]

Clearly this pastoral advice is governed by a perspective of Christian pilgrimage that views the genuine traveler as being overruled and directed by sovereign providence. Certainly the true pilgrim is responsible for "walking carefully, not as unwise men but wise" (Eph. 5:15). On the other hand, there is a higher appointment and principle concerning "those who are the called,

---

10 Ibid., p. 149.

11 Ibid., p. 143.

beloved in God the Father, and kept for Jesus Christ," and "Him who is able to keep you from stumbling, and to make you stand in the presence of His glory blameless with great joy" (Jude 1, 24). An anonymous verse describes this sovereign keeping as follows:

> Thou didst reach forth Thy hand and mine enfold;
> I walked and sank not on the storm-vexed sea;
> 'Twas not so much that I on Thee took hold
> As Thou, dear Lord, on me.

The Sovereign Revelation of Jesus Christ

1. The testimony of Hopeful.

To ward off drowsiness when traversing the Enchanted Ground, Hopeful testifies to Christian about his conversion. He explains how Faithful, at the town of Vanity, encouraged him to seek the righteousness of Christ through faith alone. Concerning his wrestlings in closing with Christ, Christian enquires: "And did the Father reveal his Son to you?" Hopeful explains that such understanding eluded him for some time, even to the point of desperation. Then Christian asks again: "And how was he [Christ] revealed unto you?" Hopeful tells how the light of gospel truth eventually dawned upon his soul so that, "now was my heart full of joy, mine eyes full of tears, and mine affections running over with love to the name, people, and ways of Jesus Christ." To this Christian responds: "This was a revelation of Christ to your soul indeed."[12]

Here Bunyan teaches that the true knowledge of the Lord Jesus Christ is not ultimately a matter of personal discovery, but rather particular divine revelation, just as he taught: "All things have been handed over to Me by My Father, and no one knows who the Son is except the Father, and who the Father is except the Son, and anyone to whom the Son wills to reveal Him" (Luke 10:22).

2. The testimony of Ignorance.

Here we discover a stark contrast with Hopeful's testimony. Again along the Enchanted Ground, Christian and Hopeful are reacquainted with Ignorance and a long discussion ensues concerning the precise nature of the gospel. Ignorance scornfully repudiates the doctrine of justification by faith alone and defends a gospel of infused righteousness whereby cooperation with grace

---

[12] Ibid., pp. 155-6.

produces works that gradually justify. Christian, with no uncertainty, roundly condemns this "other gospel" (Gal. 1:8-9), at which Hopeful suggests: "Ask him [Ignorance] if ever he had Christ revealed to him from heaven." To this Ignorance responds: "What! you are a man of revelations! I believe that what both you, and all the rest of you, say about that matter, is but the fruit of distracted brains." Hopeful replies: "Why, man! Christ is so hid in God from the natural apprehensions of the flesh, that he cannot by any man be savingly known, unless God the Father reveals him to them."

Finally Christian asserts:

> You [Ignorance] ought not so slightly to speak of this matter; for this I will boldly affirm, even as my good companion hath done, that no man can know Jesus Christ but by the revelation of the Father (Matt. 11:27); yea, and faith too, by which the soul layeth hold upon Christ, if it be right, must be wrought by the exceeding greatness of his mighty power; the working of which faith, I perceive, poor Ignorance, thou art ignorant of (I Cor. 12:3; Eph. 1:18-19)."[13]

Here the illegitimate pilgrim indicates his aversion for the sovereignty of God in salvation; he does not merely express ignorance, but also a distaste for the truth concerning God that He, "will have mercy on whom He will have mercy" (Rom. 9:15-16).

THE SOVEREIGNTY OF GOD IN BUNYAN'S OTHER WRITINGS

That John Bunyan had a particular sense of divine calling is indicated by a revealing comment in *The Doctrine Of The Law And Grace Unfolded* published in 1659. He recounts that, following the early turbulent period in his Christian life, when stability in the saving grace of God came to his soul,

> methought I heard such a word in my heart as this—I have set thee down on purpose, for I have something more than ordinary for thee to do; which made me the more marvel, saying, What, my Lord, such a poor wretch as I. Yet still this continued, I have set thee down on purpose, and so forth, with more fresh incomes of the Lord Jesus and the power of the blood of his cross upon my soul. . . . Reader, I speak in the presence of God, and he knows I lie not; much of this, and such like dealings of his could I tell thee of; but my business at this time is not so to do, but only to tell what

[13] Ibid., pp. 158-9.

operation the blood of Christ hath had over and upon my conscience, and that at several times, and also when I have been in several frames of spirit.[14]

Sovereignty in *Grace Abounding to the Chief of Sinners*

1. *Experiences of deliverance.*

This personal testimony is saturated with the unquestioned belief that God is ordering the whole process of Bunyan's life. To begin with, consider four juxtapositioned incidents described at the commencement of *Grace Abounding.*

> 12. But God did not utterly leave me, but followed me still, not now with convictions, but judgments; yet such as were mixed with mercy. For once I fell into a creek of the sea, and hardly escaped drowning. Another time I fell out of a boat into Bedford river, but mercy yet preserved me alive. Besides, another time, being in the field with one of my companions, it chanced that an adder passed over the highway; so I, having a stick in my hand, struck her over the back; and having stunned her, I forced open her mouth with my stick, and plucked her sting out with my fingers; by which act, had not God been merciful to me, I might, by my desperateness, have brought myself to mine end.
> 13. This also have I taken notice of with thanksgiving; when I was a soldier, I, with others, were drawn out to go to such a place to besiege it; but when I was just ready to go, one of the company desired to go in my room; to which, when I had consented, he took my place; and coming to the siege, as he stood sentinel, he was shot into the head with a musket bullet, and died.[15]

2. *Concern about personal election.*

Prior to his conversion, Bunyan was disturbed concerning whether he was one of God's elect.

> [T]hough I was in a flame to find the way to heaven and glory, and though nothing could beat me off from this, yet this question did so offend and discourage me, that I was, especially at some times, as if the very strength of my body also had been taken away by the force and power thereof. This scripture did also seem to me to trample upon all my desires, 'It is not of him that willeth, nor of him that runneth, but of God that showeth mercy' (Rom. 9:16). . . . Therefore, this would still stick with me, How can you tell that you

---

[14] Ibid., I, p. 549.

[15] Ibid, I, §§ 12-13, p. 7.

> are elected? And what if you should not? How then? . . . Why, then, said Satan, you had as good leave off, and strive no further; for if, indeed, you should not be elected and chosen of God, there is no talk of your being saved. . . . By these things I was driven to my wits' end, not knowing what to say, or how to answer these temptations. Indeed, I little thought that Satan had thus assaulted me, but that rather it was my own prudence, thus to start the question.[16]

However, it is significant that following his conversion, Bunyan seemed no longer troubled by this doctrine, but rather fully endorsed it.

3. Revelation through Scripture.

Throughout *Grace Abounding* there are over thirty references to the truth of Scripture bursting upon Bunyan's soul. Often he declares, "That scripture did also tear and rend my soul," or "these words broke in upon my mind," or "suddenly this sentence bolted in upon me," or "this word took hold upon me," or "this scripture would strike me down as dead," or "that scripture fastened on my heart," or "these words did, with great power, suddenly break in upon me," etc.[17] The point here is that because of the divine initiative necessary for the soul to embrace the truth of the Bible, Bunyan recognized that the light of truth breaking in upon him was a sovereign revelation, and not simply due to self-discovery.

Sovereignty and Particular Election

In *A Confession Of My Faith* published in 1672, Bunyan provides a definitive statement concerning his belief in the doctrine of election under seven headings,[18] which proves to be very much in agreement with the particular or Calvinistic Baptists of his day. A parallel statement is found in *The Work Of Christ As An Advocate* published in 1688 which also is covered under seven headings.[19] The following summary comparison indicates that the later delineation of 1688, the year of Bunyan's death, is a fresh presentation rather than a revision. However, both lists emphasize the certain decree of God, election being in Christ, the rejection of foreseen faith, and grace being sufficient to guarantee glory.

---

[16] Ibid, §§ 58-61, p. 13.

[17] Ibid., §§ 68, 104, 143, 185, 201, 206, pp. 14-32.

[18] Ibid., II, pp. 598-9.

[19] Ibid., I, pp. 163-4.

Confession Of Faith
1672

1. Election is free, being founded in grace, and the unchangeable will of God (Rom. 11:5-6; Eph. 1:11; II Tim. 2:19)
2. This decree, choice or election, was before the foundation of the world; and so before the elect themselves, had being in themselves (Rom. 4:17; Eph. 1:4; II Tim. 1:9).
3. The decree of election is so far off from making works in us foreseen, the ground or cause of the choice: that it containeth in the bowels of it, not only the persons, but the graces that accompany their salvation (Rom. 8:29; Eph. 1:4; 2:10; 3:8-11; II Tim. 1:9).
4. Jesus Christ is he in whom the elect are always considered, and that without him there is neither election, grace, nor salvation (Acts 4:12; Eph. 1:5-7, 10).
5. There is not an impediment attending the election of God, that can hinder their conversion, and eternal salvation (Jer. 51:5; Acts 9:12-15; Rom. 8:30-35; 9:7).
6. No man can know his election, but by his calling. The vessels of mercy, which God afore prepared unto glory, do thus claim a share therein (Rom. 9:24-25).
7. Election does not forestall or prevent the means which are of God appointed to bring us to Christ, to grace and glory; but rather putteth a necessity upon the use and effect thereof; because they are chosen to be brought to heaven that way: that is by the faith of Jesus Christ, which is the end of effectual calling (II Thess. 2:13; I Pet. 1:12; II Pet. 1:10).

Christ As An Advocate
1688

1. Election is eternal as God himself, and so without variableness or shadow or change, and hence it is called "an eternal purpose," and a "purpose of God" that must stand (Eph. 3:11; Rom. 9:11).
2. Election is absolute, not conditional; and, therefore, cannot be overthrown by the sin of the man that is wrapt up therein. No works foreseen to be in us was the cause of God's choosing us; no sin in us shall frustrate or make election void (Rom. 8:33; 9:11).
3. By the act of election the children are involved, wrapped up, and covered in Christ; he hath chosen us in him; not in ourselves, not in our virtues, no, not for or because of anything, but of his own will (Eph. 1:4-11).
4. Election includes in it a permanent resolution of God to glorify his mercy on the vessels of mercy, thus fore- ordained unto glory (Rom. 9:15, 18, 23).
5. By the act of electing love, it is concluded that all things whatsoever shall work together for the good of them whose call to God is the fruit of this purpose, this eternal purpose of God (Rom. 8:28-30).
6. The eternal inheritance is by a covenant of free and unchangeable grace made over to those thus chosen; and to secure them from the fruits of sin, and from the malice of Satan, it is sealed by this our Advocate's blood, as he is Mediator of this covenant, who also is become surety to God for them (John 10:28-29; Rom. 9:23; Heb. 7:22; 9:15, 17-24; 13:20).
7. By this choice, purpose, and decree, the elect, the concerned therein, have allotted them by God, and laid up for them in Christ, a sufficiency of grace to bring them through all difficulties to glory (Acts 14:22; Eph. 1:4-5, 13-14; II Tim. 1:9).

Sovereignty and Free Will

John Bunyan's understanding of particular election inevitably involved a denial of "free will" as commonly understood by those holding to an Arminian concept of human autonomy. In other words, the appropriation of the gospel by God's elect was ultimately the consequence of sovereignly and particularly endowed faith rather than a universal, inherent human ability to believe or not believe. Moreover, it was the gospel of salvation by pure grace that required that no human cooperation with the saving message, even faith on the basis of free will, could be construed as a necessary and independent human contribution. So Bunyan writes: "Faith, as the gift of God, is not the Savior, as our act doth merit nothing; faith was not the cause that God gave Christ at the first, neither is it the cause why God converts men to Christ; but faith is a gift bestowed upon us by the gracious God, the nature of which is to lay hold on Christ."[20] Such a perspective did not negate faith or its necessity, as Bunyan's evangelistic urging indicates; rather it made faith subservient to the power of God to save according to the ultimate truth of His good will and decree.

Thus Bunyan frankly confesses in the last sermon he preached in 1688, "I am not a freewiller; I do abhor it."[21] He advises, "keep company with the soundest Christians, that have most experience of Christ; and be sure thou have a care of Quakers, Ranters, Freewillers."[22] Further he is even sensitive to that which "savors too much of a tang of free will" about it.[23] In response to the latitudinarian Edward Fowler's *The Design Of Christianity*, Bunyan writes in 1672:

> That there is no such thing in man by nature, a liberty of will, or a principle of freedom, in the saving things of the kingdom of Christ, is apparent by several scriptures. Indeed there is in men, as men, a willingness to be saved their own way, even by following, as you, their own natural principles, as is seen by the Quakers, as well as yourself; but that there is a freedom of will in men, as men, to be saved by the way which God hath prescribed, is neither asserted in

---

[20] Ibid., p. 519.

[21] Ibid., II, p. 756.

[22] Ibid., III, p. 383.

[23] Ibid., II, p. 652.

> the scriptures of God, neither standeth with the nature of the principles of the gospel.[24]

It ought not to be forgotten that as in other aspects of Bunyan's doctrine of *sola gratia* salvation, here his understanding is likewise more akin to the teaching of Luther at this point, and it is not unreasonable to surmise that the Bedford tinker may well have imbibed much of the German Reformer's polemic *On The Bondage Of The Will.* Richard Greaves comments along this line of thinking as follows: "In rejecting any notion of free will which would detract from the graciousness and sovereignty of God in salvation, Bunyan spoke more from a soteriological concern in a soteriological context (as did Luther) than from the scholastic principles of a philosophical-theological system (as did Owen).[25]

THE AUTHENTICITY OF REPROBATION ASSERTED

In the prior heads of this chapter, no reference has been made to *Reprobation Asserted* and its disputed authenticity so that the clear evidence offered for Bunyan's understanding of sovereignty, election, and free will might stand beyond challenge. In rejecting as unreliable the publication date of *Reprobation Asserted* in 1674 according to George Offor,[26] Richard Greaves informs us concerning this work as follows:

> The first independent claim of Bunyan's authorship appeared in a catalogue of his works printed by Nathaniel Ponder in the third edition of *One Thing is Needful: or, Serious Meditations upon the Four Last Things* in 1688. Ponder's criterion for attribution was whether or not a title-page printed Bunyan's name in full. *Reprobation Asserted* therefore qualified, in Ponder's judgment, as a genuine work of Bunyan. Although Ponder's reasoning is not compelling, it is a point in favor of Bunyan's authorship of *Reprobation Asserted* that the publisher of at least eight of his works regarded it as his. Ponder's testimony is additionally important in view of the fact that he published *The Pilgrim's Progress* (1678 and 1684) and was therefore acquainted with Bunyan's concern about pseudonymous imitations.[27]

---

24 Ibid., p. 312.

25 Richard L. Greaves, *John Bunyan*, p. 59.

26 Bunyan, *Works,* II, p. 335.

27 Richard Greaves, *John Bunyan and English Nonconformity,* p. 186.

Conjecture as to Bunyan being the author of this work commenced with the rejection of its authenticity in 1885 by his principal biographer to date, John Brown. Subsequent study of this matter led the late Roger Sharrock, general editor of the Oxford (Clarendon) edition of Bunyan's *Miscellaneous Works* completed in 1994, to exclude it from this collection on the grounds that it was spurious.[28]

The Modern Rejection of *Reprobation Asserted*

1. John Brown.

George Offor's belief that *Reprobation Asserted* was first published in 1674 is based upon a catalog of Bunyan's works compiled by Charles Doe, a friend of Bunyan's. However, Brown comments concerning Doe that, "I venture to think that he was mistaken, as he might very well be in reference to a book published several years before his personal acquaintance with Bunyan began."[29] Brown further challenges what he claims are spurious publication details, and then comments regarding the style of composition:

> It [*Reprobation Asserted*] neither begins nor ends in Bunyan's characteristic fashion, nor is there in it a single touch to remind us of his own peculiar vein. Let him write on what subject he may, he writes not long before he either melts with tenderness or glows with fire. This writer never deviates into anything of the kind. He is hard and cold in style, thin in scheme and substance.[30]

2. Roger Sharrock.

Richard Greaves, drawing upon personal correspondence with the general editor of the recent Oxford (Clarendon) edition of Bunyan's *Works,* relates that Sharrock, while "rejecting Brown's arguments as inconclusive, decided after a more intensive analysis that the work was, in fact, not Bunyan's."[31] The exact details upon which Sharrock based his conclusion do not appear to have been published, though perhaps Greaves relates all that is relevant.

---

[28] Greaves, *Bunyan and English Nonconformity,* pp. 185-6. It would be helpful if more details of Sharrock's investigation and conclusions in this regard were made available.

[29] John Brown, *John Bunyan*, p. 228.

[30] Ibid.

[31] Greaves, *Bunyan and English Nonconformity*, p. 185.

3. Richard Greaves.

This editor of four volumes of the Oxford (Clarendon) edition of Bunyan's *Miscellaneous Works* cautiously rejects the authenticity of *Reprobation Asserted*. While offering grounds for rejecting Brown's charge concerning spurious publication details, yet concerning stylistic differences he concludes: "Its logical and well-ordered structure, involving eleven chapters in forty-four pages, is essentially without parallel in Bunyan's other writings. . . . Only when Bunyan was directly embroiled in a theological controversy did he tend to omit popular phraseology, a direct appeal to the audience, and use of colorful metaphors."[32]

Concerning some doctrinal inconsistency, Greaves writes:

> The most important difference is the affirmation of a general atonement in *Reprobation Asserted*, which conflicts with Bunyan's concept of a limited atonement. According to the author of the disputed treatise, 'Christ died for all [II Cor. 5:15], tasted death for every man [Heb. 2:9]; is the Savior of the World [I John 2:2]'. The writer employs these verses to support a doctrine of general atonement. Elsewhere, Bunyan quoted Hebrews 2:9 and I John 2:2 when referring to the extent of the atonement, but qualified the latter verse by stating that Christ 'as a Propitiation' is 'not ours only, but also for the Sins of the whole World; to be sure, for the Elect throughout the World'. Furthermore, the author of *Reprobation Asserted* clearly stated that, 'the death of Christ did extend itself unto them [that is, the reprobate]: for the offer of the Gospel cannot, with God's allowance, be offered any further than the death of Jesus Christ doth go; because if that be taken away, there is indeed no Gospel, nor grace to be extended.' (*Works*, II, 348). According to Bunyan, however, Christ 'died for all his elect' (*Miscellaneous Works*, xi, p. 216). . . . Bunyan may, of course, have changed his mind on this issue; most of the statements expressing his belief in a limited atonement come from a period subsequent to that when *Reprobation Asserted* was written. Yet he made at least two comments reflecting the concept of a limited atonement in 1672 and 1674, so that such a possibility is remote. (*Miscellaneous Works*, iv, p. 64 (but cf. a statement on the same page: 'So he dyed for all'); viii, p. 61).[33]

So Greaves concludes:

---

[32] Ibid., p. 188.

[33] Ibid., pp. 189-90.

When all the facts are analyzed it is possible to argue plausibly either for or against Bunyan's authorship of *Reprobation Asserted.* Yet the discrepancies in style and theology, coupled with the uncertain external evidence and the distinct possibility that the treatise was written shortly after the publication of *Peaceable Principles and True* [1674] by an open-membership, open-communion Particular Baptist who admired Bunyan's role in that debate, point to the likelihood that *Reprobation Asserted* is a spurious, pseudonymous work.[34]

The Modern Validation of *Reprobation Asserted*

1. Henri Talon.

This French author of *John Bunyan: The Man and His Works,* first published in 1948, simply rejects John Brown's arguments on the basis of Charles Doe's attestation and G. B. Harrison's brief arguments.[35]

2. G. B. Harrison.

This English author of *John Bunyan: A Study of Personality*, published in 1928, rejects John Brown's arguments, especially with regard to style:

> But the same hard, logical style [of *Reprobation Asserted*] is to be found in *Questions About the Nature and Perpetuity of the Seventh-day Sabbath*, wherein Bunyan was again arguing a point of doctrine. The arguments for reprobation and election arise quite naturally from Bunyan's doctrine of grace. Others of his disciples have felt no difficulty about the book; Doe included it in the list of Bunyan's works, though not in his folio, and Offor, who was the first to reprint it, calls down the Divine Blessing on his 'attempt to spread this important, although to many, unpalatable doctrine.'[36]

3. Paul Helm.

In a far more substantial assessment of the problem than Talon or Harrison, Paul Helm has offered a detailed response to Greaves which, while giving plausible explanations to several matters, inevitably focuses on the chief problem and that being the charge that the writer of *Reprobation Asserted*, particularly in Chapter

---

[34] Ibid., p. 191. Would a Particular Baptist uphold a general atonement?

[35] Henri Talon, *John Bunyan: The Man and His Works*, p. 261n.

[36] G. B. Harrison, *John Bunyan: A Study in Personality*, pp. 125-6.

IX, gives evidence of believing in a general atonement.[37] Helm declares that: "This is the only place in the work in which a general atonement is asserted, if indeed it is asserted here."[38] This being the case, he further heightens the tension of the problem with the challenge:

> In the work objections to the doctrine of reprobation are constantly and candidly faced [and refuted]. But apparently the doctrine of general atonement, which is (to say the least) in extreme tension with the Calvinistic view of the decrees of God, is slipped in without a word of apology. . . . Where else in this period, and from this theological quarter, is there another such work, a work that argues *both* that from all eternity God has decreed to elect some of the fallen race to salvation through Christ, and to pass over others who will be eternally condemned on account of their sin *and* that Christ's atonement was not for the elect but was general or indefinite in intent?[39]

Helm's *modus operandi* is first to discover if a limited atonement is taught elsewhere in *Reprobation Asserted*. In the absence of explicit examples, he quotes two instances in Chapters I and V where he suggests that this doctrine is *implicit*. Second, he attempts to avoid a contradiction by suggesting that the language of Chapter IX describes a "tender" or general *offer* of the gospel to all men without distinction, even as most Calvinists do who believe in a limited atonement. It is pointed out that the main thrust of this chapter is concerned with the offer of the gospel to elect and non-elect alike. "[T]he gospel is to be proffered to both, without considering elect or reprobate, even as they are sinners. . . . [T]he gospel is to be tendered to all in general, as well as to the reprobate as to the elect, *to sinners as sinners*."[40] But is this merely an offer of theoretical intention? Or is it a sincere offer? Helm responds: "Christ's death extends itself to the reprobate in the sense that if

---

37 By the term "general atonement" is generally meant God's sincere offer of salvation through Christ to all men who, in spite of being sinners, retain an autonomous and decisive capacity to believe or not believe.

38 Paul Helm, "Bunyan and *Reprobation Asserted*," *The Baptist Quarterly*, Vol. XXVIII, April, 1979, p. 88. Pieter de Vries does not agree with Greaves that here we have a doctrinal conflict since the author of *Reprobation Asserted,* unlike Bunyan, expresses belief in universal redemption. *John Bunyan on the Order of Salvation*, p. 73.

39 Ibid., pp. 88-9.

40 Bunyan, *Works*, II, p. 349.

they *were* [emphasis added] to believe then Christ's death would suffice for their salvation."[41] To this Greaves replies: "Helm rightly acknowledges that nowhere in this tract does the writer explicitly indicate that Christ died for the elect alone; . . . if Christ died for the elect alone, any offer of the benefits of his death to the reprobate would be fraudulent."[42] This point aside since it is not really germane to the main argument here,[43] Helm convincingly quotes a parallel passage from the bona fide *The Jerusalem Sinner Saved* to prove Bunyan's practical concern, as here in *Reprobation Asserted*, that the call and invitation must go out to all without distinction before the matter of election is considered.[44]

Probable Bunyan Authorship

For this writer, the claim that Bunyan is not the author of *Reprobation Asserted* because of the principal reason that Chapter IX appears to profess belief in a general atonement is not convincing. In particular it virtually ignores the unmistakable Calvinism of the work as a whole. More important than the question as to whether there is explicit or even implicit reference to a limited atonement in *Reprobation Asserted* overall, is the vital question concerning whether this work clearly asserts particular election, involving the denial of universal ability or autonomy, in which case the offer of a general atonement would still appear anomalous and an issue to be dealt with. Particular election presupposes universal inability save for grace given to the elect. Hence the problem would still remain concerning the proposed "fraudulent" offer of the gospel to the impotent non-elect. However the author here is an emphatic believer in particular election and for this reason he feels bound to consider the very charge of a "fraudulent" offer that Greaves proposes.

---

[41] Helm, "Bunyan And Reprobation Asserted," p. 91.

[42] Richard Greaves, *John Bunyan and English Nonconformity*, pp. 190-1.

[43] This charge of a fraudulent or insincere offer is that which Hyper Calvinists have brought against Calvinists such as John Owen who taught the free offer of the gospel to all while believing in a limited atonement. This led to the Hyper Calvinist belief in a proclaimed gospel that does not invite, with the expectation that only the elect would respond. Refer to Peter Toon, *The Emergence of Hyper-Calvinism in English Nonconformity*, pp. 70-103, 134-5

[44] Helm, "Bunyan And Reprobation Asserted," p. 91.

Consider the heading of Chapter IX. "*Whether God would indeed and in truth, that the gospel, with the grace thereof, should be tendered to those that yet he hath bound up under Eternal Reprobation?*"[45] Surely this is not the concern of a believer in a general atonement. The heading of Chapter X reads: "*Seeing then that the grace of God in the gospel, is by that to be proffered to sinners, as sinners; as well as to the reprobate as to the elect; Is it possible for those who are indeed not elect, to receive it, and be saved?*" Then follows the heading of Chapter XI. "*Seeing* [that] *it is not possible that the reprobate should receive this grace and live, and also seeing* [that] *this is infallibly foreseen of God; and again, seeing God hath fore-determined to suffer it so to be; Why doth he yet will and command that the gospel, and so grace in the general tenders thereof, should be proffered unto them?*"[46] Bunyan answers in closing:

> God willeth and commandeth the gospel should be offered to all, that thereby distinguishing love, as to an inward and spiritual work, might the more appear to be indeed the fruit of special and peculiar love. For in that the gospel is tendered to all in general, when yet but some do receive it; yea, and seeing these some are unable, unwilling, and by nature, as much averse thereto, as those that refuse it, and perish; it is evident that something more of heaven and the operation of the Spirit of God doth accompany the word thus tendered for their life and salvation that enjoy it (I Thess. 1:4-7).[47]

Thus further explanation is given that in some respects the elect and reprobate receive differing grace:

> [T]here is present grace and present mercy [for the reprobate], eternal grace and eternal mercy [for the elect]. . . . [T]he non-elect perish by reason of sin, notwithstanding present mercy, because of eternal justice; and that the elect are preserved from the death, though they sin and are obnoxious to the strokes of present justice, by reason of eternal mercy. What shall we say then? Is there unrighteousness with God? God forbid: 'He hath mercy on whom he will have mercy, and compassion on whom he will have compassion (Rom. 9:15).'[48]

---

45 Bunyan, *Works*, II, p. 348.

46 Ibid, pp. 348-9, 352.

47 Ibid., p. 355.

48 Ibid., p. 358.

Again, this is the reasoning of a thorough Calvinist who is confronting the antinomy of particular redemption and the explicit command of Scripture to invite elect and non-elect sinners universally to the gospel feast (Matt. 22:9).[49] It must be admitted that Bunyan's pastoral ministry epitomized this emphasis, namely undoubted Calvinism by persuasion along with proclamation of Jesus Christ that included passionate, unrestricted invitations to sinners of every stripe.

CONCLUSION

It seems quite plain that while *The Pilgrim's Progress* does not contain explicit teaching on Calvinistic aspects of the sovereignty of God, yet Bunyan's overall commitment to the essential doctrines of sovereign grace was uncompromising to say the least. In presenting the gospel to the unbeliever, he was fervent in his unqualified offer of grace to earnest sinners and at the same time vigorous in the solicitation of faith from indifferent sinners. Often he would reason about difficulties and objections from the unbeliever in much the same way as Spurgeon does in *Around The Wicket Gate.* Yet, in his evangelistic endeavors, he did not see the necessity of forcefully injecting details concerning election, reprobation, free will, and foreknowledge, especially in *The Pilgrim's Progress*. It could well be that, as Greaves has pointed out, the primacy of free grace was more important to Bunyan in his gospel witness than the proclamation of reasoned matters concerning God's decree. However, once a child of God began to mature, truth concerning the sovereignty of grace was plainly expounded as necessary for stability and assurance.

---

[49] In *The Death of Death in the Death of Christ*, John Owen counsels on this vital matter: "A minister is not to make inquiry after, nor to trouble himself about, those secrets of the eternal mind of God, namely,—whom he purposeth to save, and whom he hath sent Christ to die for in particular. It is enough for them to search his revealed will, and thence take their *directions*, from whence they have their *commissions*. . . . They command and invite all to repent and believe; but they know not in particular on whom God will bestow repentance unto salvation, nor in whom he will effect the work of faith with power." *Works*, X, p. 300.

CHAPTER TEN

The Despairing Reprobate in the Iron Cage

OF all the scenes in *The Pilgrim's Progress*, this one presents the most solemn mystery. John Kelman declares it to be, "the darkest of all Bunyan's pictures."[1] And it obviously was Bunyan's intention to produce a sober response even as Christian concludes, "Well, . . . this is fearful! God help me to watch and be sober, and to pray that I may shun the cause of this man's misery!"[2] Of course this stimulation to "fear" according to Bunyan was part of his pastoral intention that found its balance with the encouragement to "hope" as well in the preceding scenes.[3] In this regard, it is noteworthy that Christiana, with the four children and Mercy, were also exposed to this portrayal.[4] However, the response of readers through the centuries to this particularly grave episode has not always been so submissive.

The Essence of the Problem

In its classical religious sense, "despair" results from heinous sinners comprehending irrecoverable abandonment by God; thus while they have been previously offered grace, now they are forever without hope. God refrains from making any further particular saving moves toward such reprobates so that their condition has become irremediable. There is also a lesser form of despair whereby a man *believes* that he is beyond the hope of God's grace, even though grace is in fact still offered. Such despair is born more of stubborn unbelief rather than God's turning from a sinner.

---

1 John Kelman, *The Road*, I, p. 64.

2 John Bunyan, *The Works of John Bunyan*, ed. George Offor, III, p. 101.

3 Ibid., p. 102.

4 Ibid., p. 184.

In the case of the man in the iron cage, while having formerly professed hope in grace, now he believes he is beyond the reach of mercy, and so declares that, "God hath denied me repentance. His Word gives me no encouragement to believe; yea, himself hath shut me up in this iron cage; nor can all the men in the world let me out. O eternity! eternity! How shall I grapple with the misery that I must meet with in eternity?"[5] While it could be maintained that the whole of this comment still remains within the realm of the man's *opinion* of his condition and God's attitude, other writings leave no doubt that Bunyan did believe that in certain instances, a man could be, to use his term, "beyond grace"[6] or permanently abandoned, according to God's determination.

Responses to the Problem

Several commentators have expressed their dislike for Bunyan's teaching at this point, though out of respect for the tinker as a whole, such opinions are stated in terms of what Bunyan is not supposed to have meant, even though his writings plainly state that a man may be abandoned by God while still living on earth. George Cheever declares that, "Bunyan intended not to represent this man as actually beyond the reach of mercy, but to show the dreadful consequences of departing from God, and of being abandoned of him to the misery of unbelief and despair."[7] Robert Maguire defensively comments: "Surely God's mercy is universal, extending through time, through life, even to the end. There is no case that we would pronounce hopeless; no sin beyond the reach of pardon."[8] Kelman similarly responds: "It is certain that Bunyan did not believe that such a state of mind as this, represented the truth of the case as a necessary and final doom."[9] Here personal doctrinal preference seems to intrude so as to obscure the plain teaching that the author of *The Pilgrim's Progress* states propositionally: "The day of grace ends with some men before God taketh them out of the world. I shall give you some instances of

---

[5] Ibid., p. 101.

[6] Ibid., pp. 579-585.

[7] George B. Cheever, *Lectures on The Pilgrim's Progress*, p. 174.

[8] Robert Maguire, *Lectures on Bunyan's Pilgrim's Progress*, p. 40.

[9] Kelman, *The Road*, I, p. 67.

this. . . . First. I shall instance Cain. . . . Second. I shall instance Ishmael. . . . Third I shall instance Esau."[10]

THE HISTORICAL IDENTIFICATION OF THE MAN IN THE IRON CAGE

Since *The Pilgrim's Progress* closely parallels the real life experiences of John Bunyan described in his spiritual autobiography *Grace Abounding To The Chief Of Sinners*, it is probably true that the "Despairing Reprobate in the Iron Cage" is representative of a real character of his time, or a personal acquaintance. Bunyan was a penetrating observer of human nature. In *The Life And Death Of Mr. Badman*, he gives details of several unsavory individuals who he had come across in everyday life. But who in particular does this despairing captive in the iron cage represent? There are two recognized possibilities.

The case for John Child

1. The support of George Offor.

George Offer, editor of the standard three volume set, *The Works Of John Bunyan*, first published in 1854, supposes that the man in the iron cage is an allusion to an apostate named John Child:

> He had been a Baptist minister, and was born at Bedford in 1638. . . . he appears to have been an intimate friend of Bunyan's, so that when his *A Vindication of Gospel Truths* was published, John Child united in a recommendatory preface—this was in 1657. From a dread of persecution he conformed to the Church of England. . . . This poor wretch afterwards became terrified with awful compunctions of conscience. He was visited by Mr. Keach, Mr. Collins, and a Mr. B. (probably Bunyan.) When pressed to return to the fold of Christ, he said, 'If ever I am taken at a meeting, they will have no mercy on me, and triumph, *This is the man that made his recantation*; and then ruin me to all intents and purposes, and I cannot bear the thought of a cross nor a prison.' . . . His cries were awful. '*I shall go to hell; I am broken in judgment: when I think to pray, either I have a flushing in my face, as if it were in a flame, or I am dumb and cannot speak.*' In a fit of desperation he destroyed himself on the 15th October 1684.[11]

---

[10] Bunyan, *Works*, III, pp. 577-78.

[11] Ibid., pp. 72-73.

2. The repudiation of John Stachniewski.

While John Brown confirms this apostasy according to the records of the Bedford church,[12] yet there is no reference to this sad episode in any of Bunyan's writings, and especially *Grace Abounding To The Chief Of Sinners*. Although others hold this viewpoint, such as N. H. Keeble, who suggests that Roger Sharrock was of the same opinion,[13] John Stachniewski has more recently offered conclusive evidence that John Child was not the despairing reprobate in the iron cage, that is documentation indicating that *The Pilgrim's Progress* was written too early for such a parallel to be incorporated.[14] Rather, a far more specific and plausible identification is available.

The case for Francis Spira

1. Spira identified in Bunyan's writings.

In 1548, a lawyer in Italy of great repute named Francis Spira professed conversion to biblical and Protestant gospel truth. However, he later relapsed into Roman Catholicism and as a consequence became a victim of extreme despair. An account of his apostasy titled *A Relation Of The Fearful Estate Of Francis Spira*, tells of his subsequent remorse that found no hope in God's mercy. George Offer notes that his copy of this book, "has added to it a narrative of the wretched end of John Child, a Bedford man, one of Bunyan's friends."[15] It is highly significant that in all of his published works, Bunyan refers to Francis Spira on five occasions spanning from 1666 to 1682, and each time with regard to his irrecoverable condition. Let us separately consider each of these references.

a. In *Grace Abounding To The Chief Of Sinners*, published 1666.

As noted in Chapter 6, here the conversion of Bunyan, or his entrance through the Wicket Gate, took place in approximately 1650 shortly before he came under the helpful influence of John Gifford's ministry (§§ 113-117). However, it was not until 1653 that Bunyan experienced lasting assurance that God had lifted

---

[12] John Brown, *John Bunyan*, pp. 120-21.

[13] John Bunyan, *The Pilgrim's Progress*, ed. N. H. Keeble, p. 268.

[14] John Stachniewski, *The Persecutory Imagination*, pp. 199-200n.

[15] Bunyan, *Works*, I, p. 118.

away his burden of guilt; only subsequent to this did he become a member of the Bedford church (§§ 229-235, 253). In this intervening period of approximately four years, he experienced times of near despair since he believed that he had "sold Christ" (§§ 132-139), and committed the unpardonable sin (§§ 147-154).

At that time Bunyan also believed that he had sinned even as Judas, and especially Esau (Heb. 12:16-17). He laments:

> It is too late, I am lost, God hath let me fall; not to my correction, but condemnation; my sin is unpardonable; and I know, concerning Esau, how that, after he had sold his birthright, he would have received the blessing, but was rejected. About this time, I did light on that dreadful story of that miserable mortal, Francis Spira; a book that was to my troubled spirit as salt, when rubbed into a fresh wound"(§ 163).[16]

b. Again in *Grace Abounding To The Chief Of Sinners.*

Here an oblique reference is made to Spira as Bunyan continues through his early period of ambivalence following conversion. In thinking to ask for prayer by the fellowship of nonconformist believers in Bedford on account of the unsettled state of his soul, he anxiously comments:

> I feared that God would give them no heart to do it; yea, I trembled in my soul to think that some or other of them would shortly tell me, that God had said those words to them that he once did say to the prophet concerning the children of Israel, 'Pray not thou for this people,' for I have rejected them (Jer. 11:14). So, pray not for him, for I have rejected him. Yea, I thought that he had whispered this to some of them already, only they durst not tell me so, neither durst I ask them of it, for fear, if it should be so, it would make me quite besides myself. Man knows the beginning of sin, said Spira, but who bounds the issues thereof?[17]

c. In *The Heavenly Footman*, published 1671.

Here Bunyan considers what it means when Christ is described as he "who shuts and no one opens" (Rev. 3:7). He concludes that the Son of God excludes with finality. "And how if thou shouldst come but one quarter of an hour too late? I tell thee, it will cost thee an eternity to bewail thy misery in. Francis Spira can tell thee

---

[16] Ibid., § 163, pp. 25-26.

[17] Ibid., § 179, p. 28.

what it is to stay till the gate of mercy be quite shut; or to run so lazily, that they be shut before thou get within them."[18]

d. In *The Barren Fig-Tree*, published 1673.

Subtitled "The Doom And Downfall Of The Fruitless Professor," here Bunyan demonstrates that a person may be excluded from saving grace long before their earthly life is ended. Of some who grievously sin against a profession of the gospel,

> they are denied the power of repentance, their heart is bound, they cannot repent; it is impossible that they should ever repent, should they live a thousand years. It is impossible for those fall-aways to be renewed again unto repentance, 'seeing they crucify to themselves the Son of God afresh, and put him to an open shame' (Heb. 6:4-6). Now, to have the heart so hardened, so judicially hardened, this is as a bar put in by the Lord God against the salvation of the sinner. This was the burden of Spira's complaint, 'I cannot do it! 0h! now I cannot do it!'"[19]

Here then are words that closely resemble the confession of the "Miserable Reprobate in the Iron Cage" to Christian: "I cannot get out; O, now I cannot. . . . I have crucified him [the Son of God] to myself afresh.[20]

e. In *The Greatness Of The Soul*, published 1682.

Here Bunyan considers the sensitivity of the soul in the nether regions:

> Miseries as well as mercies sharpen and make quick the apprehensions of the soul. Behold Spira in his book, Cain in his guilt, and Saul with the witch of Endor, and you shall see men ripened, men enlarged and greatened in their fancies, imaginations, and apprehensions, though not about God, and heaven, and glory, yet about their loss, their misery, and their woe, and their hells.[21]

2. Spira identified as the Man in the Iron Cage.

Hence it seems most likely that Bunyan's forlorn captive was, in fact, a representation of the spiritual derelict, Francis Spira. Certainly John Child may have some secondary application.

[18] Ibid., III, pp. 382-83.

[19] Ibid., p. 582.

[20] Ibid., p. 101.

[21] Ibid., I, p. 118.

However, it is obvious that the author of *The Pilgrim's Progress* has been indelibly impressed by the truth concerning such a hopeless and abandoned soul as Spira. Furthermore, Bunyan was undoubtedly chilled by reading the following poem that introduces the account of this religious man who, being spiritually and physically dead, yet speaketh.

Here see a soul that's all despair; a man
All hell; a spirit all wounds; who can
  A wounded spirit bear?
Reader, would'st see, what may you never feel
Despair, racks, torments, whips of burning steel!
Behold, the man's the furnace, in whose heart
Sin hath created hell; O in each part
  What flames appear:
His thoughts all stings; words, swords;
  Brimstone his breath;
His eyes flames; wishes curses, life a death;
A thousand deaths live in him, he not dead;
A breathing corpse in living, scalding lead.[22]

THE DOCTRINAL IDENTIFICATION OF THE MAN IN THE IRON CAGE

For Bunyan, this man is in a cage very different from that which Christian and Faithful found themselves in for a brief period at Doubting Castle.[23] It represents everlasting rather than temporary hopelessness, and herein lies its horror. It cannot be doubted that Bunyan taught here, and in detail in *The Barren Fig-Tree*, that there are caged reprobates in this present earthly life who are beyond the rescue of divine mercy, and this notwithstanding, as earlier quoted, the opinions of Cheever, Maguire, and Kelman. Again, he expressly states that, "the day of grace ends with some men before God takes them out of this world."[24] His support from Scripture includes Exodus 9:14; Deuteronomy 29:18-19; I Samuel 28:4-6; Isaiah 66:4; Romans 1:28-31; 2:3-5; Ephesians 4:18-19; II Thessalonians 2:10-12; I Timothy 4:2; Hebrews 6:4-6; Jude 5-6, 13.[25]

---

[22] Ibid., III, p. 583.

[23] Ibid., pp. 128-29, 131-32.

[24] Ibid., p. 579.

[25] Bunyan, *Works*, III, pp. 560-85.

The Influence of the Unpardonable Sin

1. Bunyan's personal experience.

After his conversion, Bunyan's ambivalence in terms of his assurance led to the consideration that he may well have committed the unpardonable sin of Mark 3:29.[26] The reason appears to be that, in being tempted "to sell and part with Christ," while resisting for a period, he felt that he eventually yielded and consented to Satan's overtures. Thus he comments, "Now was the battle won, and down fell I, as a bird that is shot from the top of a tree, into great guilt and fearful despair."[27] The ongoing turmoil led him to compare himself with Judas, and Esau in particular who, "found no place for repentance, though he sought it with tears" (Heb: 12:17). Finally delivered from his fears and doubts through grasping the assurance that trust in Christ's perfect righteousness brings, Bunyan seems to have been delivered from any further personal concern in this matter.

2. Bunyan's early teaching.

In 1659, just prior to his long imprisonment, Bunyan's *The Doctrine of the Law and Grace Unfolded* was published in which a definitive statement reveals his understanding of the unpardonable sin. It clearly parallels his belief of certain reprobates being past grace in this life as detailed in *The Barren Fig Tree*. He declares:

> But that [unpardonable] sin is a sin that is of another nature [from the sin of David and Peter], which is this—For a man after he hath made some profession of salvation to come alone by the blood of Jesus, together with some light and power of the same upon his spirit; I say, for him after this knowingly, wilfully, and despitefully to trample upon the blood of Christ shed on the cross and to count it an unholy thing [as the man in the iron cage confesses], or no better than the blood of another man, and rather to venture his soul any other way than to be saved by this precious blood. And this must be done, I say, after some light (Heb. 6:4-5), despitefully (Heb. 10:29), knowingly (II Pet. 2:21), and wilfully (Heb. 10:26 compared with v. 29), and that not in a hurry and sudden fit, as Peter's was, but with some time beforehand to pause upon it first, with Judas; and also with a continued resolution never to turn or be converted

[26] Ibid., I, §§ 147-48, p. 24.

[27] Ibid., I, § 140, p. 23.

again; 'for *it is* impossible to renew such again to repentance,' they are so resolved and so desperate (Heb. 4).[28]

Certainly this parallels the reprobate in the iron cage who was "once a fair and flourishing professor," and yet resolutely "sinned against the light of the Word, and the goodness of God;" thus "I have provoked God to anger, and he has left me; . . . I have despised his [Christ's] person (Luke 19:14); I have despised his righteousness; I have 'counted his blood an unholy thing;' I have 'done despite to the Spirit of grace" (Heb. 10:28-29).[29]

3. *Bunyan's later teaching.*

In 1688, the year of his death, Bunyan's *The Jerusalem Sinner Saved* was published in which he wrote:

> [H]e that has sinned the sin against the Holy Ghost cannot come [John 6:37; Rev. 21:6; 22:17], has no heart to come, can by no means be made willing to come to Jesus Christ for life; for that he has received such an opinion of him [Christ], and of his things, as deters and holds him back. . . . He counteth this blessed person, this Son of God, a magician, a conjuror, a witch, or one that did, when he was in the world, what he did, by the power and spirit of the devil. . . . His blood, which is the meritorious cause of man's redemption, even the blood of the everlasting covenant, he counteth 'an unholy thing,' . . . of no more worth to him, in his account, than was the blood of a dog, an ass, or a swine.[30]

The Indications of Being Past Grace

What evidence then are we to expect concerning a person who is, to use Bunyan's expression, "past grace"? In *The Barren Fig-Tree,* which is subtitled, "The Doom and Downfall of the Fruitless Professor," based on Luke 13:6-9 and published in 1682, he describes five signs, which are summarized as follows.[31]

a. A person may be past grace when he has withstood and abused and worn out God's patience. Having come to the fig-tree for fruit, and found none, God repeatedly shakes and

---

[28] Ibid., p. 566. Refer to George Butler, "The Iron Cage Of Despair and 'The Unpardonable Sin' In The Pilgrim's Progress," *English Language Notes*, XXV, Sept. 1987, pp. 34-38.

[29] Bunyan, *Works*, III, pp. 100-1.

[30] Ibid., I, pp. 102-3.

[31] Ibid., III, pp. 579-85.

warns it, yet still without result, so that He eventually calls for his axe!

b. A person may be past grace when God lets him alone and allows him to do anything without the restraint of difficulties, or concern with regard to holiness. The fig-tree is no longer tended, but left to grow wild.

c. A person may be past grace when his heart becomes so hard and stony that it is discarded by God as impenetrable. This is the hardness of a Lot's wife or Pharaoh. It is a hardness which God judicially hardens to a point of hopelessness.

d. A person may be past grace when he determines to garrison his heart against the Word of God. This person purposely shuts out the light so as to enjoy darkness. This fig-tree has a root that bears gall and wormwood.

e. A person may be past grace when he scoffs against the Lord and despises His messengers while being determined to pursue his own course. Thus God sets himself against such as these by causing them to perish rather than savingly believe.

The Qualifications Concerning Abandonment

1. Abandonment always follows persistent rebellion.

In every instance of a suggested hopeless reprobate, such as with Cain, Ishmael, or Esau,[32] or even Saul and Judas, Bunyan clarifies that God's abandonment follows after man's most heinous, barefaced, and persistent rebellion. This is also evident in Romans 1:24, 26, 28, where God "gives over" or abandons certain men and women who persist in flagrant and extreme depravity.

2. Despair and distraction must be distinguished.

A distinction must be made between a despairing and a distraught soul. The former case is abandoned by God and claimed by Satan, whereas the latter case is kept by God and assailed by Satan. In *The Life And Death Of Mr. Badman*, Bunyan comments:

> And here I would put in a caution. Every one that dieth under consternation of spirit; that is under amazement and great fear, do not therefore die in despair. For a good man may have this for his bands in his death, and yet go to heaven and glory (Ps. 73:4). For, as I said before, he that is a good man, a man that hath faith and

---

[32] Ibid., pp. 577-79.

holiness, a lover and worshiper of God by Christ, according to his Word, may die in consternation of spirit; for Satan will not be wanting to assault good men upon their deathbed, but they are secured by the Word and power of God; yea, and are also helped, though with much agony of spirit, to exercise themselves in faith and prayer, the which he that dieth in despair can by no means do.[33]

THE GREATNESS OF THE GRACE OF CHRIST

As there is grace, so there is justice in God; and man having sinned, God concluded to save him in a way of righteousness; therefore it was absolutely necessary that Jesus Christ should put himself into our very condition, sin only exempted. He was Prince of life, so he for our sakes laid down that also ; for so stood the matter, that he or we must die, but the grace that was in his heart wrought with him to lay down his life. Again, he was Prince of peace, but he forsook his peace also. He laid aside his peace with the Father, and made himself the object of his Father's curse.

Thou Son of the Blessed, what grace was manifest in thy condescension! Grace brought thee down from heaven, grace stripped thee of thy glory, grace made thee poor and despicable, grace made thee bear such burdens of sin, such burdens of sorrow, such burdens of God's curse as are unspeakable. O Son of God! Grace was in all thy tears, grace came bubbling out of thy side with thy blood, grace came forth with every word of thy sweet mouth (Ps. 45:2; Luke 4:22). Grace came out where the whip smote thee, where the thorns pricked thee, where the nails and spear pierced thee. O blessed Son of God! Here is grace indeed! Unsearchable riches of grace! Grace to make angels wonder, grace to make sinners happy, grace to astonish devils. And what will become of them that trample under foot this Son of God?

John Bunyan
Saved by Grace
Works, I, pp. 245-6

---

[33] Ibid., p. 661

CHAPTER ELEVEN

Images of Jesus Christ in The Pilgrim's Progress

IT appears nothing short of astonishing that one modern author should so myopically deny the pervasiveness of Jesus Christ in John Bunyan's most famous allegory. Brian Nellist comments:

> So interiorized does he [Bunyan] make his model of the religious life it often seems close to those very Quakers and Ranters whom he so controverted so strenuously in his youthful days. . . . One result of this interiorizing is remarkable—the comparative absence of Christ from the immediate experience of the Pilgrim. In *Grace Abounding* He is everywhere acknowledged, but in *The Pilgrim's Progress* He is only occasionally in Christian's mind. If we ask what takes His place in the work, then the answer is, I would suggest, the Road itself.[1]

Hence, it is hoped that the following summary of Bunyan's Christology in allegory will, once and for all, do away with such an obviously careless proposal.

THE IMAGES OF JESUS CHRIST IN THE PILGRIM'S PROGRESS

When Jesus Christ declared that, "he [Moses] wrote of Me" (John 5:46), he undoubtedly referred to a fullness of meaning and variety of literary expression that far transcended any one explicit prophetic reference. J. C. Ryle expounds upon the sense of this verse as follows:

> At the very least we may conclude He meant that throughout the five books of Moses, by direct prophecy, by typical persons, by typical ceremonies, in many ways, in divers manners Moses had written of Him. There is probably a depth of meaning in the Pentateuch that has never yet been fully fathomed. We shall

---

[1] Brian Nellist, "The Pilgrim's Progress and Allegory," *The Pilgrim's Progress, Critical And Historical Reviews*, ed. Vincent Newey, p. 150.

probably find at the last day that Christ was in many a chapter and many a verse, and yet we knew it not.[2]

In the same way, John Bunyan also uses a variety of literary expressions, most being biblically sourced and styled, to describe this same Christ. *The Pilgrim's Progress* is more than a seamless robe of biblical truth; rather it is a full-orbed Christology. Richard Greaves accurately declares: "Bunyan's thought as a whole was based on the doctrine of the grace of God revealed in Christ—a concept which permeated the whole of his writings and which was the focal point of his preaching and thinking."[3] As we shall now see, this emphasis is well illustrated in the famous allegory in no less a degree than Bunyan's other writings. Of course there is a degree of hiddenness inherent in the allegorical form; but this is intentional on Bunyan's part, and he expects us to "lift the veil" and peer at the substance of the "Lord" of the hill, the "King" of glory, the "Holy One," "Mighty One," "Prince," "Redeemer," which titles are used over forty times in Part One.

The "Yonder Shining Light"

When Evangelist directs the sight of Christian from the City of Destruction toward "yonder shining light" in the distance, Bunyan intends here that we should identify this situation with II Peter 1:19 which reads: "We have also a more sure word of prophecy; whereunto ye do well that ye take heed, as unto a light that shineth in a dark place, until the day dawn, and the day star arise in your hearts." While this passage of Scripture has, it would seem, primary reference to the return of Jesus Christ at the end of this age,[4] that is with brilliance and splendor, yet Bunyan appears to apply this verse to the first dawning of Christ in the heart of a seeking unbeliever.

Christian is too dim of sight to behold clearly the Wicket-gate, that is Christ as the exclusive way of salvation, let alone the inscribed invitation at its head; but he can make out something of Christ in "the prophetic word." He has some light of the truth in the midst of a particularly squalid world. Early in *Grace Abounding to the Chief of Sinners*, Bunyan relates how historical parts of the Bible first appealed to him, and only later did Paul's

---

2 J. C. Ryle, *Expository Thoughts On John*, I, p. 324.

3 Richard Greaves, *John Bunyan*, p. 159.

4 Charles Bigg, contra Joseph B. Mayor.

epistles have any appeal.[5] So Evangelist encourages Christian to pursue this light which he presently perceives, that is until it bursts forth into the glory of the gospel of Christ that gives entry into the narrow way.

The Wicket-gate Complex

Just as John 10 presents Jesus Christ as "the door" vs. 7-9, of the sheep, "the life-giver" v. 11, for the sheep, and "the good shepherd" vs. 11, 14, of the sheep, so at the Wicket-gate this same Christ is presented in a manifold way. It is a Christocentric collage, a multifaceted representation of Jesus Christ as the entrance to the narrow way (Matt. 7:13-14).

1. Christ as the Word.

The first revelation of truth that Christian receives at the Wicket-gate is the inscription over the entrance that reads, "Knock and it shall be opened unto you" (Matt. 7:7). This word of Christ taken from the Sermon on the Mount is a most encouraging invitation that advises the earnest traveler to avail himself of the Son of God's bidding.

2. Christ as Good-will.

The porter Good-will, both a grave or serious, and a welcoming person, is in fact the Son of God, as explained in Chapter 6. Alexander Whyte adds: "So much was Christian taken with the courtesy and the kindness of Good-will, that had it not been for his crushing burden, he would have offered to remain in Good-will's house to run his errands, to light his fires, and to sweep his floors. So much was he taken captive with Good-will's extraordinary kindness and unwearied attention."[6]

3. Christ as the Wicket-gate.

According to Bunyan's dream in *Grace Abounding*, the narrow gap that he passes through from darkness to sunshine is in fact, "Jesus Christ, who is the way to God the Father,"[7] also detailed in Chapter 6. In Part Two, when Christiana and Mercy come to the

---

5 John Bunyan, *The Works of John Bunyan*, ed. George Offor, I, §§ 29, 46, pp. 9, 11.

6 Alexander Whyte, *Bunyan Characters*, I, p. 69.

7 Bunyan, *Works*, I, § 55, p. 13.

Keeper of the Gate, we read: "Then Christiana made low obeisance, and said, Let not our Lord be offended with his handmaidens, for that we have knocked at his princely gate."[8]

The Interpreter's House Complex

Being representative of the teaching ministry of the Holy Spirit, whose ministry is to focus on Christ (John 15:26; 16:13-14), all seven scenes here, either implicitly or explicitly speak of Christ. The implicit references are: a. The portrait of the godly pastor, who faithfully serves his Master. b. The distinction between the law and the gospel, in which there is the sprinkling of the grace of Christ. c. The virtue of patience contrasted with passion, who are subject to Christ the Governor. d. The persevering valiant pilgrim, who seeks entrance into Christ's palace. e. The despairing reprobate in the iron cage, who spurns the mercy of the Son of the Blessed. However, two explicit scenes are as follows.

1. Christ as the conqueror of the assailed heart.

When Satan attempts to extinguish the true pilgrim's heart that gospel grace has ignited, Christ provides the oil of grace that maintains the blaze. That is, Christ continually intercedes for the child of God (Heb. 7:25) and strengthens the heart by grace (Heb. 13:8-9).

2. Christ as the judge at the end of the age.

For Bunyan, the great final assize at the end of this age will be executed by Jesus Christ in glory, that is by he who four times is identified as the "Man" who sits upon the cloud (Acts 17:30-31; Rev. 14:14-16). This particular aspect of the work of Christ is to be constantly kept in sight by professing pilgrims as a sober reminder.

The Place of Deliverance Complex

At this juncture, while the portrayal of Christ's saving work is multi-faceted, yet the focus remains singular upon his atoning sacrifice. Furthermore, what is perceived here by Christian is to be recalled frequently for his ongoing edification. Every benefit described here, whether experiential or declared, is rooted in Christ. Two in particular are:

---

8 Ibid., III, p. 179.

1. Christ as the burden bearer

While it is not until Christian arrives at the Palace Beautiful that he mentions the man who did "hang bleeding upon the tree," nevertheless the praise of Christ is preeminent. This crucified Son of God grants rest, saves with power, supplies living water, forgives sin, imputes righteousness, sanctifies and secures.

2. Christ as the clothier with righteousness.

Again, while it is not until Christian arrives at the Palace Beautiful that his change of raiment is perceived to be a beautifully "*embroidered* coat," yet he rejoices that he who strips away filthy rags is also able to cover with righteousness. So in praise of Christ he sings:

> Blest cross! Blest sepulchre! Blest rather be
> The man that there was put to shame for me![9]

The Palace Beautiful Complex

Christian is told by the Porter of the Palace Beautiful that this edifice "was built by the Lord of the Hill."[10] Hence, its beauty (Ps. 48:1-3) is its character as the Body of Christ, the Church, while its every feature reflects the glory of Jesus Christ. In his *Discourse Of The Building, &c., Of The House Of God*, a poem of 1310 lines, Bunyan describes the particular beauty of this spiritual building as follows:

> Lo her foundation with saphires are;
> Her goodly windows made with agates fair,
> Her gates are carbuncles, or pearls; nor one
> Of all her borders but's a precious stone:
> None common, nor o' th' baser sort are here,
> Nor rough, but squar'd and polish'd everywhere.
>
> The doors, the walls, and pillars of this place;
> Forbidden beasts here must not show their face.
> With grace like gold, as with fine painting, he
> Will have this house within enriched be;
> Fig-leaves nor rags, must here keep out no cold,
> This builder covers all with cloth of gold,

---

9 Ibid., p. 103.

10 Ibid., p. 107.

Of needle-work, prick'd more than once or twice
(The oft'ner prick'd, still of the higher price)
Wrought by his SON, put on her by his merit,
Applied by faith, revealed by the Spirit.[11]

1. Christ as the Lord of the Hill.

That is, Jesus Christ is sovereign over the death that wicked mankind inflicted upon him on Mt. Calvary.[12] This person is the object of glad talk during supper time, as well as the subject of discussion in the Palace study, over which he reigns. In a similar pastoral sense he is the owner of the Delectable Mountains. In his triumphant resurrection, this Lord caused the wrath of man to praise him (Ps. 76:10; Acts 4:27-28). Thus, in partaking of the emblems of this Lord, both bread and wine, there is true feasting in the heart by faith; here is soul nourishment indeed; here Christian is satisfied with the true bread of life in the remembrance of this Lord (John 6:48-51, 54-58).

2. Christ as the Warrior.

His spiritual military rank and prowess, his great conquests, his subjection of his enemies, his dispersal of spoils to his subjects, his evident wounds, his triumphant enthronement, his whole recorded history, all delight the Palace residents to such an extent that they fellowship late into the night (I Cor. 15:25-28; Heb. 2:14-15; Rev. 19:11-16). Here Christian learns in particular of Christ's militant supremacy; this is timely in view of his impending encounter with Apollyon (Rom. 8:31-37).

3. Christ as the Savior.

He is especially devoted to the rescue of poor and beggarly pilgrims who, although corrupt in origin, yet are elevated to princely rank (I Sam. 2:8; Ps. 113:7-8). The extent of this condescension is indicated by his becoming stripped naked and mortally wounded so that he might gather into his kingdom a multitude of royal citizens (Rev. 5:9-10). All of this redeeming activity was for the adoption of sons "according to the kind

---

[11] Ibid., II, p. 578.

[12] The expression "Lord of the hill" is used on four occasions and in context refers to the hill where Christian looked at the cross and was released of his burden, not the hill on which the Celestial City is located, Bunyan, *Works*, III, pp. 107, 109, 110, 143.

intention of his will, to the praise of the glory of His grace" (Eph. 1:4-6).

4. *Christ as the Protector.*

As members of his body, the Church, there is confidence expressed in intercessory prayer, by his subjects, that he will protect them (II Tim. 4:18). As for the Head of this Body, Bunyan elsewhere writes in *The Saints Privilege And Profit* that, "his church is part of himself; it is his own concern, it is for our own flesh. . . . Because we are part of himself, he cannot but care for us, nature puts him upon it; yea, and the more infirm and weak we are, the more he is touched with the feeling of our infirmities, the more he is afflicted for us."[13]

5. Christ as the eternal Son.

The records of his great antiquity, as cataloged in the Palace library, transcend time and enter into eternity. For he is the Son of God, the Son of "the Ancient of Days" (Dan. 7:9, 13-14). As such, his "origin" or sonship is by means of an "eternal generation" (John 5:26).

The Opposer of Apollyon

The great controversy that ensues here concerns Apollyon and Christian's Prince. Christian himself is but a pawn, albeit a significant one, in a struggle involving far greater stakes. Even Apollyon acknowledges this to be the case when he fiercely rages, "I am an enemy to this Prince [Christian's Lord]; I hate this person, his laws, and people."[14] In response, Christian speaks very knowledgeably and dependently of his King: "O thou destroying Apollyon! To speak the truth, I like his service, his wages, his servants, his government, his company, and country, better than thine; and, therefore, leave off to persuade me further; I am his servant, and I will follow him."[15]

1. *Christ as the King of princes.*

Christian's whole rebuttal of Apollyon's claims upon him concerns the reasons for his new allegiance to the "King of

---

[13] Ibid., I, p. 674.

[14] Ibid., III, p. 113.

[15] Ibid., p. 112.

princes." The point here is that whereas Apollyon has claimed to be the "Prince and God" of the City of Destruction, along with its evil alliances, yet Christian is now subject to one greater than this despot, namely the "King of kings and Lord of lords" (I Tim. 6:14-16; Rev. 19:11-16).

2. Christ as the merciful Prince.

With regard to Apollyon's charge of evident sin and suffering in Christian's earthly pilgrimage, two major rejoinders are offered. First, the King of princes is, unlike Apollyon, justly able to pardon offences, and especially those committed in the environment of the evil kingdom. Second, yes, it is true that the likes of Christian often suffer in their conflicts with Apollyon, but only for a proving season until their promised glory comes at the conquering appearance of their King.

The Vanquisher of Moses

Faithful's inclination to yield to the desires of his flesh by means of the overtures of Adam the first earns for him not only carnal pain, but also the repeated assaults of Moses who declares, "I know not how to show mercy."[16] But then comes a greater and stronger one than Moses, with justifying nail prints in his hands, who commands the law-enforcer to forbear (John 1:17; Rom. 7:1-4; Heb. 3:1-3). So Moses flees and Faithful is then enabled to ascend the remainder of the Hill Difficulty. Concerning the role of the Mosaic Law in the life of the Christian, Bunyan elsewhere writes:

> Whenever thou who believest in Jesus, dost hear the law in its thundering and lightening fits, as if it would burn up heaven and earth; then say thou, I am freed from this law, these thunderings have nothing to do with my soul; . . . when this law with its thunderous threatenings doth attempt to lay hold on thy conscience, shut it out with a promise of grace; cry, the inn is took up already, the Lord Jesus is here entertained, and here is no room for the law.[17]

The Transient at Vanity Fair

The necessity of all bona fide pilgrims passing through Vanity en route to the Celestial City brings to Bunyan's mind the thought

---

[16] Ibid., pp. 118-119.

[17] Ibid., II, p. 388.

that the Prince of princes passed this same way. Though it would seem that, having descended from the Celestial City, he went in reverse through Vanity toward the Place of Deliverance and there was directly translated back to the glory from whence he had come. The point here is that pilgrims, in meditating on their Prince, are comforted by the knowledge that their Savior has been touched with the feeling of their infirmities; as a consequence he has become a sympathetic high priest who offers grace to help in time of need (Heb. 4:14-16).

Bunyan further explains in *The Saint's Privilege And Profit*:

> Are we tempted to distrust God? So was he [the Lord Jesus]: are we tempted to murder ourselves? So was he: are we tempted with the bewitching vanities of this world? So was he: are we tempted to commit idolatry, and to worship the devil? So was he (Matt. 4:3-10; Luke 4:1-13). So that herein we also were alike; yea, from his cradle to his cross he was a man of affliction throughout the whole course of his life.[18]

Hence, "since He himself was tempted in that which He has suffered, He is able to come to the aid of those who are tempted" (Heb. 2:17-18).

The Saving Object of Hopeful's Testimony

As a citizen of Vanity, Hopeful traded heavily at the Fair. But Faithful's ominous preaching disturbed him and aroused conviction of sin which he sought to suppress. Increasingly tormented in his soul, he attempted religious self-reformation. But persistent inward conviction caused him to seek counsel from Faithful, who told him his only hope was the obtaining of the righteousness of a perfectly righteous man. Thus Faithful declared Christ to Hopeful as follows:

1. Christ as the righteous Savior.

The Lord Jesus is revealed as the only sinless man who, having come from the right hand of the Most High God, is uniquely qualified as a justifier of those who believe in his substitutionary atonement (Rom. 3:21-26; I Tim. 2:5).

---

[18] Ibid., I, p. 673.

2. Christ as the willing Savior.

Hopeful doubts Christ's particular interest in him. But Faithful points out that the Lord Jesus died for others, not himself, and that he personally invites sinners to come and be welcomed by him (John 6:37; 7:37-39).

3. Christ as the revealed Savior.

While Hopeful earnestly seeks for salvation, yet Faithful enquires as to whether Christ has sovereignly revealed himself (Luke 10:22). Hopeful is not immediately welcomed, yet he is prepared to die while seeking saving grace. Even so prevenient grace upholds him (Hab. 2:3).

4. Christ as the embraced Savior.

Then light from heaven reveals the invitation, "Believe on the Lord Jesus Christ, and thou shalt be saved " (Acts 16:30-31). Now the answers to Hopeful's objections flood from the Spirit of God through the Word, and not mediately through Faithful (John 6:35-37; Rom. 4:5; 10:4; II Cor. 12:9; I Tim. 1:15; Heb. 7:24-25).

5. Christ as the transforming Savior.

Now Hopeful joyfully muses on the enlightenment and revelation that has come to his soul. Now he sees the world, God, and himself in their true light (Rom. 6:17-18). Now his love for Christ is full, personal, and submissive.

The External Object of Christian's Testimony.

The closely disputed exchange between Christian and Ignorance concerns, not a vague and general understanding of "faith in Christ for justification," but rather a vital distinction between a subjective justification that works with and in man and a justification that is objectively a work of God that originates from outside of man. When Ignorance scoffs at Christian's hope in "what Christ in his own person has done without [external to] us,"[19] and the supposed licentious implications of such a faith, he strikes at the very heart of a right understanding of the doctrine of justification by faith. At this point, it is perhaps most evident just how intensely Christ conscious Christian is as he travels the Road. To say otherwise is

[19] Ibid., III, p. 158.

simply to indicate one's ignorance of the essential doctrine of Bunyan's text.

The Lord of Death.

As Christian and Hopeful prepare to traverse the River of Death, they are told that its apparent terror will be felt in proportion to the degree to which they "believe in the King of the place."[20] As they are in transit, Christian despairs of being welcomed on the other side. But Hopeful reassures his brother with the confident assertion, "Be of good cheer, Jesus Christ maketh thee whole." Then Christian's dullness vanishes as he cries out, "O I see him again, and he tells me, 'When thou passest through the waters, I will be with thee; and through the rivers, they shall not overflow thee' (Isa. 43:2)."[21] In all of the Christian life Jesus Christ is the great forerunner (Heb. 6:20), that is he has prepared the way ahead and made clear his steps in which we are to follow. And when we come to the last enemy, which is death, how comforting it is to understand that the Lord Jesus has gone ahead of us and prepared for our crossing of the bar (I Cor. 15:26, 54-57).

The Lord of Glory

On the other side, Christian and Hopeful are by no means satisfied with their newfound immortality. Their conversation with the escorting angels is still of the glory of the heavenly Jerusalem just ahead of them. Certainly the anticipation of the citizenry and accouterments there is thrilling, yet supremely, they are told, "you must wear crowns of gold, and enjoy the perpetual sight and vision of the Holy One, for 'there you shall see him as he is' (I John 3:2)."[22] So they are eventually received into the Celestial City with the singing of, "Enter ye into the joy of your Lord." Then the new citizens join in singing, "Blessing, and honor, and glory, and power, be unto Him that sitteth upon the throne, and unto the Lamb, for ever and ever" (Rev. 5:13). Now journeying has culminated in arrival, and faith is supplanted by sight.

In Bunyan's *Dying Sayings* it is recorded:

> O! Who is able to conceive the inexpressible, inconceivable joys that are there [in heaven]? None but they who have tasted of them.

[20] Ibid., p. 163.

[21] Ibid., p. 164.

[22] Ibid., p. 164.

Lord, help us to put such a value upon them here, that in order to prepare ourselves for them, we may be willing to forego the loss of all those deluding pleasures here. How will the heavens echo of joy, when the Bride, the Lamb's wife, shall come to dwell with her husband forever? Christ is the desire of nations, the joy of angels, the delight of the Father; what solace then must that soul be filled with, that hath the possession of him to all eternity?[23]

CONCLUSION

It hardly needs saying that Bunyan's writings in general simply pulsate with Christ. The contemplation of the Lord Jesus enthralls him at every turn. So he declares in a poem, "Of the Love of Christ":

> The love of Christ, poor I! may touch upon;
> But 'tis unsearchable. O! there is none
> Its large dimensions can comprehend
> Should they dilate thereon world without end.[24]

George Cheever further adds:. "In all things [connected with Bunyan's allegory] we are brought to Christ, and thrown upon him; and this is the sweet voice of the Pilgrim's Progress, as of the Gospel."[25]

On the other hand, those who have neglected this aspect in their pursuit of lesser concerns in Bunyan studies have usually reflected a degree of impoverishment that is certainly rooted in the neglect of this passion for the Redeemer of sinners.

And so it is the case with regard to *The Pilgrim's Progress* and its undoubted Christocentric emphasis. To study the allegory and avoid this vital core is to likewise be impoverished. On the other hand, to submit to Bunyan's fervent presentation of Christ is to experience a memorable encounter with the essence of the gospel of Paul and Luther.

---

[23] Ibid., I, p. 66.

[24] Ibid., III, p. 760.

[25] George Cheever *Lectures on The Pilgrim's Progress*, p. vi.

CHAPTER TWELVE

Pastoral Emphases in The Pilgrim's Progress

IN the course of seminar teaching on *The Pilgrim's Progress*, one pastor's comment has remained with this writer that has been of great encouragement. It was to the effect that because of the strong pastoral emphasis in the famous allegory, such teaching ought to be a mandatory study requirement for candidates entering the Christian ministry. However, such perception has not always been so readily forthcoming. Consider the following statement taken from B. R. White's article in the esteemed and learned collection of articles titled *John Bunyan, Conventicle and Parnassus*. Under the heading of "The Fellowship of Believers: Bunyan and Puritanism," this Oxford scholar writes: "Christian, Bunyan's pilgrim, was essentially a lonely figure. Admittedly he had counselors such as Evangelist and the Interpreter and, importantly, friends on the way such as Faithful and Hopeful, but the sense of the surrounding presence of a church fellowship was almost completely absent."[1]

It is the last comment that gives cause for concern since it is this writer's opinion that Part One of *The Pilgrim's Progress* is replete with references, both emphatic and indirect, that indicate the significant and edifying role of local church fellowship for earnest pilgrims. Yet in the nineteen pages of this article, while there is detailed consideration of Bunyan Meeting, its origins, setting, and distinctive characteristics, as reflected in an assortment of Bunyan's writings, and apart from the above introductory reference, *The Pilgrim's Progress* does not rate so much as one considered mention, and especially that magnificent and substantial portrayal

[1] B. R. White, "The Fellowship of Believers: Bunyan and Puritanism," *John Bunyan, Conventicle and Parnassus*, ed. N. H. Keeble, p. 1. Pieter de Vries is similarly mistaken when he writes that, "In *The Pilgrim's Progress* the church plays a very modest role," *John Bunyan on the Order of Salvation*, p. 80.

of a faithful nonconformist church, the Palace Beautiful. Due courtesy can only call this omission astonishing!

So we gladly take up the challenge that White's assessment presents, and assert that the doctrine of the church, or the roles of the pastor and the pastorate, are pervasive in *The Pilgrim's Progress*, even as they were in the life and ministry of John Bunyan. This is obviously the stance of Richard Greaves when, in his established doctrinal study of Bunyan, he devotes one of his six main subject heads to the doctrine of the church and calls it, "The Pilgrim's Stately Palace."[2] The problem of perception here is simply a matter of paying attention to Bunyan's introductory poetic exhortation to, "Put by the curtains, look within my veil,"[3] and he intends that some effort will be required. However a certain pastoral sensitivity is also necessary. For this reason a comment of historian Christopher Hill ought to be challenged at this point as well. He states that, "I am neither a literary critic nor a theologian, the two persons best qualified to talk about Bunyan."[4] With the greatest respect, let it be affirmed that the person best qualified to talk about Bunyan is that evangelical pastor who can, to a reasonable degree, enter into the spiritual animus that so dominated his mentor.

PASTOR AND PASTORATE IN THE PILGRIM'S PROGRESS

The Ministry of Evangelist

It would be a fundamental error to impose a modern understanding of the concept of an evangelist upon Bunyan's character, that is an itinerant, somewhat flamboyant and American styled preacher who pursues a decision harvesting trail. Rather, Evangelist here represents a significant facet of the pastoral office indissolubly related, whether traveling or not, to the local church.

To be more specific, the representation here is most likely that of the evangelistic emphasis of Pastor John Gifford. In *Grace Abounding To The Chief Of Sinners* Bunyan relates, himself having been burdened and searching for relief in his soul:

> About this time I began to break my mind to those poor people in Bedford, and to tell them my condition, which, when they had

---

2 Richard L. Greaves, *John Bunyan*, pp. 123-151.

3 John Bunyan, *The Works of John Bunyan*, ed. George Offor, I, p. 167.

4 Christopher Hill, 'John Bunyan and the English Revolution,' *The John Bunyan Lectures 1978*, p. 15.

> heard, they told Mr. Gifford of me, who himself also took occasion to talk with me, and was willing to be 'well' persuaded of me, though I think but from little grounds: but he invited me to his house, where I should hear him confer with others, about the dealings of God with the soul; from all which I still received more conviction, and from that time began to see something of the vanity and inward wretchedness of my wicked heart, for as yet I knew no great matter therein; but now it began to be discovered unto me, and also to work at that rate for wickedness as it never did before.[5]

All three of Evangelist's appearances are pastoral in nature, while each reflects a distinctive aspect of the pastoral office.

His *first* appearance, at the City of Destruction, is as a *seeking evangelist/pastor* who is on the lookout for burdened sinners. The parchment-roll he gives to Christian represents his proclamation ministry from the Word of God, namely, "Fly from the wrath to come" (Matt. 3:7).

His *second* appearance is as a *guiding evangelist/pastor* who rescues wayward sinners. This follows after Mr. Worldly-Wiseman has seduced Christian with a false gospel. Evangelist is a faithful antithesis, while Mr. Worldly-Wiseman represents a professional latitudinarian minister, most likely an Anglican vicar named Edward Fowler, later a Bishop.

His *third* appearance, just before Vanity Fair, is as a *shepherding evangelist/pastor* who nurtures saved sinners. This ongoing concern indicates pastoral integrity through the support of his spiritual offspring after they have been converted. He not only exhorts Christian and Faithful, but also takes on a prophetic role.

The House of the Interpreter

This ministry is that which Good-will (Jesus Christ) at the Wicket-gate has recommended to Christian; that is, here is Jesus Christ's promised legacy of the Holy Spirit (John 14:16-18, 26; 15:26; 16:7-11, 13-14). These seven scenes all represent teaching that Bunyan considers to be necessary for a new convert, as well as that which he received at the Bedford nonconformist church under the pastoral ministry of John Gifford; here indeed was a godly mentor. Not surprisingly it is the first scene that reveals the priority which Bunyan gave to the significance of the godly pastor.

---

[5] Ibid., I, § 77, p. 15.

1. The priority of the portrait of the godly pastor.

This initial scene is declared by Bunyan, via Interpreter, to be of primary importance. "I have showed thee this picture first, because the man whose picture this is, is the only man whom the Lord of the place whither thou art going, hath authorized to be thy guide in all difficult places thou mayest meet with in the way."[6] Such pastoral nurture was only to be found within the confines of this man's residence, that is the forthcoming Palace Beautiful and subsequently the Delectable Mountains.

2. The substance of the portrait of the godly Pastor.

Surely Pastor Gifford, in whom the student tinker's aspirations were embodied, is partly portrayed here. In *Grace Abounding To The Chief Of Sinners*, Bunyan describes how some Christian friends, "told Mr. Gifford of me, who himself took occasion to talk with me, and was 'well' persuaded of me, though I think from but little grounds: but he invited me to his house, where I should hear him confer with others, about the dealings of God with the soul." Following conversion he expresses gratitude for, "holy Mr. Gifford, whose doctrine, by God's grace, was much for my stability."[7]

Bunyan's statue, erected at the corner of St. Peter's Green, Bedford in 1874, is modeled after this scene, and rightly so. Everything about this pastor is rooted in the life of a faithful nonconformist church, especially his capacity to, "beget children, travail in birth with children, and nurse them himself when they are born. . . . his work is to know and unfold dark things to sinners."[8] In other words, he is a spiritual midwife whose business is chiefly conducted in a suitable care center, the local church.

The Palace Beautiful

Here is an exquisitely beautiful and extensive portrayal of a faithful biblical local church, a nonconformist assembly, an outpost of the Celestial City, so necessary for sustained progress.[9]

---

6 Ibid., III, p. 98.

7 Ibid., I, §§ 77, 117, pp. 15, 20.

8 Ibid., III, p. 98.

9 Greaves, *John Bunyan*, p. 123. C. H. Spurgeon devotes two chapters to this matter in his *Pictures from Pilgrim's Progress*, pp. 113-29.

It is fascinating to consider why, in contrast, Faithful does not reside here. In this regard, refer to Chapter 14.

A careful distinction is made here between Bunyan's belief in a separated church gathered out of sinful society and the comprehensive Church of England establishment that was wedded to the monarchial state. In other words, local church membership in a nonconformist fellowship required a testimony to regeneration and personal salvation, in contrast with mere nominal association with the Church of England by the populace in general through the formal administration of water baptism.

Hence, Christian, poised outside the Palace Beautiful, portrays the new convert about to be carefully interviewed before membership in a separated church is granted. Notwithstanding this precautionary investigation, he perceives this edifice to be highly attractive, that is a desirable spiritual oasis in the midst of a wilderness world.

1. Christian's Distressing Approach.

Here the savage opposition of civil and ecclesiastical tyranny, portrayed by two snarling lions, attempts to oppose pilgrims in their desire to associate with a nonconformist fellowship. However, Watchful, the pastor/porter at the Palace gate, like Gifford, encourages Christian to persevere in resisting the opposition and attain edification and rest within God's spiritual retreat, a place built "for the relief and security of pilgrims."[10]

John Brown graphically describes this conflict in his chapter entitled, "The Church in the Storm." He gives instances of the most inhumane enforcement of penalties that were imposed upon people for being guilty of participation in an "unlawful conventicle [religious gathering]."

> Thus, "Justices of the Peace and constables were empowered to break open doors in carrying out its [the *New Conventicles Act*] provisions [of distraining, extracting money or goods in payment of penalties], and Lieutenants and Deputy-lieutenants of Counties were to disperse assemblies with horse and foot, if necessary. . . . This resolute spirit of oppression was met, as is usual in the case of Englishmen, with an equally resolute spirit of resistance.[11]

[10] Bunyan, *Works*, III, p. 106.

[11] John Brown, *John Bunyan*, p. 204.

2. *Christian's initial examination.*

First the porter Watchful, then Discretion, followed by Prudence, Piety, and Charity (reminiscent of the 'three or four poor women' whose godly conversation impressed Bunyan on a sunny day in Bedford?)[12] cautiously examine this pilgrim. Entrance into church membership was not designed to be an easy process.

a. The investigation.

The primary concern here is the discovery that the applicant is a legitimate pilgrim by virtue of his entrance through the Wicket-gate into the way, persevering faith, and a desire to reach the Celestial City. Personal testimony of conversion was a vital concern, since the Palace residents, particularly the pastor and four virtuous ladies, well understood that the entrance of an unconverted member would bring leavening defilement (I Cor. 5:5-8).

b. The Bunyan Meeting pattern.

Gordon Campbell comments:

> An examination of *The Church Book of Bunyan Meeting* shows that Bunyan drew the house rules of the Palace Beautiful from his own church, for it appears that those who desired to join the Bedford church had to wait outside till they were called in. The congregation decided
>
>> that such persons as desire to joyne in fellowship, if upon the conference of our friends with them . . . our saide friends be satisfyed of the truth of the worke of grace in their heartes . . . they shall desire them to come to the next church-meeting, and to waite neare the place assigned for the meeting, that they may be called in. (folio 17)
>
> Bunyan himself was admitted to Gifford's church by such a process.[13]

3. *Christian's examination for edification.*

Following reception into membership, there commences a most beautiful literary vignette describing the ideal internal ministry of a

---

[12] Bunyan, *Works*, I, §§ 37-38, p. 10.

[13] Gordon Campbell, "The Theology of *The Pilgrim's Progress*," *The Pilgrim's Progress, Critical and Historical Views*, ed. Vincent Newey, pp. 251-2.

faithful local church. However, equally attractive, though less well known, is Bunyan's ability to convey the reality of local church life in a poem of 1,310 lines entitled, *A Discourse of the Building, Nature, Excellency, and Government of the House of God.* The following extract well illustrates its insightful teaching:

> Alas! Here's children, here are great with young;
> Here are the sick and weak, as well as strong.
> Here are the cedar, shrub, and bruised reed;
> Yea, here are such who wounded are, and bleed.
> As here are some who in their grammar be,
> So here are others in their A, B, C.
> Some apt to teach, and others hard to learn;
> Some see far off, others can scarce discern.
>
> Although this house thus honorable is,
> Yet 'tis not sinless, many things amiss
> Do happen here, wherefore them to redress,
> We must keep to our rules of righteousness;
> Nor must we think it strange, if sin shall be
> Where virtue is; don't all men plainly see
> That in the holy temple there was dust,
> That to our very gold, there cleaveth rust?
>
> This is the house of God, his dwelling place,
> 'Tis here that we behold his lovely face;
> But if it should polluted be with sin,
> And so abide, he quickly will begin
> To leave it desolate, and then woe to it,
> *Sin and his absence quickly will undo it.*[14]

Having gained entrance, Christian's varied experiences now come under scrutiny so as to reveal the Puritan emphasis on "cases of conscience," that is close examination of personal spiritual problems and a consideration of suitable remedies, cf. William Perkins, Richard Baxter, etc.[15] This searching of Christian prepares him for supper time (I Cor. 11:28).

---

[14] Ibid., II, pp. 583, 587.

[15] One of Bunyan's later writings is entitled, *A Case Of Conscience Resolved*, in which he considers the appropriateness of women conducting their own separate prayer meetings and the like. Bunyan, *Works*, II, pp. 658-74.

a. Concerning his journey thus far.

Here the young pilgrim recounts his travel experiences thus far before very sympathetic, though more mature auditors. Here Christian also reveals his inner desires, struggles, victories, and delights. A local church is a place where the members of the body of Christ are concerned about the spiritual nurture of each other (I Cor. 12:25).

b. Concerning his spiritual interests.

Then follows more sensitive probing with regard to heart experience in which Christian reveals not only problems, but also solutions that are sourced in faithful local church ministry. Of particular encouragement is the pilgrim's anticipation of the Celestial City; such a perspective is given clearer focus within the assembly of God's people.

c. Concerning his family relationships.

Even more sensitive questioning concerns the absence of Christian's wife and children, in response to which he explains the opposition they expressed to going on pilgrimage. Emphasis is placed upon the church member's responsibility to conduct himself before his family, unlike Talkative, in a godly, virtuous, and winsome manner.

4. Christian's enrichment at supper.

Here is a precious jewel in Bunyan's allegorical casket. Following a period of examination, Christian shares in a banquet, that is the Lord's Supper which is a remembrance of the mercy and glories of Christ, as a warrior, savior, and protector. There is nothing sacramental here, rather rich remembrance, by means of spiritually nourishing emblems, concerning Christ's redeeming glory and generous, gracious benefits.

a. The discussion at the Lord's table.

As a warrior, Christ triumphed over the prince of death, though he shed much blood in the process. As a savior, he determined to exalt poor pilgrims, even though they were born beggars and their nature originated from the dunghill. As a protector, he became the sovereign guardian of the Palace, resisting even the very gates of hell (Matt. 16:18).

In *Christian Behavior*, Bunyan writes:

> It is the ordinance of God, that Christians should be often asserting the things of God each to others; and that by their so doing they should edify one another (Heb. 10:24-25; I Thess. 5:11). The doctrine of the gospel is like the dew and the small rain that distilleth upon the tender grass, wherewith it doth flourish, and is kept green (Deut. 32:2). Christians are like the several flowers in a garden, that have upon each of them the dew of heaven, which being shaken with the wind, they let fall their dew at each other's roots, whereby they are jointly nourished, and become nourishers of one another. For Christians to commune savorily of God's matters one with another, it is as if they opened to each other's nostrils boxes of perfume.[16]

b. The blessings of the Lord's table.

The resultant blessing is that of Christian finding both peace and rest in his own heart as well as in the midst of corporate fellowship. The source of this peace and rest has been the focusing of the pilgrim's vision upon the gospel mercies of Jesus Christ. Here is the dynamic which causes, "all bitterness and wrath and anger and clamor and slander . . . with all malice" to be done away with in local church life (Eph. 4:30-5:2). Thus participation in the Lord's Supper ought to be productive of peace, rest, refreshment, and spiritual renewal for further travel.

It is not surprising that Christian awakes, as the next day dawns, with a newfound invigoration that expresses itself in joyful song. The words exalt in the ecstasy of church fellowship that may be likened to residing "next door to heaven."[17]

5. Christian's instruction for edification.

The emphasis concerning local church activity now changes from one of fellowship in the truth to that of instruction in the truth, that is "the apostles' doctrine" (Acts 2:42), via "pastors and teachers," so that the members might be "edified" (Eph. 4:11-12). While Christian is presently unaware of his impending contest with Apollyon, yet his Palace guides seem to appreciate the need of every available means of grace. Thus he is equipped with personal information, fortification, and vision. These remain abiding priorities for local church ministry.

---

[16] Bunyan, *Works*, II, p. 570. Offor rightly lauds this exquisite portrayal.

[17] Ibid., III, p. 110.

a. The study.

Here is a presentation of Bible truth that every pilgrim ought to know about, including the valiant acts of servants of the Lord, the mercies of the Lord toward great sinners, Palace (church) history, prophecies concerning their Lord, the nations, and the climax of the ages.

b. The armory.

Here the supply of suitable weaponry for pilgrims is inexhaustible. There is also a display of encouraging memorabilia associated with valiant saints of the past. In a later writing entitled *The House of the Forest of Lebanon*, Bunyan comments:

> The church also in the wilderness, even in her porch or first entrance into it, is full of pillars, apostles, prophets, and martyrs of Jesus. There also hang up the shields that the old warriors have used, and are plastered upon the walls the brave achievements which they have done. There are also such encouragements there for those that stand, that one would think none that came thither with pretense to serve there would, for very shame, attempt to go back again.[18]

c. The rooftop vista.

Christian's guides suggest an edifying rooftop perspective, having a heavenward focus, in the face of the pilgrim's eagerness to be on his way. While due to sin and dissension, the view could be hazy, on this occasion the closeness and unity of genuine fellowship have ensured that the way ahead may be viewed with breathtaking clarity. So the Delectable Mountains, another encouraging pastoral port of call, are recognized in the midst of Immanuel's Land, from where the Celestial City may be viewed.

6. Christian's personal equipping.

The pilgrim is then personally equipped in the armory with the weapons necessary for warfare, "the full armor of God," as described in Ephesians 6:10-18. Further, a supply of Christ's emblems, "a loaf of bread, a bottle of wine, and a cluster of raisins," are also provided.[19] Thus Christian's departure is from the

---

[18] Ibid., III, p. 535.

[19] Ibid., p. 111.

protective and strengthening fellowship of a local church out into the howling wilderness of this world.

The Pastoral Deception of By-ends and Company

A devotee of the comfortable religion of mammon, By-ends unashamedly confesses that, being a citizen of the town of Fair-speech, he is also related to Mr. Two-tongues, the local parson; most likely he is also another Bunyan representation of a Latitudinarian minister within the Church of England. Having been joined with his three former school friends, Mr. Hold-the-World, Mr. Money-love, and Mr. Save-all, this foursome recommends the pastoral wiles of a professional pastor who uses religion for self-advancement. Doubtless Bunyan portrays here establishment ministers who are ambitious for promotion by means of flexible convictions and accommodation to human carnality. This portrayal represents the pastoral office in a way that is so antithetical to Bunyan's biblical convictions and practice.

In particular, Mr. Money-love admiringly hypothesizes about a minister who aspires to be appointed to a more prosperous church. As a consequence, he adjusts his preaching and principles to gain acceptance. He further propounds that a tradesman who attends church to profit materially from marrying a wealthy lady is to be commended for his initiative. Thus all four agree that these situations represent church life as it ought to be, only to find themselves under the withering condemnation of Christian.

The Awakening in Doubting Castle

While the week days of captivity under Giant Despair are arid and depressing to Christian and Hopeful, even to the point of contemplating suicide, yet as Saturday evening concludes there commences a change of circumstances. So we read:

> Well, on Saturday, about midnight, they began to pray, and continued in prayer till almost break of day. Now, a little before it was day, good Christian, as one half-amazed, brake out in his passionate speech: What a fool, quoth he, am I, thus to lie in a stinking dungeon, when I may as well walk in liberty! I have a key in my bosom, called Promise, that will, I am persuaded, open any lock in Doubting Castle.[20]

The strong inference of Bunyan here is that, while the week up to Saturday had been parched and depressing, following prayer at

---

[20] Ibid, p. 142.

the dawning of the Lord's day, that is on Sunday morning, suddenly the light of God's promises in His word, pastorally proclaimed, dispels the captivity that darkness has brought; indeed it brings the paralysis of despair. In *The Jerusalem Sinner Saved*, Bunyan writes:

> Despair! When we have a God of mercy, and a redeeming Christ alive! For shame, forbear; let them despair that dwell where there is no God, and are confined to those chambers of death which can be quenched by no redemption. . . . Oh! So long as where we are where promises swarm, where mercy is proclaimed, where grace reigns, and where Jerusalem [big] sinners are privileged with the first offer of mercy, it is a base thing to despair.[21]

The Fellowship at the Delectable Mountains

Here is another perspective on the separatist local church which Bunyan pastored at Bedford. However John Kelman rightly points out, "the former [representation at the Palace Beautiful] was elementary and preparatory: this is advanced enlightenment and guidance among spiritual heights. It is a place of contemplation such as is possible only after ripe experience."[22]

The plurality of pastors comprises Knowledge, Experience, Watchful, and Sincere, whose "oversight" is from the tops of these peaks. They care for their flocks that graze by the side of the highway. By means of their hospitable ministry, both hope and fear are stimulated. In Part Two they welcome Mr. Great-heart with his large company of pilgrims and, having invited both weak and strong to enjoy their entertainment, "had them to the palace door."[23] Bunyan clearly identifies this gathering as a fellowship in association with the Palace Beautiful.

Here is instruction, comfort, and rest. For these and other reasons true pilgrims find this place of residence to be exceedingly "delectable," that is tasty to the redeemed soul. In *The Desire Of The Righteous Granted*, Bunyan writes: "Church fellowship, rightly managed, is the glory of all the world. No place, no community, no fellowship, is adorned and bespangled with those beauties as is a church rightly knit together to their head, and lovingly serving one another. . . . Hence the church is called the

---

21 Ibid., I, p. 92.

22 John Kelman, *The Road*, II, p. 67.

23 Bunyan, *Works*, III, p. 230.

place of God's desire on earth (Ps. 132:13-16)."[24] Thus follows a tour of the region that includes instruction from the heights designed to preserve the pilgrims from the unholy depths of a shipwrecked faith.

1. *The hill called Error.*

Below this peak are the dashed remains of heretics such as Hymenaeus and Philetus (II Tim. 2:16-18) who pervert the doctrine of the resurrection. Concerning this passage of the Apostle Paul, William Hendriksen comments: "They resembled those present-day liberals who, while refusing to be caught saying, 'There is no resurrection.' allegorize the concept."[25] These torn remains also represent the strewn wreckage of sectarian folly (Rom. 16:17), scholastic idolatry (II Tim. 3:7), and fascination with doctrinal novelty (Acts 17:21).

2. *The mountain called Caution.*

Here is a sequel to the previous episode of Christian and Hopeful's escape from Doubting Castle. Below this peak are blind men stumbling amongst tombs, gashing themselves, and appearing to be beyond rescue. To the mouth-stopping horror of the escorted pilgrims, these are but other doomed captives of Giant Despair. Not surprisingly we read, "Then Christian and Hopeful shamefully looked upon one another, with tears gushing out, but yet said nothing to the Shepherds."[26] Their gaunt and palid expressions, accompanied with bodily tremors, shrowded the inner silent chorus of, 'There but for the grace of God go we' (I Cor. 15:10).

3. *The By-way to Hell.*

In a valley adjoining an unnamed hill is a door to Hell which, when opened, spews forth flame, sulphur fumes, and the cries of tormented souls. Previous entrants have included Esau, Judas, Alexander the blasphemer, and Ananias and Sapphira. This sober vista warns that many false pilgrims can persevere for great distances, even beyond this point. Thus Christian and Hopeful exclaim, "We had need to cry to the Strong for strength."[27]

---

[24] Ibid., I, pp. 757-8.

[25] William Hendriksen, *I & II Timothy and Titus*, p. 265.

[26] Bunyan, *Works*, III, p. 145.

[27] Ibid., p. 145.

4. The telescopic view from the hill Clear.

By way of contrast is an encouraging vista, one which faithful pastors will always continue to offer to their flocks. From the hill Clear, with hands still trembling on account of the sobering effect of the previous revelation, yet Christian and Hopeful are able catch a glimpse, through the "perspective glass [telescope]," of the glory of the Celestial City. As a result they burst into song:

Thus, by the Shepherds, secrets are reveal'd,
Which from all other men are kept conceal'd.
Come to the Shepherds, then if you would see
Things deep, things hid, and that mysterious be.[28]

In Bunyan's poetic discourse concerning *The Building, Nature, Excellency, And Government Of The House Of God*, he describes this same pastoral priority, of a faithful seventeenth century church, that longingly looks from earth toward heaven:

Such mountains round about this house do stand
As one from thence may see the holy land.[29]

5. The parting pastoral exhortation.

Each Shepherd provides the pilgrims with his own distinctive piece of farewell counsel. Knowledge supplies a map of the way before them. Experience warns of the Flatterer ahead. Watchful cautions against sleeping on the Enchanted Ground. Sincere prays that God will give them speed and safety. Again from *The Building, Nature, Excellency, And Government Of The House Of God*, Bunyan describes these shepherd/pastors thus:

This officer is call'd a steward too,
Cause with his master's cash he has to do,
And has authority it to disburse
To those that want, or for that treasure thirst.[30]

The Fellowship at Beulah Land

Here is the choicest of territory this side of the Celestial City. It is almost a suburb of heaven. The former terrors of the Valley of

---

[28] Ibid.

[29] Ibid., II, p. 579.

[30] Ibid., p. 581.

the Shadow of Death, Giant Despair and Doubting Castle cannot reach pilgrims in this region. Here is rich refreshment, by means of orchards and gardens, for pilgrims just prior to their crossing of the River of Death. Further, the King's gardener gives every assistance including a personally escorted tour of the local features. His identification is most likely another aspect of the pastoral office, as was the case with Evangelist. Here he cultivates nourishment and focuses upon comforting senior pilgrims as they anticipate the final stage of their journey.

PASTOR BUNYAN IN THE PILGRIM'S PROGRESS

It is abundantly clear that the whole pastoral vision of John Bunyan is interwoven throughout *The Pilgrim's Progress*. After the doctrine of the gospel, it appears to be the doctrine of the church and its biblical administration that so often occupies his thoughts.

The Pastoral Influences on John Bunyan

While the Bible dominated Bunyan's every consideration, yet there were other factors that directed his thinking concerning the role of the local church and its shepherd. In a fraternal sense, there were the friendships of John Gifford, John Burton, William Dell and John Owen. All of these were thoroughly convinced concerning the matter of church independency. From an opposite perspective was the nonconformist assessment, born of fearful experience, that the Church of England gave obvious evidence of its episcopal system being irreconcilable with the biblical pattern.

The Pastoral Influence of John Bunyan

Who can tell just how many at the pastoral level have themselves been pastored by John Bunyan? Preeminent in this regard would be C. H. Spurgeon whose indebtedness will be dealt with in Chapter 13. However, numerous other Christian leaders have confessed their gratitude, not only for Bunyan's works in general, but especially *The Pilgrim's Progress*.

1. George Whitefield.

> Perhaps, next to the first publishers of the gospel of the blessed God, these sayings were never more strongly exemplified in any single individual (at least in this, or the last century) than in the conversion, ministry and writings of that eminent servant of Jesus Christ, Mr. John Bunyan, who was of the meanest occupation, and a notorious sabbath-breaker, drunkard, swearer, blasphemer, &c.

by habitual practice; and yet, through rich, free, sovereign, distinguishing grace, he was chosen, called, and afterwards formed, by the all-powerful operations of the Holy Spirit, to be a scribe ready instructed to the kingdom of God. The two volumes of his works formerly published [in 1736], with the success that attended them in pulling down Satan's strong-holds in sinners' hearts, when sent forth in small detached parties, are pregnant proofs of this. Some of them have gone through a great variety of editions. His *Pilgrim's Progress,* in particular, has been translated into various languages, and to this day is read with the greatest pleasure, not only by the truly serious, of different religious persuasions, but likewise by those to whom pleasure is the end of reading. Surely it is an original, and we may say of it, to use the words of the great Doctor Goodwin in his preface to the Epistle to the Ephesians, that it smells of the prison. It was written when the author was confined in Bedford gaol. And ministers never write or preach so well as when under the cross: the spirit of Christ and of glory then rests upon them.[31]

2. John Newton

Soon after I returned from Yorkshire, I began to expound the Pilgrim's Progress in our meetings on Tuesday evenings; and though we have been almost seven months traveling with the pilgrim, we have not yet left the house Beautiful; but I believe we shall set off for the Valley of Humiliation in about three weeks. I find this book so full of matter, that I can seldom go through more than a page, or half a page at a time. I hope the attempt has been greatly blessed among us; and for myself, it has perhaps given me deeper insight into John Bunyan's knowledge, judgment, and experience in the Christian life, that I should ever have had without it.[32]

3. J. Gresham Machen.

"[T]hat tenderest and most theological of books, the 'Pilgrim's Progress' of John Bunyan . . . is pulsating with life in every word."[33]

Only in eternity will the full extent of Bunyan's ministry be estimated, when innumerable pastors thank God for his biblical legacy and wise pastoral guidance. This is not to say that such a

---

31 John Bunyan, *The Works of that Eminent Servant of Christ, Mr. John Bunyan*, I, pp. v-vi.

32 John Newton, *The Works Of The Rev. John Newton*, VI, pp. 37-8.

33 J. Gresham Machen, *Christianity and Liberalism*, p. 46.

godly icon was void of any indiscretion. His innocent though perhaps unguarded encounter with Agnes Beaumont provides an illustration of how necessary it is for a pastor to be circumspect at all times.[34] However, an elegy at Bunyan's death is the best measure of the man.

> He in the pulpit preached truth first, and then
> He in his practice preached it o'er again.[35]

ACTIVE CHURCH MEMBERSHIP

> *This house then is no nurse to idleness:*
> *Fig-trees are here to keep, and vines to dress;*
> *Here's work for all; yea, work that must be done;*
> *Yet work, like that, to playing in the sun;*
> *No drone must hide himself under those eaves;*
> *Who sows not, will in harvest reap no sheaves.*
> *The slothful man himself, may plainly see,*
> *That honey's gotten by the working bee.*

John Bunyan
A Discourse of the Building, &c.,
Of the House of God
Works, II, p. 587

---

[34] In 1674, when single Agnes Beaumont, aged 21, urgently needed a ride from her brother's farmhouse to a Bedford Church meeting at Gamlingay, on seeing Pastor Bunyan ride up, she pressed for a ride on the back of John's horse. He reluctantly agreed. However, Agnes' father was enraged when he espied the manner of his daughter's riding away and so locked her out of his house that evening. Though she was soon received home, within a week Agnes' father suddenly died. As a result, opponents of Bunyan started rumors concerning a poisoning and adultery. Eventually John was fully cleared, though he must have regretted giving that ride to begin with. Refer to Brown, *John Bunyan*, pp. 225-7; John Bunyan, *Grace Abounding to the Chief of Sinners*, ed. Roger Sharrock, pp. 176-80.

[35] Bunyan, *Works*, I, p. lxxiv.

CHAPTER THIRTEEN

C. H. Spurgeon and The Pilgrim's Progress

THE most notable preacher of Victorian England was surely Charles Haddon Spurgeon, pastor of the Metropolitan Tabernacle located at Newington in the south bank region of London. From the boy preacher wonder aged nineteen to the seasoned Baptist leader of British nonconformity, with 6000 regularly being packed into his Sunday services, this prince of the evangelical pulpit gave constant acknowledgment of his indebtedness to John Bunyan as to no other spiritual mentor. This is no idle proposal since his son Thomas suggests that, "I am pretty sure that his answer to the query, 'Who is your favorite author?' was, 'John Bunyan.' He has spoken of him over and over again as 'my great favorite,' and has left on record that he had read *The Pilgrim's progress* at least one hundred times."[1]

In *Grace Abounding To The Chief Of Sinners*, Bunyan gives ready appreciation concerning his spiritual benefactor and counselor, Pastor John Gifford. So, in like manner, Spurgeon seems to have sat at the feet of the Bedford tinker to the point where there is easily recognized a passion that both held in common for the saving grace of God that must be earnestly pressed upon sinners of every kind. In this regard consider Spurgeon's gospel tract "Around The Wicket Gate" that not only draws upon Bunyan's famous scene in *The Pilgrim's* Progress, where Christian becomes an authentic pilgrim, but also contains a similar fervency that urges hesitating sinners to delay no longer, but rather heed the welcoming call of the Lord Jesus Christ.

Most likely the preeminent quality of *The Pilgrim's Progress* in the mind of Spurgeon was its seamless weaving of the Word of God in such an appealing manner that he freely acknowledged it as having second rank, after the Bible, because of this unique

---

1 Thomas Spurgeon, Editor's Introduction, C. H. Spurgeon, *Pictures from Pilgrim's Progress*, p. 5.

characteristic. Thus he confesses: "It [The Pilgrim's Progress] is a volume of which I never seem to tire; and the secret of its freshness is that it is so largely compiled from the Scriptures."[2]

The Formative Years

1. As a young lad in his grandfather's library.

When living for several years with his grandfather, who was a Baptist pastor at Stambourne, Essex, the boy Spurgeon loved to spend time in a small dark room, the study in which there was a collection of books that greatly attracted him. Among many volumes representing classic English Protestantism, an illustrated version of *The Pilgrim's Progress* especially captured his attention. He recalls, following his conversion:

> John Bunyan could not have written as he did if he had not been dragged about by the devil for many years. I love that picture of dear old Christian. I know, when I first read *The Pilgrim's Progress*, and saw in it the woodcut of Christian carrying the burden on his back, I felt so interested in the poor fellow, that I thought I should jump with joy when, after he had carried his heavy load so long, he at last got rid of it; and that was how I felt when the burden of guilt, which I had borne so long, was for ever rolled away from my shoulders and my heart.[3]

A friend also related that at the age of fifteen Spurgeon was heard to recite long passages from *Grace Abounding*.[4]

2. As a young pastor nearing marriage.

In 1854, when Spurgeon first preached at New Park Street Chapel in London, a young lady named Susannah Thompson was in attendance who would eventually become his beloved wife on January 8, 1856. Courtship was possible through their frequent meeting since Susannah was often a visitor at the home of Deacon Olney where the young Spurgeon was periodically entertained. Eighteen months before their marriage, Spurgeon gave this young lady a gift being an illustrated copy of *The Pilgrim's Progress* with the following inscription: "Miss Thomson, with desires for her progress in the blessed pilgrimage, from C. H. Spurgeon, April 20,

---

[2] C. H. Spurgeon, *Pictures from Pilgrim's Progress*, p. 11.

[3] C. H. Spurgeon, *The Great Change—Conversion*, p. 9.

[4] C. H. Spurgeon, *C. H. Spurgeon's Autobiography*, I, pp. 24-5, 56-7.

1854."[5] Mrs. Spurgeon later writes: "I do not think that my beloved had at that time any other thought concerning me than to help a struggling soul Heavenward; but I was greatly impressed by his concern for me, and the book became very precious as well as helpful."[6]

The Common Characteristics

Both Bunyan and Spurgeon were probably of French extraction. John Brown writes concerning the Bedford preacher that, "in 1219 the form of the name was Buignon, really an old French word. . . . [I]t is more probable that the Bunyans sprang from those Northmen who came to us through Normandy."[7] The London pastor of the Metropolitan Tabernacle was a descendant of the Protestant Hugenots who fled from persecution in France.[8] Both were of baptistic convictions, believing in nonconformity, baptism by immersion upon confession of faith, though Bunyan was less rigid in not requiring baptism for church membership. Both lacked formal university and theological education, though it is apparent that extraordinary natural ability, which God was able to harness, enabled them to learn from godly colleagues and pursue self-study with intense earnestness. Neither scorned the learning of the godly, yet they could be severe on sterile establishment religion that trusted more on water baptism and formality rather than heart transforming conversion.

1. As pastors.

Both were gifted preachers possessing great fluency and powers of expression. While Spurgeon drew immense crowds in London, even as many as 24,000 at the Crystal Palace, yet Bunyan, who is said to have turned down invitations to pastor churches much larger than the Bedford meeting, could draw 1,200 in London on a working day at 7.00 am in the dark of winter with 24 hours notice; on a Sunday he would draw 3,000.[9] Both were gifted writers whose publications were circulated world wide. If Bunyan could claim to have produced the second most widely published piece of literature after the English Bible, *The Pilgrim's Progress*, Spurgeon could

---

5 Ibid., II, pp. 11-12.

6 Charles Ray, *Mrs. Surgeon*, p. 9.

7 John Brown, *John Bunyan*, p. 19.

8 E. C. Dargan, *A History of Preaching*, II, pp. 534-5.

9 Charles Doe, 'The Struggler,' Bunyan, *Works*, III, pp. 766-7.

claim to have produced the most widely circulated collection of sermons in the history of the Christian Church, the *Metropolitan Tabernacle Pulpit*. Both were beloved and able pastors whose pulpit and literary skills did not lead to isolation in study resulting in the neglect of shepherding. Certainly Spurgeon had secretarial help and considerable financial support. However both were accessible, with Bunyan never forgetting the pastoral encouragement of John Gifford when spiritually adrift, while Spurgeon regularly counseled congregants, enjoyed the company of orphans at the Stockwell Orphanage, and invested much time in the lives of students at the Pastor's College when in training, as well as when pastoring in close and distant regions.

Furthermore, it should not be forgotten that both Bunyan and Spurgeon were blessed with godly wives who provided unfailing support even as did their children.

2. As Calvinists.

However, in terms of that which most closely knit these two souls together, it would most certainly be their passion for the gospel of the sovereign grace of God. In plain terms, Bunyan and Spurgeon were both thoroughgoing Calvinists, perhaps with Bunyan having closer alignment with Luther. Spurgeon recounts:

> Well can I remember the manner in which I learned the doctrines of grace in a single instant. . . . I can recall the very day and hour when first I received those truths in my own soul,—when they were, as John Bunyan says, burnt into my heart as with a hot iron; and I can recollect how I felt that I had grown on a sudden from a babe into a man.[10]

Nevertheless this emphasis on the sovereignty of God was never merely cerebral or academic. Both Bunyan and Spurgeon were fervent in their proclamation of free grace through Christ, especially in doctrinal terms that were rooted in the Reformation. At the same time there was an immediacy with both that pressed the gospel upon hesitating and burdened sinners with great urgency and experiential expectation; there was to be no delay on account of preparationism or qualified and stilted offers of redemption due to reasonings concerning God's regard for the elect and non-elect. Rather, Bunyan declares in *Come and Welcome to Jesus Christ*, "Coming sinner, see here the willingness of Christ to save; see here how free he is to communicate life, and all good things, to such as

---

[10] C. H. Spurgeon, *C. H. Spurgeon's Autobiography*, I, pp. 181-2.

thou art. He complains, if thou comest not; he is displeased if thou callest not upon him."[11] Likewise Spurgeon writes in *Around The Wicket Gate*, after the manner of his mentor:

> It comes to this, my friend, as it did with John Bunyan; a voice now speaks to you, and says, 'Wilt thou keep thy sin and go to hell? Or leave thy sin and go to heaven?' The point should be decided before you quit the spot. In the name of God, I ask you. Which shall it be—Christ and salvation, or the favorite sin and damnation?[12]

The Pulpit Ministry

The formal preaching of C. H. Spurgeon at New Park Street Chapel and the Metropolitan Tabernacle spanned over 35 years, from 1854-1891. A close study of this ministry reveals a pervasive influence by John Bunyan that not only proves the earlier contention of his son Thomas, that the Bedford pastor was his father's favorite author, but also that this seventeenth century nonconformist was more influential in the depths of Spurgeon's soul than any other individual. Consider the following details which are derived from *The New Park Street Pulpit* and the *Metropolitan Tabernacle Pulpit* that are presently published in 63 volumes.[13]

1. Frequent references.

Within the 3561 published sermons that comprise Spurgeons's pulpit ministry, the name of John Bunyan occurs 779 times and far exceeds the mentioning of numerous other revered saints such as Luther, Calvin, Owen, Baxter, Charnock, Henry, Whitefield, Gill, Newton, etc. Making certain allowances, this means that Spurgeon made reference to Bunyan, on average, every sixth sermon he preached for thirty-five years. Other publications such as *Lectures*

---

[11] Bunyan, *Works*, I, p. 298. Andrew Fuller rejected the denial of gospel invitations by Hyper Calvinists: "I had read pretty much of Dr. Gill's Body of Divinity, and from many parts of it had received considerable instruction. I perceived, however, that the system of Bunyan was not the same with his; for that while he maintained the doctrines of election and predestination, he nevertheless held with the free offer of salvation to sinners without distinction." *The Complete Works of the Rev. Andrew Fuller*, I, p. 15.

[12] C. H. Spurgeon, *Around The Wicket Gate*, p. 36.

[13] These 63 volumes were accessed using *The C. H. Spurgeon Collection*, a compact disc published by Ages Digital Library. All page numbers refer to this pagination.

To My Students, *An All-Around Ministry*, *Morning and Evening*, *Spurgeon's Autobiography*, *The Treasury of David*, and the monthly magazine *The Sword and Trowel,* all indicate frequent references to Bunyan and his ministry.

2. Detailed exposition.

There is a profound understanding of *The Pilgrim's Progress,* both parts, *Grace Abounding To The Chief Of Sinners*, and *The Holy War.* All of these works are frequently referenced, and often the mention of one incident or character will stimulate the recollection of another. The range of characters that Spurgeon references is truly kaleidoscopic. Often a page of exposition and application will focus on a multiplicity of personalities derived from a notable allegorical scene, while Bunyan aphorisms abound. In particular there are six sermons that are devoted to specific allegorical situations. They are:

a. Sermon 64, 1856, "The Enchanted Ground," with the text, I Thessalonians 5:6. Believers are exhorted to beware of slumbering even as were Christian and Hopeful by one of the Shepherds at the Delectable Mountains. Supporting references include the Hill Difficulty, the savage lions, Apollyon, Giant Despair, and Beulah land.

b. Sermon 205, 1858, "A Lecture For Little-faith," with the text, II Thessalonians 1:3. Little-faith is compared with Ready-to-halt, Mr. Fearing, Mr. Despondency, Miss Much-afraid, Mr. Feeble-mind, Great-heart, Valiant-for-truth, while Spurgeon also constructs his own Great-faith, Strong-faith, and Mr. Great-trouble.

c. Sermons 297-8, 1860, "Mr. Evil Questioning Tried And Executed," with the text, II Kings 5:12. Based upon *The Holy War*, Mr. Evil-questioning is a Diabolonian with the deceitful alias of Honest-enquiring; he is married to No-hope having children named Legal-life, Unbelief, Wrong-thoughts-of-Christ, Clip-promise, Carnal-sense, Live-by-feeling, and Self-love. Having despised the work of the Holy Spirit, he is judged guilty and hanged in Bad-street.

d. Sermon 777, 1867, "Helps," with the text, I Corinthians 12:28. The spiritual gift that Paul defines is associated with Christian's rescuer at the Slough of Despond. Thus, "'helps,' if I understand Bunyan aright, are stationed all round the borders of the Slough of Despond, and it is their business to keep watch all round and listen for the cries of any poor benighted travelers who may be staggering in the mire."[14]

e. Sermon 3449, 1870, "Buying The Truth," with the text, Proverbs 23:23. The resistance of Christian and Faithful to worldly overtures at Vanity Fair prompts their cry to "buy the truth." Spurgeon interprets this as preference for biblical truth that is doctrinal, experimental, and practical, being sourced in Christ, "without money and without price."

3. *Distinctive reverence.*

There is profound esteem for the author of *The Pilgrim's Progress* that knows no other human parallel. For instance, Bunyan is named the "half-inspired" master in the realm of allegory,[15] whose brilliant simplicity is acknowledged as follows:

> Why did John Bunyan become the apostle of Bedfordshire, and Huntingdonshire, and round about? It was because John Bunyan, while he had a surpassing genius, would not condescend to cull his language from the garden of flowers, but he went into the hayfield and the meadow, and plucked up his language by the roots, and spoke out in words that the people used in their cottages.[16]

The foundation of such singular devotion on Spurgeon's part is later explained: "Next to the Bible, the book that I value most is John Bunyan's 'Pilgrim's Progress,' and I imagine I may have read that through perhaps a hundred times; it is a book of which I never seem to tire, but then the secret of that is, that John Bunyan's 'Pilgrim's Progress' is the Bible in another shape. It is the same heavenly water taken out of this same well of the gospel."[17]

4. *Experiential identification.*

There is an empathetic attitude on Spurgeon's part since in the Bedford tinker he found a kindred spirit in much the same way that Bunyan found a kindred spirit in Luther. So he affectionately refers to "honest John" or "Master John" and will not suffer literary critics who opine that Bunyan was too self-absorbed:

---

14 C. H. Spurgeon, *Metropolitan Tabernacle Pulpit*, V.13, p. 729.

15 Ibid., V. 9, p. 293; V. 11, p. 93.

16 Ibid., V. 3, p. 99.

17 Ibid., V. 47, pp. 259-60.

> Southey, [the British poet laureate] in his "Life of Bunyan," seems at a difficulty to understand how Bunyan could have used such depreciating language concerning his own character. For it is true, according to all we know of his biography [*Grace Abounding*], that he was not, except in the case of profane swearing, at all so bad as the most of the villagers. Indeed, there were some virtues in the man which were worthy of all commendation. Southey attributes it to a morbid state of mind, but we rather ascribe it to a return of spiritual health. Had the excellent poet seen himself in the same heavenly light as that in which Bunyan saw himself, he would have discovered that Bunyan did not exaggerate, but was simply stating as far as he could a truth which utterly surpassed his powers of utterance.[18]

Another instance of heartfelt loyalty concerns the flight from Doubting Castle by Christian and Faithful where,

> according to Master Bunyan, the key [promise] turned in the great lock which locked the [outer] iron gate. To use John Bunyan's own words, he says, "That lock went damnable hard." In all the new editions of "Pilgrim's Progress," it is put, "That lock went desperate hard." That is the more refined way of putting it, but John Bunyan meant just what he said, and implied that there was a sense of the wrath of God upon the soul of man on account of sin, so that he felt as if he were near even to perdition itself. And yet, at such a time, the key did turn in the lock, and the iron gate was opened.[19]

The Lecture Series

Following Spurgeon's death in 1891, discovery was made of manuscripts of addresses on *The Pilgrim's Progress*, including both parts, that he most likely gave "at Monday evening prayer-meetings with the special purpose of edifying such as had just begun to go on pilgrimage."[20] Many of these were subsequently published in *The Sword And Trowel.* They all exude a spiritual enthusiasm that found the allegorical master providing such a catalyst by which Spurgeon could be evangelistically ignited.

---

[18] Ibid., V. 14, p. 185. This same opinion is repeated in V. 15, p. 601; V. 26, p. 911. Like Southey, Richard Greaves expresses this doubtful estimate. *John Bunyan and English Nonconformity*, p. 194.

[19] Ibid., V. 59, pp. 472-3.

[20] Thomas Spurgeon, Editor's Introduction, *C. H. Spurgeon, Pictures from Pilgrim's Progress*, p. 4.

Concerning Christian's jubilant response at his being delivered of his burden at the cross, Spurgeon declared:

> Well might poor Pilgrim, having lost his load, give three great leaps for joy and go on singing:—
>
> Blest Cross! Blest sepulcher! Blest rather be
> The man that there was put to shame for me!
>
> Believer, do you recollect the day when your fetters fell off? Do you remember the place where Jesus met you and said, "I have loved thee with an everlasting love; I have blotted out as a cloud thy transgressions, and as a thick cloud thy sins; they shall not be mentioned against thee any more for ever?" Oh! What a sweet season is that when Jesus takes away the pain of sin. When the Lord first pardoned my sin, I was so joyous that I could scarce refrain from dancing. I thought on my road home from the house where I had been set at liberty, that I must tell the stones in the street the story of my deliverance.[21]

Encouragement to Believe

Coming sinner, the Jesus to whom thou art coming is lowly in heart, he despiseth not any. It is not thy outward meanness, nor thy inward weakness; it is not because thou art poor, or base, or deformed, or a fool, that he will despise thee: he hath chosen the foolish, the base, and despised things of this world, to confound the wise and mighty. He will bow his ear to thy stammering prayers; he will pick out the meaning of thy inexpressible groans; he will respect thy weakest offering, if there be in it but thy heart. Now, is not this a blessed Christ, coming sinner? Art thou not like to fare well, when thou hast embraced him, coming sinner?

John Bunyan
Come and Welcome to Jesus Christ
Works, I, p. 297

---

[21] C. H. Spurgeon, *Pictures from Pilgrim's Progress*, p. 85.

CHAPTER FOURTEEN

The Companionship of Christian and Faithful

THERE is something very attractive and endearing about the warmth of spiritual friendship that develops between Christian and Faithful, fellow-citizens from the City of Destruction, when they eventually meet just beyond the Valley of Humiliation. George Cheever describes this initial acquaintance as follows: "What happiness it was for these Christians to meet each other! What delightful comparison of each other's experience, what strengthening of each other's faith and joy!"[1] This being so, it would seem difficult to avoid the real possibility that such a relationship reflects intimate details concerning a valued friendship of Bunyan himself. But more of this speculation later on.

Christian First Leaves the City of Destruction

Although Christian is deeply distressed at having to leave behind his wife and children, separation with regard to other social relationships in the City of Destruction does not appear to trouble him. Hence, knowing that Faithful is also residing in the same city at that time, we conclude that any knowledge they had of each other was quite insignificant. The next incident that presents some connection between these two as pilgrims, quite a distance ahead, concerns Christian's lone fearful passing of the savage lions and immediate relief on lodging at the Palace Beautiful for four nights.

Here Christian is informed by the Porter at the Palace Beautiful that Faithful has recently passed by without taking up temporary residence. Having passed through the Valley of Humiliation with considerable trial, subsequently in the Valley of the Shadow of Death Christian hears Faithful cry out a short way ahead, "Though I walk through the valley of the shadow of death, I will fear no evil, for thou art with me" (Ps. 23:4). Emerging from this trial he

---

1 George B. Cheever, *Lectures on The Pilgrim's Progress*, p. 230.

sees Faithful a short distance ahead and eventually catches up with him in circumstances that are both humiliating and comforting.

Faithful follows from the City of Destruction

In later testimony Faithful indicates that it was the influence of Christian's warning of imminent judgment, just before this pilgrim's departure from the City of Destruction, that led to his own ensuing flight as well. His meeting with Madam Wanton, Adam the First, Moses, Discontent, and Shame, suggests a carnal weakness while lacking the pride of Christian. On this occasion Faithful discovers the lions to be asleep, and so passes by without any harassment; he is then greeted by the Porter of the Palace Beautiful, but on account of it still being midday, he declines the invitation to seek residence and join Christian. Instead Faithful resolutely presses on, avoiding Apollyon and the cave of Pope and Pagan. Rather, he enjoys more sunshine than did Christian. And then he hears the cry of his trailing friend, "Let me catch up, and I will be your companion."[2]

The Tender Meeting of the Two Pilgrims

Here is a characteristic instance of Bunyan's ability to amuse and edify simultaneously. He portrays determined Faithful as a pilgrim who will not for a moment halt in his journey, even when the accelerating Christian does not lag too far behind. Then Christian races past, admires his advance on his colleague, and stumbles on account of his gloating. Cheever comments: "Then did Christian vain-gloriously smile! Ah what a smile was that? But now see how he that exalteth himself shall be abased, and how surely along with spiritual pride comes carelessness, false security, and a grievous fall."[3] But without the slightest thought of offering a rebuke, the gentle Faithful raises his brother up, and so "they went very lovingly on together."[4] As Charles Wesley has written:

> All praise to our redeeming Lord,
> Who joins us by His grace,
> And bids us, each to each restored,
> Together seek His face.

---

2 Bunyan, *Works*, III, p. 116.

3 Cheever, *Lectures,* p. 230.

4 Bunyan, *Works*, III, p. 117.

He bids us build each other up;
And, gathered into one,
To our high calling's glorious hope
We hand in hand go on.[5]

The Unresolved Puzzle

Now while a truly memorable lesson has been taught here concerning Paul's admonition, "Therefore let him who thinks he stands take heed that he does not fall" (I Cor. 10:12), some obvious questions still remain unanswered. For instance, while we now understand how Faithful was able to get ahead of Christian, even so, what is Bunyan indicating here with regard to this avoidance by Faithful of the blessings of true local church fellowship available at the Palace Beautiful that were greatly appreciated by Christian? This is not a question that goes beyond the substance of Bunyan's intent.

Further, why were the lions angry with Christian, yet asleep when Faithful passed by? And again, assuming that Christian represents Bunyan, then who might Faithful represent? Was there any close acquaintance of Bunyan's whom we know about who could be identified as a portrayal of Faithful? Of one thing we can be sure, knowing Bunyan's intention to goad and arouse curiosity, these questions involve details that the author intends for us to wrestle with and seek a resolution. And this we intend to do.

THE SAVAGE AND THE SLEEPING LIONS

In Part Two of *The Pilgrim's Progress*, Great-heart defends Christiana and her company in the Valley of the Shadow of Death against a prowling lion. This beast is identified by Bunyan, according to I Peter 5:8-9, as 'the devil.' However, most commentators agree that the two lions on either side of the narrow way, about a furlong before the Palace Beautiful, are to be otherwise identified. They are correctly recognized by Roger Sharrock, and most other commentators, as that wedding of church and state, that union of ecclesiastical and civil power, that found fierce expression in the English monarchy under Charles I and Charles II.[6] In his introduction to *Grace Abounding To The Chief Of Sinners*, Bunyan describes himself as writing, while

[5] *The Methodist Hymn-Book*, p. 648.

[6] John Bunyan, *The Pilgrim's Progress*, eds. J. B. Wharey and R. Sharrock, p. 320.

imprisoned, "from the lions' dens." He continues, "I thank God upon every remembrance of you [Bedford church believers]; and rejoice, even while I stick between the teeth of the lions in the wilderness."[7]

Christian is Troubled

Clearly the lions are determined to restrict pilgrim Christian, as epitomized by Bunyan, from reaching the security of the Palace Beautiful, that is a faithful nonconformist church. Upon the accession of Charles II to the throne as the first restoration monarch in 1660, opposition by independents to legally mandated conformity led to Bunyan's immediate imprisonment as well as the ejection of about 1,760 dissenting ministers from their pastorates. Establishment religion was exceedingly savage!

Faithful is Untroubled

Following after Christian, in broad daylight, Faithful finds that the lions are asleep. Most likely they sense that this pilgrim will not seek to reside at the Palace Beautiful; he is not so much in direct opposition to them. And this being the case, then what is Faithful's local church affiliation? There can only be one possibility, and that is he represents a non-separatist Puritan, an Anglican Puritan after the likes of the more moderate Richard Baxter and William Gurnall.

THE PORTER GAINS A GUEST AND LOSES A GUEST

In seventeenth century terms, John Bunyan was a thoroughgoing separatist and independent. That is, he evaluated the establishment Anglican church as being unbiblical in its essential structure and beyond redemption. Hence, in the Palace Beautiful we see attractively described the biblical ideal to which, no doubt, he desired that the Bedford separatist congregation he pastored should represent. Therefore the Porter's solicitation of both Christian and Faithful sets up an interesting matter for consideration since he is only successful with one of these authentic pilgrims. And we are also faced with the question as to whether Christian the separatist can yet have true and intimate fellowship with Faithful the non-separatist?

---

7 Bunyan, *Works*, I, p. 4.

Christian Resides Several Nights

To the trembling Christian, Watchful the Porter gives great encouragement: "Is thy strength so small? Fear not the lions, for they are chained, and are placed there for trial of faith where it is, and for discovery of those that have none. Keep in the midst of the path, and no hurt shall come unto thee."[8] Thus following careful investigation, the pilgrim enters into the bliss and blessing of genuine local church fellowship. Here edification is found to be many-faceted, substantial, and faithful.

Faithful Passes By

To the transient Faithful, it seems most likely that Watchful the Porter was just as solicitous in his conversation. Surely he mentioned the name of his recently arrived lodger. But Faithful is not sufficiently interested; he courteously declines the invitation and immediately commences to descend into the Valley of Humiliation. Sad to say, members of the true body of Jesus Christ do not always adhere to the best earthly representation of that fellowship designated the Body of Christ. Often many traditional impediments get in the way.

WHO THEN IS FAITHFUL?

From an overall point of view, he is a saint equally as admirable as Christian. Richard Greaves proposes he is a representation of Martin Luther,[9] though this seems rather unlikely since the German reformer, in his own European setting, was definitely separated, that is by means of excommunication from the church of Rome. Faithful is somewhat beguiled by Talkative, yet his testimony at Vanity is both Stephen-like (Acts 6:8-15; 7:54-60) and triumphant. And though Faithful was a nonseparatist, yet Bunyan the separatist intends that we should appreciate the rich fellowship that developed between two so unlikely candidates. And why is this so? Because Bunyan himself entered into friendships with some nonseparatist Anglicans. And one such pastoral relationship may indeed have involved the very person that Faithful is intended to personify. His name is William Dell.

---

[8] Ibid., III, p. 106.

[9] John Bunyan, 'I Will Pray with the Spirit; The Doctrine of the Law and Grace Unfolded,' *Miscellaneous Works,* ed. Richard L. Greaves, p. xviii.

William Dell the Anglican

He was a native of Bedfordshire who became a Fellow of Emmanuel College, Cambridge, and was episcopally ordained. In 1642 he became the rector at Yelden, being about eleven miles north of Bedford. Through the Earl and Countess of Bolingbroke who attended his ministry, Dell became influential amongst the Commonwealth leaders:

> In 1645-46 he was chaplain to the army under General Fairfax, and was the person appointed to bring the articles of the surrender of Oxford to Parliament. In 1649, . . . he was made master of Gonville and Caius College [Cambridge], still retaining his Bedfordshire rectory, and was one of the commissioners sent to attend Charles I before his execution. . . . his sermons both before the House of Commons and in the country were matter of frequent debate in Parliament.[10]

However from an establishment point of view, Dell's opinions were regarded as tending toward radicalism so that he was ejected from the Yelden pastorate in 1662. At heart he was more of an independent. Brown quotes him as follows:

> In earthly governments there is no sameness: . . . how much more evil it is to insist upon uniformity in the life of a Christian, and of the Churches of Christ, taking away all freedom of the Spirit of God, who, being one with God, works in the freedom of God. . . . What wild and woeful work do men make when they will have the church of God thus and thus, and get the power of the magistrate to back theirs, as if the new heavens wherein the Lord will dwell must be the work of their own fingers, or as if the New Jerusalem must of necessity come out of the Assembly of Divines at Westminster.[11]

William Dell the Friend of John Bunyan

Although approximately twenty years older than Bunyan, Dell clearly appreciated the fraternal relationship that developed between the two of them, for it appears that their hearts were in close agreement on many things, particularly with regard to church order and baptism, as well as esteem for Luther. Dell "opposed kingship and tithes. . . . He taught that 'all churches are equal, as

---

[10] John Brown, *John Bunyan*, pp. 74-75. See also Eric C. Walker, *William Dell, Master Puritan*, 238 pp.

[11] Ibid., p. 75.

well as all Christians. Union with the church flows from our union with Christ, not vice versa.'"[12]

Regardless of Cambridge dons who sneered at the tinker's aspiration to preach, the Yeldon rector was pleased to have Bunyan minister at his church on Christmas Day, 1659. In spite of some disgruntled parishoners, Dell responded that he would,

> "rather choose to be in fellowship with poor plain husbandmen and tradesmen who believe in Christ . . . than with the heads of universities and highest and stateliest of the clergy." He rejected the accepted idea that universities should be "the fountain of the ministers of the Gospel." . . . His parishoners reported in 1660 that Dell had said Charles I "was no King to him, Christ was his King. A republic was good enough for Venice and Holland, why not England?"[13]

Hence, it is highly likely that Bunyan was strongly influenced by his senior and more learned friend. Yet while Dell in many ways does maintain his Anglican connection, that is until the establishment separates itself from him by ejection in 1662, we may guess that as Faithful passed by the Palace Beautiful, still he looked at its outward appearance with considerable appreciation and longing. Yet for some unknown reason he could not bring himself to accept the Porter's invitation.

CONCLUSIONS CONCERNING BUNYAN'S ECUMENICITY

Upon the meeting of Christian and Faithful it is written: "they went very lovingly on together, and had sweet discourse of all things that had happened to them in their pilgrimage."[14] So also the relationship between Bunyan and Dell appears to have been equally as spiritually satisfying. While Bunyan had little time for broad and high churchmen, yet in Dell we see that the tinker's ecumenical relationships were not separatist in some iron cast, second degree of separation sense. Rather, we conclude:

Separatist Bunyan Fellowshipped with a Non-separatist

He offered companionship to a brother who had come along a pathway that considerably differed from his own. Dell was originally of the establishment mold. However, Bunyan's own

---

[12] Christopher Hill, *A Tinker And A Poor Man*, p. 167.

[13] Ibid., pp. 166-67.

[14] Bunyan, *Works*, III, p. 117.

separatist views notwithstanding, he also received profitable fellowship and most likely considerable tutelage. In turn, upon Dell's ejection, who could better offer comfort and encouragement than John Bunyan?

Separtist Bunyan Preached for a Non-separatist

The fact that Bunyan agreed to preach at Yelden on Christmas Day, 1659, as a result of Dell's invitation, knowing that some of his congregation would be antagonistic, indicates the tinker's open-mindedness insofar as the uncompromising proclamation of the Word of God is concerned. So Vera Brittain has reasonably speculated concerning this occasion: "At the end of the service, John accompanied William Dell to the Rectory to take Christmas dinner with him and his family. . . . After dinner the two men sat alone over the table, discussing the local anti-Puritans and the state of the nation. The present anarchy could not continue."[15] They probably sensed the imminent return of the monarchy and consequent intolerance of nonconformity.

Separatist Bunyan Learned from a Non-separatist

That Bunyan, to some degree, embraced the terminology of covenant theology, so prevalent during the seventeenth century, is evident from his writings and particularly that of *The Doctrine of the Law and Grace Unfolded* published in 1659.[16] However, he appears to equate the Covenant of Grace exclusively with the New Covenant and not superimpose it upon "the covenants of promise" (Eph. 2:12) in some comprehensive sense. Refer to Chapter 8 for a more detailed consideration of this matter. Nevertheless, from where Bunyan derived his understanding of the elements of this doctrinal system remains a matter of conjecture. Quite likely he not only read according to the recommendations of Dell, as well as Burton, Gifford and Owen, but frequently entered into discussion with these pastoral associates concerning such matters. Certainly he would have been stimulated by their learned discourse.

The extensive discourse between Christian and Faithful accentuates the distinctive experiences that pilgrims encounter, but more importantly the spiritual profit that results from the sharing of testimony concerning these events. Doubtless Bunyan was particularly grateful for those times of fellowship with William

---

[15] Vera Brittain, *In The Steps of John Bunyan*, p. 180.

[16] Ibid., I, pp. 520-34.

Dell of Cambridge, as well as John Owen of Oxford, whereby he became aware of pilgrimage experiences that differed from his own.

SINGING IN THE CHURCH

The songs sung in the temple were new, or such as were compiled after the manner of repeated mercies that the church of God had received, or were to receive. And answerable to this, is the church to sing now new songs, with new hearts for new mercies (Ps. 33:3; 40:3; 96; 144:9; Rev. 14:3). New songs, I say, are grounded on new matter, new occasions, new mercies, new deliverances, new discoveries of God to the soul, or for new frames of heart; and are such as are most taking, most pleasing, and most refreshing to the soul.

These songs [in the temple] also were called "the songs of Zion," and the "songs of the temple" (Ps. 137:3; Amos 8:3). And they are so called as they were theirs to sing there; I say, of them of Zion, and the worshippers in the temple. I say, to sing in the church, by the church, to him who is the God of the church, for the mercies, benefits, and blessings which she has received from him. Zion-songs, temple-songs, must be sung by Zion's sons, and temple-worshippers.

To sing to God, is the highest worship we are capable of performing in heaven; and it is much if sinners on earth, without grace, should be capable of performing it, according to his institution, acceptably. I pray God it be done by all those that now-a-days get into churches, in spirit and with understanding.

John Bunyan
Sololom's Temple Spiritualized
Works, III, p. 496

CHAPTER FIFTEEN

The Poems and Songs of The Pilgrim's Progress

THOMAS GOODWIN, classic Puritan of Cambridge and Oxford, comments during the early years of Bunyan's life that while instrumental music was part of the Levitical form of worship for ancient Israel, yet "musical instruments are not to be in the worship of God now, no more than incense."[1] The typical Puritan worship service was exceedingly simple; the only music was unaccompanied singing of the metrical psalms. Hence, because of this "acappella singing in their churches, while Anglicans admitted instrumentalists, an idea has passed current that they were hostile to music. The truth is otherwise. Puritans produced the first Italian opera in England, Cromwell supported an orchestra at court, and in this country [America] music, both secular and sacred, was encouraged."[2]

No doubt the banning of drama and a downplaying of the graphic arts in general may have contributed toward this false impression of musical stiltedness. However, as Christopher Hill puts it:

> Myths have a way of living on long after they have been disproved. Some Puritans disliked certain types of music in church services, since they believed that polyphony or choral singing, for instance, or the playing of organs distracted the attention of auditors from the intellectual content of worship; but under Puritan rule in the 1640s "music flourished as never before" [Quoting Scholes, *The Puritan and Music*]. Bunyan, like John Owen, played the flute, and the Bedford prisoner is said to have made himself a flute out of a chair-leg to play in jail. There survive a metal violin and a cabinet decorated with musical instruments which are believed to have

1 Thomas Goodwin, *The Works of Thomas Goodwin*, III p. 215.

2 Perry Miller and Thomas H. Johnson, eds., *The Puritans – A Sourcebook Of Their Writings.*, II, p. 394.

belonged to him. The very title of *Grace Abounding* may come from a book of madrigals [part-songs].[3]

THE METRICAL INNOVATION OF JOHN BUNYAN

John Milton notwithstanding, the Puritans in general made no effort to excel in poetry for the purpose of communicating divine truth. Rather, passionate pastoral prose always remained their forte.[4] However, John Bunyan was certainly an exception in this regard. As with the over forty poems and songs included in both parts of *The Pilgrim's Progress*, so the whole of his *Works* reflect a strong conviction that both poetic and hymnic verse are suitable and arresting vehicles for the communication of the Word of God as well as being helpful stimuli for worship.

Examples of Bunyan's Poetic Expression

1. Profitable Meditations, 756, lines ,1661.[5]

This first venture into verse commences with an apology reminiscent of that which introduces *The Pilgrim's Progress*. Then follows doctrinal exhortation on a variety of subjects concerning man, sin, Christ, the church, death, and judgment. The application is characteristically repeated and direct.

> Take none offence, Friend, at my method here,
> 'Cause thou in Verses simple Truth dost see:
> But to them soberly incline thine ear,
> And with the Truth it self affected be.
>
> 'Tis not the Method, but the Truth alone
> Should please a Saint, and mollifie his heart:
> Truth in or out of Meeter is but one;
> And this thou knowest, if thou a Christian art.
>
> When Doctors give their Physick to the Sick,
> They make it pleasing with some other thing:
> Truth also by this means is very quick,
> When by Faith it in their hearts do sing.

---

3 Christopher Hill, *A Tinker And A Poor Man*, p. 261.

4 Miller and Johnson, *The Puritans*, I, pp. 77-79.

5 John Bunyan, *The Miscellaneous Works of John Bunyan*, "The Poems," ed. Graham Midgley, VI, pp. 1-35.

2. Prison Meditations, 280 lines, 1663.[6]

In responding to a friend who had written a word of encouragement, incarcerated Bunyan expresses gratitude for such kindly counsel.

Thou dost encourage me to hold
  My head above the flood,
Thy counsel better is than gold,
  In need thereof I stood.

I am, indeed, in prison now
  In body, but my mind
Is free to study Christ, and how
  Unto me he is kind.

For though men keep my outward man
  Within their locks and bars,
Yet by the faith of Christ I can
  Mount higher than the stars.

3. One Thing Is Needful, 1190 lines, 1665.[7]

Bunyan describes this as "Serious meditations upon the four last things, death, judgment, heaven, and hell." Thus he commences:

These lines I at this time present
  To all that will them heed,
Wherein I show to what extent
  God saith, Convert with speed.

For these four things come on apace,
  Which we should know full well,
Both death and judgment, and, in place
  Next to them, heaven and hell.

4. Ebal And Gerizim, 870 lines, 1665.[8]

These mountains, representing blessing and cursing (Deut. 11:29: 27:12-13), are illustrative of the mercy and severity of God.

---

[6] John Bunyan, *The Works of John Bunyan*, ed. George Offor, I, pp. 63-6.

[7] Ibid., III, pp. 726-37.

[8] Ibid., pp. 737-45.

Thus having heard from Gerazim, I shall
Next come to Ebal, and you thither call,
Not there to curse you, but to let you hear
How God doth curse that soul that shall appear
An unbelieving man, a graceless wretch;
Because he doth continue in the breach
Of Moses' law, and also doth neglect
To close with Jesus; him will God reject.

5. A Caution To Stir Up To Watch Against Sin, 132 lines, 1684.[9]

Using a verse recommended to him, Bunyan then continues on the theme of the subtleties and deceitfulness of sin.

The first eight lines one did commend to me,
The rest I thought good to commend to thee:
Reader, in reading be thou rul'd by me,
With rhimes nor lines, but truths, affected be.

Sin will at first, just like a beggar, crave
One penny or one half-penny to have;
And if you grant its first suit, 'twill aspire
From pence to pounds, and so will still mount higher
To the whole soul: but if it makes its moan,
Then say, here is not for you, get you gone.
For if you give it entrance at the door,
It will come in, and may go out no more.

6. A Book For Boys And Girls, 49 poems, 1686.[10]

Numerous editions, many with attractive engravings, have proved the popularity of this volume, with the author's introduction being comprised of 96 lines.

UPON THE FROG

The frog by nature is both damp and cold,
Her mouth is large, her belly much will hold;
She sits somewhat ascending, loves to be
Croaking in gardens, though unpleasantly.

---

[9] Ibid., II, pp. 575-6.

[10] Ibid., III, pp. 746-62.

Comparison

The hypocrite is like unto the frog,
As like as is the puppy to the dog.
He is of nature cold, his mouth is wide
To prate, and at true goodness to deride.
He mounts his head as if he was above
The world, when yet 'tis that which has his love.
And though he seeks in churches for to croak,
He neither loveth Jesus nor his yoke.

7. *A Discourse Of The Building, Nature, Excellency, And Government Of The House Of God, 1310 lines, 1688.*[11]

Here is a delightful and comprehensive description of the doctrine of the Christian church that is strongly nonconformist.

The builder's God, materials his Elect;
His Son's the rock on which it is erect;
The Scripture is his rule, plummet, or line,
Which gives proportion to this house divine,
His working tools his ordinances are,
By them he doth his stones and timber square,
Affections knit in love, the couplings are;
Good doctrine like to mortar doth cement
The whole together, schism to prevent.

This place, as hospitals, will entertain,
Those which the lofty of this world disdain:
The poor, the lame, the maimed, halt and blind,
The leprous, and possessed too, may find
Free welcome here, as also such relief
As ease them will of trouble, pain and grief.

Art thou bound over to the great assize,
For hark'ning to the devil and his lies;
Art thou afraid thereat to show thy head,
Fear thou then be sent unto the dead?
Thou may'st come hither, here is room and place,
For such as willingly would live by grace.

[11] Ibid., II, pp. 577-90.

The Development of Bunyan's Poetic Expression

Popular poetic resources were readily available to Bunyan in his youth in the form of ballads, broadsides (polemic pamphlets), and chap-books (pedlar's popular literature). In *Grace Abounding*, Bunyan relates how he, as newly married, attended the Elstow parish church, "and there should very devoutly, both say and sing as others did, yet retaining my wicked life."[12] Most likely the version of the metrical psalms used at that time was the Sternhold and Hopkins edtion dating back to 1563. Hill gives evidence for believing that Bunyan's earlier poetic form drew heavily upon Sternhold and Hopkins, while his later verse indicates a more free and developed style.[13] This fact seems especially evident when we consider the obviously superior verse composition that is found in Part Two of *The Pilgrim's Progress* when compared with that of Part One.

The Development of Bunyan's Hymnic Expression

Bunyan's first recorded interest in instrumental music is his expressed delight in bell-ringing at the Elstow parish church following his attempt at outward religious reformation. However, he soon gave up this practice since it took on superstitious proportions and became in his mind a vain pursuit.[14] However, by this time the past turbulent decade in the tinker's life had witnessed a novelty in church life that became the cause of much controversy:

> Congregational hymn singing flourished during the breakdown of ecclesiastical controls in the 1640s, when congregations could take their own decisions. Hymn-singing then was regarded by the authorities as potentially dangerous. It was associated with the lower classes, with Baptists and Muggletonians [apocalyptic, anti-trinitarians]. . . . Among Baptists in particular the subject led to disagreements. There had been disputes over this in the Bedford church from its earliest days. Gifford warned against them in his deathbed letter.[15]

Both Hanserd Knollys and Benjamin Keach, the latter being pilloried and imprisoned for his trouble, were Baptists who

---

[12] Ibid., I, § 16, p. 7.

[13] Hill, *Tinker And A Poor Man*, pp. 266-67.

[14] Bunyan, *Works*, I, §§ 33-34, p. 10.

[15] Hill, *Tinker And A Poor Man*, pp. 262-64.

encouraged congregational hymn singing, and there is little doubt that John Bunyan was of the same opinion. In *Light For Them That Sit In Darkness* he writes of the "peace of God" as follows: "It is also expressed by "singing;" because the peace of God when it is received into the soul by faith putteth the conscience into a heavenly and melodious frame."[16] That the author here intends that hymns be understood as the type of singing he has in mind is most obvious when the context of verse in *The Pilgrim's Progress* is understood.

THE POEMS OF THE PILGRIM'S PROGRESS

The introductory poems of Part One and Part Two are of similar length and wholly comprised of rhyming couplets. Part One includes 20 verse sections, all rhyming couplets, of which 12 are specifically designated for singing. Part Two includes 23 verse sections of which 7 are couplets, 14 are quatrains, and 8 are designated for singing. Assuming a minimum of six years separating the writing of Part One and Part Two of *The Pilgrim's Progress*, it is obvious that this period saw a considerable development in Bunyan's ability to compose poetic verse. Significantly, his most notable composition, "Who would true valor see," is the most complex in its construction.

Hill is certainly correct when he declares that, "his [Bunyan's] poems are enjoyable because he himself obviously enjoyed observing and writing them. He wrote with gusto and wit."[17] But Louis Benson is much closer to the truth when he writes that Bunyan's verse, "is best described as being didactic rather than poetic in motive and accomplishment."[18] The tinker was not interested in "art for art's sake," but rather the poetic encapsulation of truth for the cause of enticing evangelism and stimulating edification.

THE SONGS OF THE PILGRIM'S PROGRESS

The twelve separate verse sections in Part One that enjoin singing must have been considered in Bunyan's time as a clear recommendation of congregational singing, especially since there is not so much as one reference to a metrical psalm in all of *The Pilgrim's Progress*. Hill refers to a credible comment in this regard

---

16 Bunyan, *Works*, I, p. 424.

17 Hill, *Tinker And A Poor Man*, p. 272.

18 Louis Benson, *The Hymns of John Bunyan*, p. 3.

as follows: "Tindall [*John Bunyan: Mechanick Preacher*] suggested that the songs in *The Pilgrim's Progress* were intended as propaganda on behalf of church singing."[19] Sharrock is of the same opinion.[20] Notice that when Christian finds refreshment and rest at the Palace Beautiful, a representation of a faithful nonconformist church, he awakens the next morning and immediately bursts into song. Similarly in Part Two, when Christiana and her sons, and Mercy feast at the house of the Interpreter, they are entertained with minstrel music. Again, at the Palace Beautiful, following rest, they hear music so that Mercy happily responds: "Wonderful! music in the house, music in the heart, and music also in heaven, for joy that we are here."[21]

At the conclusion of Part One, as if like the strains of a finale, there is the welcoming music of "the King's trumpeters" by which Christian and Hopeful are accompanied to the very gates of the Celestial City. Once inside they receive "harps to praise; . . . then the bells in the city rang again for joy. . . . I also heard the men themselves, that they sang with a loud voice, saying, 'Blessing, and honor, and glory, and power, be unto him that sitteth upon the throne, and unto the Lamb, for ever and ever.'"[22] Similarly at the conclusion of Part Two, several pilgrims cross the River of Death including Christiana, Mr. Valiant-for-truth, and Mr. Stand-fast, who find that the other side "was filled with horses and chariots, with trumpeters and pipers, with singers and players on stringed instruments, to welcome the pilgrims as they went up."[23]

The Emphasis in Part One

The singing that is expressly stated as such commences with Christian's hymn of praise to Christ at the Place of Deliverance. Every other similar instance involves only the three principal pilgrims, namely Christian, Faithful and Hopeful. It is Christian and Hopeful who frequently sing together. Concerning content, while several songs offer praise and thanksgiving, many more are concerned with exhortation, lament, and warning.

---

[19] Hill, *Tinker And A Poor Man*, p. 264.

[20] John Bunyan, *The Pilgrim"s Progress*, eds. J. B. Wharey and Roger Sharrock, pp. 343-44.

[21] Bunyan, *Works*, III, pp. 188, 198.

[22] Ibid., pp. 165-6.

[23] Ibid., p. 244.

1. Christian sings in praise of Christ's saving benefits at the Place of Deliverance.
2. Christian sings upon awakening from rest at the Palace Beautiful.
3. Christian sings having traversed the Valley of the Shadow of Death.
4. Faithful sings having resisted the persistent censure of Shame.
5. Christian sings about Faithful's triumphant martyrdom at Vanity Fair.
6. Christian sings to Hopeful when By-ends and friends fall into the silver mine.
7. Christian and Hopeful sing having been refreshed at the river of God.
8. Christian and Hopeful sing having escaped from Doubting Castle.
9. Christian and Hopeful sing at the telescopic sight of the Celestial City.
10. Christian sings about the lesson of seeking more faith than Little-faith.
11. Christian and Hopeful sing having been disciplined for heeding the Flatterer.
12. Christian sings to Hopeful an awakening song on the Enchanted Ground.

The Emphasis in Part Two

There is now a greater stress on singing in fellowship while the poetic quality of the songs is considerably improved. Three hymns in particular that have gained some degree of recognition, described by Graham Midgley as a "lyrical breakthrough,"[24] are as follows:

[24] Bunyan, *Miscellaneous Works*, VI, lvi-lvii.

1. Mercy's hymn, "Let the Most Blessed be my Guide."[25]

Benson suggests that this is most suitably sung at the admission of members to a church.[26]

Let the Most Blessed be my guide
If't be his blessed will;
Unto his gate, into his fold,
Up to his holy hill.

And let him never suffer me
To swerve or turn aside
From his free grace, and holy ways,
Whate'er shall me betide.

And let him gather them of mine
That I have left behind;
Lord, make them pray they may be thine,
With all their heart and mind.

2. The Shepherd Boy's hymn, "He that is down needs fear no fall."[27]

This being the first hymn of Bunyan's to gain wide acceptance, it gives positive expression to life in the Valley of Humiliation.

He that is down needs fear no fall,
He that is low, no pride;
He that is humble ever shall
Have God to be his guide.

I am content with what I have,
Little be it or much;
And, Lord, contentment still I crave,
Because Thou savest such.

Fulness to such a burden is
That go on pilgrimage;
Here little, and hereafter bliss,
Is best from age to age.

---

[25] Bunyan, *Works,* III, p. 178.

[26] Benson, *Hymns of John Bunyan,* pp. 5-6.

[27] Bunyan, *Works,* III, p. 206.

3. Valiant-for-Truth's hymn, "Who would true valor see."[28]

Beyond dispute, this, Bunyan's most irregular hymn, has become his most famous; it has found its way into the outstanding English hymnals of the past century. Furthermore, it exquisitely reflects the essential pilgrim quality of *The Pilgrim's Progress*, and for this reason ought to be acknowledged as Bunyan's life theme.

Who would true valor see,
  Let him come hither;
One here will constant be,
  Come wind, come weather.
There's no discouragement
  Shall make him once relent,
His first avow'd intent
  To be a pilgrim.

Who so beset him round
  With dismal stories,
Do but themselves confound,
  His strength the more is;
No lion can him fright,
  He'll with a giant fight;
But he will have the right
  To be a pilgrim.

Hobgoblin nor foul fiend
  Can daunt his spirit;
He knows he at the end
  Shall life inherit.
Then fancies fly away,
  He'll fear not what men say;
He'll labor night and day
  To be a pilgrim.

[28] Ibid., p. 235.

CHAPTER SIXTEEN

Seventeenth Century Communication of The Pilgrim's Progress

CONVINCED that *The Pilgrim's Progress* ought to be proclaimed today, we must now consider in greater detail whether such faithful communication is really possible in a modern era that is so addicted to polychrome marketing of literary fast food. The content of Bunyan's allegory may well be timeless, yet its stylistic packaging may nevertheless be perceived as outdated and unappealing.

Famous eighteenth century essayist Samuel Johnson, himself a High Church Tory and not a Calvinist, although he is described as one "who had no patience to read a book through," yet is said to have "found himself so fascinated by [*The Pilgrim's Progress*] . . . that he could not put it down until it was finished."[1] The next century, historian and essayist Thomas Macaulay writes: "In the wildest parts of Scotland *The Pilgrim's Progress* is the delight of the peasantry. In every nursery *The Pilgrim's Progress* is a greater favorite than Jack the Giant-killer. Every reader knows the straight and narrow path as well as he knows a road in which he has gone backward and forward a hundred times."[2]

However, honesty compels us to confess that today there is no such spontaneous interest. To be sure, reprint sales remain steady and universal. Nevertheless, in general there is only indifference and ignorance concerning *The Pilgrim's Progress*, as a recent survey indicates. Christopher Hill relates that, "In the USA less than one in seven of a recent [1987] cross-section of 17-year olds

---

1 Ezra S. Tipple, "Pilgrim's Progress a book for Preachers," *Methodist Review*, July, 1908, p. 591.

2 Thomas Macaulay, *Casebook, Bunyan, The Pilgrim's Progress*, ed. Roger Sharrock, p. 67.

could identify the book."[3] Then there is the more direct opposition from the secular fringe of literary criticism.[4]

So what response is appropriate here? An immediate reply, certainly in tune with the ethos of this closing century, would be the suggestion that Bunyan's product needs new packaging. And many evangelicals would join this chorus in calling for relevant communication. But before we respond to such a timely question in a premature manner, first let us consider the nature and purpose of seventeenth century English Puritan literature as represented by Bunyan. For to neglect this fundamental matter is to be in danger of responding in ignorance with the result that we venture into communicative novelties that Bunyan would doubtless never countenance.

SEVENTEENTH CENTURY PURITAN LITERATURE

To begin with, let us readily admit the prolixity of Bunyan's nonconformist contemporaries, even as he himself could be wordy and intricate in some of his more polemical works when compared

---

3 Christopher Hill, *A Tinker And A Poor Man*, pp. 372-3.

4 L. R. Gardiner, in noting the literary hostility of the 1960's toward evangelical religion quotes the pungent criticism of *The Pilgrim's Progress* by Brophy, Levey, and Osborne in their *Fifty Works of English (and American) Literature We Could Do Without*. Ian Breward, ed., *John Bunyan - A Commemorative Symposium*, p. 2. More recently has been the sharp, historical psychoanalysis of Bunyan by Stachniewski. The author of *The Pilgrim's Progress* is said to have suffered a severe persecutory complex on account of his perspective of an oppressive God derived from Calvinism and a literalist interpretation of the Bible. John Stachniewski, *The Persecutory Imagination - English Puritanism and the Literature of Religious Despair*, pp. 1-84, 127-216. In reply, Bunyan's terse prefatory comment in *Grace Abounding* is simply that, "the Philistines understand me not." Bunyan, *Works*, I, p. 4. George Offor adds: "He [Bunyan] lived in an atmosphere, and used a language, unknown to the wisdom of this world. . . . His mind was deeply imbued with all that was most terrific, as well as most magnificent in religion. In proportion as his Christian course became pure and lovely, so his former life must have been surveyed with unmitigated severity and abhorrence. These mental conflicts are deeply interesting; they arose from an agonized mind – a sincere and determined spirit roused by Divine revelation, opening before his astonished but bewildered mind, solemn, eternal realities. He that sits in the scorner's seat may scoff at them, while he who is earnestly enquiring after the way, the truth, and the life, will examine them with prayerful seriousness." Bunyan, Works, III, p. 10.

with modern English; but he was never florid with the pretense of learning. In comparison with today's literary climate, representative writers of this period could be verbose in the extreme. Their sentences were long and circuitous, and their logic, while being finely tuned, yet could stretch the able mind to great lengths. J. I Packer lists: "Joseph Caryl's 6,000 quarto pages on Job; 2,000 plus in folio on Hebrews from John Owen; Hildersam's 152 sermons on Psalm 51:1-7; over 800 pages of small print in all modern editions of William Gurnall's treatment of Ephesians 6:10-20, *The Christian in Complete Armor*."[5]

Yet on the other hand, who can read the last mentioned work and not be impressed with Gurnall's legitimate expansion of his text, his masterful use of illustration, and his constant practicality? Furthermore, it ought to be well considered that most secular writers of that period were equally wordy and yet very acceptable; in the same way these Puritan writings were both avidly read and widely distributed even beyond Great Britain in continental churches by means of various translations.[6] And further, ought not some contemporary honesty be in place here? For why are we today so critical of such "ponderous" and "heavy" tomes when in fact it would seem more likely that the fault is largely our own? We ought to be able to read such literature with ease; but our present shallow roots in good literary soil have weakened both our abilities and interest.

In Bunyan's case, he reads more easily than his scholarly friend John Owen,[7] and undoubtedly it was this unadorned yet winsome manner, even so evident in his popularity as a preacher, that helped to gain such broad approval for his writings. This stylistic purpose was intentional since he writes to his more learned readers:

> I have not so beautified my matter with acuteness of language as you could wish or desire. . . . I have not given you, either in the line or in the margent, a cloud of sentences from the learned fathers. . . . Sir, words easy to be understood do often hit the mark, when high and learned ones do only pierce the air. . . . I honor the godly as Christians, but I prefer the Bible before them; and having that still with me, I count myself far better furnished than if I had without it all the libraries of the two universities. Besides, I am for drinking

[5] J. I. Packer, *A Quest For Godliness*, p. 73.

[6] Ibid., pp. 62-3.

[7] C. H. Spurgeon makes a delightful comparison between Bunyan and Owen in his *Eccentric Preachers*, p. 33.

water out of my own cistern; what God makes mine by the evidence of his Word and Spirit, that I dare make bold with.[8]

Hence, in *The Pilgrim's Progress* there are no ornate literary flourishes, only plain prose that sparkles with the beauty of its purity and clarity. Here then is a work that is so composed as to be most suitable for communication to future generations.

The Form of Puritan Writings

Like numerous prolific Christian writers such as Luther, Calvin, Edwards, Spurgeon, Lloyd-Jones, and especially the contemporaneous fellow Puritans, Thomas Manton, Stephen Charnock, and Richard Baxter, many of Bunyan's writings were probably the fruitage of extensive and didactic preaching, including that which he performed in prison. Most likely *The Pilgrim's Progress* incorporates many illustrations that were part of earlier sermons. This is even implied by the strange fact that in all of the three volumes of Bunyan's works edited by George Offor, there is only one designated sermon, and that being his last based on John 1:13, delivered just twelve days before his death in August of 1688.[9] However, with his fellow nonconformists, the Bedford pastor employed communicative method that was characteristic of his time, and remains readily adaptable for the late twentieth century.

1. Bunyan was analytical.

Like a dog with a bone, he wrestled with his text until every vestige of meat was obtained from it. Consider his dealing with the text, "So run, that ye may obtain" (I Cor. 9:24), which writing was published under the title of *The Heavenly Footman*. The whole concept of "running," that is spiritual progress for the seeker and believer, is analyzed with great penetration and discernment.

> [A]ll or every one that runneth doth not obtain the prize; there be many that do run, yea, and run far too who yet miss of the crown that standeth at the end of the race. You know that all who run in a race do not obtain the victory; they all run, but one wins. And so it is here; it is not every one that runneth, nor every one that seeketh, nor every one that striveth for the mastery, that hath it (Luke 13).

---

8 John Bunyan, *The Works of John Bunyan*, ed. George Offor, III, p. 398.

9 On occasion Bunyan does admit that a particular writing is based upon sermons previously delivered.

> Though a man do strive for the mastery, saith Paul, '*yet* he is not crowned, except he strive lawfully;' that is, unless he so run, and so strive, as to have God's approbation (II Tim. 2:5). What, do you think that every heavy-heeled professor will have heaven? What, every lazy one; every wanton and lazy professor, that will be stopped by anything, kept back by anything, that scarce runneth so fast heaven-ward as a snail creepeth on the ground? Nay, there are some professors do not go on so fast in the way of God as a snail doth go on the wall; and yet these think, that heaven and happiness is for them. But stay, there are many more that run than there be that obtain; therefore he that will have heaven must RUN for it.[10]

2. Bunyan was systematic.

Puritans were often called "precisians" because of the scrupulousness of their lifestyles. And Bunyan was no exception in this respect. In other words he was orderly and, like Manton, Charnock, and Baxter, committed to thorough outlining in his writing. Again, consider the outline of *The Heavenly Footman.*[11] However, *The Pilgrim's Progress* is not so rigidly structured this way, though refer to the careful arrangement of the description of Temporary; here are four reasons why he departed from the faith and nine progressive stages in his falling away.[12]

3. Bunyan was illustrative.

While his verbal illustrations are legion throughout his *Works*, yet he was not averse to visual illustration in a supplementary sense. His *Map Shewing the Order and Causes of Salvation* published in 1664,[13] being similar to one produced earlier by William Perkins toward the end of the sixteenth century,[14] is certainly avant-garde for its time and easy to comprehend. Further, Bunyan would certainly have approved of "The Sleeping Portrait" as it is called which was included in the third edition of *The*

---

[10] Bunyan, *Works*, III, pp. 381-2.

[11] Ibid., p. 380.

[12] Ibid., pp. 160-1.

[13] Ibid., inserted between p. 559 and p. 560, but excluded from the recent Banner of Truth reprint.

[14] John Stachniewski, *The Persecutory Imagination*, pp. 196-7.

Pilgrim's Progress published in 1679.[15] It not only depicts Bunyan in a dreaming posture, but also pictures Christian progressing from the City of Destruction toward the Wicket-gate.

4. Bunyan was poetic.

Milton notwithstanding, the Puritans in general made no effort to excel in poetry for the purpose of communicating divine truth. Rather, passionate though often ponderous pastoral prose always remained their forte; Miller and Johnson write that: "It is as writers of prose that the Puritan's literary art finally must be judged. Prose was the vehicle of their finest thoughts."[16] However, Bunyan was certainly an exception in this regard. As with the over forty poems and songs included in both parts of *The Pilgrim's Progress*, so the whole of his *Works* reflect a strong conviction that both poetic and hymnic verse are suitable vehicles for the communication of the Word of God. His *Book For Boys And Girls* especially reflects his fervent interest in this regard. Refer to Chapter 15, as well as Volume VI of the Oxford Press (Clarendon) publication of *The Miscellaneous Works of John Bunyan.*[17]

5. Bunyan was not dramatic.

While lively prosaic drama found one of its ablest exponents to be John Bunyan, yet undoubtedly he would have shunned any suggestion of a staged production of *The Pilgrim's Progress*. For him, the theater was a favorite pastime of the inhabitants of Vanity; at their Fair were all sorts of "juggling, cheats, games, plays, fools, apes, knaves, and rogues."[18] The Cromwellian interregnum was iconoclastic toward the stage:

> During the twenty years of Puritan rule at mid-century, most of the theaters were closed and hardly anything was written for the stage; . . . then the theaters were shut, abruptly and apparently forever. When they opened in 1660, they were forced at first to rely on a backlog of twenty-year old plays. But gradually they built up a

---

[15] John Bunyan, *The Pilgrim's Progress*, eds. Wharey and Sharrock, pp. 151-4.

[16] Perry Miller and Thomas H. Johnson, eds., *The Puritans - A Sourcebook Of Their Writings*, I, pp. 77-79.

[17] John Bunyan, *"The Poems," The Miscellaneous Works of John Bunyan*, ed. Graham Midgley, 345 pp.

[18] Bunyan, *Works*, III, p. 127.

> repertoire of comedies (generally bawdy) and tragedies in the rhetorical declamatory manner.[19]

The Purpose of Puritan Writings

There is little doubt that the overriding purpose in the writings of Puritans such as Bunyan was pastoral rather than professional. That is, they were intensely concerned about spiritual shepherding and the welfare of redeemed children of God, both themselves and those committed to their care. Peter Lewis well describes this heart-possessing animus as follows:

> Puritanism was not merely a set of rules or a larger creed, but a life-force: a vision and a compulsion which saw the beauty of a holy life and moved towards it, marveling at the possibilities and thrilling to the satisfaction of a God-centered life. . . . Every area of life came under the influence of God and the guidance of the Word. Each day began and ended with searching, unhurried and devout personal and family prayer. Each task, whether professional or manual, was done to the glory of God and with a scrupulous eye to his perfect will.
>
> Every relationship, business or personal, was regulated by spiritual principles. Hours free from labor were gladly and zealously employed in the study of the Scriptures, attendance upon public worship, 'godly converse' or intense witness and every other means which contributed to the soul's good. In a word, the 'great business of godliness' dominated the ardent believer's ambitions and called forth all his energies. We may say that to a large extent Puritanism succeeded where other more cloistered ideologies failed, because here men embodied true doctrine so that Puritanism was visible before men. Men saw on earth lives that were not earthly, lives that touched their own at so many points, yet which rolled on into a moral and spiritual continent of breathtaking landscape. Indeed, it is not too much to say that Puritans were Puritanism proper – for Puritanism was sainthood visible.[20]

It is for this reason that we would kindly suggest that J. I. Packer may be guilty of a tautology when he entitles a very fine chapter in his *A Quest For Godliness*, "The Practical Writings of the English Puritans."[21] In other words, we would ask which writings, at least

---

19 M. H. Abrams, ed., *The Norton Anthology of English Verse*, I, pp. 1055-6.

20 Peter Lewis, *The Genius Of Puritanism*, p. 12.

21 Packer, *Quest For Godliness*, p. 49.

in any substantial sense, were not practical? Even so, in laying this minor point aside, let us turn to this same chapter and make use of the author's excellent characterization, under five headings, of the practical purposes of Puritan writings, and especially as they are reflected through the pen of John Bunyan.[22]

1. Bunyan was a physician to the soul.

According to Acts 20:28, he understood his first priority to be concern for his own relationship with God. Sensitivity in this regard permeates all of his works, especially *Grace Abounding To The Chief Of Sinners* being based on Psalm 66:16, "Come and hear, all ye that fear God, and I will declare what he hath done for my soul." At the conclusion of this work he writes:

> I find to this day seven abominations in my heart: 1. Inclinings to unbelief. 2. Suddenly to forget the love and mercy that Christ manifesteth. 3. A leaning to the works of the law. 4. Wanderings and coldness in prayer. 5. To forget to watch for that I pray for. 6. Apt to murmur because I have no more, and yet ready to abuse what I have. 7. I can do none of those things which God commands me, but my corruptions will thrust in themselves, 'When I would do good, evil is present with me.'
>
> These things I continually see and feel, and am afflicted and oppressed with; yet the wisdom of God doth order them for my good. 1. They make me abhor myself. 2. They keep me from trusting my heart. 3. They convince me of the insufficiency of all inherent righteousness. 4. They show me the necessity of flying to Jesus. 5. They press me to pray unto God. 6. They show me the need I have to watch and be sober. 7. And provoke me to look to God, through Christ, to help me, and carry me through this world. Amen.[23]

As a consequence, Bunyan loved the souls of men and especially those who were deeply conscious of being lost, even as he once was. Consider the following appeal that concludes his *Justification By An Imputed Righteousness*:

> Sinners, take my advice, with which I shall conclude. . . . Call often to remembrance that thou hast a precious soul within thee; that thou art in the way to thy end. . . . put thyself in thy thoughts into the last day thou must live in this world, seriously arguing thus – . . . How if the first voice that rings tomorrow morning in my heavy

[22] Ibid., pp. 64-77.

[23] Bunyan, *Works*, I, p. 50.

> ears be, 'Arise, ye dead, and come to judgment?' . . . O how serious should sinners be in this work of remembering things to come, of laying to their heart the greatness and terror of that notable day of God Almighty, and in examining themselves, how it is like to go with their souls when they shall stand before the Judge indeed! To this end, God make this word effectual. Amen.[24]

2. Bunyan was an expositor addressing the conscience.

Because the Bible was inerrant and truthful, that is verbal and propositional revelation exhaled from the mouth of God (II Tim. 3:16) who cannot lie (Heb. 6:18), refer to Chapter 3, such an authoritative foundation resulted in a homiletic method that gave unswerving commitment to the exposition of this sacred text. Consider the following examples:

a. *The Greatness of the Soul*, based on Mark 8:37.[25]

b. *The Strait Gate*, based on Matthew 7:13-14.[26]

c. *The Pharisee And The Publican*, based on Luke 18:10-13.[27]

d. *Paul's Departure And Crown*, based on II Timothy 4:6-8.[28]

e. *An Exposition On The First Ten Chapters Of Genesis.*[29]

f. *The Heavenly Footman*, based on I Corinthians 9:24.[30]

g. *The Holy City, or the New Jerusalem*, based on Revelation 21:10-27; 22:1-4.[31]

Moreover, Bunyan believed that the Word of God had a unique ability to lance sorely festering souls in such a way as to lead from conviction of conscience to resultant repentance:

> Now when the hand of the Lord is with the Word, then it is mighty: it is 'mighty through God to the pulling down of strong holds' (II Cor. 10:4). . . . It sticks like an arrow in the hearts of sinners, to the causing of the people to fall at his foot for mercy (Heb. 4:12). . . .

---

[24] Ibid., p. 334.

[25] Ibid., pp. 104-50.

[26] Ibid., pp. 362-90.

[27] Ibid., pp. II, pp. 215-77.

[28] Ibid., I, pp. 721-2.

[29] Ibid., II, pp. 413-502.

[30] Ibid., III, pp. 375-94.

[31] Ibid., pp. 395-459.

> When seconded by mighty power, then the same is as the roaring of the lion, as the piercing of a sword, as a burning fire in the bones, as thunder and as a hammer that dashes all to pieces (Jer. 25:30; Amos 1:2; 3:8; Acts 2:37; Jer. 20:9; Ps. 29:3-9)."[32]

But to what end is this convicting work? It is that, "by [God's] breaking of the heart he openeth it, and makes it a receptacle of the graces of his Spirit; this is the cabinet, when unlocked, where God lays up the jewels of the gospel.[33]

3. Bunyan was an educator of the mind.

In today's existential, relational, subjective world governed by self-interest, sensuality, and sentiment, this emphasis tends to be scoffed at on account of being unnecessarily cerebral and remote from contemporary reality along with the hurting masses. At this point, Puritanism is in sharp conflict with the status quo posture of contemporary evangelical Christianity. Packer explains as follows:

> All the Puritans regarded religious feeling and pious emotion without knowledge as worse than useless. Only when the truth was being felt was emotion in any way desirable. When men felt and obeyed the truth they knew, it was the work of the Spirit of God, but when they were swayed by feeling without knowledge, it was a sure sign that the devil was at work, for feeling divorced from knowledge and urging to action in darkness of mind were both as ruinous to the soul as was knowledge without obedience. So the teaching of truth was the pastor's first task, as the learning of it was the layman's.[34]

Hence Bunyan would be in full agreement here. His earliest two writings which opposed the extreme interiorizing of Christian truth by the Quakers, *Some Gospel Truths Opened*[35] and *A Vindication Of Gospel Truths*,[36] make plain that genuine subjective experience is grounded upon objective Scripture truth, that the knowledge of an indwelling Christ is rooted in an historic and external Christ seated at the right hand of the Father. He himself embodied what

---

32 Ibid., I, p. 694.

33 Ibid., p. 709.

34 Packer, *Quest For Godliness*, p. 70.

35 Bunyan, *Works*, II, pp. 129-74.

36 Ibid., pp. 176-214.

today might be called "a walking Bible," except that he would not allow for any disjunction between the cognitive intaking and practical outworking of divine truth.

There is content and substance and doctrine in all that Bunyan writes; however, this meat is well seasoned with illustrations, full of vital spiritual nutrients, made readily digestible for soul assimilation, and strenuously recommended with great force of exhortation and evangelistic proclamation. For example, refer to his catechism *Instruction For The Ignorant* subtitled, "A Salve to that Great Want [Lack] of Knowledge which so much Reigns both in Young and Old," and especially the section on "Faith in Christ." Here all sorts of spurious faith are distinguished from the true, which is described as, "faith [which] quickeneth to spiritual life, purifies and sanctifies the heart; and worketh up the man that hath it, into the image of Jesus Christ (Col. 2:12-13; Acts 15:9; 26:18; II Cor. 3:18)."[37]

4. Bunyan was an enforcer of the truth.

In other words, his manner of communication was intentionally unadorned with sophisticated terms and learned phraseology. The claims of the truth of God upon his life were far too important for literary flourish, homiletic performance, and pastoral posturing. So in his preface to *Grace Abounding To The Chief Of Sinners* he explains:

> I could also have stepped into a style much higher than this in which I have here discoursed, and could have adorned all things more than here I have seemed to do, but I dare not. God did not play in convincing of me, the devil did not play in tempting of me, neither did I play when I sunk into a bottomless pit, when the pangs of hell caught hold upon me; wherefore I may not play in my relating of them, but be plain and simple, and lay down the thing as it was.[38]

Following the death of John Gifford in 1655, Bunyan's next pastor in Bedford was John Burton, who wrote a forward to the novice preacher's first published work mentioned earlier, the polemical tract directed against the Quakers and Ranters titled *Some Gospel Truths Opened*. In this recommendation he writes:

---

[37] Bunyan, *Works*, II, p. 686.

[38] Ibid., I, p. 5.

> Reader, in this book thou wilt not meet with high flown airy notions, which some delight in, counting them high mysteries, but the sound, plain, common, (and yet spiritual and mysterious) truths of the gospel. . . . Neither doth this treatise offer to thee doubtful controversial things, or matters of opinion, as some books chiefly do, which when insisted upon, the weightier things of the gospel have always done more hurt than good: But here thou hast things certain, and necessary to be believed, which thou canst not too much study. . . . This man is not chosen out of an earthly, but out of the heavenly university, the church of Christ. . . . And though this man hath not the learning or wisdom of man, yet through grace he hath received the teaching of God, and the learning of the Spirit of Christ, which is the thing that makes a man both a Christian and a minister of the gospel. . . . He hath, through grace taken these three heavenly degrees, to wit, union with Christ, the anointing of the Spirit, and experience of the temptations of Satan, which do more fit a man for that mighty work of preaching the gospel, than all university learning and degrees that can be had.[39]

While men of formal learning, as so many of the Puritans were, yet they took the similarly learned Apostle Paul to be their model when he wrote to the Corinthians: "And when I came to you, brethren, I did not come with superiority of speech or of wisdom, proclaiming to you the testimony of God. . . . And my message and my preaching were not in persuasive words of wisdom, but in demonstration of the Spirit and of power" (I Cor. 2:1, 4). So untutored Bunyan took this same stance; together they shunned "pulpiteering," that is preaching in a grand and oratorical style since, as Packer quotes John Flavel: "A crucified style best suits the preachers of a crucified Christ."[40]

5. Bunyan was a man of the Spirit.

By this it is meant that he was not only well endowed with spiritual gifts, but also he was a pastoral exemplar of spiritual graces. George Offor makes special mention of Bunyan's self-renouncing persona as follows:

> The finest trait in Bunyan's character was his deep, heartfelt humility. This is the more extraordinary from his want of secular education, and his unrivaled talent. . . . He acknowledged to Mr. Cockayn [a London pastor and friend], who considered him the

39 Ibid., II, 140-1.

40 Packer, *Quest For Godliness*, p. 75.

> most eminent man, and a star of the first magnitude in the firmament of the churches, that spiritual pride was his easily besetting sin, and that he needed the thorn in the flesh, lest he should be exalted above measure. . . . His self-abasement was neither tinctured with affectation, nor with the pride of humility. His humble-mindedness appeared to arise from his intimate communion with Heaven.[41]

In other words, Bunyan's total submission to the Bible as pure objective truth led to a subjective self-evaluation that is so honestly recorded in *Grace Abounding To The Chief Of Sinners*. There his transparency is primarily before God. To be sure, the immediate experience is withering humiliation, near to the point of despair, yet the ultimate end is the triumph and praise of sovereign grace. Hence for the purpose of maintaining the house of the Lord or local church, he shares some "of the spoils won in battles."[42]

It is for this reason that just as Bunyan declares, "I preached what I felt, what I smartingly did feel, even that under which my poor soul did groan and tremble to astonishment,"[43] so he writes with the same amalgam of revelation from God and intimate encounter with God. There is no pretension, no scripting of what others might expect him to write, only a subdued soul that, having been stripped naked of any sham, desires and grasps for the gracious righteousness of God in company with those of like mind. He describes this quest as follows:

> For my part, I find it one of the hardest things that I can put my soul upon, even to come to God, when warmly sensible that I am a sinner, for a share in grace and mercy. Oh! methinks it seems to me as if the whole face of the heavens were set against me. Yes, the very thought of God strikes me through, I cannot bear up, I cannot stand before him, I cannot but with a thousand tears say, 'God be merciful to me a sinner' (Ezra 9:15; Luke 18:13). At another time when my heart is more hard and stupid, and when his terror does not make me afraid, then I can come before him and talk of my sins, and ask mercy at his hand, and scarce be sensible of sin or grace, or that indeed I am before God: But above all, they are the rare times, when I can go to God as the Publican, sensible of his

41 Bunyan, *Works*, I, p. lxxvii.

42 Ibid., § 339, p. 49.

43 Ibid., § 276, p. 42.

glorious majesty, sensible of my misery, and bear up, and affectionately cry, 'God be merciful to me a sinner.'[44]

Hence, it may be truly said of Bunyan that he never addressed hearers and readers with vital truth except he had first addressed his own heart concerning the very same matter. Thus when Packer describes the Puritan contemporaries of the Bedford tinker, he at the same time precisely describes the tinker himself, for he also gave personal priority to, "conscientious faithfulness to the Bible; vivid perception of God's reality and greatness; inflexible desire to honor and please him; deep self-searching and radical self-denial; adoring intimacy with Christ; generous compassion manward; forthright simplicity, God-taught and God-wrought, adult in its knowingness while childlike in its directness."[45] Therefore it should again be remembered that, upon Bunyan's death, one appreciative elegy rightly declared:

He in the pulpit preached truth first, and then
He in his practice preached it o'er again.[46]

THE PILGRIM'S PROGRESS AS PURITAN LITERATURE

It is probably far more difficult for the twentieth century western mind to grasp the setting of communication in the Puritan seventeenth century than might at first be thought. Our view today of Puritan writings through a visual graphics and image orientation would likely assess such literature as unattractive, verbose, dull, difficult to read, lacking in a sense of humor, boring, antiquated, and highly moralistic. Yet how would the Puritan assess our writings today? Surely the graphic presentation would for a while amaze him, as would the quality of printing and production. But with regard to content, apart from the numbing advance in technology, he would most likely rate our books in general as juvenile, so often trivial, quite apart from his obvious revulsion at our raw paganism and moral decadence.

Hence *The Pilgrim's Progress* remains a Puritan work that had great seventeenth century appeal, though it was somewhat in advance of its time nevertheless. So what might be said about it in preparation for considering how it ought to be communicated in this late twentieth century?

---

[44] Ibid., II, p. 261.

[45] Packer, *Quest For Godliness*, p. 77.

[46] Bunyan, *Works*, I, p. lxxiv.

It Addresses the Reader Typographically, Not Visually

By modern standards, the first edition of *The Pilgrim's Progress* was extremely plain and uninviting. No larger than 5½" x 4¼", it was printed with new, though to our appreciation, rough type on yellowish-gray paper; it initially included poor spelling and misprints, and lacked a number of narrative incidents that are included in the subsequent second and third editions. Bound in sheepskin, without any illustration,[47] it included 232 pages in addition to the author's apology and conclusion, and cost one shilling and sixpence. The circulation of the eleven editions published during Bunyan's lifetime was approximately 100,000.

In the light of this relatively plain, even tawdry presentation, *The Pilgrim's Progress* sharply contrasts with the visual image emphasis of this century. This paperback sized volume with cold black type lacking the warmth of full color, vivid illustration, and the appeal of sophisticated layout, more narrowly relies upon the alternative attraction of allegorical illustration, purity and simplicity of prose, and the foundation of pervasive, authoritative biblical substance. The appeal concerns content rather than visual enticement.

It Addresses the Reader Cognitively.

During the seventeenth century, the reader expected to be informed rather than impressed. He had no background of modern advertising that "sells the sizzle, not the steak," of twentieth century publishing that attracts by illustration rather than objective truth, of modern television that entices by image sensation rather than a truth message. However, a book composed of unadorned pages that are repetitively crammed with small type and large paragraphs, did *not* present a problem for the literate English commoner.

Why was this so? Neil Postman gives the answer, and while he focuses upon the literacy of eighteenth century America compared with today, yet his response is obviously applicable with regard to the literary acuity of the seventeenth century Puritan and his audience compared with the relative cognitive dullness of evangelicals today. He writes:

---

[47] This assumes the conclusion of Sharrock that the "Sleeping Portrait" was not included until the third edition. Bunyan, *The Pilgrim's Progress*, ed. Sharrock, p. xxxviii-xxxix. While illustrated versions, especially for children, were forthcoming, it was literary rather than graphic illustration that brought rapid popularity.

The name I give to that period of time during which the American mind submitted itself to the sovereignty of the printing press is the Age of Exposition. Exposition is a mode of thought, a method of learning, and a means of expression. Almost all of the characteristics we associate with mature discourse were amplified by typography, which has the strongest possible bias toward exposition: a sophisticated ability to think conceptually, deductively and sequentially; a high valuation of reason and order; an abhorrence of contradiction; a large capacity for detachment and objectivity; and a tolerance for delayed response. Toward the end of the nineteenth century, for reasons I am most anxious to explain, the Age of Exposition began to pass, and the early signs of its replacement could be discerned. Its replacement was to be the Age of Show Business.[48]

It Addresses the Reader with an Allegory to Reality Order

That is, whereas the present age desperately attempts to escape reality and ultimate truth by means of Hollywood fantasy, television escapism, theme park adventure, science fiction make-believe, drug induced hallucination, or even funeral parlor cosmetology, in contrast *The Pilgrim's Progress* uses allegory and an adventure image that are intended inevitably to lead the reader to confrontation with the reality of biblical truth and salvation. The allegorical adornment is but a means to a substantial and objective end; it is *not* an end in itself.

In the same vein, this reality concerns truth which alone can give rise to legitimate experience. The allegorical road to reality leads from the truth of a wilderness world to the truth of citizenship in a holy heaven, from the truth of condemnation by God to the truth of saving grace from God, from the knowledge of this truth to the personal embrace of this truth. From the very beginning of *The Pilgrim's Progress*, Bunyan makes this intent quite clear.

> Would'st thou see a truth within a fable?
> Would'st thou be in a dream, and yet not sleep?[49]

---

[48] Neil Postman, *Amusing Ourselves To Death*, p. 63.

[49] Bunyan, *Works*, III, p. 87.

CHAPTER SEVENTEEN

Twentieth Century Communication of The Pilgrim's Progress

To be transported rapidly from the literary culture of seventeenth century England, and particularly the Puritan sermonic/typographic style of that period, to the ubiquitous multi-media jungle of the twentieth century as it impacts evangelical Christianity, is to experience a truly Copernican revolution. To consider the "advance" from the God of Stephen Charnock to the God of Robert Schuller, from Thomas Manton to the drama and glitz of designer churches, from John Bunyan to the religious professionals of today who shamelessly promote the gospel using the marketing strategy of Vanity Fair, is to be confronted with a leap of quantum proportions. And this being so, in our desire to communicate most effectively *The Pilgrim's Progress* today, the vital question arises as to what degree we can utilize modern communication methods while at the same time not dishonoring God and disregarding Bunyan's expressed purposes. In other words, how can we employ communicative means that complement a sacred message and attain a holy, God glorifying end that focuses on the substance of this peerless allegory?

The Legacy of Dominant Print

It is no exaggeration to state that the two hundred year period following the publication of *The Pilgrim's Progress* in 1678 was dominated by and increasingly saturated with the printed page. This was really the only popular medium available. Neil Postman explains: "From the seventeenth century to the late nineteenth century, printed matter was virtually all that was available, There were no movies to see, radio to hear, photographic displays to look at, records to play. There was no television. Public business was channeled into and expressed through print, which became the model, the metaphor and the measure of all discourse."[1] While advances were made, during this period, in designing more efficient printing presses, in illustration and graphic design, in paper production and binding, yet the message imprinted by handset type was one to be mentally digested.

Postman well characterizes this period as follows:

> From Erasmus in the sixteenth century to Elizabeth Eisenstein in the twentieth, almost every scholar who has grappled with the question of what reading does to one's habits of mind has concluded that the process encourages rationality. . . . To engage the written word means to follow a line of thought, which requires considerable powers of classifying, inference-making and reasoning. It means to uncover lies, confusions, and over-generalizations, to detect abuses of logic and common sense. It also means to weigh ideas, to compare and contrast assertions, to connect one generalization to another. . . . In a culture dominated by print, public discourse tends to be characterized by a coherent, orderly arrangement of facts and ideas.[2]

It should also be kept in mind that during these successive centuries mentioned above, apart from the Bible, *The Pilgrim's Progress* was unquestionably the most widely read book in the English speaking world. Further, in the realm of graphic layout considerable advance was made, and no better indication of this could be gained than by perusal of the exquisite nineteenth century illustration of Barnard, Bennett, Copping, Dalziel, Friston, Linton, Priolo, the Rhead brothers, Selous, Watson, and Wentworth.

The Dawning of Audio-visual Stimulation

Suddenly, as the nineteenth century began to set, beside this surging torrent of print, another stream of a different sort commenced to cascade forth with the result that these two rivers converged. This mingling of two strong currents, typographic and audio-visual media, was productive of greater variety of impression and style, sensual as well as cognitive appeal, and increased choice for the human psyche that was all too ready for stimulation. The cumulative effect was overwhelming with the result that the informative and educational process experienced a revolution The following diagram indicates the rapid succession of these new means of communication.

---

[1] Neil Postman, *Amusing Ourselves To Death*, p. 41.

[2] Ibid., p. 51.

MEDIUM	INAUGURATION	COMMENTS
PRINT		
Flatbed	1450	Gutenberg
Rotary	1850	Letterpress only
Rotary - high speed	1920's	Letterpress, Gravure, Litho
PHOTOGRAPHY	1841	Negative/Positive copying
TELEGRAPHY	1845	Public Corp., Morse code
TELEPHONE		
Wire	1878	Bell Telephone Incorporated
Radio	1927	Between U.S. and England
PHONOGRAPH	1877	Edison's first cylinder
MOTION PICTURES		
Silent	1903	"The Great Train Robbery"
Color	1922	"The Toll of the Sea"
Sound	1927	"The Jazz Singer"
RADIO	1920	First scheduled programs
TELEVISION		
Black and White	1936	Public Broadcast, England
Color	1951	Public Broadcast, U.S.
SATELLITE	1962	Telstar
COMPUTER	1983	Internet, Email

NEW MEDIA INVADE THE TWENTIETH CENTURY

However further consider even more recent developments with digital audio and surround sound, video cassettes and discs augmented by big screens, high definition video, mobile telephones, computers, compact discs, fax machines, and the imminent prospect of virtual reality. Does this revolution in communications technology present a window of opportunity for a more welcome and clear contemporary proclamation of *The Pilgrim's Progress*? Some would, with great creative enthusiasm, undoubtedly think so.

The Embrace of Sensible Communication.

What then has been the fall out effect of this new wave of communications technology upon print, the former prima donna of the cognitive world? Mitchell Stephens of the *Los Angeles Times* provides a good sitcom illustration:

> What's missing from these pictures? Three people sit in a doctor's waiting room. One stares at the television that rests on an end table, the second fiddles with a hand-held video game; the head of the third is wrapped in earphones. A couple of kids, waiting for bedtime, lie on the floor of a brightly painted room, busily manipulating the controls of a video game. Two hundred people sit in an airplane. Some have brought their own tapes, some doze, most stare up at a small movie screen. What is missing from these pictures, and increasingly from our lives, is the activity through which most of us learned much of what we know of the wider world. What's missing is the force that, according to a growing consensus of historians, established our patterns of thought and, in an important sense, made our civilization. What's missing is the venerable, increasingly dated activity that you . . . are engaged in right now [reading].[3]

However, these major contemporary media rivals have taught the elder typographic statesman a thing or two, though more by way of seduction than refinement of breeding. For the new generation of communication vehicles, and especially television, has distinguished itself by offering expertise in suggestive imagery, sensual impression, disjointed immediacy, varnished reality, and commercial profitability. David Wells describes this distinctive capability as follows:

> Television entertainments tend to avoid problems that can't be solved by the end of an hour; in some ways they turn their backs on messy reality altogether, weaving a fiction of happy automatons with gleaming teeth, well-kept homes, shiny new cars, and hair that is never mussed for long. . . . In television's fantasy world, gangsters are sophisticated and intelligent, and prostitutes are glamorous and healthy, untouched by the violence, manipulation, and fear that plagues the real world's mean streets. On the whole, television

---

[3] Mitchell Stephens, "The Death of Reading," *Los Angeles Times Magazine*, September 22, 1991, p. 10.

> makes no pretense of having a social conscience. Its perspective on life is not moral. It is not even real. . . . Television serves up a stream of fleeting images that . . . are arranged more to produce a dramatic effect than to convey consistent ideas in a logical manner. It is of the very essence of television that it is impermanent. Viewers are meant to experience the programming, not to think about it.[4]

As a result, the print media have not been slow to learn. Newspaper formats now present "print-bites," rather than extended narrative or prose, supported by spot color layout and full color illustrations. *USA Today* has become the *CNN* of the press. Magazines and specialty newspapers place heavy emphasis on graphics and photography, almost to the point where the text has become of subsidiary importance. In children's literature, graphics, especially cartooning and vivid color, have taken on a primary role in communicative method.

Yet has this shift of emphasis resulted in a resurgence of reading, even of the more popular sort? Has this mixture of television style and typography worked? In no way. Stephens explains:

> The Gulf War provided further evidence of how far the newspaper has fallen. According to a survey by Birch/Scarborough, a grand total of 8.9% of us [in the U.S.] said we kept up with the war news primarily through newspapers. The days when we found most of our news set in type on a page are long gone. . . . Here is perhaps the most frightening of the statistics on books: According to the Gallup Poll, the number of Americans who admitted to having read no books during the past year—and this is not an easy thing to admit to a pollster—doubled from 1978 to 1990, from 8% to 16%.[5]

Postman thoroughly agrees, though he is far more specific with regard to explaining not only why this conflict remains, but also why it offers no prospect of reconciliation:

> Television's way of knowing is uncompromisingly hostile to typography's way of knowing; . . . television's conversations promote incoherence and triviality; . . . the phrase "serious television" is a contradiction in terms; . . . television speaks in only one persistent voice—the voice of entertainment. . . . to enter the great television conversation, one American cultural institution after

[4] David F. Wells, *No Place For Truth*, pp. 200-201.

[5] Stephens, "The Death of Reading," p. 12.

> another is learning to speak its terms. Television, in other words, is transforming our culture into one vast arena for show business.[6]

This being so, then ought the communication of *The Pilgrim's Progress* to this twentieth century generation include similar flirtation with the media style of modernity? Should Bunyan's typography be wedded to a sensual/image priority?

The Seduction of Sensual Communication.

The seeming triumph of the phosphorous screen over the typographic page, of the picture over print, of image over cognition, has far broader consequences that relate to human behavior in general than merely a necessary change in communicative strategy. In Postman's *Amusing Ourselves To Death*, his title prophetically directs us to his main thesis that western man's destiny, by means of media direction, is one of blissful giddiness born of hedonistic intoxication. He writes:

> What I am claiming here is not that television is entertaining but that it has made entertainment itself the natural format for the representation of all experience. . . . The problem is not that television presents us with entertaining subject matter but that all subject matter is presented as entertaining, which is another issue altogether. . . . No matter what is depicted or from what point of view, the overarching presumption is that it is there for our amusement and pleasure. . . . Everything about a news show tells us this—the good looks and amiability of the cast, their pleasant banter, the exciting music that opens and closes the show, the vivid film footage, the attractive commercials—all these and more suggest that what we have just seen is no cause for weeping. A news show, to put it plainly, is a format for entertainment, not for education, reflection or catharsis.[7]

Postman further concludes that, because of this encroaching entertainment mind-set, Aldous Huxley's forecast of man's future direction in his *Brave New World* is far more probable than that of George Orwell in his *Nineteen Eighty-Four*:

> What Orwell feared were those who would ban books [in a police state]. What Huxley feared was that there would be no reason to ban a book, for there would be no one who wanted to read one [in an indulgent state]. Orwell feared those who would deprive us of

---

6 Postman, *Amusing Ourselves To Death*, p. 80.

7 Ibid., pp. 87-88.

> information. Huxley feared those who would give us so much that we would be reduced to passivity and egoism. Orwell feared that the truth would be concealed from us. Huxley feared the truth would be drowned in a sea of irrelevance. Orwell feared that we would become a captive culture. Huxley feared that we would become a trivial culture, preoccupied with some equivalent of the feelies. . . . In *1984*, Huxley added, people were controlled by inflicting pain. In *Brave New World*, they are controlled by inflicting pleasure. . . . This book [*Amusing Ourselves To Death*] is about the possibility that Huxley, not Orwell, was right.[8]

That western society has moved in a more light-hearted direction, in parallel with greater exposure to the audio/visual media, is not difficult to demonstrate. The trend is now, even in the workplace as well as church life, toward a more relaxed atmosphere, informal protocol, and casual dress. A recent syndicated newspaper article originating from Boca Raton, Florida is headlined, "Office laughter helps employees enjoy their work." Author Amy Ellis explains that employers are finding,

> that lightening up and encouraging their employees to do the same is an effective way to boost morale and worker productivity. "There's been a dramatic turn away from fear as a way to motivate the work force," says Bill Wood, president of the Delray Beach, Fla., Chamber of Commerce. "Things have loosened up at the workplace, and there's a general understanding that its OK to laugh and have a good time." Behind all the jocularity, however, there is a serious message. In his book, "Lighten Up," C. W. Metcalf maintains that "silliness in the face of seriousness is a mark of mental health, and the failure to find humor in threatening situations can indicate dullness, rigidity and sometimes even mental illness." . . . Workers at Boca Raton First National Bank are encouraged to "dress down" on Fridays and "dress up" on major holidays. Staff members at Boca Raton Magazine relieve stress by starting water gun fights or playing with the company intercom.[9]

If this tendency continues, it may well happen that the military will be next to incorporate a philosophy of humor into its training for battle preparedness! Even funerals are now euphemistically designated as "celebrations of life." So one may realistically wonder just how long it will take for grief therapy to incorporate

---

[8] Ibid., pp. vii-viii.

[9] Amy Ellis, "Office laughter helps employees enjoy their work," Escondido *Times Advocate*, September 26, 1993, pp. G2-3.

clowning, and for the graveside ceremony to be reconstituted as a jovial "ringing down of the curtain" upon the life of a person who entertained well. For after all, is not entertainment what life is all about?

The Dilemma of Cognitive Literary Communication.

That the print media are strong on stimulating retained understanding and weak on creating visual impression goes without need of further proof. That the audio/visual media are strong on stimulating visual impression and weak on creating retained understanding is now a matter that is well supported by reliable evidence. In a *U.S. News & World Report* article entitled, "What is TV Doing To America?", author James Mann writes:

> Until recently, there was little research on how the human brain absorbs information from TV. Many scholars long have been convinced that viewers retain less from television than from reading, but evidence was scarce. Now, a research project from Jacob Jacob, a Purdue University Psychologist, has found that more than 90 percent of 2,700 people tested misunderstood even such simple fare as commercials or the detective series "Barnaby Jones." Only minutes after watching, the typical viewer missed 23 to 36 percent of the questions about what he or she had seen. One explanation is that TV's compelling pictures stimulate primarily the right half of the brain, which specializes in emotional responses, rather than the left hemisphere, where thinking and analysis are performed. By connecting viewers to instruments that measure brain waves, researcher Herbert Krugman found periods of right-brain activity outnumbering left-brain activity by a ratio of 2 to 1. Another difficulty is the rapid linear movement of TV images, which gives viewers little chance to pause and reflect on what they have seen. Scientists say this torrent of images also has a numbing effect, as measured electronically by the high proportion of alpha brain waves, normally associated with daydreaming or falling asleep. The result is shortened attention spans—a phenomenon increasingly lamented by teachers trying to hold the interest of students accustomed to TV.[10]

So for the modern communicator who desires to get his message across in clear print, because he believes that understanding is of primary importance, a dilemma arises. On the one hand, the medium of the printed page will best accomplish his desired end

---

[10] James Mann, "What is TV Doing To America?", *U.S. News & World Report*, August 2, 1982, p. 28.

while yet reaching a diminishing audience that is unrepresentative of society in general. On the other hand, audio/visual media will reach an expanding audience which, while being impressed to some degree, will yet lack high comprehension of the intended message.

To focus even more closely on this problem, consider the dilemma as it applies to the communication of *The Pilgrim's Progress* to a modern audience. Shall the primary thrust be print for the sake of better impartation of the truth to a more limited audience, or shall capitulation be made to the more in vogue audio/visual media for the sake of making a broad impression upon a large audience? And further, can a "both-and" resolution of this problem be forged that effectively does away with the "either-or" impasse? The next heading gives definitive answers to these questions, though it introduces a feature which is peculiarly Christian, and that is the vital element of the Spirit of God that animates authentic proclamation of the truth of God to sinful mankind.

Of course the dilemma just unfolded equally applies to the communication of the Word of God, that is the printed Bible. To consider it in parallel with *The Pilgrim's Progress*, while according it reverence that no other book merits, will yet help us in our quest to best honor God through the right portrayal of Bunyan's classic allegory.

TWENTIETH CENTURY CHRISTIAN LITERARY COMMUNICATION

Of all Christian literature that has been published over the past nineteen hundred years of church history, it would be hard to find a volume that lends itself to visual expression more than does Bunyan's *The Pilgrim's Progress*. The literary imagery alone of this work is quick to engrave indelible pictures on the mind. Hence, it is no surprise that those with an artistic and enterprising bent have attempted to employ audio/visual media of almost every kind for the purpose of obtaining enhanced and relevant communication of this classic allegory. Illustration and representation of various styles including cartooning, drama, music, and film, have all been employed. However, the degree to which these means have accomplished Bunyan's declared purposes, they being rooted in typographic expression, still remains a most debatable point. And this being the case, it would seem that further reflection upon the conflicting principles involved may help to bring about a right resolution.

The Present Audio/Visual Indulgence.

In general, contemporary Christianity, whether it be liberal, moderate, or conservative, has readily bought into the overtures of opportunity marketed by the audio/visual media. Recall again the statement of Postman that, "to enter the great television conversation, one American cultural institution after another is learning to speak its terms."[11] That Postman includes the Christian church as one such entrant is beyond doubt, especially when he further devotes one whole chapter to American Christianity's romance with "show biz" communication. His conclusion, apparently not one of a conservative evangelical, is frank and to the point. It is cause for serious reflection.

> First, . . . on television, religion, like everything else, is presented, quite simply and without apology, as an entertainment. Everything that makes religion an historic, profound and sacred human activity is stripped away; there is no ritual, no dogma, no tradition, no theology, and above all, no sense of spiritual transcendence. On these shows, the preacher is tops. God comes out as second banana.[12]

In other words, television cannot be tamed or subdued, though it does transform and subdue those who would attempt to sanctify its secularity. It does wed well with its own kind. Coleen Cook, an evangelical Christian and former TV news anchor, comments:

> One reason Charismatics dominate much of Christian TV is that charismatic expression is simply more theatrical and visual than the worship style of some other Protestant groups. Charismatic theology also tends to be less preoccupied with complex theological

---

[11] Postman, *Amusing Ourselves To Death*, p. 80.

[12] Ibid., pp. 116-117, 121. In response to Postman's pessimistic appraisal of television in terms of it being a relative failure as a cognitive medium of communication is *Redeeming Television* by Quentin Schultze. From a Reformed and cultural mandate perspective, Schultze argues for the redemption of television for communicative usefulness by means of the employment of certain principles, pp. 165-80. 1. Let Christians become discerning viewers. 2. Let Christians be educated concerning television. 3. Let Christians help to redeem television institutions. 4. Let Christians cultivate commercial alternatives. 5. Let Christians encourage informed media criticism. However, this writer would still side with the view of Postman that television, because of its essential visual, image and entertainment character, cannot supplant the priority of word/truth in print.

concepts and systematized theology. Since it is less complicated, it tends to work better on television.[13]

1. The case of Christianity Today.

In David Wells' *No Place For Truth*, he carefully documents the effect of the audio/visual media, over a thirty year period, upon evangelical Christianity's premier magazine, originally a classic print medium:

> *Christianity Today* was born in 1956 at almost exactly the moment when Americans entered the Age of Television; 1955 was the year when 50 percent of Americans owned television sets, and by 1960 the overwhelming majority had purchased passports to the new Promised Land of video experience. The early years of *Christianity Today*, perhaps out of financial exigency, showed no recognition of the new Age that had dawned, but as black and white sets increasingly gave way to color, so too did *Christianity Today*. The cheap, pulpy paper on which it had begun its life gave way to bright, colorful coated stock in the 1970s."
>
> . . . By 1989, then the transition had been completed. *Christianity Today* now looked like a poor cousin to *Time* magazine, basically a news magazine that was simply a little more pious and a little less interesting than the genuine article. And, like *Time*, it has repackaged its content for the video age, using abbreviated stories and lots of color graphics to encourage a leisurely, recreational reading of the magazine. This is not a particularly happy development in the pages of a magazine covering the secular fabric of society, but it is a cause for considerably graver concern when the Christian faith is used as a matter for our distraction and entertainment.[14]

However, even more disturbing for Wells is his discovery of a shift of emphasis with regard to content, from the doctrinal to the relational, from the objective to the subjective, from essays to more segmentation.

> By 1989, gone was the vision in which the magazine was born, gone was its moral and intellectual fiber, and gone was its ability to call the evangelical constituency to greater Christian faithfulness. Reflecting the nostrums of the therapeutic society had been transformed from a vice into a virtue, and popularity had been

[13] Coleen Cook, *All That Glitters*, p. 195.

[14] Wells, *No Place For Truth*, pp. 207, 210-211.

transformed from something incidental to Christian truth to something central to it.[15]

2. *The case of Marvel Comics' The Pilgrim's Progress.*

A review article in the July 19, 1993 issue of *Christianity Today* describes a joint publishing venture between Thomas Nelson Publishers and Marvel Comics. They have just released an all-color comic-book version of *The Pilgrim's Progress* which is hailed as the first in a series of Christian classics. We are told that, "the primary difference in story line between the comic-book and the original is that the story has been updated to the twentieth century."[16] In other words, we are to expect the application of audio/visual media principles of communication to a pure print medium in such a way that image focused teens who dimly comprehend text can more easily understand the essential truth of Bunyan's biblical allegory. So to what degree is this goal faithfully accomplished?

Image adaptation is vivid in the extreme, as is characteristic of comic-book style. Christian, Faithful, and Hopeful (a black man), on account of frequently being depicted as bare-chested, are all evidently on high protein diets and preoccupied with body-building. Conflict receives extreme and grotesque portrayal; heaven seems galactic, while the biblically substantial discourses are totally missing. The great virtue appears to be virility rather than a meek and humble spirit that Bunyan so epitomized.

Truth content confronts us with far more serious problems, and especially perversion of catastrophic proportions. We are not considering here merely the use of contemporary expressions for the sake of relevance, but obvious revisionism. In a slough of industrial waste, Christian is rescued by a man, presumably Help, who is labeled "Our Earth Ecology, Inc." The man in the iron cage in the original text describes himself as once a "fair and flourishing professor [confessing believer];" however, the ignorance of the reviser is indicated when he has the man confess, "I was once a flourishing scholar." Then in total contradiction of what Bunyan wrote, the despairing man explains, "I have built this cage

---

[15] Ibid., p. 211.

[16] Ross Pavlac, "Bang! Zow! Christian Comic Books Join Fight for Teens," *Christianity Today*, July 2, 1993, p. 48.

to live in [not, 'God himself hath shut me up in this iron cage']. Here, I can hide and be safe from troubles."[17]

When a demon attacks Christiana and Mercy and exclaims, "Hahh!! They're just women!!," to the rescue comes nubile Great-heart clad in shapely armor, yes a woman, and not a man-servant of Interpreter. The gospel too, being portrayed more synergistically, places greater emphasis upon faith than, as is Bunyan's overwhelming interest, faith's atoning object. The truth of justification by faith in Christ's personal substitutionary righteousness, including mention of the embroidered coat, is obviously omitted on account of it being considered as theology that is too complex. It is not surprising that Mr. Valiant-for-truth does not receive a mention. Surely the tinker of Bedford would cry out in dismay, "And as I slept I dreamed a dream, . . . and behold it has now been turned into a nightmare!"

The Challenge of Capitulation.

From the outset of what follows, let it be understood that this writer's proposal, although containing strong criticism of popular "Christian" communications theory, is nevertheless not a call to blind obscurantism, the avoidance of change for the sake of the preservation of historic tradition. The social status quo of this century must be honestly addressed, and not only idealism. However, the case that follows is, without apology, a call for the resistance of communications theory overtures that, even with the best of intentions, revise the truth, dilute the truth, demean the truth, and employ media that conflict with the truth.

Admittedly, the whole contemporary media culture employs enormous amounts of energy in soliciting participation in its stimulating delights. And the Christian church has in no way been immune from feeling the tremendous force of this industry's siren-like argument, namely, that if you want to reach the world, then you must communicate using the world's language. However, to this proposition two additional truths must be added. First, the language of this world is primarily molded and transmitted by the audio/visual media, and this means that its essential thrust is entertainment, certainly before truth cognition. Second, the research information of George Barna concerning the basic focus of most Americans must be considered here as well. He concludes: "Two out of three adults (63%) concur that the purpose of life is enjoyment and personal fulfillment. They have little sense that we

---

[17] John Bunyan-Martin Powell, *The Pilgrim's Progress*, Marvel Comics.

have been placed on earth with a higher mission, or to fulfill the goals of an omnipotent and omniscient God."[18] In other words, even at a religious level, most Americans are primarily interested in entertainment, in psyche massage, in egocentricity. So that, in the absence of some jolting prophetic jeremiad, some awakening pulpit fire from a John the Baptist, then the only alternative is capitulation to the allure of the visual, media style agenda.

1. Visual performance enticement.

Unfortunately, some Christians seem ready to yield to the beckoning call of, if not the primary electronic media, then the kindred means of audio/visual communication that similarly engage interest through entertainment. Referring again to Coleen Cook, she thoroughly agrees with Postman's analysis of television, and especially its genre identification as entertainment.[19] She further adds: "I know that television is best at creating illusions, not at communicating truth. Since Jesus was in the truth business, television might have presented some very perplexing problems for him."[20]

However, the conclusion of *All That Glitters* leads us in a change of direction, almost a complete about turn, when the author recommends church drama as a means of reaching baby-boomers and seekers. What is the rationale for this proposal?

> The church must recognize that this new breed of church seeker has been subliminally conditioned to the look and feel of television information and will be unconsciously drawn to church initially by the style of presentation, not by the substance of the teaching. This is not to suggest that there should be no substance in what we present during church, but that we need to adapt our style of presentation to the conditioned expectations of the audience—especially the unchurched—if we are to reach them.[21]

That is to say, the church must entice the unbeliever by means of the medium to which he is accustomed. If the world is attracted by the mode of entertainment, then let the church clothe substance in entertainment. But, to draw upon Postman's essential conviction, what happens to the substance that Cook would make inclusive

---

[18] George Barna, *What Americans Believe*, p. 30.

[19] Cook, *All That Glitters*, pp. 241-43.

[20] Ibid., p. 202.

[21] Ibid., p. 262.

here? Surely it is that the communication of that substance by means of an entertainment medium results in that same substance being identified by the congregation *as* entertainment. The medium inevitably intrudes upon the message. In this way the truth becomes polluted.

Cook continues: "The church can learn from 'preachers' such as Norman Lear [humanist producer of the television series *All In The Family*]—people today accept information more readily if they are being entertained."[22] But furthermore, the intention here is not merely to entertain as a prelude, but also package the gospel in a manner that makes it more digestible. Thus Cook explains:

> I believe that the church is standing at a crossroads in communicating the gospel. We are faced with the difficult, but not impossible, task of drawing secular people to the point of faith by first recognizing where their frame of reference is. Bowing to the demands of a TV-conditioned culture and being contemporary in our approach can give a face-lift to the gospel presentation that is a starting point but not the ending.[23]

This sort of reasoning would have been unthinkable for the apostles of the early church, even though they encountered cultural diversity of no lesser proportion than today, especially when one

---

[22] Ibid., p. 264.

[23] Ibid., p. 264. The author musters several arguments to support her case. New Testament evidence of any sort is conspicuous by its absence. (1) In the Old Testament, both tabernacle and temple worship were audio/visual in nature and appealed to all five senses. However, in the New Testament these matters are described as part of "the weak and worthless things" (Gal. 4:3, 9) which, for Christians, have been superceded by worship "in spirit and truth" (John 4:21-24). (2) The illiterate medieval church resorted to passion and morality plays. However, the remedy for this situation was the Reformation when the truth of God's Word initiated earth-shaking revival and supplanted ineffectual drama with the glories of the gospel. (3) The Old Testament prophets proclaimed truth using a variety of visual media. Presumably Jeremiah's visit to the potter (Jer. 18:1-6), Ezekiel's tile city (Ezek. 4:1-4), and Amos' beholding of the Lord's plumb line (Amos 7:7-9) are in mind here. However, most emblems of this sort were beheld in visions; they, together with the relatively few tangible items, were undoubtedly revealed to the prophets for the purpose of establishing permanency through inscripturation. It should be remembered that verbal imagery, as opposed to visual imagery, plays a significant part in Scripture. So it is the case with *The Pilgrim's Progress.*

considers the Hebrew, Greek, and Roman life-style variations. They would have considered such reasoning as bordering on heresy, and particularly the suggestion that the gospel needed an updated, world-appealing dress.

John MacArthur, Jr. addresses this capitulation of the evangelical church in America very plainly in his recent book, *Ashamed Of The Gospel.* Of his courageous stance, we need many tribes of forthright preachers, and not pastoral C.E.O.'s. whose expertise is marketing and communications strategy.

> Some will maintain that if biblical principles are presented, the medium doesn't matter. That is nonsense. If an entertaining medium is the key to winning people, why not go all out? Why not have a real carnival? A tattooed acrobat on a high wire could juggle chain saws and shout Bible verses while a trick dog balanced on his head. That would draw a crowd. And the content of the message would still be biblical. . . . What's wrong with that? For one thing, the church has no business marketing its ministry as an alterative to secular amusements (I Thess. 3:2-6). That corrupts and cheapens the church's real mission. . . . Moreover, instead of confronting the world with the truth of Christ, the market-driven megachurches are enthusiastically promoting the worst trends of secular culture. Feeding people's appetite for entertainment only exacerbates the problems of mindless emotion, apathy, and materialism. Quite frankly, it is difficult to conceive of a ministry philosophy more contradictory to the pattern our Lord gave us.[24]

2. *Visual performance emptiness.*

It is significant to contemplate that the numerous visual/dramatic presentations of *The Pilgrim's Progress*, virtually without exception, have been characterized by extravagant form while at the same time lacking much original substance. This is especially true with regard to the considerable pruning of the discourse sections; the long though meaty discourse on the Enchanted Ground especially suffers in this regard. It seems that when the visual/dramatic mode takes control, it cannot suffer cognitive matters that draw attention away from its seductive dress.

a. A theme park parody.

This writer finds it surprising that, to date, no one appears to have suggested that a commercial theme park be developed that is based upon *The Pilgrim's Progress*. It boggles the mind to imagine

---

[24] John F. MacArthur, Jr., *Ashamed Of The Gospel*, pp. 69, 71.

the various rides and exhibits that could be constructed. At the park entrance, a roller-coaster would, at high speed, whisk away visitors from solicitous hucksters and furrow its way through the parting sludge of the Slough of Despond. More athletic types could attempt the impossible, that is the climbing of the snow-capped hill (Mt. Sinai) beyond which glistens the illuminated Village of Morality. Various characters, both admirable and disgusting, would mingle with the crowd readily agreeing to be photographed with tourists, the old and the young.

The tour of the house of the Interpreter, all seven dazzling rooms, would elicit screams of both delight and horror. At the wayside Place of Deliverance Chapel, meditation would be possible, or a wedding ceremony. Then would follow, after passing through a lane of caged lions, the glittering Palace Beautiful with its happy fountains, martial arts demonstrations, full service restaurant, and overnight accom-modation. A high tech exhibit, employing the very latest in robotic engineering, would pit chrome-armored Christian, complete with laser sword, against the luminiforous green, fire and curse belching Apollyon. Then would follow the fiendish Doubting Castle, incorporating a Bible exhibit with a variety of video dramatizations for sale. At Beulah Land, a theater in the round would project dazzling vistas of the Celestial City. The River of Death would be crossed near the exit by means of a pleasant boat ride leading to awaiting winged angels who bid the pilgrims farewell with gospel tracts and discount coupons for passing on to friends. Of course the declared purpose of this whole enterprise would be, perish the thought that it could be mercenary or otherwise, the presentation of the gospel in the modern idiom. After all, is not audio/visual communication, garnished with entertainment, the only way to go?

Surely the response to the above proposal must be, if it take seriously the essential character of biblical Christianity, an emphatic repudiation. Such a disturbing parody, though reflective of much contemporary evangelism, yet conjures up a sense of revulsion in the heart of the earnest child of God. And why is this so? Because the audio/visual/entertainment mix not only attempts to use unholy means to attain a holy end, with resulting contamination, but also it is grossly deficient in truth content.

b. Stage and drama presentations.

The same problems arise, as dealt with above, if a dramatic stage presentation of *The Pilgrim's Progress* is suggested. The medium remains an audio/visual/entertainment mix that is in essential conflict with Bunyan's sacred purposes, even his allegorical style. Postman comments:

> Most Americans . . . have difficulty accepting the truth, if they think about it at all, that not all forms of discourse can be converted from one medium to another. . . . Moreover, the television screen itself [and we would add the stage] has a strong bias toward a psychology of secularism. The screen [and the stage] is so saturated with our memories of profane events, so deeply associated with the commercial and entertainment worlds that it is difficult for it to be created as a frame for sacred events.[25]

Furthermore, the dramatic stage, as well as television, will, on account of its very nature, dethrone the priority of truth content and supplant it with the priority of entertainment. Truth will by no means be absent, but it will be subservient to the interests of presentation, impression, sensual experience, and satisfaction.

In this same vein, let it be proposed that Bunyan would in no way approve of an oratorio style of presentation of *The Pilgrim's Progress* that, while employing the most accomplished of musical style, yet eviscerated the text of eighty percent of its content while rearranging the remaining twenty percent. Such a work has indeed been produced by the eminent English composer Ralph Vaughan Williams. Simply titled *The Pilgrim's Progress*, it was first performed in four acts in 1951 at the Royal Opera House, Covent Garden, London, lasting approximately two and one half hours. The production was well received, especially in America, but the medium, as entertainment, overshadowed the diminutive role of truth.[26] Perhaps more revealing in this regard is the composer's response in correspondence with a friend who comments, "By the way your Pilgrim seems to be afraid of his Christian name." To this Vaughan Williams replied that, "I on purpose did not call the pilgrim 'Christian' because I want the idea to be universal and apply to anybody who aims at the spiritual life [as a pilgrimage] whether he is Xtian, Jew, Buddhist, Shintoist, or 5th Day Adventist."[27] Thus the essential Christian purposes of Bunyan were of no concern to this composer. In plain terms, the result is revisionism which generally all literary and musical composers object to when their own works are subject to truth evisceration.

---

25 Postman, *Amusing Ourselves To Death*, pp. 117, 119.

26 R. Vaughan Williams, *The Pilgrim's Progress*, pp. i-vii.

27 Michael Kennedy, *The Works of Ralph Vaughan Williams*, pp. 312-314.

3. The essential issue.

This then brings us to the point of great cleavage whereby the purposes of Bunyan, clearly expressed in *The Pilgrim's Progress,* are separated from the purposes of the modern apologists for the audio/visual/entertainment media. Bunyan's overriding concern in composing *The Pilgrim's Progress* is objective, biblical truth, doctrinal truth, gospel truth, and yes, transforming truth. At the same time he is not afraid to incorporate subsidiary adornment, whether it be an allegorical style, occasional droll humor, or even interpretive illustrations. But the important point here is that these elements most definitely remain subsidiary. They do not distort or overwhelm. However, with the enthusiast for the use of the audio/visual/entertainment media, the reverse of this point is true. For these people, whether they have religious investment here or not, their first interest is in human contentment and approbation, even at the expense of truth. They fear about giving offence; they are concerned about being responsible for boredom; they worry about being rejected. So to remedy any such problem they change the original performance and contextualize, or more truthfully, adjust the facts to suit the audience. Such an attitude is the very reverse of being prophetic, especially in a biblical sense.

Hence, it is concluded that to be faithful today to Bunyan's purposes for the proclamation of *The Pilgrim's Progress*, those media which best communicate truth ought primarily to be employed. Audio/visual support media are also to be used, but only in a secondary sense and as long as they remain supportive without offering conflict.

The Lesson from Divine Revelation

The God of the Bible has made himself known to mankind, that is He has disclosed or revealed himself in ways of his determining. Thus God has made communication with man, and He has determined specific media by which the infinite God might inform finite man, the eternal God might be known by temporal man, the spiritual God might have fellowship with material man, and the heavenly God might reach down to earthly man. However, our specific concern here is both the identification and analysis of these divine media, most commonly designated as general and special revelation, and especially their relationship to the relative usefulness of human audio/visual and print media that evangelical Christianity chooses to use today.

While God has implanted some knowledge of himself within the soul of man (Rom. 2:14-15), yet original sin and its universal inheritance has caused that understanding to be thoroughly perverted (Rom. 21-23). However, external to man God has mediated the truth about himself principally by means of general or natural revelation, that is the created order (Ps. 19:1-6; Acts 14:15-17; Rom. 1:18-21), and special or personalized revelation, that is the written Word of God and the incarnate appearing of the Lord Jesus Christ (Ps. 19:7-14; John 1:14; II Tim. 3:16-17; Heb. 1:1-2).

That God was very particular in his attitude toward man receiving a true self-disclosure of His person is evident by the fact that He utterly forbad, on pain of death (Deut. 17:2-5), any attempt to make a visual or substantial representation of himself. Postman presses home this point in a very relevant way:

> In studying the Bible as a young man, I found intimations of the idea that forms of media favor particular kinds of content and therefore are capable of taking command of a culture. I refer specifically to the Decalogue, the Second Commandment of which prohibits the Israelites from making concrete images of anything. "Thou shalt not make unto thee any graven image, or likeness of any thing that is in the heaven above, or that is in the earth beneath, or that is in the water beneath the earth." I wondered then, as so many others have, as to why the God of these people would have included instructions on how they were to symbolize, or not symbolize, their experience. It is a strange injunction to include as part of an ethical system unless the author assumed a connection between forms of human communication and the quality of a culture.[28]

As previously mentioned, God has seen fit to communicate himself in a variety of ways. Nevertheless, He has mandated against *man* having this same freedom and flexibility with regard to selecting media for the human communication of God. Even so, in God's self-disclosure, he has evidently chosen certain media and excluded others for very definite purposes. And these purposes seem to indicate clear guidelines for the Christian church's selection of appropriate media for the proclamation of the truth of God.

---

[28] Postman, *Amusing Ourselves To Death*, p. 9.

1. God's medium of His creation.

Here is God's audio/visual communication involving impressive orchestration concerning the glory of His sovereignty, intricate providence, and transcendence. So Calvin writes: "We must therefore admit in God's individual works—but especially in them as a whole—that God's powers are actually represented as a painting."[29] Yet he concludes: "It is therefore in vain that so many burning lamps shine for us in the workmanship of the universe to show forth the glory of its author. Although they bathe us wholly in their radiance, yet they can of themselves in no way lead us into the right path. . . . we have not the eyes to see this unless they be illumined by the inner revelation of God through faith"[30] Why is this so? Because while the man of this world patronizes the painting, he scorns the Painter. And furthermore, the painting does not instruct man of his insulting and proud attitude, nor does it specify the remedy of saving grace. While this media proclaims awesome imagery, yet it lacks necessary truth content concerning man's predicament and God's remedy. Here is mouth-stopping spectacle sans specific, applicatory truth.

2. God's medium of His Word.

In contrast, here is that objective, propositional revelation concerning the moral state of the universe and the moral character of God. This was to be the appointed means for the disclosure of the heart of God as distinct from his handiwork. Postman adds:

> The God of the Jews was to exist in the Word and through the Word, an unprecedented conception requiring the highest order of abstract thinking. Iconography thus became blasphemy so that a new kind of God could enter a culture. People like ourselves who are in the process of converting their culture from word-centered to image-centered might profit by reflecting on this Mosaic injunction.[31]

Even the coming of the incarnate Son of God, the "Word made flesh" (John 1:14), did not alter this media stance. The truth was simply personified to a supreme degree and then maintained as before through inscripturation (II Pet. 1:17-19).

---

[29] John Calvin, *Institutes of the Christian Religion*, I, V, 10.

[30] Ibid.

[31] Postman, *Amusing Ourselves To Death*, p. 9.

What then does this divine mandate for the priority of word/print media over audio/visual media suggest? Again, that capitulation in reversing this order will continue to produce disastrous consequences, and especially for evangelical Christianity. As we shall next see, in *The Pilgrim's Progress* itself Bunyan was quite insistent on this priority.

The Lesson from Vanity Fair

The arrival of Christian and Faithful at the town of Vanity, with its notorious Fair, is in reality another encounter with the City of Destruction which now parades itself in a more festive and embellished manner. The spirit of this community is one of gaiety, carnal indulgence, novel amusement, or in a word—entertainment. Now Bunyan's representation here instructs us, concerning the nature of this world of whatever generation, that there is no essential difference in terms of basic interests. That is, unbelieving man has always craved for pleasurable stimulation in a primary and selfish sense. And at Vanity-Fair, as with this present modern age, there is that same narcissistic and lusty pursuit.

However, in terms of communication, what media does Bunyan indicate here that both Christian and Faithful should employ in their witness as transient pilgrims? Negatively, there is no suggestion that they should incorporate the lifestyle of Vanity into their methodology; they are not to reach out with the media that is so popular in Vanity. But positively, they are to focus upon one medium only, the individual pilgrim, who is to transmit upon three different wavelengths. These transmissions are:

1. The witness of evident holiness.

Christian and Faithful were distinguishable by means of their unusual clothing, or close identification with Christ, even as fools (I Cor. 4:10); their uncommon speech, its biblical and heavenly quality (Col. 4:6); their genuine disinterest in Vanity-Fair merchandise (Matt. 6:19-20), that is worldly possessions. It was their holy distinctiveness that testified of their holy God, not their unholy incorporation of the world even as a witnessing style.

2. The witness of inscripturated truth.

Both for import and for export, their only stock-in-trade was the objective Word of God. They sought the truth by crying out, "We buy the truth" (Prov. 23:23), and at the same time proclaimed the truth, even as Faithful effectively did in his preaching to Hopeful.

They freely marketed the produce of divine truth that, when digested, nourishes and enlivens the soul (John 17:17). They did not offer candy-cane platitudes with fleeting sweetness and temporary roller-coaster thrills that must inevitably come down to earth's harsh reality.

3. The witness of manifest graciousness.

They exchanged kindness for malice received, and patience for abuse inflicted (Rom. 12:20-21; I Pet. 3:8-9), thereby gaining a sympathetic following. Later in the account of Part Two, when Mercy, along with Christiana, resides at Vanity in the house of Mr. Mnason, she so cares for the poor that they call her blessed. By these means, the names of Faithful and Christian, formerly cursed, become to be admired by many. As a result of this overall testimony, a small fellowship is gradually established in Vanity that gains some honorable recognition.[32]

Again we see the priority, for Bunyan, of truth proclaimed over visual exhibition such as Vanity-Fair was well equipped to stage. In this situation, it is particularly the uncluttered consistency of the truth, its uncompromising proclamation even unto death, that begins to encroach upon Satan's entrenched domain.

The Riposte for Word/Truth Priority

While we readily admit the distinctive mix of *The Pilgrim's Progress* as a literary whole, yet, as has been cumulatively demonstrated, the great passion of its author is the truth of God as revealed in the Bible. The various component parts of allegory, occasional humor, intrigue, adventure, contrast and continuity, beauty of expression, human interest, and poetic interlude, are but subsidiary adornments that adhere to the supremely important, concrete foundation of divine revelation external to man.

Now the definiteness of this proposition is made on account of the contemporary climate, the Christian church not being excluded from it, which has moved this focus of Bunyan from outward, concrete assertion toward inward and sensual stimulation, that is from objective reality toward subjective relativism. Throughout the seventies Francis Schaeffer warned evangelical Christendom of this insidious development. In one of his later writings he challenged Christians: "We must not finally even battle [humanism] on the front for freedom, and specifically not only our freedom. It must be

[32] Bunyan, *Works*, III, pp. 132, 224-5.

on the basis of Truth. Not just religious truths, but the Truth of what the final reality is. Is it impersonal material or is it the living God?"[33]

More recently, a voice for the nineties has appeared similarly to warn us of the further progress of corrosive modernity in humanizing, and therefore destroying, the solid foundation of biblical Christianity. In his recent book already mentioned, *No Place For Truth*, David Wells concludes:

> The bottom line for our modernized world is that there is no truth; the bottom line for Christian consciousness is precisely the opposite. The Christian predisposition to believe in the kind of truth that is objective and public and that reflects ultimate reality cuts across the grain of what modernity considers plausible. . . . Today, reality is so privatized and relativized that truth is often understood only in terms of what it means to each person. A pragmatic culture will see truth as whatever works for any given person. Such a culture will intercept the statement that Christianity is true to mean simply that Christianity is one way of life that has worked for someone, but that would not be to say that any other way of life might not work just as well for someone else. . . . The contraction of reality into the self, whether in its Liberal or evangelical versions, introduces nothing more or less than the reordering of reality by our modernized world, and the first casualty of this reordering, with respect to the mind, is the belief that truth is something that should be found outside of our own subjective consciousness.[34]

Hence, it is emphatically proposed that in conformity with Bunyan's basic intention, contemporary proclamation of *The Pilgrim's Progress* must reclaim a word/truth priority, while by no means jettisoning appropriate graphic support. To do otherwise would be to commit cognitive suicide, even if, for a time, a well decorated though antiquated corpse did remain. For biblical Christianity there can be no yielding whatsoever at this point.

In our increasingly unrighteous society, the primary need is a revival of manifest righteousness that is clearly sourced in the God

---

[33] Francis Schaeffer, *A Christian Manifesto*, p. 54. It is ironic that this very book, in making a plea for the recovery of truth, should so suffer at the hands of error. Carol Flake reports that, "although *A Christian Manifesto* outsold *Jane Fonda's Workout Book* by two to one in May 1982, Fonda was number one on *The New York Time's* bestseller list and Dr. Schaeffer 'was relegated to ignominious oblivion.'" Carol Flake, *Redemptorama*, p. 165.

[34] Wells, *No Place For Truth*, pp. 280-281.

of all righteousness. However, such a moral revolution cannot result, a relational/subjective gospel notwithstanding, except the roots of truth, in channeling understanding through the trunk and branches of proclamation, bring about the flowering of ethical godliness. It is for this reason that Isaiah declared: "Truth has stumbled in the street, and uprightness cannot enter" (Isa. 59:14). The parallelism here clearly suggests that "truth" is productive of "righteousness." In other words, the truth of God must have priority in proclamation or else a moral community cannot be born, sustained and flourish (Ps. 85:11).

Outside of the Bible then, what better vehicle of Bible truth could there be for world-wide consumption than *The Pilgrim's Progress*? The medium has already proved its universal and timeless appeal. All that now needs to be accomplished is its honest proclamation. Yes, *The Pilgrim's Progress* ought not to be simply made available on bookstore shelves. It can certainly reach seeking people this way. However, in accord with its author's wishes, it should be expounded as never before. In his concluding poem Bunyan writes:

> Now, Reader, I have told my dream to thee;
> See if thou canst interpret it to me,
> Or to thyself, or neighbor;[35]

In other words, readers of *The Pilgrim's Progress* are to become proclaimers to their neighbors. They are to use it as engaging literature for both adult evangelism and edification, as a narrative compendium of the truth of God revealed only in Holy Scripture. These modern times desperately call for those who have a sense of prophetic urgency concerning the truth of Scripture and, like their Old and New Testament mentors, while directed by God to communicate with a variety of suitable media, will never veer from the bottom line of priority for word/truth proclamation.

THE SOLUTION FOR CONTEMPORARY PROCLAMATION

In summary, the following principles are suggested for the proper proclamation and teaching of *The Pilgrim's Progress* to this present modern generation. In all of this, it should go without saying that it is the truth of the Word of God that is to prevail in terms of the message being declared.

---

[35] John Bunyan, *The Works of John Bunyan*, ed. George Offor, III, p. 167.

Maintain Bunyan's Purposes

Frequently review the allegorical purposes of Bunyan expressed in the closing lines of his introductory apology as well as the conclusion of Part One of *The Pilgrim's Progress*. Encourage the reading of other non-allegorical writings by this author.

Let Word/Truth have Priority

Aim at guiding people back to a word/truth priority that first engages the mind, then brings weight to bear upon the conscience and persuasively invites submission. Encourage the supplementary reading, where appropriate, of relevant parts of the writings of Schaeffer, Postman, and Wells, etc., that expose the distinctive biases and fallacies of this closing twentieth century.

Beware of Modern Media Impressionism

Encourage people to be critical of the contemporary image/sensuality/subjectivist priority, as they presently face it, that subordinates the mind to impression and feeling and thus opposes, to many quite unknowingly, biblical priorities.

Proclaim *The Pilgrim's Progress* with Personal Conviction

First let the truth of *The Pilgrim's Progress* become a personal stimulus after careful study; then ignite interest in others through proclamation and teaching using direct exposition of the narrative that continuously draws attention to the revealed Word of God.

Encourage the Reading of *The Pilgrim's Progress*

Recommend an accurate revision of *The Pilgrim's Progress* as well as the reading of other related works of Bunyan including Part Two of *The Pilgrim's Progress*, *Grace Abounding To The Chief Of Sinners*, *The Holy War*, and *The Heavenly Footman*, etc.

Maintain Bunyan's Truth Content

Always heed Bunyan's exhortation to "look within my veil, turn up my metaphors," that is continually dig for the Bible truth that is buried below the allegorical surface. Give special emphasis to the teaching of the discourse sections.

Endeavor to Understand Bunyan's Doctrinal Emphases

Especially draw attention to Bunyan's teaching on the gospel, sanctification, the pastorate, and reaching heaven. Communicate this truth according to its integral relationship to the allegorical framework rather than systematic formulations.

Employ Well Structured Outlining

In other words, as an equivalent to media sound-bites with which society is so familiar, do not hesitate to outline the text of *The Pilgrim's Progress*. At the same time maintain the order and truth of the narrative.

Let Visual Imagery Supplement Truth

Supplement *The Pilgrim's Progress* with visual images such as suitable illustrations that faithfully correspond to, but never overwhelm the original text. Such an approach is certainly not mandatory, though the times and audience may require it.

A WORD OF ADVICE

1. Dost thou love thy own soul? Then pray to Jesus Christ for an awakened heart, with a heart so awakened with all the things of another world, that thou mayest be allured to Jesus Christ. 2. When thou comest there, beg again for more awakenings about sin, hell, grace, and about the righteousness of Christ. 3 Cry also for a spirit of discerning that thou mayest know that which is saving grace indeed. 4 Above all studies apply thyself to the study of those things that show thee the evil of sin, the shortness of man's life, and which is the way to be saved. 5 Keep company with the most godly among professors. 6 When thou hearest what the nature of true grace is, defer not to ask thine own heart if this grace be there.

John Bunyan
The Strait Gate
Works, I, p. 390

CHAPTER EIGHTEEN

Modern Assessments of The Pilgrim's Progress

IN discussion and analysis concerning *The Pilgrim's Progress* since its publication in 1678, there has been an increasing bifurcated interest in Bunyan's classic, that is a disjunction between the literary/historical and biblical/theological entities. At the allegory's inception and on into the eighteenth century of evangelical awakening, while literary/historical considerations were of serious interest, yet they were unquestionably subordinated to overwhelming regard for biblical/theological truth.

Concerning this period C. Stephen Finley comments, while drawing special attention to the nineteenth century:

> John Bunyan benefited, as much as any figure associated with the dramatic Puritanism of the seventeenth century, from the Evangelical majority culture of the Victorians. Indeed, for many of the Victorian faithful, including many of the men and women who were to go on to greatness in Victorian literary and religious circles, Bunyan played a role in their religious formation and in their personal mythologies of quest and development second only to that of the Bible itself. A complete list of such persons would be very long indeed, but would include, to cite only the literary, Macaulay, Carlyle, Ruskin, Froude, [and] Charlotte Bronte."[1]

However, for all of this "Evangelical majority culture," the Victorian era increasingly witnessed a reversal of interest in *The Pilgrim's Progress* that resulted in the ascendancy of literary/historical concern over that of biblical/theological truth, certainly in parallel with an increasing social secularity.

As a result, by the time of the publication of J. A. Froude's *Bunyan, English Men of Letters* in 1880, he could write:

---

[1] C. Stephen Finley, "Bunyan Among The Victorians: Macaulay, Froude, Ruskin." *Journal of Literature & Theology*, Vol. 3, No. 1, March 1989, pp. 77-94.

> [Bunyan's] doctrine was the doctrine of the best and strongest minds in Europe. It had been believed by Luther, it had been believed by Knox. . . . Few educated people use the language of it now. In them it was a fire from heaven shining like a sun in a dark world. With us the fire has gone out; in the place of it we have but smoke and ashes. . . . Unfortunately, parents [now] do not read Bunyan, he is left to the children. . . . The conventional phrases of Evangelical Christianity ring untrue in a modern ear like a cracked bell."[2]

Of course George Offer's definitive three volume edition of Bunyan's *Works* published in 1854 produced a scholarly product that equally exuded warm evangelical sympathy. However, by the turn of the century comparable enthusiasm for the truth of *The Pilgrim's Progress* is difficult to find, at least in academic circles.

In 1905 Robert Bridges, poet and man of letters, writes:

> Bunyan's chief merit . . . is his prose style, which is admired by all who prefer the force of plain speech to the devices of rhetoric. . . . It is pleasanter to write about Bunyan without reference to his theology; . . . his theology needs so much allowance that anything which isolates him from his time does him vast injury; and this some of his warmest friends do not perceive, when they Victorianise his spelling and parade his Calvinism on shiny paper."[3]

So as this century has progressed, it has become increasingly expected that correct procedure in Bunyan studies should require a writer to be scrupulously dispassionate except, that is, when disagreement is expressed with the tinker's literalist hermeneutic concerning the Bible and his Calvinistic doctrine.

However, if the Bedford pastor were alive today, he would undoubtedly reprimand those who only offer their literary patronage and exhort them to repent and humble themselves before the righteous hand of God and seek His mercy. It is in this sense that the twentieth century has proved to be a wilderness period since, for all of its academic contributions, and they have been considerable, yet the focus has studiously avoided the nerve of Bunyan's passion for the saving grace of the Lord Jesus Christ and thus contributed toward present spiritual sterility. Froude's

---

[2] J. A. Froude, *John Bunyan, English Men of Letters*, pp. 49-50, 55-56, 62, 29.

[3] Robert Bridges, *Bunyan, The Pilgrim's Progress, A Casebook*, ed. Roger Sharrock, pp. 112-15.

comment remains profoundly true, "the fire has gone out; in the place of it we have but smoke and ashes."[4]

THE TWENTIETH CENTURY ANALYSIS

Modern scholastic infatuation with John Bunyan divides itself into five areas of specialization that, for the most part, have both a common secularity and an uncommon sympathy with Bunyan's essential purposes. To some degree, conservative Christianity is to blame for this captivity since, in neglecting the adult character of *The Pilgrim's Progress*, considerable numbers in academia have tended to adopt the Bedford tinker for themselves, very much as an adult, while at the same time denuding him of his vital gospel dress. Consider for a moment then these distinctive subdivisions of contemporary enquiry, and at the same time always keep in focus Bunyan's biblical and gospel passion as a basis of judgment which he would certainly bring to bear on his critics.

Literary Criticism

The predominant contribution in the field of modern Bunyan studies comes from lecturers and professors in university English departments. In *The Pilgrim's Progress, Critical And Historical Reviews*, 1980, edited by Vincent Newey, all fourteen essays are from authors employed in university English departments. In *John Bunyan, Conventicle and Parnassus*, 1988, edited by N. H. Keeble, over half of this collection of twelve tercentenary essays comes from university English specialists. In *Bunyan in Our Time*, 1989, edited by Robert G. Collmer, this collection of tercentenary essays has nine contributing scholars, eight of which are English lecturers or professors. Amongst all of the contributors to these three volumes, it would be difficult to recognize one author who discloses his clear, evangelical sympathy with Bunyan's specific gospel. At the same time, secular and theologically liberal sympathies are evident throughout all of these writings.

While one may be tempted to accept this as an expected emphasis, in view of the formative role of Bunyan in the field of English composition, yet it needs to be understood that the author of *The Pilgrim's Progress* never intended that he be awarded this distinctive honor concerning literary form and development sans evangelical truth. Granted that he intended a plainness of style in his magnum opus, which the scholars seem incapable of

---

4 Froude, *John Bunyan, Men of Letters*, pp. 55-56.

reproducing in their writing about him, yet it is sadly significant that the field he was most concerned about, that is Bible truth, has today undoubtedly slid to a position of relative insignificance.

The distinct secular and surgical character of twentieth century analysis of Bunyan in the field of literary and historical criticism is especially noticeable in the light of intentional detachment from any evangelical sympathy in this pursuit. The exception here is when the author cannot refrain from polite disparagement and a patronizing manner with regard to seventeenth century theology in view of modern critical enlightenment. At the more scholarly level, there seems to have developed even a certain manner of expression when Bunyan is under scrutiny, a "literary-speak" style that English specialists seem so adept at producing. Certainly the new Oxford Press (Clarendon) publication of Bunyan's works has been an outstanding achievement that has employed many scholars who are both accomplished and dedicated in their fields of either English or history. Yet, by itself, this product will simply be assessed as a notable academic monument, an admirable anachronism, unless the heartwarming truth of Bunyan returns to its rightful place of prominence.

Of course it is clear that Bunyan intends that the reader carefully delve into his allegory and thus "look within my veil," but in this method it is his design that "the substance of my matter" be discovered, not ever novel nuances, sometimes quite bizarre, that are often couched in terms of reference that only the scholastically initiated can understand.

Historical Investigation

After university English department personnel, the most prolific contributors to contemporary Bunyan studies would be specialist historians, obviously those who focus on seventeenth century England. Concerning this period, who would deny the vastness and helpfulness of Christopher Hill's comprehension of Bunyan's era, notwithstanding the necessity to filter his conclusions through Marxist presuppositions, social class consciousness, and a decidedly materialist perspective. Similarly Richard Greaves has offered a constant stream of judicious and perceptive writings that have been most illuminating; his doctrinal sensitivity in this regard has greatly enhanced his contribution.

But still, as far as Bunyan is concerned, we are dealing with an important yet secondary matter. While the historic foundation of biblical Christianity is of vital concern, yet it still must yield to the greater importance of the interpretation of those events, and especially the Apostle Paul's passionate emphasis upon the saving grace of God offered to great sinners such as himself. So in the understanding of *The Pilgrim's Progress*, it is that same truth from the pen of Paul, thence via Augustine and Luther at a human level, that is so incomparably important. To investigate history surrounding Bunyan and his allegory, and yet at the same time to repudiate his central message of gospel truth, is ultimately merely to toy with the bones of a slaughtered animal while people starve for want of nourishing flesh.

Psychological Analysis

One of the most appealing characteristics of John Bunyan is the sheer honesty of his writing, warts and all, and especially as it is so evident in *Grace Abounding To The Chief Of Sinners*. This being so, it is not surprising that students of human psychology, whether professional or otherwise, have found this writing, as well as others of a confessional type, to be a happy hunting ground for conjecture. A classic, though clinically secular, estimate is that of William James who, as a psychologist focusing on religious experience, describes Bunyan's post-conversion troubles by means of terms that border on describing a psychotic frame of mind.[5]

A more recent analysis is by another university English lecturer, the late John Stachniewski, who in his *The Persecutory Imagination,* reviewed later in this chapter, stridently opposes the Calvinistic biblicism, so representative in Bunyan, that, he alleges, led a generation to despair excessively. Even Roger Sharrock cannot resist the temptation to attempt a diagnosis that is symptomatic of modern psychoanalysis.[6] However it is difficult to

---

5 "He was a typical case of the psychopathic temperament, sensitive of conscience to a diseased degree, beset by doubts, fears and insistent ideas, and a victim of verbal automatisms, both motor and sensory. These were usually texts of Scripture which, sometimes damnatory and sometimes favorable, would come in a half-hallucinatory form as if they were voices, and fasten on his mind and buffet it between them like a shuttlecock. Added to this were a fearful melancholy, self-contempt and despair." William James, *The Varieties of Religious Experience*, p. 136.

6 "Bunyan speaks in the autobiography of being troubled in childhood by fearful dreams and visions. It may be that there was a pathological side to the nervous intensity of these fears; in the religious crisis of his maturity his guilty terrors took the form of hallucinations and auditory and tactile delusions." John Bunyan, *Grace Abounding to the Chief of Sinners*, ed. Roger Sharrock, p. xiii.

avoid the conclusion that so much of this type of investigation, the above being merely typical, is based upon a subjective and humanistic estimate that has not the faintest understanding of what it is to be deeply convicted of sin according to biblical standards.

In this same vein, consider the secular critics and analysts who foist their own standards upon a gullible public, and come up with similar analyses of the Apostle Paul and his Damascus road conversion. Such was the case with Dr. William Sargant's book published in 1957, *Battle for the Mind,* in which he explained Paul's "total collapse, hallucinations and an increased state of suggestibility due to exhaustion," followed by the "implanting of new beliefs and imposed indoctrination" by Ananias. Dr. Martyn Lloyd-Jones' able refutation of this whole approach should be consulted in this regard.[7]

It seems that Bunyan anticipated this type of criticism, for in his introduction to *Grace Abounding To The Chief Of Sinners,* written after having already spent six years in Bedford county jail, he specifically addresses "My dear children" in his preface, that is the nonconformist congregation of which he was a member and yearned to encourage. So he keeps his account "plain and simple," encouraging the believers to profit from recalling "the very beginnings of grace in their souls." Then he adds, "The Philistines understand me not. . . . He that liketh it, let him receive it; and he that does not, let him produce a better."[8]

Political and Sociological Theory

In terms of remoteness from the heart of John Bunyan's purposes, it is probably this more recent field of investigation that is the most distressing. The reason is that it is a willful exercise in using the Bedford preacher as some sort of literary utility in a way that he himself would strenuously denounce. It is typical of the times in which we live that a disjunction is made between idealism and reality. Hence through socialist/materialist spectacles, admiration of and extrapolation concerning Bunyan's social environment, proletarian courage, and literary inventiveness, is accompanied with a total rejection, even loathing of his passionate and dominant biblical convictions.

A foremost exponent of this methodology is Christopher Hill, whose Marxist beliefs undergird his recent exposition of Bunyan,

---

[7] Refer to D. Martyn Lloyd-Jones' refutation of Sargant's book in, *Knowing The Times*, pp. 61-89.

[8] John Bunyan, *The Works of John Bunyan*, ed. George Offor, I, pp. 4-5.

and are dealt with in more detail later in this chapter. In this same vein, consider David Herreshoff's essay, "Marxist Perspectives on Bunyan," which focuses on an array of Marxists over the past fifty years who have, in a variety of ways, admired the Bedford tinker's social role and allegorical skills, though definitely not his evangelical doctrine, and thus have attempted to baptize him with socialist ideology. The audacity in this regard is reflected by the fact that the author should even raise the question: "[I]s Bunyan 'ours' or 'theirs' or perhaps both?" In other words, does Bunyan belong to "secular and proletarian" or "Christian and bourgeois [interests]?"[9]

Marxist talk using biblical/Bunyanesque expressions abounds:

> [T]he revolution is the work of a conscious class incarnating an idea, the proletariat as collective messiah. . . . Another reason for Marxists' being attracted to Bunyan is that he is seen by them as a guide who can show them to a wicket gate beyond which they can get a clear view into the political landscape of the English Revolution and its aftermath. . . . Readers of recent Marxist Bunyan scholarship will discover that the ideological clothing [embroidered coat?] metaphor is alive and well in the prose of some. . . . If the Puritan revolutionaries could see their world only through a glass, darkly [I Cor. 13:12], the proletarian revolutionaries will see historical reality face to face [I Cor. 13:12].[10]

The agenda in this incongruous relationship is well described by Herreshoff's reference to the German Marxist, Georg Seehase:

> Aware that German editions of *The Pilgrim's Progress* which serve the cause of Christian propaganda continue to appear, Seehase believes it is feasible to prepare an edition at least of the First Part to serve the needs of socialist publishing policy. It would be provided with a suitable and appealing commentary. . . . If one concedes that Bunyan is ineradicably possessed of a religious false consciousness, however, *The Pilgrim's Progress* can only be understood as, at the most, a belles-lettristic [literary essay] tract illustrative of the Bible. Seehase wants more for the book than that; he wants to annex it to the domain of the socialist heritage.[11]

---

[9] David Herreshoff, "Marxist Perspectives on Bunyan," *Bunyan in Our Time*, ed. Robert G. Collmer, pp. 161-2.

[10] *Ibid.*, pp. 162-3.

[11] *Ibid.*, p. 183.

The only fitting response to such bold revisionism is the assessment that this mentality is typical of a system that has no objective morality and therefore does not blush or even faintly blink when literary rape is proposed.

Theological Appreciation

In contrast with the above categories, serious and sympathetic consideration of Bunyan's doctrinal stance is difficult to find, and even within conservative Christendom. Exceptions concern Richard Greaves' *John Bunyan* and Pieter de Vries' *John Bunyan on the Order of Salvation* which are reviewed later in this chapter. U. Milo Kaufmann's *The Pilgrim's Progress And Traditions In Puritan Meditation* is certainly insightful, but hardly sympathetic with Bunyan's evangelicalism. He writes:

> No religious awakening is likely to be an awakening of a seventeenth-century Puritan sensitivity and a recovery of its categories. Too much has happened in the meantime. A more rewarding course, it seems to me, is to affirm that *The Pilgrim's Progress* offers us the handsomely-articulated structure of literature's basic plot: the career of a human life.[12]

Similarly, former seminary principal Gordon Wakefield's more recent *Bunyan the Christian*, also reviewed in this chapter, while reflecting affection, yet clearly is an interpretation based upon obvious liberal presuppositions, not to mention Wakefield's Arminianism, that are quite opposite to those of Bunyan.

So while a deep evangelical appreciation of Bunyan is sadly lacking, at the same time children's versions of *The Pilgrim's Progress* abound in ever more simplistic forms that are undoubtedly leading to misrepresentation amongst adults in general. This writer's seminar experience amongst adults in teaching *The Pilgrim's Progress* has repeatedly proved this assertion to be true. Time and time again, people who have been led through the allegory have freely confessed their previous ignorance and misunderstandings in this regard. It is also probable that, in an age that has become so intoxicated with visual stimulation, even to a point of bondage, it is more difficult for people today to move beyond Bunyan's imagery to the deeper levels of objective, biblical truth.

---

[12] U. Milo Kaufmann, *The Pilgrim's Progress And Traditions In Puritan Meditation*, p. vi.

One of the features of George Offor's edition of Bunyan's *Works* is the obvious warmth of regard which he felt, not only for the Bedford pastor's person, but also his doctrine. And it is this quality that will continue to endear his devoted contribution to Bunyan lovers, whatever the scholastic shortcomings may be. The same could also be said of John Brown's biography; clearly this author profoundly loved his subject. But when one considers by comparison two more contemporary and parallel works, the Oxford (Clarendon) publication of Bunyan's *Works*, as well as Michael Mullett's *John Bunyan in Context*, the distinguishing feature in these instances is the absence of that warmth and affection so obvious in the earlier works, no doubt justified in the name of impartial scholarship. Be that as it may, while being grateful in part, we ought not to be so congratulatory concerning present accomplishments that are more sterile even if learned. It would be better that we return to "heart work," as Bunyan calls it, as a matter of primary concern while certainly not neglecting the importance of an accurate text and historical enlightenment.

THE RECOGNITION OF PRESUPPOSITIONS

In lain Murray's recent biography *Jonathan Edwards*, he commences with a most necessary introduction titled, "On Understanding Edwards."[13] His concern is that some of the more contemporary scholarly writings on the life of Edwards, such as by Ola Winslow and Perry Miller, fail to acknowledge their naturalistic presuppositions which are doctrinally alien to those of the Bible and early eighteenth century Calvinism in New England.

So Murray explains:

> Those who consider that modern enlightenment has superseded the possibility of the supernatural and displaced the Bible as a revelation from a living God, ought at least to have considered the alternative reason which Edwards proposes for disbelief [namely deadness and darkness of the soul through pride]. Instead, they simply assume that Christianity is 'discovered to be fictitious'. And they proceed to write about Edwards as though this makes no difference to any genuine understanding of his life and thought. They never address themselves to the question, What would follow if Edwards' religion is in accord with Christ and the Bible and if it be true? Any references which they make to the Bible at all are commonly as superficial as that of Henry Churchill King who at the

---

[13] Iain Murray, *Jonathan Edwards*, pp. xix-xxxi.

> Edwards' Bicentenary regretted that Edwards lacked 'Christ's wonderful faith in men.'[14]

So it is the case today with regard to modern estimates of *The Pilgrim's Progress* and Bunyan. He died only fifteen years before the birth of Edwards and his mishandling is not at all unlike that of the Massachusetts divine which Murray describes. And the reason for this is not hard to discover. The plain fact is that like Edwards, Bunyan believed the Bible to be truthful and without error. It is not surprising to discover then that these two choice saints, their different educational levels notwithstanding, were in close agreement regarding essential Christian doctrine.

However, when the modern biographer of Bunyan, Gordon Wakefield, is confronted with this biblical world-view, he raises a very appropriate point: "The chief question for our time is whether Bunyan's view of the universe [and God and the Bible and sin and the gospel] has any meaning for us."[15] In real and objective terms for this modern scholar, the answer must surely be negative. Nevertheless, in subjective terms the published answer of Wakefield is positive, that is when an existential and relativistic extrapolation is applied.

Consistent with his theology, it is this latter course for which Wakefield certainly opts. He briefly describes Bunyan's "Mapp Shewing the Order and Causes of Salvation and Damnation." Then he illustrates:

> Some people are helped by maps even if they do not correspond to the actual terrain to be traversed. In *Bugles and a Tiger* John Masters told of a Gurkha prisoner of the Japanese in Burma, who managed to escape and made his way by an arduous journey through the Burmese jungle back to base. They asked him how he had done it. He said he had a map. Astonished and eager they asked to see it. He produced it. It was a street map of London.[16]

While Wakefield readily admits that *The Pilgrim's Progress* is a more popular guide than Bunyan's "Mapp," yet he concludes: "There are those who may live good and Christian lives and attain health and peace of soul according to a plan of salvation which does not bear any relation to what seem to most people to be the objective and believable realities of God and the world. And

---

[14] Ibid., p. xxvi.

[15] Gordon Wakefield, *Bunyan The Christian*, p. 125.

[16] Ibid.

though it may be fearsome it may lead, as with Bunyan, to a life of integrated fulfilment and at any rate a sight of journey's end."[17]

In other words, though the famous allegory clearly presents a very specific conservative biblical theology,[18] yet one may approach it and ambiguously incorporate into it a contrary theology and still travel to a journey's end. Of course the fact that one may travel in this manner, according to Bunyan, as an Ignorance, for whom Wakefield has sympathy,[19] does not strike the author as contradictory. Though for Bunyan such an imposition upon his dream would be understood as nothing short of error to be condemned like that of the Latitudinarian, Edward Fowler. The point then is that, as Murray warns, it is vital that the underlying bias of modern Bunyan scholars be recognized. For instance, in spite of Christopher Hill's encyclopedic understanding of seventeenth century England and his modest style, yet as a confessed Marxist his proletarian infatuation from a materialist stance needs to be understood since it inhibits the author from entering into the animus of Bunyan as does George Offer.

EIGHT CONTEMPORARY BUNYAN SCHOLARS

The following eight vignettes are representative of various shades of modern Bunyan scholarship. The field as a whole is vast, though, sad to say, almost totally lacking in evangelical warmth. This is not meant to demean the positive contribution of predominant textual, stylistic, and historical study. Nevertheless, it remains true that most contributions in this area come from scholars who are decidedly opposed to Bunyan's doctrine, and this it would seem militates against a true presentation of Bunyan's total and essential message.

This writer believes that for the author of *The Pilgrim's Progress* it is this aspect of authoritative Bible truth at an experiential level that ought to predominate.[20] To deny this is to treat the classic

---

[17] Ibid., p. 126.

[18] Ibid., pp. 34-36.

[19] Ibid., p. 89.

[20] George Marsden has vainly attempted to call secular scholarship back to an inclusion of an experiential Christian emphasis, and doubtless his plea will go unheeded by an audience that in general is fundamentally opposed to historic evangelical truth and resultant experience, that is unless an unorthodox twist on experience is offered. His tame solution, hardly demonstrated in the history of Christian revival, is explained as

allegory more as a literary cadaver suitable only for dispassionate dissection and twentieth century cosmetology. However, this will never bring back the life of God to this corrupt and listless generation, just as the author intended for the seventeenth century. Rather, we must heed Bunyan's exhortation: "Do thou the substance of my matter see," which is to return to the gospel he so fervently proclaimed, which is Luther's gospel, and the Apostle Paul's gospel, the one and only gospel of the sovereign grace of God.

Roger Sharrock

The late professor of English at King's College, University of London, probably ranks as the foremost Bunyan scholar of the twentieth century. His monumental contribution has been not only as General Editor of the Oxford Press (Clarendon) publication of the full works of Bunyan that is intended to replace the standard three volume set produced during the last century by George Offor, but also as the particular editor of the 1960 revision of the critical text of *The Pilgrim's Progress* originally edited by J. B. Wharey in 1928. This volume, also published by Oxford Press (Clarendon), is not only the definitive text of the famous allegory, with full critical apparatus, but also a mine of information that includes a supplementary commentary.

Second in importance to this would be Sharrock's editorship of *Grace Abounding To The Chief Of Sinners*, Bunyan's spiritual autobiography, published in 1962. Sharrock's numerous other books and articles of a textual, literary, and historical nature, including a biography of Bunyan, have always been regarded, from the point of view of his areas of expertise, judicious and insightful, drawing upon a profound knowledge of seventeenth century England and the best of primary resources.

A representative sample of Sharrock's writing would be his introductory essay in the Penguin edition of *The Pilgrim's*

---

follows: "Religious-political conservatives who complain about the establishment of 'secular humanism' are partially correct. . . . The religious right [presumably biblicists] does not help by suggesting, in effect, that we go back to a Christian establishment. That is not the only alternative and it is not a desirable one. Rather, we should recognize that we are dealing with an over-correction and look for a way to restore a better balance among both religious and nonreligious voices." *The Outrageous Idea Of Christian Scholarship*, p. 24.

Progress.[21] He repeatedly acknowledges the foundational role of the Bible in the allegory. It is Bunyan's "reliance on the literal text of the Bible which is the prime motive of the autobiography [*Grace Abounding*, as well as *The Pilgrim's Progress*]" (p. 11). Further, "*The Pilgrim's Progress* is soaked in the imagery of the Bible and deeply pervaded by the Puritan belief that the Bible provided a key to every problem of life and thought" (p. 23). Moreover, and the tilt of his opinion seems to show here, "Bunyan's intense, *peculiar* [emphasis added] reading of Scripture has guided the very structure of his narrative" (p. 25).

In the same subjective vein we read: "Puritanism has been misconceived as restrictive moral prohibitions, weighed down by sexual guilt; in the mid seventeenth century it was a fiery religious and social dynamic resembling Marxism more than modern Fundamentalism" (p. 13). But this seems a very inappropriate parallel. True, the Revolution under Cromwell was militant, social as well as religious, though these elements were definitely subordinate to an authoritative Bible that was revered in a manner similar to twentieth century biblical fundamentalism; Bunyan would have abominated dialectical materialism, that is the philosophic root of Marxism derived from Feuerbach and Hegel.

However, the heart of Christian's quest is well described. In parallel with Luther, "it is his [Bunyan's] tremendous need to find a righteousness not his own by which to be saved, which is the force irresistibly driving Christian along the road to his final entry into the Celestial City" (p. 11). Further, for the novice contemporary reader a most important principle concerning Bunyan's multi-layered style is well described. "For the modern reader, the human working compromise between realism and allegory is likely to conceal the firm outlines of the theological structure which were more obvious to Bunyan's contemporaries and especially to his fellow-Nonconformists. What is on the surface an episodic series of adventures, a folk-tale of ups and downs such as Bunyan himself enjoyed in the popular romances of his unregenerate youth, has a tough skeleton of which each articulated joint precisely indicates a stage in the Puritan psychology of conversion" (p. 18).

Certainly objection ought to be raised at the suggestion that following Christian's fierce engagement with Apollyon using various weapons, his subsequent recourse to a distinctive weapon

---

[21] John Bunyan, *The Pilgrim's Progress*, (Penguin) ed., Roger Sharrock, pp. 7-26.

named "All-prayer" in the Valley of the Shadow of Death is allegorical inconsistency, "clumsiness," a "gaffe," and a "blunder" (p. 17). The truth is that Bunyan is using biblical consistency when he consecutively moves from reference to "the sword of the Spirit" to the need of "all prayer" as both are described in Ephesians 6:17-18. Nevertheless, Sharrock has left us with a legacy of textual, literary, and historical clarification that will greatly profit students of Bunyan and his writings for many generations to come.

Christopher Hill

As the pre-eminent modern historian in the field of seventeenth century English history, with an appealing communicative ability that enhances his conclusions, Christopher Hill has particularly focused his attention upon the English Revolution during the close of which period John Bunyan's pen began to flourish so imaginatively. This former Master of Balliol College, Oxford, published in 1989, under the American title of *A Tinker And A Poor Man*, an acclaimed study of "John Bunyan and his Church, 1628-1688." It continues to be acknowledged as both innovative in much of its interpretation and encyclopedic with regard to the sources it references.

It should be noted that Hill, a humanistic Marxist and former member of the Communist Party of Great Britain, not surprisingly views Bunyan and his environment by means of a secular and social context. This is in no way meant to depreciate the author's vast understanding of Bunyan's times which he unveils with such fascinating detail. Hill comprehends the Bedford pastor's doctrinal stance in a formal sense, though it is not difficult to perceive that the author has no real sympathy with this biblical world-view whatsoever. Even so, it is readily acknowledged that Hill's style is peaceable.

Christopher Hill's grand thesis is that Bunyan and his writings, sans the prominent top layers of Christian doctrine and allegorical enticement, when carefully analyzed, provide a fascinating scenario of social and class tension in the light of the pervasive Puritan economic dynamic. He states:

> We must therefore be alert to the devices of allegory, use of Biblical myths, parable, metaphor, and irony which Bunyan regularly employed. His main themes are simple, clear, and straightforwardly expressed: but their application contains a wealth of overt and covert allusions, some of which I have tried to bring out. There are risks in trying to read between the lines. But there was a chasm

between Bunyan's thinking and that of the JPs who sent him to jail; between him and the Latitudinarian clergy, the more liberal wing of the Church of England. I am not suggesting that Bunyan's interests were primarily political; far from it. . . . But the mere fact of being a protestant dissenter forced political decisions on him."[22]

So while the author knows full well of the priority of spiritual and gospel truth for Bunyan, yet he is content to concentrate on backdrop scenery while ignoring the performance on center stage. Thus when we come to the chapter on *The Pilgrim's Progress*, the focus upon social context is heavy indeed, to the intentional avoidance of Christian's main problem which is the burden of personal sin. So we read:

> Running through *The Pilgrim's Progress* is a strong sense of the superiority of the poor to the rich. . . . The pilgrim, like the whole book, is firmly set in a lower-class ambiance. . . . When we first see him the Pilgrim is in rags—allegorical rags, to be sure, but they also represent real poverty. . . . The Pilgrim is a "laboring man", of "base and low estate and condition". . . . Undesirable characters in *The Pilgrim's Progress*, as later in *The Holy War*, are almost obsessively labeled as lords and ladies, gentlemen and gentlewomen.
>
> In the most helpful analysis of *The Pilgrim's Progress* I have read for a long time [it not being difficult to guess why], James Turner describes Bunyan as "a despised itinerant manual worker, excluded from landownership, exposed to the rigors of the open road as he traveled and the violence of property-owners [Giant Despair] if he deviated; yet he was a householder and artisan, descended from yeomen and small traders."[23] . . . In Emmanuel's Land, on the Delectable Mountains and in Beulah, lands and their produce are "rent free", "common . . . for all the pilgrims". In the Celestial City, it is said, pilgrims have houses of their own [but surely a reference to John 14:2]. . . . The burden [on Christian's back] is sin, the product of centuries of unequal society [not according to Bunyan's doctrine].[24]

So with a great socialist and revisionist flourish, Hill concludes: "Puritanism, tenacious especially in defeat, combined to make *The Pilgrim's Progress* not only a foundation document of the English working-class movement but also a text which spoke to millions of

[22] Christopher Hill, *A Tinker And A Poor Man*, pp. 14-15.

[23] James Turner, "Bunyan's Sense of Place," *The Pilgrim's Progress, Critical and Historical Views*, ed. Vincent Newey, p. 97.

[24] Hill, *A Tinker And A Poor Man*, pp. 212-213, 215, 219-220, 377.

those poor oppressed people whom Bunyan . . . wished to address."[25]

Again, let it be repeated that Hill provides a wealth of intriguing and helpful background information concerning Bunyan and his writings. But "background" rather than "foreground" is precisely the right term to be used in this situation. The author confessedly plays with the flesh rather than the heart or soul of his topic. But then, Hill would not believe that there is such an entity as a "soul," nor is there original sin or a redeeming Christ or a truthful Word of God. He may as well rightly understand the inner core of Bunyan as it is possible for a camel to pass through the eye of a needle.

Neil H. Keeble

A lecturer in English at Stirling University in Scotland, Neil Keeble has focused his studies on seventeenth century Puritanism in England with considerable emphasis being given to a literary focus on the life and times of John Bunyan. He is presently President of The International John Bunyan Society. In 1980 he published an essay entitled "Christiana's Key: The Unity of The Pilgrim's Progress,"[26] in which diversity within unity concerning Part I and Part II is well attested. He puts it this way, alluding to I Corinthians 13:13: "If Part I had handled faith and hope, Part II turns to charity. . . . He 'who would true valor see' had best read the whole of *The Pilgrim's Progress.*"[27]

His most substantial contribution appears to be *The literary culture of nonconformity in later seventeenth century England* published in 1987.[28] Whereas there has been a tendency to isolate Bunyan and *The Pilgrim's Progress* in their Puritan setting, Keeble here presents the Bedford pastor as an integral part of the literary scene and nonconformist struggle within Restoration England.

In 1988 he edited a notable volume *John Bunyan, Conventicle and Parnassus*, being a collection of essays dedicated to the tercentenary of the death of the Bedford tinker. His own

---

[25] Ibid., p. 380.

[26] N. H. Keeble, "Christiana's Key: The Unity of The Pilgrim's Progress," *The Pilgrim's Progress, Critical And Historical Views*, ed. Vincent Newey, pp. 1-20.

[27] Ibid., pp. 14, 18.

[28] N. H. Keeble, *The literary culture of nonconformity in later seventeenth-century England,* 356 pp.

contribution, "'Of him thousands daily Sing and talk': Bunyan and his reputation" is an excellent and detailed description of the growth of influence and circulation of *The Pilgrim's Progress* since its first publication in 1678.[29] The outline of this essay describing the evolution of Bunyan's reception is worthy of mention here.

> *The Seventeenth-century Bunyan.* While the common people heard him gladly, the educated considered him vulgar.
>
> *The Augustan Bunyan.* Improving regard and acceptance finds Dr. Samuel Johnson giving his approval along with the disguised recognition of William Cowper. However Edmund Burke considers him degraded and David Hume in bad taste.
>
> *The Evangelical Bunyan.* As the darling of the Great Awakening, there is high regard from the leaders such as John Wesley, George Whitefield, and later John Newton.
>
> *The Romantic Bunyan.* A period of heightened taste and aesthetics provides the approval of Robert Southey, William Blake, Charles Lamb, Sir Walter Scott, Thomas Macaulay, and Samuel Coleridge.
>
> *The Victorian Bunyan.* Now he makes impression upon the works of Nathaniel Hawthorne, Charlotte Bronte, William Thackeray, Louisa M. Alcott. Scholarly affection flows from George Offor and John Brown.
>
> *The Modern Bunyan.* Roger Sharrock, William York Tindall, Christopher Hill, and U. Milo Kaufmann give social and literary analysis.

Of special note is Keeble's editorship of the Oxford University Press edition of *The Pilgrim's Progress* in The World's Classics series, published in 1984, the actual text being that of the 1960 Wharey and Sharrock edition. While granting his indebtedness to Sharrock, yet a distinctive contribution in commentary is made here. The introductory essay, very much following the twentieth century mode which is emphatic on nuances of style, culture, history and motives, yet avoids the specifics of Bunyan's supreme passion for gospel grace and truth. The comment, "Puritanism was a pre-eminently social movement whose considerable literature was characterized by a fascinated interest in the actual experiences of

---

[29] N. H. Keeble, "'Of him thousands daily Sing and talk': Bunyan and his reputation," ed. N. H. Keeble, *John Bunyan, Conventicle and Parnassus*, pp. 241-64.

men,"[30] is far too removed from the heart of the matter. Rather, Puritanism was a conservative Christian movement born of a desire for reformation within Anglicanism, doubtless with social consequence, rooted in a thoroughly authoritative Bible and Reformation theology.

Richard Greaves

Presently the Robert O. Lawton Distinguished Professor of History and Courtesy Professor of Religion, Florida State University, Richard Greaves obtained his Ph.D. degree from the University of London for his research into Puritan theology as represented by John Bunyan. An edited version of his doctoral thesis was published in 1969 simply under the title of *John Bunyan*. However, the scarcity of such a study, focusing on historical theology, within the vast array of Bunyan investigative literature makes it to be of distinct importance. For this reason, a modified outline of the main chapters is as follows:

A. The Pilgrim's God.
   1. Divine wrath and grace.
   2. Divine extension of grace.
   3. Necessity of satisfaction.
   4. Extent of grace.

B. The Pilgrim's Call.
   1. Predestination and election.
   2. Predestination and reprobation,
   3. Free will.
   4. Divine call.

C. The Pilgrim's Response.
   1. Faith.
   2. Repentance.
   3. Justification.
   4. Forgiveness.
   5. Sanctification.
   6. Perseverance.

D. The Pilgrim's Covenant.
   1. Covenant of works.
   2. Covenant of grace - divine aspect.

---

[30] John Bunyan, *The Pilgrim's Progress*, ed. N. H. Keeble, pp. xii-xiii.

3. Covenant of grace - human aspect.
4. Covenant of grace - legal aspect.

E. The Pilgrim's Stately Palace.

1. Church.
2. Ministry.
3. Sacraments.
4. Christian life.

This is an excellent study that appears to be free of liberal nuance, secular dominance, and social infatuation. Of course one could wish for at least a hint of authorial passion since the grasp of Bunyan's belief here ought to result in more than an acknowledgment of correctness. It is strange that the Bedford pastor's high view of Scripture, which is so foundational to his doctrine and a thorn to modern critics, is neglected, or perhaps assumed. The chapter on Bunyan's covenant theology is open to some question since the tendency is to associate it with the prevailing understanding of the distinctive systematic doctrine at that time. However, although Bunyan does frequently use the term "covenant of grace" in his *The Doctrine Of The Law And Grace Unfolded*, yet it is intended to describe chiefly the new covenant according to the influence of Luther, and not an overarching covenant under which subsume many administrations according to the definition of *The Westminster Confession of Faith*. Further, it is noteworthy that Bunyan does not at all use or even hint at covenant terminology in *The Pilgrim's Progress*, notwithstanding Greaves' confession of a failed attempt to derive such an association. Refer to page 138.

Concerning the tinker's Calvinism, Greaves gives a very fine analysis of Bunyan's understanding of divine sovereignty; again it is more rooted in Luther's predestinarian appreciation of grace rather than the Westminster divines' teaching on God's eternal decree. He suggests that this is the reason for Bunyan's distinctive vibrancy. So Greaves concludes: "Always there remained that motivating force of transforming grace which neither maturity nor theological awareness diminished. This, coupled with his skill 'in the direct colloquial expression of truth,' was the key to the success which he achieved as a writer and a preacher."[31]

Mention should also be made of Greaves' substantial editorial involvement with the completed publication by Oxford Press (Clarendon) of Bunyan's *Miscellaneous Works*; this includes his

[31] Richard Greaves, *John Bunyan*, p. 160.

editorship of Volumes II, VIII, IX and XI, within *The Miscellaneous Works of John Bunyan.* Another volume of stimulating essays entitled *John Bunyan And English Nonconformity* includes his cautious opinion, in agreement with Sharrock, that *Reprobation Asserted* is a spurious work.[32] Further, he has published both *An Annotated Bibliography Of John Bunyan Studies* (84 pp.) and, with James Forrest, *John Bunyan A Reference Guide* (478 pp.).

Gordon Campbell

As a lecturer in English at the University of Leicester, Campbell is worthy of mention for two particular reasons. First, he has contributed essays on Bunyan in two significant scholarly volumes in the realm of Bunyan studies, namely *The Pilgrim's Progress, Critical and Historical Views*, 1980, edited by Vincent Newey, and *John Bunyan, Conventicle and Parnassus*, 1988, edited by N. H. Keeble. Second, both of these essays, "The Theology of The Pilgrim's Progress," and "Fishing in Other Men's Waters: Bunyan and the Theologians," are obviously concerned with Bunyan's theological beliefs and sources, and this emphasis is very much related to the concerns of this writer.

Now it is readily acknowledged that Campbell appreciates the problem of confronting a Puritan biblicist faith: "Because Bunyan's theology impinges to some extent on *The Pilgrim's Progress*, students of literature too often dismiss it as a book which champions a faith to which they feel hostile, if they are non-believers, or which they find distastefully evangelical, if they subscribe quiescently to a liberal form of Christianity."[33] However, because it is obvious that he is also troubled with such unabashed evangelicalism, an approach is suggested that is certainly not novel in the modern arena of Bunyan studies. It is simply ideological extrapolation that pushes to one side the doctrinal specificity:

> But the redeeming literary quality of *The Pilgrim's Progress* resides in the fact that Bunyan's imagination transcends his theological convictions, in much the same way that his energetic pursuit of souls shows a compassion for the fate of the dispossessed which

[32] Richard Greaves, *John Bunyan And English Nonconformity*, pp. 185-91.

[33] Gordon Campbell, "Fishing in Other Men's Waters: Bunyan and the Theologians," *Conventicle and Parnassus*, ed. N. H. Keeble, p. 150.

> arises from his cold theological conviction that an overwhelming proportion of humanity has been consigned irrevocably to hell.[34]

Hence, Campbell's essays soon reveal a bias away from Bunyan's evangelical doctrine that colors the whole of his writings. He declares:

> Puritans deemed the Bible to be the sole and sufficient source of doctrine. In practice, however, the process of exegesis did not consist in teasing doctrines out of the Bible, but rather in reading doctrines in which they already believed into the Bible. The Bible is not, after all, a theological work, but rather a collection of narratives and epistles from which, at best, doctrines can be inferred; even the relatively explicit teaching of the apostle Paul stands in need of strenuous explication if it is to be transformed into the dogmas of the Christian faith. . . . His [Bunyan's] affirmation of the Trinity is a good example of a belief which cannot be traced to the Bible for the simple reason that there is no biblical doctrine of the Trinity. It is possible on biblical evidence to mount an argument of some respectability for the divinity of Jesus, but it is a long step from that doctrine to a belief in a triune godhead.[35]

Therefore we will consider just this one notable case where the Bedford tinker suffers scrutiny that quickly discards his faith on the grounds that it is more traditional and not really biblical, when in fact the criticism is born of doctrinal antipathy and misrepresentation.

In one of Bunyan's earliest publications, *Some Gospel-Truths Opened according to the Scriptures*, he rhetorically questions a nominal Christian: "But when did God shew thee that thou wert no Christian? When didst thou see that: And in the light of the Spirit of Christ, see that thou wert under the wrath of God because of original sin? (Rom. 5:12)."[36] Campbell claims that because Romans 5:12 is quoted in support here, therefore Bunyan's doctrine was based upon a faulty translation of v. 12b where "in whom [presumably Adam] all sinned" was understood rather than the more correct, "because all sinned." Thus he declares, "The fact that the doctrine of original sin rested on a mistranslation did not impede its influence, and it became a central doctrine of the faith.

---

[34] Ibid.

[35] Ibid., pp. 137-8, 144.

[36] Bunyan, *Works*, II, p. 166.

Bunyan believed it, and believed it to be biblical."[37] Thus the impression clearly conveyed, based upon references to J. N. D. Kelly's *Early Christian Doctrines*,[38] is that the doctrine of original sin has rested principally upon a mistranslation of Romans 5:12b by Ambrosiaster c. 375 A.D. with the subsequent support of the linguistically unskilled Augustine. Thus a longstanding doctrine has really no biblical basis and as a consequence unlearned Bunyan has been misled by poor exegesis.[39]

To begin with, to read Kelly is to discover that he is not so reckless as to claim that a whole doctrine arose in Christendom on account of Ambrosiaster's poor exegesis at this one point, though he does see it as significant, even pivotal and influential concerning Augustine. There were other Scriptures used for proof at that time.[40] Campbell's inference that had Romans 5:12b been correctly interpreted, the doctrine of original sin would not have arisen, cannot be supported. Further, while the prevailing contemporary opinion is that Romans 5:12b should be translated "because all sinned," this understanding also includes that of more recent conservative scholars such as Moo, Morris, and Shedd.[41] who are nevertheless committed to the orthodox doctrine of original sin. Even so, it is simplistic to wipe aside the alternative "in whom all sinned" when F. W. Danker, E. Stauffer, Nigel Tuner, and W.

---

[37] Campbell, *Conventicle and Parnassus*, p. 138.

[38] J. N. D. Kelly, *Early Christian Doctrines*, pp. 354, 363.

[39] It is interesting to note that Campbell, with some justification, suggests that Bunyan's reliance upon an English text of the Bible was most likely that of the Geneva version, at least with regard to his earlier writings, *Conventicle and Parnassus*, p. 138. Yet this version's translation of Romans 5:12 does not follow that of Ambrosiaster or Augustine. It reads: "Wherefor, as by one man sinne entred into the worlde, and death by sinne, and so death went over all men: for as muche as all men have sinned."

[40] Kelly refers to the use of Psalm 51:45 by Ambrose. Concerning Ausgustine he writes, "So Augustine has no doubt of the reality of original sin. *Genesis* apart, he finds Scriptural proof of it in *Ps. 51*, *Job* and *Eph*. 2:3, but above all in *Rom*. 5:12 (where, like Ambrosiaster, he reads 'in whom') and *John* 3:3-5." *Early Christian Doctrines*, pp. 355, 363.

[41] Douglas J. Moo, *The Epistle to the Romans*, pp. 314-329; Leon Morris, *The Epistle to the Romans*, pp. 227-32; William G. T. Shedd, *Commentary on Romans*, pp. 119-30.

Manson are in essential agreement with it.[42] Turner significantly comments: "I am bound to say that this [*in whom* all men sinned] seems more consistent with the apostle's main argument when one reads the epistle to the Romans *as a whole* [emphasis added]."[43] Very much so, and it is for this reason that when Bunyan makes a further comment concerning original sin he quotes in support another significant reference:

> He [Adam] did not only leave them a broken covenant, but also made them himself sinners against it. He made them sinners—"By one man's disobedience many were made sinners" (Rom. 5:19). . . . Not only so, but also before he left them [the sons of Adam] he was the conduit pipe through which the devil did convey off his poisoned spawn and venom nature into the hearts of Adam's sons and daughters, by which they are at this day so strongly and so violently carried away, that they fly as fast to hell, and the devil, by reason of sin, as chaff before a mighty wind.[44]

John Stachniewski

A lecturer in English at Manchester University, the late John Stachniewski gained considerable limelight in the area of Puritan and Bunyan studies on account of his writing of *The Persecutory Imagination* published by Oxford Press (Clarendon) in 1991. Subtitled "English Puritanism and the Literature of Religious Despair," its main thesis is that seventeenth century English Puritanism, on account of its preoccupation with an oppressive God derived from Calvinism and a literalist interpretation of the Bible, generated excessive symptoms of despair and resultant suicide.

The author states:

> Puritans, for my purposes, were people whose minds appear to have been captured by the questions whether or not they were members of the elect, and how the life of an elect (and elect community), in contradistinction to that of a reprobate, should be ordered. In principle they took a literalist view of the Bible and were either vociferous and vigorous in their attempts to purify the Church of England of perceived accretions to the practices of the primitive

42 Moo, *Romans*, p. 322n.

43 Nigel Turner, *Grammatical Insights Into The New Testament*, p. 116.

44 Bunyan, *Works*, I, p. 505.

> church or split off into sects which they thought conformed to these most closely.[45]

Of the literary exponents of this alleged depressing emphasis, greatest attention is given to John Bunyan and his *Grace Abounding* and *The Pilgrim's Progress*. Christopher Hill makes mention of this same matter, and Stachniewski appears to be but a substantial, though more stridentt, expression of it.[46]

That the Puritans, apart from their genuine and impressive representation of Biblical Christianity, had some serious failings, is beyond doubt. Lloyd-Jones gets to the heart of the matter as follows:

> [They were] too much influenced by the analogy of the Old Testament and of Israel, and applying it to England. Was not that the real error? In the Old Testament and under that Dispensation the State (of Israel) was the church (Acts 7:38), but the State of England in the sixteenth century was not the church. In the Old Testament the two were one and identical. But surely in the New Testament we have the exact opposite. The church consists of the "called out" ones, not the total state.[47]

Now this being so, it ought to be admitted than many Puritans, and Bunyan should be excluded here, did place legal requirements on the people concerning which even the Apostles declared were, "a yoke which neither our fathers nor we have been able to bear" (Acts 15:10).[48] Yet Stachniewski does not concern himself with this

---

[45] John Stachniewski, *The Persecutory Imagination*, p. 11.

[46] Hill, *A Tinker And A Poor Man*, pp. 184-187.

[47] Martyn Lloyd-Jones, *The Puritans*, pp. 64-65.

[48] An overly romantic estimate of Puritan New England needs to consider Alice Morse Earle's *The Sabbath In Puritan New England*. For example: In "1670 two lovers, John Lewis and Sarah Chapman, were accused of and tried for 'sitting together on the Lord's Day under an apple tree in Goodman Chapman's Orchard.' . . . In Plymouth a man was 'sharply whipped' for shooting fowl on Sunday; . . . Captain Kemble of Boston was in 1656 set for two hours in the public stocks for his 'lewd and unseemly behavior,' which consisted in his kissing his wife 'publicquely' on the Sabbath Day, upon the doorstep of his house, when he had just returned from a voyage and absence of three years. . . . In 1760 the legislature of Massachusetts passed the law that 'any person able of Body who shall absent themselves from publick worship of God on the Lord's Day shall pay ten shillings fine," pp. 246, 247, 250.

aspect at all. He has his gun loaded and aimed at a different target, and that not unexcitedly, for he confesses, "I see no point in seeking to conceal, by a wholly impersonal tone, the reflexes of my own value system."[49]

Hence, with this author's object in view concerning which he expresses considerable distaste, he animatedly describes it as, "a phenomenon as bizarre as belief in the Calvinist God."[50] So for this reason he musters substantial evidence to prove that an epidemic of despair clouded Bunyan's generation. Thus, "*The Pilgrim's Progress* evolves under similar pressures, except that here the psychic persecution is more fully amplified in its social dimensions. Bunyan's allegory provided the aptest literary vehicle for the persecutory imagination, uniting the physical, psychological, and social levels on which it was simultaneously experienced."[51]

Using a style that could learn much from the more temperate, though no less committed, writing of Christopher Hill, Stachniewski provides a vast array of seventeenth century literary evidence concerning individual introspective preoccupation with the eternal purposes of God. Of course the setting at that time was certainly quite different from the more carnival spirit of today. But the cause of this supposed welter of depression is more broadly based than the author's thesis will allow. Not surprisingly, Hill suggests economic factors, though he also allows for perceived sin and Calvinism; then he concludes: "It would be useless to speculate which was the more operative cause."[52]

However, the great issue that Stachniewski does not in any way prove is whether the incidence of depression and suicide in this modern era, definitely not dominated by Calvinism, is comparatively less than that of seventeenth century Puritan England. To answer positively would certainly be brave, and expected with regard to supporting the author's basic thesis, but it would hardly be realistic. As a matter of fact, The World Health Organization has recently released a prediction that in the 21st century, depression will have risen to first place as the most

---

49 Stachniewski, *The Persecutory Imagination*, p. 14.

50 Ibid.

51 Ibid., p. 7. However, refer to John R. Knott, *Discourses of Martyrdom in English Literature*, p. 195, where it is suggested that Bunyan's persecutory imagination was derived from his admiration of the Marian martyrs as described in *Foxe's Book of Martyrs.*

52 Hill, *A Tinker And A Poor Man*, p. 185.

disabling condition, in terms of its impact on the individual, and that above road accidents, heart disease, and war.[53]

This is also the same conclusion of Gordon Wakefield:

> [Stackniewski's book] is a valuable corrective to the over-eager and selective admiration of Puritanism, which I recognize as a danger in some of my own work. . . . Yet the reaction goes too far. . . . Despair is not confined to Protestantism, nor its literature to Stachniewski's period [of concern]. If Calvinism may have aggravated his [Bunyan's] despair, did it not also deliver him from falling into the abyss of religious aberrations? Some of us may have presented the Puritan divines in too attractive a guise. But in Bunyan above all there is a tenderness as well as a humility which engages our affections still.[54]

Pieter de Vries

This Dutch scholar obtained a Ph.D. in Theology from the University of Utrecht, the title of his thesis being *John Bunyan on the Order of Salvation.* A revised English version was published in 1994.[55] Particularly noteworthy concerning this work is the delightful discovery that here we have another none too common study of Bunyan's doctrine after the manner of Richard Greaves' doctoral dissertation, though in this instance the author is less restrained in making clear his personal commitment to Bunyan's doctrinal stance; and scholarship in no way suffers on this account. At the conclusion we read:

> Those who cherish the Reformed standards of faith will be conscious of a heart-felt union with Reformed Baptists like John Bunyan. . . . May the Lord use this study to build his church. The church professes that God has blessed her with all spiritual blessings in Christ. It is the Christian's comfort that the same God who has predestinated him to be conformed to the image of his Son, has also called him, and justified him, and will some day glorify him. How good it is to serve and praise this God. Amen.[56]

---

[53] Philip Mitchell and Greg Clarke, "Comprehending the darkness," citing the World Health Organization and *New Scientist*, *The Briefing*, April 2, 1997, p. 9.

[54] Gordon Wakefield, review of Stachniewski, *Journal Of Theological Studies*, Oct., 1992, pp. 749-53.

[55] Pieter de Vries, *John Bunyan on the Order of Salvation,* pp. 234.

[56] Ibid., pp. 220-21.

Here Bunyan's convictions are considered according to the *ordo salutis* (order of salvation) with a lapsarian focus, although these technical terms were coined following Bunyan's era. Hence, here is a study of the Bedford pastor's distinctive Puritanism and his kinship with European Reformed doctrine as it is reflected in the "golden chain" of Romans 8:28-30. However, the Englishman's distinctiveness is not lost:

> Bunyan was a preacher of free grace. In answering the question how man might flee from the wrath to come, he did not refer to human properties or duties to be performed. He powerfully taught that we can only stand in the judgment of God if we are clothed with Christ's righteousness. The foundation on which we can stand before God is entirely outside of us in the work of Christ. In the history of the church law and gospel have time and again been mixed up. Christ has repeatedly been seen to be transformed into a new Moses, delineated as a taskmaster rather than a Savior.[57]

Hence, unlike a considerable proportion of Bunyan studies today, there is so much that is good, clarifying, and edifying here that a short review such as this will be forced to leave a substantial part unmentioned.

However, while the author reflects a very affectionate regard for Bunyan and his ministry, which the Dutch have especially evidenced, there are several matters raised that nevertheless ought to be questioned. For instance there is the comment: "R. L. Greaves' conclusion that Bunyan displayed Antinomian tendencies is in my opinion incorrect."[58] However, the consequences of Bunyan's later belief that the Sabbath was not a creation ordinance, but rather ordained for Israel, are at least for today grounds for making the charge of antinomianism, as is sometimes his belligerent terminology concerning Moses. Refer to Chapter 8.

Then there is the identification of Bunyan's use of the terms "covenant of works" and "covenant of grace" with the more formulated definitions.[59] Classic definitions of the "covenant of

---

[57] Ibid., p. 218.

[58] Ibid., p. 160.

[59] "The Puritans, and Bunyan is no exception, were decidedly covenant theologians," de Vries, *Order of Salvation*, p. 98. This is a confusing statement since Bunyan was not classically covenantal within the mainstream of English Puritanism, notwithstanding the covenantal terminology especially used in *The Doctrine of the Law and Grace Unfolded*. Refer to Chapter 8.

grace" speak of an overarching covenant under which subsume the specific administrations or biblically stated covenants. However for Bunyan, in a more narrow sense, "the covenant of grace" is identical with rather than inclusive of the new covenant. As detailed in Chapter 8, this "covenant of grace" was certainly transacted in heaven between the Father and the Son, yet to the exclusion of participation on the part of God's elect; it was not a derived and comprehensive covenant according to more confessional expressions as represented by the *The Westminster Confession of Faith*.

Michael A. Mullett

This senior lecturer in history at Lancaster University, England, has published extensively on religious history, with biographies of Luther, Calvin, and studies of Nonconformity. Most recently he has written, what will be regarded for many, in the intellectual arena, as the definitive analysis of Bunyan and his world. *John Bunyan in Context* is a scholarly study of the allegorist's historical setting, life, and writings, and is exhaustively referenced. The style is decidedly prolix and circuitous, like much writing in the field of modern Bunyan studies, with turns of sentence construction that would boggle the mind of Bunyan, who was such a master of attractive simplicity. This is not a book for the layman on account of the nuances that presuppose much in the realm of historic background, literary composition, and even theological expression.

It is refreshing to read of a call that directs us back to the more classic Bunyan whose involvement in political matters, notwithstanding the emphasis of Christopher Hill, is relatively minor:

> It is worth noting that, of his nearly sixty published works, none directly concerns politics, and that one early production, the 1663 *Christian Behavior* "illustrates the conservatism of Bunyan's social views" [quoting Hill]. Conservative or not, there is every indication that Bunyan was not deeply interested in political questions, in view of the overwhelming priority of spiritual and religious issues in his scheme of things.[60]

In conclusion this thought is repeated with the declaration that attempted political reconstruction of the allegorist, "lies a truth about Bunyan. But, hard though this may be for the twentieth-century *homo politicus* searching for the political element in all

[60] Michael A. Mullett, *John Bunyan in Context*, pp. 52-53.

forms of discourse to digest, the authentic Bunyan may actually be closer to the Victorian version."[61]

The breadth of Mullett's task, including commentary on a large proportion of Bunyan's writings to some degree, has inevitably resulted in instances of imbalance and skimpiness that leave the reader unfulfilled in certain areas. For instance, there is an exceedingly detailed consideration of Bunyan's arrest, trial, and imprisonment, and the space devoted to this topic substantially exceeds the whole of that one chapter apportioned to consider Part One of *The Pilgrim's Progress*. As might be expected, there is a lot to wrestle with from a historical perspective, such as the claim that, "Bunyan took a royalist line" following the Restoration of the monarchy,[62] the fact of Bunyan's medieval inheritance in relation to the matter of his literary dependency,[63] and the intriguing parallels between Luther and Bunyan that only reinforce the fundamental point concerning the substantial influence of the German theologian upon the English nonconformist.[64]

In regard to the chapter devoted to Part One of *The Pilgrim's Progress*, it is here that inadequate coverage becomes quite obvious. The treatment at this point, as in other chapters, is most eclectic. To begin with, there is the statement that "it [*The Pilgrim's Progress*] became a children's classic," the possibility being offered that this could have been Bunyan's original purpose.[65] Refer to Chapter 19 for a more detailed response to this misunderstanding. Yes, who would argue against the fact that the allegory is more substantially a discourse than an itinerary. But why take several pages to prove this. The exposition re Pope and Pagan is certainly enlightening though out of proportion. More significant is the exposition of the fact that the Palace Beautiful is a representation of the Bedford congregation. Thus, "*The Pilgrim's Progress*, then, is a Puritan book, and concerned with the life of the gathered churches."[66]

Particularly disappointing was the omission of any consideration of the issues of despair, suicide, and their remedy according to Bunyan's portrayal via Doubting Castle. In a similar vein, and

---

[61] Ibid., p. 284

[62] Ibid., p. 110.

[63] Ibid., p. 192.

[64] Ibid., pp. 10-12, 15-16, 35-36, 48.

[65] Ibid., pp. 191-2.

[66] Ibid., p. 202.

from an evangelical perspective which is surely Bunyan's perspective as well, the most unsatisfactory feature of the book as a whole is the doctrinal leanness that is so representative of much contemporary Bunyan scholarship. This lack simply betrays a spiritual void concerning a passionate appreciation of Reformation truth. For example, we read:

> Yet, although Bunyan rejected a soteriology of self-assurance which he ascribed to Fowler [the latitudinarian that Bunyan severally characterized], he himself, especially in his repudiation of the inactive and verbal religion of Talkative, seems again to move away from a Reformation doctrine of justification by faith alone, and to place confidence in the role, not of the individual's election or saving faith, but in his or her moral actions and works.[67]

This is nothing more than shallow speculation that knows not Bunyan at the doctrinal level, especially the relationship between justification and inevitable sanctification. With regard to Talkative, the confrontation that took place between he and Faithful was obviously not a gospel presentation. It was intended to facilitate exposure, to bring Talkative to repentance concerning his blindness to his own sin; should this have happened, then the truth of justification by faith would have been presented to him just as plainly as it was, later on, by Faithful to Hopeful.

Like so much of modern Bunyan scholarship, this writing is heavy on historical discovery and light on theological/biblical/experiential matters. Certainly Mullett is a historian, but his theological comment, hardly of an evangelical character, is of secondary concern, and such a priority does fundamental disservice to Bunyan. It is this poverty of emphasis that betrays the reason for the cool character of modern academic investigation sans spiritual commitment and enthusiasm. The overwhelming fact of John Bunyan, and representatively so in *The Pilgrim's Progress*, is the free saving grace of God through the Lord Jesus Christ that is offered to great sinners. If a writer does not know something of this soul-enthralling truth, it seems as though it is impossible for him adequately to do justice to the essential Bunyan. In the light of this fact, the most faithful book on the real cause of Bunyan has yet to be written in this century.

[67] Ibid., p. 200.

CONCLUSION

It is abundantly clear that the non-evangelical, theologically bland, biblically liberal, and secular spirit of this century, which seems to dominate scholarly literary analysis, is not comfortable with the doctrine of John Bunyan. Of course the same could be said with regard to the beliefs of Luther, Calvin, Edwards, etc. However the literati like the company of the truly great Christians, even if in their hearts they spurn their doctrine. They, with the arrogance of this modern age, convince themselves that had the fruits of contemporary textual criticism, with regard to the Bible, been available to our spiritual fathers, they too would have come to the enlightened, albeit soul-debilitating conclusions of today. So the older writings, such as *The Pilgrim's Progress*, are patronized for their literary and historical merit only, while the literal Bible teaching is at best regarded as *passé*.

Thus Vincent Newey, Lecturer in the Department of English Literature at the University of Liverpool, has concluded,

> that the assumptions in which *The Pilgrim's Progress* is rooted are no longer generally assumed [so that this] allows us broader sympathies. But the collapse of the work's controlling beliefs—whether we think of religion itself or of the more precise Calvinist scheme of salvation—can account only for a shift in attitude towards such figures, and not for the vividness of their continuing presence. What gives them "immortality" is Bunyan's creativity [not Bunyan's God!], appetite for life, and instinctive embrace of experience. He was restricted by his creed but was not its victim.[68]

Of course this is simply a reiteration of Sharrock, Hill, Campbell, and Stachniewski with regard to their rejection of Bunyan's regard for the Bible. This is the bottom line issue from which so much of a certain appreciation of *The Pilgrim's Progress* is derived.

So we commenced, quite unapologetically, with the assertion that in the realm of Bunyan studies, and in consideration of the Bedford tinker's most passionate concerns, this twentieth century has been a relative wilderness period. The fact is that detailed literary analysis, novel historical interpretation, and avant-garde psychological investigation have not been able to obscure a fundamental poverty of appreciation concerning what, for Bunyan,

---

[68] Vincent Newey, "Bunyan And The Confines Of The Mind," *The Pilgrim's Progress, Critical and Historical Views*, ed. Vincent Newey, p. 44.

were by far the most important issues of all. Bold confession of detachment from Bunyan's biblicist and Calvinist faith notwithstanding, the end result is a soulless and sterile contribution that will do nothing for any burdened sinner. Gordon Rupp, Luther scholar, perceives this problem when he explains, "why a Protestant Christian can understand things about Bunyan that are hidden from the innumerable literary critics who have written some very foolish pages about the measurement of Bunyan's sins, and failed altogether to understand either what it means to have a 'bruised conscience' or justification by faith."[69] George Offor understood this truth, but then his style is now regarded as "quaint" on this account. One thing is certain, Bunyan would regard the literary, historical, sociological, and psychological speculations of those who reject the plain truth of Scripture as the greatest imaginable folly.

THE COMMENTARY OF GEORGE OFFOR

How universal to fallen nature is that soul-destroying heresy—the attempt to justify ourselves by our own good works, and to make up the deficiency by the merits of the Savior! Ye might as well attempt to serve God and mammon, as to unite our impure works and those of the pure and holy Jesus. We must, as perishing sinners, fall into the arms of Divine mercy, and receive pardon as a free gift, wholly through the merits of the Savior, or we must for ever perish. It is an awful consideration.

George Offor
Justification by an Imputed Righteousness
Works, I, p. 332

---

[69] Gordon Rupp, *Six Makers of English Religion, 1500-1700*, p. 94.

CHAPTER NINETEEN

Children's Versions of The Pilgrim's Progress

IF the communication of *The Pilgrim's Progress* to adults requires a word/truth priority, then a serious case also ought to be made for arguing that the communication of Bunyan's allegory to children equally requires a word/truth priority. Unfortunately, the present deluge of fantasy oriented and audiovisual programming has tended to militate against such a concept. The media thrust has become so powerful that, unless children are fortified with solid doses of objective word/truth, they tend to subject reality to fantasy and impose fantasy upon reality.

Coleen Cook well illustrates this point as follows:

> The powerful effect of some of these artificial memories [fantasies] is vividly illustrated by a phenomenon some fire fighters call the "Darth Vader Syndrome." Increasingly, masked fire fighters are noticing that many small children caught in burning homes are running from, hiding from, or furiously fighting and resisting rescuers instead of cooperating with them in the middle of life-threatening situations. Subsequent interviews with small survivors pinpoint the problem. "I thought you were a spaceman," or "I thought you were Darth Vader," they confess.[1]

The rise of Audiovisual Education

Of course related to this problem is its alignment with the audiovisual model of learning so prevalent in adult communication. So with children, the argument has arisen that to make learning visually exciting and fun is to enhance learning. However, it ought immediately to be enquired as to what precisely is learned by means of this "fun"? One thing is certain, a child exposed to this hedonistic philosophy does learn to be dependant on hot impressionistic media and spurn cool

---

1 Coleen Cook. *All That Glitters*, p. 142.

cognitive media. As Neil Postman explains: "As a television show, and a good one, 'Sesame Street' does not encourage children to love school or anything about school. It encourages them to love television."[2]

However, this being true, the intention here is not to depreciate the proper place of imagination and fantasy in relation to audiovisual media since, at this point, we touch upon that which is so precious and memorable in childhood, and no less so in past centuries. Rather, the purpose here is to uphold the subsidiary communicative role of these elements in relation to the primary communicative role of word/truth media that present reality through cognition.

The Rise of Audiovisual Versions of *The Pilgrim's Progress*

This now brings us to the specific point of how *The Pilgrim's Progress* ought to be communicated today to children, and the obvious thrust of the foregoing has established a basic principle. It is that word/truth media must be primary and audiovisual media secondary. Again, let it be made clear that this proposition is not being presented in an either/or fashion. However, it is on account of some questionable modern versions of *The Pilgrim's Progress* for children being widely marketed that a definite stance is here proposed.

In John Brown's classic biography of Bunyan, he lists thirty-two "Editions of *The Pilgrim's Progress* for Children and Young People," the earliest being *Bunyan Explained to a Child* published in 1825.[3] Two editions published by separate authors are titled *The Pilgrim's Progress in Words of one Syllable*. Hence, with added study of these earlier Children's versions in England at the Bedford Public Library, as well as The Evangelical Library in London, it would appear that in the main, while illustrations adorned some editions of *The Pilgrim's Progress* from its third edition in 1679 onward,[4] designated versions for children in reasonable numbers did not appear until the early nineteenth century. Even then, a preponderance of these early children's versions was in fact the

---

[2] Neil Postman, *Amusing Ourselves To Death*, p. 144.

[3] John Brown, *John Bunyan*, p. 482.

[4] The third edition of *The Pilgrim's Progress*, published in 1679, appears to have been the first printing with any illustration. It included what is now known as "the sleeping portrait" which depicted not only Bunyan in a dreaming pose, but also Christian journeying from the City of Destruction toward the Wicket-gate.

full text with the added attraction of numerous appealing illustrations. However, the twentieth century has increasingly tended to publish versions strong in graphic representation and weak, or even worse, perverse with regard to the editing and alteration of the text.

In this regard, it is surprising to read contemporary Bunyan scholar Michael Mullett, comment as follows:

> Whether or not it [*The Pilgrim's Progress*] was aimed at children—as, expressly, was his *A Book for Boys and Girls* (1684)—it became a children's classic. . . . In the Romantic era, the book's apparent suitability for and appeal to children allowed for its reclassification—in terms of approval, given the Romantics' general admiration for childhood—as a children's book.[5]

Proof is then offered that includes the early nineteenth century recommendations for children of Robert Southey and George Crabbe, though doubtless they were referring to the full text and not simplified versions. However, Southey is not indicating the chief suitability of *The Pilgrim's Progress* for children, but rather its, "general popularity;—his [Bunyan's] language is every where level to the most ignorant reader, and to the meanest capacity: there is a homely reality about it; a nursery tale is not more intelligible, in its manner of narration, to a child."[6] Of that period, certainly Macaulay and Coleridge regarded Bunyan's magnum opus as being more than a novel primarily intended for children.

Let it be reiterated, as stated in Chapter I, that *The Pilgrim's Progress*, according to Bunyan's purposes, is primarily an adult book, yet at a basic level it is also capable of appealing to children. Its substance, though delightfully framed, yet concerns adult situations as everywhere portrayed. For example consider the character of Madam Wanton, the criticism of Shame, the carnality of Adam the first, the worldliness of By-ends and his friends, the subject matter of despair and suicide at Doubting Castle, and the substantial doctrine contained in the discourse entered into while traversing the Enchanted Ground.

---

5 Michael A. Mullett, *John Bunyan in Context*, p. 191.

6 Roger Sharrock, ed., *Bunyan, The Pilgrim's Progress, A Casebook*, p. 57.

SELECT CONTEMPORARY CHILDREN'S VERSIONS

The select reviews that follow are intended to be representative of the surge of children's versions of *The Pilgrim's Progress* that continue to be published. It ought to be evident that the parent who desires to teach his child the truth of Bunyan's allegory, as was intended, ought to be careful in selecting a suitable version.

Dangerous Journey, Oliver Hunkin, illustrations by Alan Parry. Grand Rapids: Wm. B. Eerdmans, 1990.

This version was originally produced for Yorkshire Television, England in 1985. A video cassette version of this series, professionally produced, is presently available being comprised of nine 15-minute episodes. The book, of large format, was published at the same time, presumably for children, though this is not stated. The main focus is on Part One while a very condensed version of Part Two is included.

To begin with, the illustrations by Alan Parry are magnificently British and undoubtedly the strength of this version. Nevertheless, the text leaves much to be desired. From beginning to end, even Bunyan's remaining doctrinal content is emptied of its specific quality and replaced with a more ecumenical brand. Simple, Sloth, and Presumption are shunted back to before Christian's arrival at the Wicket-gate. In the same vein and contrary to the original text, Pope is dead while Pagan remains alive and is made to portray Pope's stiff joints and nail-biting frustration.

The lengthy discussion on the Enchanted Ground concerning Hopeful's conversion, Ignorance's false gospel, and Temporary's regression has been completely eliminated, and herein lies the heart of the problem. Virtually all substantial discourse sections have been excluded. With this version we are confronted with impressive graphics and at best, maudlin doctrine.

The Pilgrim's Progress, illustrations by Albert Wessels. Harpenden, England: The Bunyan Press, 1993.

Here is a handsome and full presentation of the original text of Part One of *The Pilgrim's Progress* that is to be highly recommended. Published in 1993, it is typographically very readable, though the highlight is the illustrative skill of the Dutch painter, Albert Wessels. His colorful renderings of over seventy scenes draw upon many older engravings that are given new life, particularly the facial features. Several montages draw upon considerable detail taken from the text and add an interpretive touch. The only shortcoming is the "error" on page 77 where the painting of Christian passing by Pope is incorrectly titled "Pagan"!

The Pilgrim's Progress, retold by Dan Larsen, illustrated by Al Bohl. Uhrichsville, OH: Barbour & Company, 1989.

This racy version, including Parts I and II, yet commences in a most uninviting manner as follows: "The man stood in the field outside the City of Destruction and cried out in terror, 'What shall I do!'" Omissions in Part I include five scenes from the house of the Interpreter, Pope and Pagan, By-ends and his friends, Little-faith, Temporary, and the concluding scene regarding Ignorance.

Now while simplification of the text may be justified, for this reviewer omissions are another matter and tend to underestimate a child's capacity to comprehend the full panorama of Bunyan's story. If length is a problem, then why not cover the whole account episodically? This version, like so many others of this type, also omits all poetic references and thus denies a young person an attractive introduction into poetic stimulation.

Little Pilgrim's Progress, Helen L. Taylor, illustrated by W. Lindsay Cable. Chicago: Moody Press, n.d.

The cover indicates that over 350,000 of this version, designated as suitable for ages 7-12, have been sold. The distinctive feature here is the adaptation of *The Pilgrim's Progress* into the world of children by means of characterization, vocabulary, and juvenile concepts. So the commencement blandly reads: "Little Christian lived in a great city called Destruction. Its streets were full of boys and girls who laughed and played all day long. This was in the summertime when the sun was shining and the city looked bright and pleasant. On the rainy days in winter the children did not feel so happy, and they would sometimes be glad to sit down quietly and listen to stories."

However, does communication for the young require that all of the adult settings be eliminated or recast into a youthful frame of reference? Again, simplification may have a place, yet the child, for all of its enjoyment of fantasy, yet aspires to things adult, and that transitional hope is so meaningfully portrayed by Bunyan's allegory. Normal childhood is always progressive, never static. But here revision is also included, not mere simplification. For instance, why, according to this version, is Apollyon renamed "Self"? By all means change the name to the more simple "Satan". But Bunyan is most definitely portraying this foul fiend as a personal Devil, and not as mere internal conflict! At the conclusion, and in reversal of the order of the text, Ignorance faces his final destiny first, after which Little Christian gains entrance at the Celestial City, doubtless to give the story a more happy ending!

Pilgrim's Progress, retold by Mack Thomas, illustrated by Keith Criss. Sisters, OR: Gold 'n' Honey Family Classics, 1996.

Concerning this revision of Part One, we are told in the jacket: "Many contemporary editions of *Pilgrim's Progress* shorten the story, eliminating important details. Others retain the seventeenth-century English that children find difficult to understand. But this vivid retelling of *Pilgrim's Progress* offers a full text that remains faithful to the dramatic, dream-like simplicity of Bunyan's original version, while carefully presenting the story in understandable, modern English." In terms of this stated goal, it is quite well achieved, that is all of the major events and most characters are included.

However, there are literary touches and expressions that Bunyan uses, which this writer believes ought to be taught to children, that are omitted. For instance, the classic beginning reads, "As I walked through the wilderness of this world, I lighted on a certain place, where there was a den; and I laid me down in that place to sleep: and as I slept I dreamed a dream." Certainly this statement could be more smoothly written: "As I walked through the wilderness of this world, I came upon a certain place, where there was a den; and I lay down in that place to sleep; and as I slept I dreamed a dream." However, this version reads: "While walking in a forest I found a cave, where I lay down to sleep. And as I slept, I dreamed a dream." The impact of the original seems completely lost.

Further, Pope is more tamely identified as "Pompous," and Hopeful's detailed and substantial testimony of his conversion, while traversing the Enchanted Ground, is reduced to a sentence of fifteen words. Likewise the extended encounter with Ignorance that discusses the heart of the gospel becomes eight sentences, and there is no mention of Temporary. Attractively published in a large format with many colored illustrations, this version is better than many, yet by no means ideal. Rather parents should aim at teaching the complete version of *The Pilgrim's Progress* to their children as soon as is possible, using initiative and the simplification of some expressions. With added effort, such a goal is easily achievable.

The Pilgrim's Progress, retold by Martin Powell, illustrated by Seppo Makinen. New York: Marvel Comics, 1992,

Reference has already been made to this version in Chapter 17. This reviewer considers it to be one of the most objectionable and revisionist versions that has more recently become available. From a literary point of view, *The Pilgrim's Progress* is thoroughly emasculated of its essential content. The writer understands little of what Bunyan is about. From a graphics point of view, a comic world perspective imposes, not a contemporary understanding, but a degenerate portrayal of sexual nuance, physical exposure, gross representation, and identity with comic unreality rather than biblical reality.

The Game of Pilgrim's Progress, created by Marla Hershberger. Bozeman, MT: Family Time, Inc., 1994.

This is a modern, professionally produced, full fledged board game which the publisher commends as follows: "We hope that this game will not only be fun, but that it will also be used as a devotional tool. This game was purposefully designed to stimulate thoughtful discussion and generate a greater awareness of biblical principles and spiritual truths. We want to challenge each player to live a life of purity and holiness in obedience to Jesus Christ (Colossians 3:17)."

Nevertheless, this reviewer, while having enjoyed many a board game with his own children, and with anticipation of such a happy prospect with his grandchildren, yet finds it impossible to recommend a game such as this where salvation is obtained by means of the throw of a die! The salvation of a soul ought never to be framed in such a way that it is considered as a "fun thing," in much the same way as a game of Monopoly is enjoyed. It could never be said of Bunyan that he composed *The Pilgrim's Progress* in a similar way; his presentation of the gospel is in deadly earnest, not withstanding certain droll situations.

However, in the actual structure of the game several very serious problems arise. First, contrary to Bunyan's intention as explained in Chapter 6, salvation is associated with the Place of Deliverance rather than the Wicket-gate. Then, landing on any of six cross squares brings salvation; there are four at the Place of Deliverance, and two scattered apart much further ahead. We are told, "It is possible to miss landing on a 'Cross' square. In that case, the pilgrim must proceed with his burden on." Thus it is quite possible for a player to enter heaven still burdened! The author comments:

"We created *The Game of Pilgrim's Progress* to stimulate greater learning of the truths set forth in the book." One thing is certain, this game presents a false representation of the biblical gospel and Bunyan's allegorical description of it.

The Pilgrim's Progress, Accurate Text Revision, by Barry E. Horner. Lindenhurst, NY: Reformation Press, 1999.

The complete text of Part One is accurately retold with no omissions whatsoever. The format includes 36 chapters, the retention of select archaic expressions with modern equivalents, extensive biblical references, helpful footnotes, and select character illustrations.

CONCLUSION

This writer gains no pleasure in being, on the whole, more critical than complimentary with regard to these reviews. As a five year old, he well remembers his own first encounter with a colored lantern-slide presentation of *The Pilgrim's Progress* at an after school meeting in a local Baptist church. In fact it is his hope in the future to produce such a comparable visual presentation that would be suitable for projection, though probably via a CD-Rom disc. However such a production would include the full revised text and thus maintain Bunyan's truth content and emphases. Supporting graphics and audio would enhance but not overwhelm the intended dominance of word/truth. Production design would allow for a variety of segmented presentations.

Hence let the reader be reminded, as indicated earlier, that as a general rule children's versions of *The Pilgrim's Progress* did not appear till near 150 years after its first edition, and that even then these most often contained the full, unabridged text. It is only in the latter part of this twentieth century that a plethora of condensed versions has appeared. The fact is that today's generation is not so well able to read Bunyan's classic because of a comprehension disorder that has arisen as a result of audiovisual media orientation described more fully in Chapter 17. Presenting a visually projected version of *The Pilgrim's Progress* to young children is one thing, but neglecting to encourage the understanding of the full text by older children and young teens is quite another.

However, shall the Christian parent of today capitulate to the pressures and siren-like overtures of the vast audiovisual media conglomerate? Certainly not if he wants his child to grasp truth, especially Bible truth. Rather he needs to coach and encourage with books such as *The Pilgrims Progress*, and not yield to the vogue of pruning and contemporizing in such a way that authorial purposes are lost. Rather, let the following suggested principles be followed.

A. As early as possible, present a child with the full text of *The Pilgrim's Progress*, in episodes, rather than a pruned version in a short space of time.

B. By all means use a full version of *The Pilgrim's Progress* that reads in a more contemporary style, and yet in no way compromises the truth as Bunyan intended.

C. By all means use a full version that is visually augmented, but avoid any version that allows visual presentation to dominate while at the same time truth is diminished. In other words, let the child appreciate that the text is the primary point of reference.

D. Where visual augmentation is employed, make sure that it is faithful to the text and not revisionist in its representation or culturally in conflict with Bunyan's setting.

E. Lead the child from the adventurous allegorical form to the substance of doctrinal truth in such a way that he enjoys the discovery.

BUNYAN'S CONFESSION IN BEDFORD PRISON

I have sometimes seen more in a line of the Bible [in this place] than I could well tell how to stand under, and yet at another time the whole Bible hath been to me as dry as a stick; or rather, my heart hath been so dead and dry unto it, that I could not conceive the least drachm of refreshment, though I have looked it all over.

John Bunyan
Grace Abounding to the Chief of Sinners
Works, I, p. 50

CHAPTER TWENTY

150 Study Questions on The Pilgrim's Progress

THESE questions are designed to stimulate further inquiry into the overall legacy of John Bunyan, that is his times, person, writings, and especially *The Pilgrim's Progress*, though with the presumption of the allegorist's firm evangelical convictions. This book as a whole offers much that will give direction, though many questions require study in outlying fields.

The level of inquiry involved here would equate to high school and college standards. However, the inquirer ought constantly to keep in mind Bunyan's biblical purposes and not be satisfied with mere detached and academic answers. This writer would gladly interact with those who earnestly desire to study these issues from an evangelical perspective.

INTRODUCTORY CONSIDERATIONS

1. Explain why *The Pilgrim's Progress* ought to be taught and proclaimed today. Be specific in your reasoning.

2. "Because the Bible is incomparable as the inspired Word of God, we ought not to elevate a mere uninspired human work such as *The Pilgrim's Progress* to even the supposed rank of 'The second best book in all the world.'" Critique this statement, especially in the light of Bunyan's expressed publishing intentions as well as the volume's essential character and its significant involvement in the history of the Christian church.

3. "*The Pilgrim's Progress* is principally a book designed for adults rather than children." Discuss the degree to which this statement is true. Support your opinion from the text.

4. What are Bunyan's purposes in writing *The Pilgrims Progress*? Especially interact with the introductory and concluding poems. Consider why these purposes are important for the communication of the allegory today.

5. From where in the Bible does Bunyan derive his concept of "journeying" or "pilgrimage"?

6. In Bunyan's poem that concludes Part One, he warns against, "playing with the outside of my dream." What is the "inside" of his dream? How will the proper communication of *The Pilgrim's Progress* avoid a misunderstanding of this expressed purpose?

7. To what degree do Bunyan's introductory and concluding poems, in Part One of *The Pilgrim's Progress*, adequately respond to the conflicting estimates that were forthcoming at the time of publication, as well as during its illustrious ongoing history?

8. On the title page of the first edition of *The Pilgrim's Progress*, Bunyan quotes Hosea 12:10, "I have used similitudes," as justification for his allegorical method. Discuss the legitimacy of his line of reasoning here.

9. Samuel Coleridge described *The Pilgrim's Progress* as, "incomparably the best *Summa Theologiae Evangelicae* [summary of evangelical theology] ever produced by a writer not miraculously inspired." Comment on the truthfulness of this assessment.

BUNYAN'S PERSONAL EXPERIENCE

10. Compare *Grace Abounding To The Chief Of Sinners* with *The Pilgrim's Progress*. In what ways are they related, and how does *Grace Abounding* help in the interpretation of *The Pilgrim's Progress*?

11. Relate the trial of Christian and Faithful at Vanity Fair to Bunyan's own arrest, trial, and imprisonment. To what degree is such satire legitimate in Christian witness? Is there biblical justification for such an approach?

12. How does the encounter of Christian and Hopeful with Giant Despair of Doubting Castle reflect certain trials of Bunyan himself? Contrast this scene with the despair of Christian in the Slough of Despond.

13. Several modern estimates of Bunyan consider his self-analysis, such as in *Grace Abounding*, to be too extreme and reflective of a severe seventeenth century Calvinistic environment. Assess the validity of this opinion.

14. Compare Christian's experiences in the Valley of Humiliation and Valley of the Shadow of Death with those of Faithful. To what

degree are these struggles a reflection of Bunyan's experiences described in *Grace Abounding*?

15. Compare the conversion of Hopeful in *The Pilgrim's Progress* with that of Bunyan described in *Grace Abounding To The Chief Of Sinners*. Consider these contrasting perspectives with the terms of evangelical conversion that are considered normative at the end of this twentieth century.

16. Bunyan's formal education was less than modest. Compare this initial level of education with his apparent overall knowledge in later years. How did this improvement come about? What was his overall attitude to a university education and the learned?

17. What do we know of Bunyan as a family man? Consider the circumstances of his two marriages. How is his appreciation of family life reflected in both parts of *The Pilgrim's Progress*?

18. What were the major influences on Bunyan's religious development, both before and after his conversion? Consider individuals, national events, and movements such as various sects as well as the whole aura of the Church of England.

CHARACTER AND EVENT ASSESSMENTS

19. Discuss the impact of the opening paragraph of Part One of *The Pilgrim's Progress*, along with the closing paragraph that has received a less favorable estimate.

20. Bunyan's portrayal of Christian's departure from his wife and children could be misunderstood, especially when one considers the tinker's own family life. Discuss this problem with regard to both Part One and Part Two of *The Pilgrim's Progress*.

21. John Kelman writes: "On the whole, Obstinate is a better and more hopeful man than Pliable. Perverse though he be, and boorish beside this other, yet there is character in him, and more can be made of him." Discuss why you agree or disagree with this statement.

22. While Christian's unconverted name is Graceless, as we are told at the Palace Beautiful, why does Bunyan yet call the pilgrim "Christian" well before his entrance through the Wicket-gate?

23. In the early sequence of events in *The Pilgrim's Progress*, what is the significance of the placement of the Slough of Despond before the Wicket-gate? Consider the "bedaubing" of Pliable and

of Christian. What distinguishes the despondency at this scene with that which Christian experiences subsequent to his conversion?

24. Describe the essential differences between Christian and Pliable, especially with regard to motives, as they travel together and then tumble into the Slough of Despond.

25. What is the essence of Mr. Worldly-Wiseman's gospel? What seventeenth century and modern representations are there of him? Give special attention to their religious convictions.

26. The Wicket-gate is not only the place where Christian becomes an authentic pilgrim, but also a scene of intense conflict between Christ and Satan. Expand upon this thought, even as it is described in other parts of the allegory. How do the experiences of Faithful and Christiana along with Mercy differ at this point?

27. In *The Pilgrim's Progress* Jesus Christ is portrayed by several different characters and situations. Identify as many of these in Part One as you can, and comment on their individual and collective significance.

28. Expand upon the significance of the House of Interpreter as it relates to John 14-16 as well as the fact of Christian's recent conversion.

29. How do the seven scenes portrayed at the house of the Interpreter in *The Pilgrim's Progress* reflect Bunyan's own pastoral priorities, and especially with regard to the first scene of the portrait of the godly pastor?

30. Expound upon Bunyan's portrayal of the despairing reprobate in the iron cage. What historic precedents might he be drawing upon? What is his purpose here? What is Bunyan's view of reprobation in his other writings?

31. Carefully consider where Christian encounters Simple, Sloth, and Presumption, and speculate as to where they may have come from.

32. Describe the differences between Christian as an authentic pilgrim and Formalist and Hypocrisy as counterfeits. In *The Pilgrim's Progress*, what essentially distinguishes a true pilgrim?

33. How does confrontation with the Hill Difficulty affect the journey of four progressing pilgrims? What major lessons are learned in this regard?

34. Consider the symbolic meaning of the two lions that are close to the entrance to the Palace Beautiful. In particular, explain the relevance of the circumstances of Bunyan's time and experience with regard to this savage opposition to pilgrims. Also consider Faithful's contrasting experience with these same circumstance s

35. To what degree is the Palace Beautiful a faithful biblical representation of a local church? Relate your answer to other pastoral representations in Bunyan's writings.

36. Analyze the assault of Apollyon upon Christian so as to discover the different stratagems that he uses. Then describe the pilgrim responses that effectively repel this foul enemy.

37. What is the real character of the Valley of Humiliation? Consider the contrasting experiences of Christian in Part One and Christiana in Part Two.

38. Consider Bunyan's estimate of Pope and Pagan with regard to the times in which he lived and the light of subsequent centuries to date. To what degree was Bunyan influenced by history?

39. Explain the exposure of Talkative's hypocrisy, especially the strategy employed. What then is Bunyan's teaching concerning the validation of a Christian?

40. While Christian departed from the City of Destruction before Faithful, what does Bunyan intend when he describes Faithful as passing by the Palace Beautiful so as to move ahead of Christian?

41. Compare Bunyan's portrayal of Evangelist in *The Pilgrim's Progress* with his contemporary counterpart. Consider Evangelist's continuous interest in and his post-conversion involvement with the status of pilgrims.

42. What similarities and differences are there with regard to the City of Destruction and the Town of Vanity? What other localities are there that have related characteristics?

43. Explain the continuity of thought that Bunyan intends when he relates the successive events concerning By-ends and his friends, Demas and the Silver Mine at the Hill Lucre, and the Monument to Lot's wife.

44. Elaborate upon the significance of the fruit and leaves which Christian and Hopeful partake of when they are refreshed beside the River of the Water of Life. How does this experience relate to their subsequent complaining?

45. In Doubting Castle, Christian and Hopeful are directed by Giant Despair and his wife to commit suicide. Evaluate the interaction that takes place between the two prisoners on this subject. Why does Bunyan inject this topic into his allegory?

46. What is the significance of the fact that Christian and Hopeful, having been imprisoned in Doubting Castle from Wednesday until Saturday evening, escape from Giant Despair on Sunday morning?

47. What solutions does Bunyan offer for depression/despair at the Doubting Castle scene? Relate these solutions to his own experiences described in *Grace Abounding*.

48. Expound upon the contrasts that Bunyan establishes between Little-faith, Turn-away, and Temporary. What pastoral insights does this teaching suggest?

49. Explain the non-negotiable nature of Little-faith's jewels when compared with his stolen petty cash, especially in biblical terms. Consider Bunyan's biblical illustrations.

50. Assess the distinction that Bunyan makes between Little-faith and Great-grace, especially in pastoral terms. Then contrast Little-faith and Hopeful.

51. Atheist claims to have been seeking for the Celestial City for the past twenty years. In what ways might this pursuit have been misdirected?

52. What specifically are the snares of the Enchanted Ground, and their remedy? Relate these remedies to the three distinct scenes that are portrayed during this sojourn.

53. Comment on the contrasting characteristics of Hopeful, Ignorance, and Temporary as they are consecutively portrayed by Bunyan in the discourse on the Enchanted Ground.

54. To what extent do Christian and Hopeful portray a normative and mature biblical attitude when they enjoy the delights of the land of Beulah?

55. Expound upon the contrasting experiences of Christian and Hopeful at the River of Death. Also relate this to the later crossing of Ignorance at this same place.

56. Give reasons why you agree or disagree with Bunyan's portrayal of Christian and Hopeful crossing the River of Death in company rather than alone.

57. What for Bunyan are the terms of entrance into the Celestial City? Relate this to contemporary evangelism and expectations.

58. Consider the Celestial City, its repeated emphasis in *The Pilgrim's Progress*, and further descriptions of this heavenly home in Bunyan's other writings.

59. "The concluding contrast between the destiny of Christian and that of Ignorance is both awesome and breathtaking!" Comment on this opinion. Why did Bunyan not conclude *The Pilgrim's Progress* with a happy ending?

60. The three leading pilgrims in Part One of *The Pilgrim's Progress* are Christian and his two successive companions, Faithful and Hopeful. Assuming that Christian portrays the author, what other close friends of Bunyan might be represented, to some degree, by Faithful and Hopeful? Who were the tinker's intimate spiritual acquaintances?

61. Discuss the contrasts that Bunyan portrays by means of a variety of true and false pilgrims. Relate this to Bunyan's pastoral experience as well as his other writings.

DOCTRINAL ISSUES

62. What is Bunyan's attitude toward the Bible, specifically with regard to his understanding of inspiration and inerrancy? How does he interpret it?

63. Nominate and discuss the five most important doctrinal emphases in *The Pilgrim's Progress*.

64. Discuss the significance of Dr. J. Gresham Machen's statement that *The Pilgrim's Progress* is, "that tenderest and most theological of books, . . . pulsating with life in every word."

65. "*The Pilgrim's Progress* is firstly about Christian sanctification and secondly about salvation." Discuss the degree to which this statement is true.

66. Of what significance is the doctrine of justification by faith to John Bunyan in *The Pilgrim's Progress*? Explain his biblical teaching, and include reference to his other writings

67. To what extent is the ministry of Martin Luther influential in the spirit and doctrine of *The Pilgrim's Progress?* Consider the overall influence of the reformer on Bunyan, especially with regard to the nature of the gospel.

68. Compare Bunyan's teaching on sanctification, that is Christian's spiritual growth in *The Pilgrim's Progress*, with various holiness and evangelical convention emphases that are rooted, directly or indirectly, in the historic Keswick, Higher Life, and Victorious Life movements.

69. Compare Bunyan's teaching on sanctification, that is Christian's spiritual growth in *The Pilgrim's Progress*, with that of the modern Charismatic Movement.

70. What does Bunyan teach us in *The Pilgrim's Progress* concerning the Christian doctrine of assurance?

71. In what ways does *The Pilgrim's Progress* reflect a seventeenth century, nonconformist understanding of the nature and function of the church?

72. What evidence is there of Bunyan's Calvinism in *The Pilgrim's Progress*? Relate this to his pastoral ministry and other writings.

73. As a Calvinist, Bunyan gives a balanced emphasis on the doctrines of divine sovereignty and human responsibility. Indicate from *The Pilgrim's Progress* to what degree this assessment is true.

74. At what stage in *The Pilgrim's Progress* is Christian converted? Give reasons for your answer. Consider Bunyan's own experience, especially as it is related in *Grace Abounding to the Chief of Sinners*.

75. Explain the biblical basis and individual significance of the benefits which Christian receives from the three Shining Ones at the Place of Deliverance. Consider the ongoing importance of these items.

76. Expound upon the Palace Beautiful so as to indicate how many facets of the doctrine of the local church are represented by this portrayal.

77. Expound upon the importance which Bunyan places on a pilgrim being well equipped with spiritual weapons, and especially with regard to Christian's encounter with Apollyon and the Valley of the Shadow of Death.

78. Comment on the doctrinal significance of Ignorance's response to Christian: "What! Would you have us trust to what Christ in his own person has done without us?"

79. Explain the doctrinal relationship that Bunyan portrays in *The Pilgrim's Progress* with regard to Adam the First, Moses, and Christ. Give scriptural support, and especially that which Bunyan appears to draw upon.

80. Explain the characteristics that distinguish true and counterfeit faith in *The Pilgrim's Progress.*

81. What are the great doctrinal heads that are fundamental to Hopeful's testimony? With these in mind, what essentially is the gospel in this testimony?

82. Expound upon the essential distinction that Bunyan makes in *The Pilgrim's Progress* between the gospel hope of Ignorance and the gospel hope of Christian and Hopeful What historic movement(s) does Ignorance represent?

83. Expound on Bunyan's understanding of the role of women in Part One of *The Pilgrim's Progress*, while also drawing upon Part Two and his other writings.

84. What is the role of prayer in *The Pilgrim's Progress*? Refer to all instances.

85. To what degree does Bunyan portray the future glory of heaven as a fundamental goal of the authentic progressing pilgrim? Contrast this with the emphases of contemporary evangelicalism, that is with regard to being heavenly minded.

86. Expound upon the important role that Esau plays in *Grace Abounding to the Chief of Sinners* and *The Pilgrim's Progress.*

87. Designate and consider the main progressive pilgrims and the main regressive pilgrims. What characteristics distinguish these two groups?

88. Describe those areas in *The Pilgrim's Progress* where Bunyan writes as a classic Puritan, and the other areas where he seems to veer from this norm.

89. Richard Greaves writes in his doctrinal study of John Bunyan that the antecedents of the Bedford tinker's understanding of the sovereignty of God were derived more from Luther's understanding of grace rather than Calvin's views of predestination by decree. Critique this opinion, and consider Bunyan's friendship with John Burton, John Gifford, John Owen and William Dell.

90. Assess Bunyan's representation of covenant theology, especially as described in his *The Doctrine of the Law and Grace Unfolded*, and then subsequent writings.

91. Was Bunyan an antinomian to any degree? Define antinomianism, and especially relate your answer to Bunyan's understanding of the role of the law of God.

CHRISTIAN EXPERIENCE

92. What incentives does Bunyan repeatedly offer in *The Pilgrim's Progress* for pilgrims such as Christian, Faithful, and Hopeful so that they might persevere toward the Celestial City rather than regress?

93. Consider the common and distinctive characteristics and experiences of Christian, Faithful, and Hopeful. To what extent are spiritual gifts and graces an explanation of this matter? What stimulus for Christian fellowship is there here?

94. What instances of discouragement and depression in the lives of pilgrims are included in *The Pilgrim's Progress*, and what remedies does Bunyan recommend for these ailments?

95. What emphasis does Bunyan give in *The Pilgrim's Progress* to the problem of worldliness for a pilgrim? What dangers are encountered? How is deliverance described?

96. Expound upon Bunyan's understanding of separation from the world as illustrated in *The Pilgrim's Progress*. Consider both negative and positive aspects.

97. What lessons does Vanity Fair teach concerning the relationship that exists between the world and biblical Christianity? What distinctive experiences does Bunyan draw upon that are incorporated in this scene?

98. Expound upon the world-view of By-ends and his friends, especially as its religious tone may find expression in twentieth century churches.

99. What are the grounds of Christian's and Hopeful's discipline following their yielding to the Flatterer's enticement? What is the fruit of this chastisement?

100. To what extent is Bunyan concerned about covetousness in pilgrims in *The Pilgrim's Progress*?

101. Explain Bunyan's concept of "conversion" and "progress" in *The Pilgrim's Progress*. Relate biblical conversion and. progress to the modern conception of a Christian "going on pilgrimage"?

102. How would you respond to someone who commented that *The Pilgrim's Progress*, being Puritan literature over three hundred years old, is not relevant to our contemporary society?

103. Where is there exhortation to both hope and fear in *The Pilgrim's Progress*? To what degree does Bunyan communicate a pastoral balance between hope and fear to progressing pilgrims.

104. Relate instances of pilgrim experiences being recalled and mused over in *The Pilgrim's Progress*. For what reasons does Bunyan make this emphasis?

PASTORAL CONCERNS

105. What pastoral influences came upon Bunyan and in turn influenced his composition of *The Pilgrim's Progress*?

106. Summarize Bunyan's understanding of faithful pastoral oversight as depicted in *The Pilgrim's Progress*.

107. In what ways does Bunyan illustrate, in Part One of *The Pilgrim's Progress*, the crucial importance of Christian fellowship, both individual and corporate?

108. Describe the major pastoral emphases that are evident in Christian and Hopeful's encounter with By-ends and his three friends.

109. In *Grace Abounding to the Chief of Sinners*, Bunyan writes that a former pastor and mentor in Bedford, John Gifford, "made it much his business to deliver the people of God from all those false and unsound rests that, by nature, we are prone to take and make to our souls." In what ways did Bunyan fulfill this same responsibility in his own ministry, especially as indicated in *The Pilgrim's Progress*?

110. Concerning *The Pilgrim's Progress*, George Whitefield wrote: "Surely it is an original, and we may say of it, to use the words of the great Doctor Goodwin in his preface to the Epistle to the Ephesians, that it smells of the prison. It was written when the author was confined in Bedford jail. And ministers never write or preach so well as when under the cross: the spirit of Christ and of glory then rests upon them [I Pet. 4:14]." Discuss and illustrate

from the allegory, as well as the life of its author, the truth of this statement.

111. In what ways does *The Pilgrim's Progress* reflect life in a seventeenth century nonconformist church, especially with regard to the character of the Palace Beautiful?

112. How does the Palace Beautiful reflect the requirements for membership in a seventeenth century nonconformist church?

113. Establish Bunyan's homiletical method in terms of sermon arrangement and delivery according to his reputation. What sort of preacher was he?

114. Assess Bunyan's faithfulness as a pastor, and especially relate this to the pastoral ideals of *The Pilgrim's Progress.*

LITERARY CRITICISM

115. Assess the Bunyan studies movement of the twentieth century. Especially relate this evaluation to Bunyan's expressed purposes.

116. Many contemporary assessments of *The Pilgrim's Progress* have tended to admire Bunyan's style and at the same time unashamedly distance themselves from his biblical emphasis. Further, they have attempted to make secular use of this disjunction. Assess the morality and success of this movement.

117. In the introductory and concluding poems of Part One in *The Pilgrim's Progress*, Bunyan describes his style according to eight terms, namely "allegory," "similitude," "metaphor," "parable," "figure," "type," "fable," and "shadow." Consider the distinguishing meanings of these terms and establish to what extent Bunyan generally or specifically incorporates these into his style.

118. "*The Pilgrim's Progress* is an allegory of continuity, comparisons and contrasts." Demonstrate the degree to which this statement is true.

119. Discover and assess some particular examples of criticism brought against Bunyan's allegorical style in *The Pilgrim's Progress.*

120. Examine Bunyan's style of English expression in *The Pilgrim's Progress* and compare it with other notable examples of English literature. To what extent has Bunyan's literary style contributed towards the popularity of this, the most famous of all of his writings?

121. Compare the purpose, doctrine, impact, and style of *The Pilgrim's Progress* with John Milton's *Paradise Lost*.

122. Compare the purpose, doctrine, impact, and style of *The Pilgrim's Progress* with Dante Alighieri's mediaeval counterpart, *The Divine Comedy*.

123. Compare the purpose, doctrine, impact, and style of *The Pilgrim's Progress* with the religious allegorical intent of Daniel Defoe's *Robinson Crusoe*.

124. Compare the purpose, doctrine, impact, and style of *The Pilgrim's Progress* with what is regarded as Bunyan's intended sequel, *The Life and Death of Mr. Badman*.

125. Provide a careful book review of the definitive and critical text of *The Pilgrim's Progress* edited by Wharey and Sharrock and published by Oxford Press (Clarendon) in 1960.

126. Read Part Two of *The Pilgrim's Progress* and describe instances where it illuminates certain teaching and events in Part One.

127. Assess the novelty, quality, importance and character of the poems and songs included in Part One and Part Two of *The Pilgrim's Progress*.

128. How has regard for *The Pilgrim's Progress* at various levels of society changed from its inception up to the present?

129. Review two modern assessments of *The Pilgrim's Progress*. To what degree is there doctrinal sympathy with Bunyan? What most concerns these assessments in the light of Bunyan's stated purposes?

130. It is commonly suggested that in Bunyan's writing of *The Pilgrim's Progress*, in varying proportions, he draws upon his extensive Bible knowledge, his personal experience as a Puritan, and other literature of his time. Which of these three factors do you think is the principal contributor? How do the other two factors relate to your opinion? Are there any other significant contributing factors?

131. Critically assess the engravings and illustrations embodied in *The Pilgrim's Progress* since the inclusion of the "sleeping portrait" in the third edition up to the present time.

132. Bunyan acknowledges that *The Pilgrim's Progress* "may put thee into a laughter or a feud." Critically assess the degree to which the allegory is witty and serious. To what extent is this style consistent with biblical and Puritan ideals?

133. Roger Sharrock has written concerning Puritanism, with which Bunyan so closely identified, that "it was a fiery religious and social dynamic resembling contemporary Marxism more than modern Fundamentalism." Critique this statement.

134. Critique Christopher Hill's political/social assessment of John Bunyan in his *A Tinker And A Poor Man.*

135. Summarize the Agnes Beaumont incident and reflect upon her autobiographical account as well as Bunyan's role here as a pastor.

HISTORICAL BACKGROUND

136. Bunyan's life spans the end of the English monarchy at the execution of King Charles I, the establishment of the Commonwealth under Oliver Cromwell, and the restoration of the monarchy under King Charles II. How does *The Pilgrim's Progress* reflect this turbulent period in English history?

137. A significant influence on Bunyan's early Christian life was Pastor John Gifford of Bedford. Provide a summary of Gifford's life and estimate his influence upon Bunyan.

138. Bunyan's friends included two notable, learned, and contrasting Puritans, William Dell and John Owen. Describe these relationships, and to what extent they might have influenced the author of *The Pilgrim's Progress.*

139. Assess Bunyan's attitude toward the Monarchy and the Cromwellian revolution.

140. Define "latitudinarianism" according to seventeenth century England and describe how Bunyan confronted this deviant pastoral philosophy. In what ways do certain characters in *The Pilgrim's Progress* reflect this latitudinarianism?

141. Why was Bunyan so opposed to the Quaker movement? How did he respond?

142. What sectarian movements were contemporary with Bunyan, and especially those which he mentions in his writings? To what extent was he influenced or aroused by them?

143. Describe the structure and life of the Bedford congregation that Bunyan pastored.

COMMUNICATION

144. In his introductory "Poetic Apology," Bunyan uses four successive illustrations concerning dark clouds, a fisherman, a fowler, and a pearl. Explain these emblematic scenes and consider their relevance for the contemporary proclamation of *The Pilgrim's Progress*.

145. How should *The Pilgrim's Progress* be communicated to children and young people? What principles control your opinion?

146. In this modern era, several film, dramatic, and musical versions of *The Pilgrim's Progress* have been produced. Discuss their degree of success, effectiveness, faithfulness, and conformity to Bunyan's purposes?

147. Interact with Bunyan's introductory poetic apology, and especially the justification of his allegorical and enticing style. Are there limits to the communication of biblical truth using a variety of contemporary means? If so, then what are the limiting principles?

148. Assess Ralph Vaughan Williams' oratorio *The Pilgrim's Progress* according to Bunyan's stated allegorical purposes, and the related question of the communication of truth in a way that is suitable to this twentieth century.

149. Critically assess Neil Postman's estimate, in his *Amusing Ourselves To Death*, that we have moved from a past typographic mind-set to a present age of entertainment and image indulgence. Relate your answer to the effective contemporary communication of *The Pilgrim's Progress.*

150. Review a selection of four recently published children's versions of *The Pilgrim's Progress.*

CHAPTER TWENTY-ONE

Conclusion

THE purpose of this work has been to address themes and issues that arise from a serious study of *The Pilgrim's Progress* in such a way as to offer a vigorous apologetic from a conservative evangelical perspective. While it should be abundantly clear that John Bunyan was of this same evangelical opinion, and fervently so, yet this century has presented formidable obstacles to the comprehension of his distinctive writings, notwithstanding the previous centuries of unparalleled recognition. As already demonstrated, expanding secularity has invaded the media marketplace with the result that communication of sacred truth, shrouded in allegorical form, appears to have become increasingly difficult. At the same time the world has attempted to ape the allegorical form, often employing great visual skill, while investing it with an alien gospel message. One final example of this beguiling literary ruse will, it is hoped, stimulate the reader to appreciate better the superiority of Bunyan's allegorical representation of Bible truth.

John Bunyan and L. Frank Baum

It could not be said that this present generation has entirely lost sight of life being represented as a journey or a pilgrimage. However what is disturbing is the transformation of the itinerary from spiritual to mere earthly categories. Consider the following illustration of this decline in western society.

Originally published in 1900 as *The Wonderful Wizard of Oz* by L. Frank Baum, the 1939 film adaptation by MGM of *The Wizard of Oz* has been ranked as the 6th most significant movie produced in America. Without a doubt, today more young people and adults would recognize the features of this fairyland pilgrimage rather than *The Pilgrim's Progress* and this fact ought to be a matter for great concern, especially when comparisons are made and the contrasting secularity and sacredness are discovered. To begin with Baum was a Theosophist while Bunyan was a Christian. Dorothy's traveling companions in her dream are the Scarecrow, the Tin Woodman, and the Cowardly Lion; those of Christian, also in a dream, are Faithful, Hopeful, and Little-faith. For Dorothy, her pilgrimage is directed by Glinda, the Good Witch of the North, along the Yellow Brick Road, from Munchkin Land captured by the Wicked Witch of the West, to the Wizard of Oz in the Emerald City. For Christian, his pilgrimage is directed by Evangelist along the Narrow Way, from the City of Destruction captive to Beelzebul, to the Lord of the Celestial City. Along the Yellow Brick Road Dorothy is snared by sleeping in the poppy field, confronted by the Wicked Witch of the East, and imprisoned in her castle. Along the Narrow Way Christian is confronted by Apollyon, incarcerated in Doubting Castle and then warned of sleeping on the Enchanted Ground. However in stark contrast, Dorothy eventually returns to her heart's desire which is being with Uncle Henry and Aunt Em in Kansas because, "there is no place like home!" On the other hand, Christian is received into the Celestial City to be with Christ in heaven. Baum's hope is one of worldly sentimentality while Bunyan's is of, "a better [heavenly] country" (Heb. 11:16). Thus instead of western society being taught biblical reality through allegory, it has become seduced by unreal fantasy through allegory. Kansas has now become more important than heaven! Hence there is a desperate need to return to Bunyan, to reinstill his itinerary upon the souls of a Hollywood shaped generation. But only those who resonate with Bunyan's fervent evangelical faith are really qualified to carry out this task.

Bunyan and Scholasticism

As already emphasized, the Bedford tinker's zealous evangelicalism has not been so widely appreciated at the end of this century as in former times, and that in spite academic infatuation which continues unabated. However there is not the slightest doubt as to how Bunyan would address this situation today, for in his time he encountered academia on a number of occasions. On account of his genuine friendship with John Owen and William Dell because of a common basis of Christian fellowship, it could never be said that he was anti-intellectual. However, when Bunyan encountered a disjunction between a mere cognitive awareness of evangelical truth and a heart embrace of that same truth, then his rebuke could be quite severe. And so it would be the same today, because we have a similar disjunction with which scholasticism is content to live.

In the case of Talkative in *The Pilgrim's Progress*, there is a clear representation of Bunyan's attitude toward those who, while being articulate concerning truth, both secular and sacred, are yet removed from any sincere experience of that about which they so fluently converse. At Bunyan's death, as has already been mentioned, an elegy was written about him which well expresses this consistency between truth and life which he so faithfully embodied.

> He in the pulpit preached truth first, and then
> He in his practice preached it o'er again.[1]

Bunyan Studies Deficiency

For all of the emphasis of the modern Bunyan studies movement upon literary form and historic background, it has at the same time increasingly neglected the most important aspects of all, namely gospel truth, sanctifying truth, and pastoral truth at an adult level born of an authoritative Bible. Hence we will not yield this ground to scholarly infatuation in the fields of literature, history, psychology, sociology, or political science, that distances itself from experiential embrace of the saving grace of God.

A final illustration of this contemporary problem comes from an essay by the late Roger Sharrock entitled "Bunyan Studies Today: An Evaluation." To begin with, it is only partly true when he writes: "Forty years have seen a revolution in our midst in our attitude to seventeenth century Puritanism, and for that matter to the Christian tradition in general and even to Christian belief. Bunyan scholarship has benefited from this cultural and hermeneutic transformation."[2] Certainly our present understanding of Puritanism has been refined and improved, though not always accurately as secular caricature indicates, as does the influence of liberal and moderate (latitudinarian?) scholastic presuppositions. Furthermore, hermeneutic advance in our understanding of "the Christian tradition in general," as Sharrock seems to loosely yet agreeably describe it, is most questionable. A case for regression is a much better possibility. Moreover, his opinion that Barth's commentary on *Romans* as well as the writings of Kierkegaard

---

1 John Bunyan, *The Works of John Bunyan*, ed. George Offor, I, p. lxxiv.

2 Roger Sharrock, "Bunyan Studies Today: An Evaluation," *Bunyan In England And Abroad*, eds. M. Van Os and G. J. Schutte, p. 45.

were in some degree causative of this general advance is doubtful to say the least, though the mention of the influential contributions of Perry Miller and William Haller has some plausibility with regard to renewed interest in Puritanism.[3] However what of the resurgence of interest in Puritan works promoted by evangelical book publishers such as The Banner of Truth Trust?

Sharrock also mentions a further twentieth century stimulus in Bunyan studies, and that being W. Y. Tindall's *John Bunyan: Mechanick Preacher*, in portraying "a typical, competitive, scurrilously controversial mechanick preacher,"[4] which while in fact being a misrepresentation,[5] nevertheless became a catalyst for more secular and political analyses. Not surprisingly then follows a glowing celebration of Christopher Hill's writings concerning seventeenth century sectarianism. "His inquiry into the role of radical movements like the Levellers and the Diggers has been found relevant to the background of the artisan Bunyan, as has his analysis of the social and economic pressures on Puritanism and on the Puritan household and family."[6]

However, it is this emphasis on "background" that ought to be a cause for concern here since in reality "background" has become "foreground." In the whole of Sharrock's essay, the emphasis is upon the various aspects of "background" in a most prominent sense. Whereas the matter of biblical truth, being Bunyan's overwhelming passion, receives scant mention. There is a brief, even if appreciative, reference to Richard Greaves on account of him "admirably defining his [Bunyan's] theological position in relation to that of other Restoration Nonconformists." But this is a mere passing matter while the essay as a whole is dominated by these "background" matters. At the risk of sounding repetitive, let it yet once more be stated that the literary and historical movement has certainly contributed much that is helpful. On the other hand, this same movement detracts from its usefulness when it moves outside of its sphere of expertise, when it overemphasizes its importance, and when it becomes a secularizing master rather than

---

3 Ibid., pp. 45-6.

4 Ibid., p. 53.

5 Michael A. Mullett, *John Bunyan in Context*, p. 284; also Richard Greaves, *John Bunyan and English Nonconformity*, pp. 42-5, 101-26

6 Sharrock, "Bunyan Studies Today," *Bunyan In England And Abroad*, p. 52.

a servant of higher spiritual priorities, and this remains a present problem.

No clearer representation of this problem is to be found than in the area of scholars pontificating in the realm of Christian truth while at the same time having no more qualification in this matter than any average unbeliever or Christian in society. Now like anyone else, they are entitled to their opinions; but their specialized scholastic qualifications are in no way to be considered as conveying an imprimatur upon the biblical comments that they make. For instance, Roger Sharrock writes: "Not all the pictures in the Interpreter's House are biblical, but all are supported by texts. The Interpreter may be the Holy Spirit."[7] Such an opinion is entirely arbitrary as well as being reflective of presuppositions that are hardly grounded upon the evangelicalism that Bunyan has represented for over three centuries. Further, this same author is simply out of his depth in attempting to understand Bunyan's Calvinism. Consider the reasoning that, because of the security which the received certificates afford Christian and Hopeful,

> this might seem to confirm the view that for the ordinary reader Calvinism drains away all dramatic interest from the Christian life in the world. . . . How can a progress of which the end is fore-ordained keep the interest of a novel? . . . One literary consequence of Bunyan's theology is that there is no possibility of a treatment of the full life of man like that in Catholic allegory, or even in Spenser. The power of final perseverance granted to the pilgrims in election limits the range of human experience Bunyan can deal with."[8]

The dangers in this issue of scholasticism, in Christian matters, overriding and displacing biblical truth and experience, are not new. The Apostle Paul warns of those who are, "always learning and never able to come to the knowledge of the truth" (II Tim. 3:7). In other words, there is always the problem of toying with the truth, of enjoying the pursuit of truth rather than its final embrace. In romance we find those who seem to enjoy the chase rather than actual marriage. So in the realm of learning, there are those like Gotthold Lessing, a leader in German "enlightened rationalism" of the eighteenth century, of whom John Hurst writes:

> He was honest in his love of truth, but he loved the search for it more than the attainment. The key to his whole life may be found in

---

7 Roger Sharrock, *John Bunyan*, p. 79.

8 Ibid., pp. 87-9.

his own words: 'If God should hold in his right hand all truth, and in his left the ever-active impulse and love of search after truth, although accompanied with the condition that I should ever err, and should say, "Choose!" I would choose the left with humility, and say, "Give, Father! Pure truth belongs to thee alone!"'[9]

Bunyan Studies Torpor

So in the realm of current Bunyan studies, the great emphasis seems to have become the artistry of the Bedford tinker's great composition, in terms of style and setting, in such a way that it is divorced from life, and especially as the allegory defines it. G. M. Trevelyan rightly perceives this disabling distinction as follows: "None of the people who talk about 'art for art's sake' and 'the distracting influence of a moral purpose in art,' have ever yet produced art on a par with Milton's or Bunyan's, and they never will. The greatest artists are even more interested in life than art. Art seems to them as something given, by which to interpret the significance of life."[10] This is exactly so today where the endless secular dissection of the allegorist and his pen is studiously divorced from the life of Bunyan's redeemed soul that gave birth to his extraordinary writings.

To further illustrate this point, consider the confession of the Dutch scholar and theologian, Herman Bavinck as William Hendriksen describes it by translation:

> "My learning does not help me now; neither does my Dogmatics; faith alone saves me." These remarkable words, uttered by one of the greatest Reformed theologians, Dr. Herman Bavinck, should not be misinterpreted. They were uttered on his death-bed and did not imply that this humble child of God retracted anything that he had written or that he was trying to express regrets. The statement simply means that a system of doctrine, however necessary and valuable, is of no avail in and by itself. It must be translated into Christian living. There must be genuine faith in the Triune God as manifested in Jesus Christ.[11]

Hence it should be obvious, by now, that John Bunyan was of the same opinion as Bavinck. In *Grace Abounding To The Chief Of*

---

[9] John F. Hurst, *History of Rationalism*, p. 155.

[10] G. M. Trevelyan, "Bunyan's England," *The Review Of The Churches*, July, 1928, p. 319.

[11] Herman Bavinck, *The Doctrine of God*, translation ed. William Hendriksen, p. 5.

Sinners the pursuit of truth is not enough. His struggles as a young believer were a terrifying transition, though not recommended, to a place of relative stability and rest that resulted from the embrace of the truth concerning Jesus Christ's substitutionary righteousness, which he highly recommends.

However Bunyan's ultimate and dominant goal is beyond this struggle in pilgrimage. At the conclusion of the preface to *Grace Abounding* is the encouragement: "My dear children, the milk and honey is beyond this wilderness. God be merciful to you and grant that you be not slothful to go in to possess the land."[12] With similar emphasis the pre-eminent point about *The Pilgrim's Progress* is certainly not departure from the City of Destruction, nor even traveling via trials distressing and blessed, but arrival at the Celestial City resulting in unclouded fellowship with its Lord. It is for this reason that when Christian and Hopefull have entered through the gates of the Celestial City, Bunyan adds his editorial comment, "I wished myself among them."[13] Here is the reason for the spiritual sterility of modern Bunyan studies; it has no soul-longing for the biblical vista of heaven according to the terms of entrance that the Bible defines. J. I. Packer well appreciates this vital matter when he confesses: "As I move through my own seventh decade, in better health than can possibly last, I am more glad than I can say for what Puritans like Bunyan and Baxter have taught me about dying; I needed it, and the preachers I hear these days never get to it, and modern Christian writers seem quite clueless about it."[14]

Bunyan and Grace for Sinners

For Bunyan, truth must be personally appropriated; Jesus Christ studied must be embraced experientially and consummately; the pursuit of salvation must lead to nothing short of being saved by great grace that results in soul jubilation. And in emphasizing such a vital point, it is proposed that the personal discovery of this spiritual leitmotif is the only way right appreciation of the person and writings of this very useful servant of God can be obtained. If ultimate proof of this overall assertion is to be made, it will be found at the conclusion of so many of Bunyan's writings; there he repeatedly, and with great animation, exhorts his readers to act

[12] Bunyan, *Works*, I, p. 5.

[13] Ibid., III, p. 166.

[14] J. I. Packer, *A Quest for Godliness*, p. 14.

upon what he has written, to commit, to yield, to embrace this welcoming Savior. In conclusion, ponder the following examples.

The Jerusalem Sinner Saved

"Christ is Jacob's ladder that reacheth up to heaven; and he that refuseth to go by this ladder thither, will scarce by other means get up so high. There is none other name given under heaven, among men, whereby we must be saved. There is none other sacrifice for sin than this; he also, and he only, is the Mediator that reconcileth men to God. And, sinner, if thou wouldst be saved by him, his benefits are thine; yea, though thou art a great and Jerusalem transgressor."[15]

The Greatness of the Soul, and Unspeakableness of the Loss Thereof

"Sinners, would I could persuade you to hear me out! A man cannot commit a sin, but, by the commission of it, he doth, by some circumstance or other, sharpen the sting of hell, and that to pierce himself through and through, and through, with many sorrows (I Tim. 6:10). . . . I will yet add to all this; how will the fairness of some for heaven, even the thoughts of that, sting them when they come to hell!"[16]

Come and Welcome to Jesus Christ

"Coming sinner, the Jesus to whom thou art coming is lowly in heart, he despiseth not any. It is not thy outward meanness, nor thy inward weakness; it is not because thou art poor, or base, or deformed, or a fool, that he will despise thee: he hath chosen the foolish, the base, and despised things of this world, to confound the wise and mighty. He will bow his ear to thy stammering prayers, he will pick out the meaning of thy inexpressible groans; he will respect thy weakest offering, if there be in it but thy heart (Matt. 11:20; Luke 14:21; Prov. 9:4-6; Isa. 38:14-15; S. of S. 5:15; John 4:27; Mark 12:33-34; Jas. 5:11). Now, is not this a blessed Christ, coming sinner?"[17]

---

[15] Bunyan, *Works*, I, p. 103.

[16] Ibid., p. 150.

[17] Ibid., p. 297.

Justification by an Imputed Righteousness, or No Way to Heaven but by Jesus Christ

"Sinners, take my advice, with which I shall conclude this use—Call often to remembrance that thou hast a precious soul within thee; that thou art in the way to thine end, at which thy precious soul will be in special concerned, it being then time to delay no longer, the time of reward being come. I say again, bring thy end home; put thyself in thy thoughts into the last day thou must live in this world, seriously arguing thus —How if this day were my last? How if I never see the sun rise more? How if the first voice that rings tomorrow morning in my ears be, 'Arise, ye dead, and come to judgment? Or how, if the next sight I see with mine eyes be the Lord in the clouds, with all his angels, raining floods of fire and brimstone upon the world? . . . Will my profession, or the faith I think I have, carry me through all the trials of God's tribunal?"[18]

The Strait Gate

"Dost thou love thine own soul? Then pray to Jesus Christ for an awakened heart, for a heart so awakened with all the things of another world, that thou mayest be allured to Jesus Christ. . . . When thou comest there, beg again for more awakenings about sin, hell, grace, and about the righteousness of Christ . . . Cry also for a spirit of discerning, that thou mayest know that which is saving grace indeed. . . . Above all studies apply thyself to the study of those things that show thee the evil of sin, the shortness of man's life, and which is the way to be saved. . . . Keep company with the most godly among professors. . . . When thou hearest what the nature of true grace is, defer not to ask thine own heart if this grace be there."[19]

The Doctrine of the Law and Grace Unfolded

"O, therefore, let all this move thee, and be of weight upon thy soul to close in with Jesus, this tender-hearted Jesus. And if yet, for all that I have said, thy sins do still stick with thee, and thou findest thy hellish heart loath to let them go, think with thyself in this manner - Shall I have my sins and lose my soul? Will they do me any good when Christ comes? Would not heaven be better to me than my sins? And the company of God, Christ, saints, and

---

[18] Ibid., p. 334.

[19] Ibid., p. 390.

angels, be better than the company of Cain, Judas, Balaam, with the devils in the furnace of fire?"[20]

John Bunyan's Last Sermon - John 1:13

"If you are the children of God, live together lovingly; if the world quarrel with you, it is no matter; but it is sad if you quarrel together; if this be amongst you, it is a sign of ill-breeding; it is not according to the rules you have in the Word of God. Dost thou see a soul that has the image of God in him? Love him, love him; say, This man and I must go to heaven one day; serve one another, do good for one another; and if any wrong you, pray to God to right you and love the brotherhood.

Lastly, if you be the children of God, learn that lesson - Gird up the loins of your mind, as obedient children, not fashioning yourselves according to your former conversation; but be ye holy in all manner of conversation. Consider that the holy God is your Father, and let this oblige you to live like the children of God, that you may look your Father in the face, with comfort, another day."[21]

The Heavenly Footman

"That you may be provoked to run with the foremost, take notice of this. When Lot and his wife were running from cursed Sodom to the mountains, to save their lives, it is said that his wife looked back from behind him, and she became a pillar of salt; and yet you see that neither her practice, nor the judgment of God that fell upon her for the same, would cause Lot to look behind him."

"I have sometimes wondered at Lot in this particular; his wife looked behind her, and died immediately, but let what you would become of her, Lot would not so much as look behind to see her. We do not read that he did so much as once look where she was, or what was become of her; his heart was upon his journey, and well it might: there was the mountain before him, and the fire and brimstone behind him; his life lay at stake, and he had lost it if he had but looked behind him. Do thou so run: and in thy race remember Lot's wife, and remember her doom; and remember for what that doom did overtake her; and remember that God made her an example for all lazy runners, to the end of the world."[22]

---

[20] Ibid., p. 575.

[21] Ibid., II, p. 758.

[22] Ibid., III, p. 394.

A Few Sighs from Hell

"Have a care thou receive not this doctrine in notion only, lest thou bring a just damnation upon thy soul, by professing thyself to be freed by Christ's blood from the guilt of sin, while thou remainest still a servant to the filth of sin. For I must tell you, that unless you have the true and saving work of the faith and grace of the gospel in your hearts, you will either go on in a legal holiness, according to the tenor of the law; or else through a notion of the gospel, the devil bewitching and beguiling thy understanding, will, and affections, thou wilt, Ranter-like, turn the grace of God into wantonness, and bring upon thy soul double, if not treble damnation, in that thou couldest not be contented to be damned for thy sins against the law, but also to make ruin sure to thy soul, thou wouldest dishonor the gospel, and turn the grace of God, held forth and discovered to men by that, into licentiousness."[23]

SANCTIFICATION THROUGH THE MORAL LAW

Be well acquainted with the Word, and with the general rules of holiness; to wit, with the moral law; the want of this is a cause of much unholiness of conversation. Let then the law be with thee to love it, and do it in the spirit of the gospel, that thou be not unfruitful in thy life. Let the law, I say, be with thee, not as it comes from Moses, but from Christ; for though thou art set free from the law as a covenant of life, yet though still art under the law to Christ.

John Bunyan
A Holy Life the Beauty of Christianity
Works, II, p. 539

---

[23] Ibid., p. 724.

BIBLIOGRAPHY

BUNYAN'S WORKS

Bunyan, John. *The Works of John Bunyan.* Ed. George Offor. 3 vols. 1854. Edinburgh: The Banner of Truth Trust, 1991.

Bunyan, John. *The Miscellaneous Works of John Bunyan.* General Ed. Roger Sharrock. 13 vols. Oxford: Clarendon Press, 1975-94.

Bunyan, John. *The Works of that Eminent Servant of Christ, Mr. John Bunyan.* 2 vols. London: E. Gardiner, 1736-1737.

Bunyan, John. *The Pilgrim's Progress.* Ed. N. H. Keeble. Oxford: Oxford University Press (The World's Classics), 1989.

Bunyan, John. *The Pilgrim's Progress.* Ed. Roger Sharrock. Harmondsworth, Eng.: Penguin Books, 1965.

Bunyan, John. *The Pilgrim's Progress.* Eds. James Blanton Wharey, Roger Sharrock. Oxford: Clarendon Press, 1960.

Bunyan, John. *The Pilgrim's Progress.* Ed. James Inglis. London: Gall and Inglis, n.d.

Bunyan, John. *Grace Abounding to the Chief of Sinners.* Ed. Roger Sharrock. Oxford: Clarendon Press, 1962.

GENERAL REFERENCES

Abrams, M. H., ed. *The Norton Anthology of English Verse.* New York: Norton, 1993,

Allen, R. E., ed. *The Concise Oxford Dictionary.* Oxford: Clarendon Press, 1991.

Barna, George. *What Americans Believe.* Ventura: Regal Books, 1991.

Bavinck, Herman. *The Doctrine of God.* Translated by William Hendriksen. Grand Rapids: Baker Book House, 1985.

Benson, Louis. *The Hymns of John Bunyan.* New York: The Hymn Society, 1930.

Boardman, J. Harold and John, Ivor B., eds. *Macaulay's Lives of Bunyan and Goldsmith.* London: Adam and Charles Black, 1914.

Breward, Ian. *John Bunyan, A Commemorative Symposium.* Melbourne: The Uniting Church Historical Society (Victoria), 1988.

Brown, John. *John Bunyan: His Life, Times and Work.* London: Hulbert Publishing (Tercentenary Edition), 1928.

Brittain, Vera. *In The Steps of John Bunyan.* London: Rich and Cowan, 1987.

Campbell, Gordon. "Fishing in Other Men's Waters: Bunyan and the Theologians." Ed. N. H. Keeble. *John Bunyan, Conventicle and Parnassus.* Oxford: Clarendon Press, 1988,

Calvin, John. *Institutes of the Christian Religion.* 2 vols. Philadelphia: The Westminster Press, 1960.

Campbell, Gordon. "The Theology of The Pilgrim's Progress." Ed. Vincent Newey. *The Pilgrim's Progress: Critical and Historical Views.* Liverpool: Liverpool University Press, 1980.

Chantry, Walter J. *God's Righteous Kingdom.* Edinburgh: Banner of Truth Trust, 1980.

Cheever, George. *Lectures on The Pilgrim's Progress.* Glasgow: William Collins, 1860.

Collmer, Robert G., ed. *Bunyan in Our Time.* Kent, Ohio: The Kent State University Press, 1989.

Cook, Coleen. *All That Glitters.* Chicago: Moody Press, 1992.

Cowper, William. *The Poetical Works of William Cowper.* London: T. Nelson, 1852.

Dargan, Charles. *A History of Preaching.* 2 vols. New York: Hodder & Stoughton, 1905.

de Vries, Pieter. *John Bunyan on the Order of Salvation.* New York: Peter Lang, 1994.

Earle, Alice Morse. *The Sabbath in Puritan New England.* New York: Scribner's, 1900.

Edwards, Philip. "The Journey in The Pilgrim's Progress." *The Pilgrim's Progress, Critical and Historical Views.* Ed. Vincent Newey. Liverpool: Liverpool University Press, 1980.

Flake, Carol. *Redemptorama.* Garden City, N. Y.: Anchor Press, 1984.

Franklin, Benjamin. *The Autobiography of Benjamin Franklin.* Philadelphia: Henry Altemus, 1895.

Froude, A. J. *Bunyan, English Men of Letters.* London: Macmillan, 1880.

Fuller, Andrew. *The Complete Works of the Rev. Andrew Fuller.* 3 vols. Philadelphia: American Baptist Publications Society, 1845.

Furlong, Monica. *The Puritan's Progress: A Study of John Bunyan.* London: Hodder and Stoughton, 1975.

Geisler, Norman L., ed. *Inerrancy.* Grand Rapids: Zondervan, 1980.

Goodwin, Thomas. *The Works of Thomas Goodwin.* 12 vols. Edinburgh: James Nichol. 1866.

Greaves, Richard L. *John Bunyan.* Grand Rapids: Wm. B. Eerdmans, 1969.

Greaves, Richard L. John *Bunyan and English Nonconformity.* London: The Hambledon Press, 1992.

Haller, William. *The Rise of Puritanism.* New York: Harper & Row, 1957.

Harrison, G. B. *John Bunyan: A Study in Personality.* Garden City, N.Y.: Doubleday, 1928.

Hawthorne, Nathaniel. *The Celestial Railroad*. Harrisonburg, VA: Sprinkle Publications, 1990.

Hendriksen, William. *I & II Timothy and Titus*. Edinburgh: Banner of Truth Trust, 1972.

Herreshoff, David. "Marxist Perspectives on Bunyan." *Bunyan in Our Time*. Ed. Robert G. Collmer. Kent, OH: The Kent State University Press, 1989.

Hill, Christopher. *A Tinker and a Poor Man*. New York: Alfred A. Knopf, 1989.

Hill, Christopher. "John Bunyan and the English Revolution." The *John Bunyan Lectures 1978*. Bedford: Bedfordshire Education Service, 1978.

Hurst, John F. *History of Rationalism*. New York: Nelson & Phillips, 1865.

James, William. *The Varieties of Religious Experience*. New York: Collier Books, 1961.

Kaufmann, U. Milo. *The Pilgrim's Progress and Traditions in Puritan Meditation*. P. 44

Keeble, N. H. "Christiana's Key: The Unity of The Pilgrim's Progress." *The Pilgrim's Progress: Critical and Historical Views*. Ed. Vincent Newey. Liverpool: Liverpool University Press, 1980.

Keeble, N. H., ed. *John Bunyan, Conventicle and Parnassus*. Oxford: Clarendon Press, 1988.

Keeble, N. H. "'Of him thousands daily Sing and talk': Bunyan and his reputation." Ed. N. H. Keeble. *John Bunyan, Conventicle and Parnassus*. Oxford: Clarendon Press, 1988.

Keeble, N. H. *The literary culture of nonconformity in later seventeenth-century England*. Athens: University of Georgia Press, 1987.

Kelly, J. N. D. Early *Christian Doctrines*. New York: Harper, 1958.

Kelman, John. *The Road*. 2 vols. Edinburgh: Oliphant Anderson and Ferrier, 1912.

Kennedy, Michael. *The Works of Ralph Vaughan Williams*. London: Oxford, 1994,

Knott, John R. *Discourses of Martyrdom in English Literature, 1563-1694*. New York: Cambridge University Press, 1993.

Knott, jun. John R. '"Thou Must Live Upon My Word': Bunyan and the Bible." Ed. N. H. Keeble. *John Bunyan, Conventicle and Parnassus*. Oxford: Clarendon Press, 1988.

Lawrence, Anne, Owens, W. R., and Sim, Stuart., eds. *John Bunyan and His England 1628-1688*. London: Hambledon Press, 1990.

Lewis, Peter. *The Genius Of Puritanism*. Haywards Heath: Carey Publications, 1975.

Lloyd-Jones, D. Martyn. *Knowing The Times*. Edinburgh: Banner of Truth Trust, 1989.

Lloyd-Jones, D. Martyn. *Romans, The New Man, Exposition of Chapter 6*. Grand Rapids: Zondervan, 1973.

Lloyd-Jones, D. Martyn. *The Puritans: Their Origins And Successors*. Edinburgh: Banner of Truth Trust, 1987.

Luther, Martin. *A Commentary on St. Paul's Epistle To The Galatians*. Cambridge & London: James Clarke, 1972.

Luther, Martin. *Luther's Works*. 56 vols. Saint Louis: Concordia Publishing House, 1972.

MacArthur, Jr. John F. *Ashamed Of The Gospel*. Wheaton: Crossway Books, 1993.

Machen, J. Gresham. *Christianity and Liberalism*. London: Victory Press, 1925.

Maguire, Robert. *Lectures on Bunyan's Pilgrim's Progress*. London: The London Printing and Publishing Company, 1859.

Marsden, George. *The Outrageous Idea Of Christian Scholarship*. New York: Oxford, 1997.

The Methodist-Hymn-Book. London: Methodist Conference Office, 1938.

Miller, Perry and Johnson, Thomas H., eds. 2 vols. *The Puritans – A Sourcebook Of Their Writings*. New York: Harper & Row, 1965.

Moo, Douglas. *The Epistle to the Romans*. Grand Rapids: Wm. B. Eerdmans, 1996.

Morris, Leon. *The Epistle to the Romans*. Grand Rapids: Wm. B. Eerdmans, 1997.

Mullett, Michael A. *John Bunyan in Context*. Pittsburgh: Duquesne University Press, 1997.

Murray, Iain. *Jonathan Edwards*. Edinburgh: Banner of Truth Trust, 1987.

Murray, John. *Collected Writings of John Murray*. 4 vols. Edinburgh: Banner of Truth Trust, 1976.

Nellist, Brian. "The Pilgrim's Progress and Allegory." *The Pilgrim's Progress, Critical and Historical Views*. Ed. Vincent Newey. Liverpool: Liverpool University Press, 1980.

Newey, Vincent. "Bunyan And The Confines Of The Mind." *The Pilgrim's Progress, Critical and Historical Views*. Ed. Vincent Newey. Liverpool: Liverpool University Press, 1980.

Newey, Vincent., ed. *The Pilgrim's Progress: Critical and Historical Views*. Liverpool: Liverpool University Press, 1980.

Newton. John. *The Works of John Newton*. 6 vols. Edinburgh: Banner of Truth Trust, 1988.

Owen, John. The Works of John Owen. 17 vols. Edinburgh: T. & T. Clark, 1862.

Owens, W. R. "The reception of *The Pilgrim's Progress* in England." *Bunyan in England and Abroad*. Eds. M. van Os and G. J. Schutte. Amsterdam: VU University Press, 1990.

Packer, J. I. *A Quest for Godliness*. Wheaton: Crossway Books, 1990.

Packer, J. I. *Fundamentalism and the Word of God*. London: Inter-Varsity Fellowship, 1960.

Paxon, Ruth. *Life on the Highest Plain*. Grand Rapids: Kregel, 1996.

Postman, Neil. *Amusing Ourselves To Death*. New York: Penguin Books, 1985.

Ramm, Bernard. *Protestant Biblical Interpretation*. Grand Rapids: Baker Book House, 1956.

Ravitch, Diane, and Chester E. Finn, jun. *What do our 17-years-olds know?* New York: Harper & Row, 1987.

Ray, Charles. "Mrs. Spurgeon." *The C. H. Spurgeon Collection*. Albany: Ages Software, 1998.

Rupp, Gordon. *Six Makers of English Religion*. London: Hodder and Stoughton, 1957.

Rupp, Gordon. *The Righteousness of God*. London: Hodder and Stoughton, 1953.

Ryle, J. C. *Expository Thoughts On John*. 3 vols. Edinburgh: Banner of Truth Trust, 1987.

Ryle, J. C. *Holiness*. London: James Clarke, 1956.

Ryle, J. C. *Old Paths*. Cambridge: James Clarke, 1972.

Sampson, George. *The Concise Cambridge History of English Literature*. Cambridge: University Press, 1941.

Schaeffer, Francis. A. *A Christian Manifesto*. Westchester: Crossway Books, 1981.

Schaff, Philip. *The Creeds of Christendom*. 3 vols. Grand Rapids: Baker Book House, 1969.

Schultze, Quentin. *Redeeming Television*. Downers Grove: Inter-Varsity Press, 1992.

Sharrock, Roger. "Bunyan Studies Today: An Evaluation." Eds. van Os, M. and Schutte, G. J. *Bunyan in England and Abroad*. Amsterdam: VU University Press, 1990.

Sharrock, Roger., ed. *Bunyan, The Pilgrim's Progress, A Casebook*. London: Macmillan, 1976.

Sharrock, Roger. *John Bunyan*. London: Hutchinson House, 1954.

Shedd, William G. T. *Commentary on Romans*. Grand Rapids: Baker Book House, 1980.

Spurgeon, C. H. "Around the Wicket Gate." *The C. H. Spurgeon Collection*. Albany, OR: Ages Software, 1998.

Spurgeon, C. H. *Eccentric Preachers*. Pasadena, TX: Pilgrim Publications, 1978.

Spurgeon, C. H. *Metropolitan Tabernacle Pulpit*. 63 vols. Albany, OR: Ages Software, 1998.

Spurgeon, C. H. *Metropolitan Tabernacle Pulpit*. 63 vols. Pasadena, TX: Pilgrim Publications, 1980.

Spurgeon, C. H. *Pictures from Pilgrim's Progress*. Pasadena, TX: Pilgrim Publications, 1973.

Spurgeon, C. H. *C. H. Spurgeon's Autobiography*. 4 vols. London: Passmore and Alabaster, 1897.

Spurgeon, C. H. *The C. H. Spurgeon Collection*. Albany: Ages Software, 1998.

Spurgeon, C. H. "The Great Change—Conversion." *The C. H. Spurgeon Collection*. Albany: Ages Software, 1998

Spurgeon, Thomas. "Editor's Introduction." *Pictures from Pilgrim's Progress*. Pasadena, TX: Pilgrim Publications, 1973.

Stachniewski, John. *The Persecuting Imagination: English Puritanism and the Literature of Despair*. Oxford: Clarendon Press, 1991.

Swanson, Dennis Michael. *Charles H. Spurgeon and Eschatology: Did He Have a Discernable Millennial Position?* Unpublished dissertation, The Master's Seminary, CA, 1996. Internet sourced.

Talon, Henri. *John Bunyan: The Man and His Works*. Cambridge: Harvard University Press, 1951.

Toon, Peter. *The Emergence of Hyper-Calvinism in English Nonconformity*. London: Olive Tree, 1967.

Turner, James. "Bunyan's Sense of Place." *The Pilgrim's Progress: Critical and Historical Views*. Ed. Vincent Newey. Liverpool: Liverpool University Press, 1980.

Turner, Nigel. *Grammatical Insights Into The New Testament*. Edinburgh: T. & T. Clark, 1965.

van Os, M. and Schutte, G., eds. J. *Bunyan in England and Abroad*. Amsterdam: VU University Press, 1990.

Walker, Eric C. *William Dell, Master Puritan*. Cambridge: W. Heffer & Sons, 1970.

Wakefield, Gordon. *Bunyan the Christian*. London: HarperCollins, 1992.

Wallechinsky, David, Irving Wallace, and Amy Wallace. *The People's almanac presents the book of lists*. New York: Morrow, 1977.

Ward, A. R. and A. R. Waller, *The Cambridge History of English Literature*. 15 vols. New York: Macmillan, 1949.

Warfield, B. B. *Perfectionism*. Philadelphia: Presbyterian and Reformed Publishing, 1967.

Wells, David F. *No Place For Truth*. Grand Rapids: Wm. B. Eerdmans, 1993.

White, B. R. "'The Fellowship of Believers': Bunyan and Puritanism." *John Bunyan, Conventicle and Parnassus*. Ed. N. H. Keeble. Oxford: Clarendon Press, 1988.

Whyte, Alexander. *Bunyan Characters*. Grand Rapids: Baker Book House, 1981.

Williams, R, Vaughan. *The Pilgrim's Progress*. London: Oxford, 1952.

Witsius, Herman. *The Economy of the Covenants Between God and Man*. 2 vols. Escondido, CA: den Dulk Christian Foundation, 1990.

JOURNALS, MAGAZINES, ETC.

Bunyan, John and Powell, Martin. *The Pilgrim's Progress*. New York: Marvel Comics, 1992.

Butler, George. "The Iron Cage Of Despair and 'The Unpardonable Sin' in The Pilgrim's Progress." *English Language Notes*. XXV. September. 1987.

Ellis, Amy. "Office laughter helps employees enjoy their work." *Escondido Times Advocate*. September 26, 1993, pp. G2-3.

Finley, C. Stephen. "Bunyan Among The Victorians: Macaulay, Froude, Ruskin." *Journal of Literature & Theology*. Vol. 3, No. 1, March, 1989, pp. 77-94.

Helm, Paul. "Bunyan and Reprobation Asserted." *The Baptist Quarterly*. XXVII. April, 1979.

Mann, James. "What is TV Doing To America?" *U.S. News & World Report*. August 2, 1982, p. 28.

Mitchell, Philip and Clarke, Greg. "Comprehending the darkness." *The Briefing*. April 2, 1997, p. 9.

Pavlac, Ross. "Bang! Zow! Christian Comic Books Join Fight for Teens." *Christianity Today*. July 2, 1993, p. 48.

Stephens, Mitchell. "The Death of Reading." *Los Angeles Times Magazine*. September 22, 1991, p. 10.

Tipple, Ezra S. "Pilgrim's Progress a book for Preachers." *Methodist Review*. July, 1908.

Trevelyan, G. M. "Bunyan's England." *The Review Of The Churches*. July, 1928, p. 319.

Wakefield, Gordon. Review of *The Persecuting Imagination: English Puritanism and the Literature of Despair*, by John Stachniewski. *Journal Of Theological Studies*. Oct., 1992, pp. 749-53.

INDEX

THE MISSION OF GREAT CHRISTIAN BOOKS

The ministry of Great Christian Books was established to glorify The Lord Jesus Christ and to be used by Him to expand and edify the kingdom of God while we occupy and anticipate Christ's glorious return. Great Christian Books will seek to accomplish this mission by publishing Gospel literature which is biblically faithful, relevant, and practically applicable to many of the serious spiritual needs of mankind upon the beginning of this new millennium. To do so we will always seek to boldly incorporate the truths of Scripture, especially those which were largely articulated as a body of theology during the Protestant Reformation of the sixteenth century and ensuing years. We gladly join our voice in the proclamations of— Scripture Alone, Faith Alone, Grace Alone, Christ Alone, and God's Glory Alone!

Our ministry seeks the blessing of our God as we seek His face to both confirm and support our labors for Him. Our prayers for this work can be summarized by two verses from the Book of Psalms:

"...let the beauty of the LORD our God be upon us, And establish the work of our hands for us; Yes, establish the work of our hands." —Psalm 90:17

"Not unto us, O LORD, not unto us, but to your name give glory." —Psalm 115:1

Great Christian Books appreciates the financial support of anyone who shares our burden and vision for publishing literature which combines sound Bible doctrine and practical exhortation in an age when too few so-called "Christian" publications do the same. We thank you in advance for any assistance you can give us in our labors to fulfill this important mission. May God bless you.